FATED

FATED

REBECCA ZANETTI

BRAVA
KENSINGTON PUBLISHING CORP.
www.kensingtonbooks.com

BRAVA BOOKS are published by

Kensington Publishing Corp.
119 West 40th Street
New York, NY 10018

All Kensington titles, imprints, and distributed lines are available at special quantity discounts for bulk purchases for sales promotion, premiums, fund-raising, educational, or institutional use.

Special book excerpts or customized printings can also be created to fit specific needs. For details, write or phone the office of the Kensington Special Sales Manager. Attn.: Special Sales Department. Kensington Publishing Corp., 119 West 40th Street, New York, NY 10018. Phone: 1-800-221-2647.

ISBN-13: 978-0-7582-5923-3
ISBN-10: 0-7582-5923-9

First Kensington Trade Paperback Printing: March 2011

10 9 8 7 6 5 4 3 2 1

Printed in the United States of America

To Tony Zanetti, who years ago taught me to play Red Rover so he could hold my hand, and who today is the best husband I could ever imagine

To Gabe and Karlina, who inspire me every day

To Gail English, who taught me to love reading, and to Jim English, who taught me to take a chance

And finally to Debbie Smith, Stephanie West, and Brandie Chapman, who've had my back since those Red Rover days and who are as excited about this first book as I am . . .

I love you all.

ACKNOWLEDGMENTS

This book wouldn't exist without the help of many people who deserve a heartfelt thank you! So thank you to the following: Caitlin Blasdell, my amazing, talented and insightful agent; Megan Records, my wonderful, encouraging and knowledgeable editor; Jennifer Dorough, my hardworking, humorous, and talented critique partner; my beta readers and friends, Jessica Namson, Brandi Hall, and Tina Jacobson; the FF&P Critique Group and KOD's Lethal Ladies, who gave me wonderful advice. And a very special thank you to Kathy and Herb Zanetti, my supportive in-laws, who entertained Tony and the kids so that I could write about vampires, werewolves, and fate.

Chapter 1

"Mama! Mama, wake up." Tiny hands clutched at Cara's worn nightshirt, shaking with all their might.

Cara's eyes flew open, and her heart hitched in her chest. Terrified blue eyes speared her through the dusk of the morning. The little girl must have had another nightmare. "Janie, sweetheart, what?"

"They're coming. They're coming now, the bad men. We have to run." Janie's breath came in sharp gasps before she let out a high-pitched sob.

Cara shook her head, reaching out to enfold her daughter in a hug. She slowed her own breathing, the need to comfort her child overwhelming her. Poor Janie. Not another nightmare. She reached for her reading glasses on the table only to realize she'd fallen asleep with them on. Again. The newest edition of *Botanical Magazine* hadn't been the barn-burner she'd expected.

She smoothed Janie's hair down while silence echoed around them. Now more than ever, she wished Simon had lived, maybe he could have soothed their daughter's fears. She flipped on the antique pink Depression glass lamp. "It's okay, sweetheart. I'm sure it was just a bad drea—"

A loud crash came from the other room and Cara yelped. The sound of splintering wood propelled her to action. She leapt from the bed, yanked Janie into her arms, and sprinted for the master bath, barely missing the potted fern in the corner. Her heart slamming against her ribs, she locked the door and rushed toward the small window. She failed to unlock it before the thin door burst open behind her.

A broad hand stopped the door from clanging against the wall. At least six and a half feet of muscle-packed male filled the doorway.

With a cry, she dropped Janie to her feet and dodged in front of the four-year-old. The air caught in her throat and her ears started to ring as adrenaline spiked through her blood. This was not happening. She yanked her head to the side and forced herself to accept the situation. Accept that she needed to fight. She dragged oxygen into her tight lungs and searched the tiled counter for a weapon—her tweezers probably wouldn't harm anybody.

She pushed Janie back against the wall. Retreating a step, she held one hand out to ward off the threat. His size made her gulp. Brown eyes raked her from his hard cut face, and raven black hair reached his collar with a freedom that disavowed any ties to the military—although he wore the requisite flack boots and dark jeans under a bulletproof vest. She'd seen the gear on a Discovery Channel special about soldiers.

The energy emanating from him stole her breath.

"Get out," she said, shielding her child. Trying to shield herself from the feelings he threw at her. Anger, passion, and urgency all swirled together, mixing with her own panic and making her light-headed. Her knees wobbled, and her head began to ache. She usually blocked better than this. Or maybe his emotions were just that strong.

"We need to go." His tone was water over sharp rocks, as if he was trying to gentle a naturally rough voice. Then his eyes dropped to her faded nightshirt to see the image of Einstein surrounded by shopping bags—"Quantum Shopping." His top lip quirked up and a dimple winked. Her heartbeat slowed in response. Then he stalked a step closer, his hands at his sides, and her gaze flew to the gun on his hip, to the several knives secured in his vest.

Her heart leapt back into action. "You have the wrong house." She glared up at his implacable face—a face cut from granite with a jaw made to take a punch. She'd have to jump to even come close.

The scent of spiced pine and male infused the room.

He shook his head. A pit the size of a large rock settled in her stomach as adrenaline slammed the room into sharp focus. Her breath came in short pants, and her scientific mind sought an answer. A way to take his massive frame down. She stamped down on the rising panic when nothing came to mind, and again searched for a weapon, spotting the tiny Fittonia "White Anne" in the terra-cotta planter. She couldn't throw Annie at the man; the plant would never survive.

The intruder took another step to peer over her shoulder. "It will be okay. We have to go." His large hand encircled Cara's bicep before dragging her into the bedroom. Fear seized her vocal cords for a moment, and her mind scattered. Should she tell Janie to run? Could she slow him down long enough?

Then, with a muffled curse, he dropped her arm. A low growl emanated from him as he peered at his hand. He wiped it on his pant leg and grabbed her again. What had been on her shirt?

The phone near the bed caught her eye, and she lunged for it. He jerked her back, his hand warm and firm on her arm. Cara dug her feet into the carpet but their forward momentum didn't slow, so she tried to yank away as he pulled her toward a basket of clothes at the foot of the bed.

"Janie, follow us," he tossed over his shoulder.

Cara coughed out air. He knew Janie's name. This wasn't random. Fear choked her again. "How do you know her name?"

He pivoted until she smacked flush against him. Heat filled her, surrounded her. His hands settled on her arms, and his determination and intent beat at her. Damn it. She couldn't block him—she sucked as an empath. Then he lowered his head.

"I know both of your names, Cara. Listen. My name is Talen Kayrs, and I won't hurt you. I'm here to help." Determined eyes captured her while he gave her a moment. "Take a deep breath. I can feel your power. You can find the truth here. You know I won't hurt you." His voice rumbled low. Soothing.

Her body softened from his tone even as her mind rebelled. Her breathing evened out. Danger radiated out of the man, but she could sense no intention to harm her. Or Janie.

Janie tugged on her waist. "It's okay, Mama. We have to go. They're coming."

Cara stepped to the side and nodded. "Fine. We'll leave. We can follow you." If she could just get Janie to the car—

He grinned, flashing even white teeth. "You can't lie worth spit. You have one minute to throw on clothes." The sound of his rough voice shot nerve endings alive through her skin. But not from fear. He turned toward the door.

"No." She again tried to wrench away while her body tingled where it met his.

"Then you go in your pajamas." He grabbed the basket of clothes in his other arm while he towed her into the hallway. "Keep up, Janie." The little girl stumbled behind, keeping her hands glued to Cara's waist.

"Wait, no, Mama," Janie cried out, pulling on her mother. "I need Mr. Mullet." Her voice rose to a shrill sob.

Talen whirled around and squinted over Cara's shoulder. "Mr. Mullet?" He eyed the living room entrance and then focused on the little girl.

Cara pressed a hand against his chest, settling her stance to protect her child. "Mr. Mullet is her stuffed bear—she doesn't go anywhere without him." If Janie could leave the room, Cara could really fight.

Talen raised an eyebrow, his gaze thoughtful. "Hurry, Janie. Get the bear—we have to go."

Quick as a flash, Janie darted from the room. Dark eyes met Cara's and she wavered, then shot her knee upward to his groin, simultaneously punching her fist toward his face with a fierce grunt.

He shifted, allowing her knee to connect to the muscle of his upper thigh while his arm shot out to stop her punch. His broad hand enclosed her fist inches away from his chin, and the slap of skin on skin echoed around the room. The basket of clothes remained safe in his free arm.

Pain lanced through her leg, and fear cascaded down her spine. Panting out breath, she waited for retaliation. If he hit her, he'd knock her out. What about Janie?

Talen tilted his head to the side, his hand warm around hers. "Is your leg all right?"

He asked about her leg? Seriously? She'd just tried to turn him into a eunuch. "Fine," she hissed through her teeth.

"Hmmm," he said, twisting his hand to grasp her wrist and yank her into the living room. "You might want to work on not broadcasting your intent with those pretty blue eyes next time." Mere politeness colored his tone, not an ounce of anger to be found.

Cara stumbled, truly off balance for the first time that evening.

"I got him, Mama," Janie chirped, running into the room with the stuffed bear and her worn blankie. "We can go now."

The front door hung drunkenly split in two. At the sight, Cara began to struggle again. With an exasperated sigh, Talen dropped the basket of clothes, shifted her to the side, and lifted Janie into his arms.

"No!" Cara cried out, reaching for her daughter before

pounding on his broad back. Pure instinct moved her to protect Janie, and rage choked her as she beat on his dark vest.

"Get the clothes and move it," he growled over his shoulder. He crossed the front porch, heading toward a black Hummer idling at the curb.

Cara threw herself against the man holding her child, knocking over the basket. Clothes scattered across the wooden planks.

"Let her go, you bastard!"

He may not intend harm, but he had no right to kidnap them. She clutched one arm around his massive neck as her knees dug into his spine. She jerked hard against his windpipe. A rush of anger slammed through her body, pushing out the fear.

Even with her struggling on his back, his long strides continued toward the vehicle unhampered. He yanked open the rear door, placed Janie in a booster seat, and buckled her in with quick motions. Cara moved to jump off him, only to have him close the door, grab her arm, and pull her around. Two strong hands held her aloft. Hard steel met her backside when he stepped into her, his face lowering to hers. "Stop fighting me."

His strength was unbelievable. Her own vulnerability beat into her as she realized her nightshirt had risen to reveal pale pink panties. The cool night air rushed across her bare legs. Dark denim scratched the tender skin of her inner thighs, and she opened her mouth to scream.

One swift movement and his mouth covered hers. Hot, firm, and somehow restrained. The effort of his restraint belted into her. He fought to control himself. Heat slammed through her. A roaring filled her ears and her breath hitched. Her heart slowed, and time stopped. For a brief moment, *his* heartbeat echoed throughout her body to a spot below her stomach.

He growled low and his mouth moved over hers, no longer silencing her, but tasting. Exploring. One thick arm swept around her waist and pulled her into him; the other lifted to tangle a hand in her hair. He tugged, angled her head more to the side. He went deeper.

She moaned as his tongue met hers. He explored her mouth like he owned it. For a moment, he did. She forgot everything. There were only his lips on hers, demanding. Promising. His heat warmed her as she returned his kiss, pushing closer into his hard body, forgetting reality.

Pure strength surrounded her. Hot. Dangerous. Tempting. Then a bird screeched high above and awareness crashed into her.

She jerked her head back, her lips tingling, her mind spinning. Deep brown eyes kept her gaze. His arm tightened around her waist while he raised his head farther.

"Don't scream." His voice had deepened to something guttural, something that added to the fluttering in her lower stomach.

"Mama?" Janie's voice wavered from inside the vehicle.

"She can't see us—I have the privacy screens up," Talen murmured.

Great. So no one could see in, either. Smart kidnapper.

"Tell her it's all right." He released Cara's hair to allow space between them.

"No. Let us go." Reality cascaded back with the coldness of his moving away. What had she done? She brought her elbow down on his collarbone. Hard. A shaft of pain shot up her arm, and her eyes widened. How did that not injure him?

He grinned, amusement softening his hard mouth. Releasing her, he yanked open the passenger side door and lifted her inside, snapping the seat belt before she could blink. Then his face was in hers again. "Undo this belt and I'll bind you."

The door slammed, and he was back in the car before she drew another breath. His words should have frightened her. But instead, fury threatened to explode out of her. She tamped down on it with a scientist's mind—she'd get out of this.

With a screech of tires, he pulled the Hummer into the quiet street. She searched frantically for some type of weapon. Mere minutes had passed since Janie had awoken her—they were taken so quickly, nobody would even know they were gone. She flashed her gaze toward the now silent man. The early light of dawn filtered through the tinted windows and danced across the hard planes of his face. She studied him, searching for a weakness. Any weakness.

"Janie, you'll be safe soon." Kindness wove through his words.

Cara swung her head around. "It's going to be okay, Janie," she whispered to her daughter, fighting tears.

Janie, her blue eyes sparkling, grinned back. "I know, Mama. I knew Talen was coming."

"You did?"

"Yeah. I dreamed about him. But I didn't know when." Grinning, she clutched her worn teddy bear to her chest, snuggling her nose into his fluffy hair.

Cara faced the front, her mind whirling. She was in the middle of an experiment at work—she needed to be there tomorrow. What if she rolled down the window and screamed? Would anybody hear?

"I'm not going to hurt you, Cara." He entered the empty highway.

She worried her lip with her teeth. Miss Kimmie would be the first to know they were gone when Janie didn't show up for preschool tomorrow. She'd call someone, right? Or just assume Janie was home sick with the stomach virus going around the class? "So how about you let us go, um, Talen?" She wondered if he were crazy, if she could somehow reason with him.

He flashed her a glance at the use of his name and heat rushed to her face. "I can't let you go."

Nope, no reasoning with him. "Why not?" She slid her hand down to her belt buckle.

"I wasn't kidding about binding you." His warning rumbled through the small space. She jerked her hand back to her lap. "You're in danger, more than you can understand right now."

Oh, she understood all right. She straightened in her seat when he exited the highway at the edge of Mercy Lake, her safe little town on the outskirts of Boston. Her stomach dropped as she realized there was only one place they could be going. "You're taking us to the private airport?"

"Yes."

"Why?" The exclusive airport was used only for corporate jets and small water planes.

"Because that's where the plane is." His tone didn't invite further discussion.

"I can't fly somewhere in my nightshirt." The comment slipped out before she could stop herself.

He turned in surprise, flashing a smile that did odd things to her belly. Man, she was losing it. "I told you to bring the basket of clothes."

"Listen," she tried reasoning with him again. "Let us go, and we won't tell anybody. I promise."

"I appreciate that," Talen said dryly. "But I told you I can't. You're in danger."

"Right. Danger." Dread pooled in her stomach as they rolled to a stop before a sleek silver jet. He switched off the ignition and silence echoed throughout the space. He turned to her, raising an eyebrow.

"Are we going to have a problem getting on the plane?"

"We are not getting on that plane." She needed to get Janie out of the car so they could run for help. She unsnapped her belt.

A hand on her arm and one at her hip easily lifted her over the console to settle on his lap where her ass briefly rested against the hard ridge of a well-built man. Another smooth motion and they were outside the vehicle with her cradled in his arms. His broad hand had protected her head from the steel carriage, even as she fought his hold.

She jammed an elbow into his ribs.

His face dipped to confront hers. "Cara. Enough. I doubt you want your daughter to see you slung over my shoulder being carried onto the plane. Flashing those pretty pink panties."

Cara gaped at him, her breath coming in short gasps. He took advantage of the reprieve to drop her to her feet and open the rear door. "Unbuckle Janie."

His warm body trapped her in place; she had no choice but to unbuckle her daughter. She lifted Janie up and small arms clutched her neck. "They're still coming," Janie whispered.

"I feel them, too," Talen said, his breath stirring her hair. One hand enclosed her arm in a vise. "Let's get out of here." He slammed the door shut.

Waves of urgency battered Cara from both sides, propelling her toward the silent plane even as her mind rolled with questions. With reservations. Maybe she and Janie should try to take the Hummer.

"Stop thinking so hard." Talen released her arm while giving her a gentle push up the small steps. "We're leaving. Now."

"Go, Mama. Hurry," Janie implored.

Cara gave in. She climbed up the steps to sit on a thick grey couch. Janie snuggled up to her side with a sigh of relief, and Cara buckled them both in. Talen secured the door and reached into a cubby above the windows for a blue blanket, which he handed to Cara with a grin. No threat came from him, at least none directed at her. As he dropped into a seat facing her on the couch across the narrow aisle, the engines roared to life, and the plane taxied toward the runway.

Chapter 2

Talen allowed himself to relax as the plane leveled off. They were safe. He smiled at Janie while the girl studied him. She was awful tiny to have demolished three centuries of peace. Crocus blue eyes shot curiosity and daring from her young face as she spoke. "So, are you going to protect us?"

Cara jumped at the child's voice. The small jet lifted into the air like a predator on a mission while two pairs of identical blue eyes focused across the tiny aisle.

"Is that all right with you?" He turned his gaze on the child. She fascinated him. So fragile, even the whispering wind would threaten her. A real child. Human.

Janie squinted before looking his frame up and down, and reaching a decision, she nodded solemnly, her "yes" a bare whisper of sound. The knuckles on her tiny fingers clenched white on her mother's hand.

Talen remained silent for a moment, taking in the pale features of the two females. The blue blanket enfolded them both. Knowing full well what he pledged, he spoke. "Yes. I'm here to protect you." His vow threaded through the cozy cabin, and the child let out her breath with a smile while Cara frowned, glancing around. Probably for a weapon.

He knew what he'd promised, and since he hadn't broken a promise in his long life, he refused to start now. He studied the two as the plane gained altitude. Both had long, curly hair the color of burnished teak, deep blue eyes, and delicate bones. Something close to protectiveness nudged his conscience.

Janie gave him a toothless grin. "So you comed for us. Finally."

She tugged the tattered brown bear closer to her chest, and Talen grinned. Mr. Mullet did indeed wear a faded blue mullet as his hairstyle. Talen settled into the plush couch. "I'm here for you, Janie."

"Who are you?" Cara pulled Janie even closer.

Talen sighed. "I'll explain once we get to DC, Cara. All I can tell you right now is that you're safe."

"I don't think so. What the hell's in DC?"

"Who is in DC."

"All right"—her pretty eyes narrowed to daggers—"who the hell is in DC?"

The muted interior lights illuminated her fragile features. The stirring in his loins now made sense to him. He'd felt the change in his skin, in his blood the second he'd touched her, and now had proof of their connection on his palm. Forever. He refrained from studying his hand again—he'd do so later. "The Director of the U.S. Marshal's Service."

"You aren't a U.S. Marshal." She hurled the words as an accusation. A dare, even.

He grinned. "Not even close, darlin'."

"Explain."

The accusation and dare he could've ignored, but the plea, the concern from a mother attempting to protect her child, well, even he couldn't disregard that. And considering they had just become *his*, he should try to make them happy.

"I don't know all of the details, only that you're in danger. The life you've been leading is now over."

"What kind of danger?"

He studied her, wondering how much he should reveal. The woman looked to be on the edge, and unfortunately, there wasn't much he could do about it—if he told her everything, well . . .

"Your eyes are wrong." Janie's soft voice wound through the shrill sound of high-end jet engines.

"My eyes?" He fought a grin. His brother Dage was correct, as usual. Janie was beyond gifted, beyond a normal psychic.

"Yes. They're not sposta' be brown."

"Maybe they aren't," he agreed.

"Contacts—like on TV?" Janie scrunched her face in a frown.

"Contacts," he affirmed.

"Can you take 'em out?"

"Not yet. Later I will."

"Okay." The little girl leaned against her mother before closing her eyes with a sigh.

A chill skittered along Cara's spine as she listened to the exchange. What was wrong with his eyes? Why did Janie know about it already? Why did the sweet child have to see the future at all?

If Miss Kimmie didn't call to check on them, then surely Dr. Phillips, Cara's boss, would call. The jerk was under a deadline to keep his grant, and he needed her at work. Her research into creating a virus that would enhance the crop yield of corn showed enough promise to glean two solid grants for the next year. And oh God. Her sister Emma would go freaking crazy. She'd tear apart the U.S. Marshal's Service to find them.

Cara straightened in her seat, digging her nails into her moist palms as Talen kept his gaze on her. She lifted her chin to glare at the large man sitting so relaxed across the aisle. His size made her feel small. Vulnerable. Feminine.

He had a body designed for billboards. His thick chest, narrow waist, and long legs showed power and strength. Bold eyes sat in a hard face softened not at all by its own beauty; a masculine starkness that would render an observer speechless from afar. This close the effect was devastating.

"It's going to be all right, Cara." His voice gentled as he settled farther back in the couch. "You're safe now."

She refused to answer and continued to study him. Dark eyebrows slashed over those brown eyes that apparently weren't quite right. High cheekbones protruded as ridges over deep hollows, and his jaw clenched strong and formidable. And his mouth. God. Full lips didn't hint at a hidden sensuality; they boldly promised heated sex. Without apology. Minutes before those same lips had been on hers, and as they tipped up at her appraisal, a stirring tickled in her belly. An unfamiliar stirring the scientist in her yearned to investigate.

The woman deep within knew better.

He gave a full grin. "I suggest you get some rest, darlin'. Life just became very interesting."

"What about my plants?" she mumbled, hating the words even as they tumbled out of her mouth. What the heck? She and Janie had just been taken by an enormous soldier who kissed like the devil, and she was worried about her plants.

Talen lifted an eyebrow. "Your plants at your house?"

She nodded, biting her lip.

"I'll take care of it." At her frown, he nodded. "I promise, Cara. Your plants will be cared for." He cleared his throat. "Any other concerns?"

Pure arrogance, this man. "Yes. My sister Emma will go crazy trying to find us." As soon as tomorrow night, when they were supposed to have dinner. "I need to call her." Their parents had died just before Cara had turned sixteen; eighteen-year-old Emma had raised her from that point. As always, they'd make a plan together.

A slow shake of Talen's head had the nerves jumping along Cara's skin. "No. Let's get to the Marshal's service, and we'll figure everything out from there. Don't worry about the plants or your sister—you can trust me. Now try to get some rest." He crossed his long legs at the ankles and closed his eyes.

She had no choice but to trust him. Her plants would be

all right, and she'd figure out a way to get a hold of Emma. Next to her, Janie mumbled in her sleep. Damn it. Janie had a play date with a new friend tomorrow. And Cara had a grown-up date. The first one in—God, how long? The accountant who'd been calling her for months suddenly seemed, well, small. Boring. Pasty. Cara turned away from the bulky soldier relaxing across the aisle. Wide awake, she watched the clouds flash by out the window.

Two hours later Cara stared at the maple conference table while Janie happily ate a doughnut next to her. Crumbs dropped like snow on the smooth surface. They had been waiting for thirty minutes in the innocuous metal building to the left of the small runway, but at least new jeans and sweaters had been provided for them. The quiet of the room lulled her toward a much needed sleep.

She hoped she'd be able to keep her daughter safe. Danger swirled around them with a breath of its own. She may not have the clear sense of Janie, but she knew it was there. Her gaze focused on a pretty row of African violets lined up against the window—purple, pink, and white. Calmness settled over her.

She stroked Janie's wild curls as the steel door opened, and a slender, older man in his mid-sixties entered in front of a grim-faced Talen. The man's gunmetal hair was mussed, the lines on his face carved with a dull knife. She straightened in her chair as they took seats across the small conference table, waiting for one of them to speak.

"Ms. Paulsen, I'm Director McKay, and I want to apologize for this morning's drama." He reached out to pat her knuckles, his liver-spotted hand chilled. Unease wound through his body while his breath came in short bursts. Her own body tensed in reaction—now she couldn't even block this guy's emotions? The director's gaze flicked to Talen and back again.

"Director," Cara pinned the man with her best "mom

stare." "I want an explanation." He may be afraid of the silent menace next to him, but she wasn't.

Director McKay cleared his throat before smiling. His lips wavered a bit. "Well, simply put, Janie and you have been targeted by the Merodize gang out of New York."

"The who out of what?" Cara shook her head. "A gang? There's no way some city gang has ever heard of us, trust me. What's really going on here?" She swung a narrowed gaze at the motionless man next to the director. "Well?"

"Ms. Paulsen," the director huffed before grimacing at Talen. It was obvious who was in charge.

Talen leaned forward. "The gang is irrelevant; it just serves as foot-soldiers for the Kurjans."

"The Kurjans? Sounds like some weird terrorist group. What could they want with us?" Cara asked, just as Janie sucked in her breath, causing all eyes to turn to her.

"They're real?" Janie asked Talen, her face paling to the color of wet paste.

"They're real," Talen confirmed, his jaw firming. "But I promise they won't hurt you, Janie. You're safe, on my life."

Every motherly instinct came alive in Cara when her daughter began to tremble. "Who the hell are the Kurjans?" She slammed her hand on the table before rising.

"Sit down." She found herself obeying Talen's sharp command before thinking about it. He scowled. "The Kurjans are a mutual enemy. For reasons we don't need to go into now," he nodded subtly at Janie, "their main goal is to kidnap women. Those with enhanced abilities are especially sought. They now want you, Cara." He narrowed his gaze on her. "And your research abilities would be an added bonus."

The blood pounded in her head as her eyes widened on the two men. Her research abilities? There was no way some Iraqi terrorist group was searching for women with enhanced abilities. Or for those, like her, working to alter plant genetics to be more resistant to diseases. What in the hell was going on? Fine, she'd play along for the moment, at least until she could grab her daughter and run. "What enhanced abilities?"

"Come on, Cara. You don't need to hide anymore." Talen's jaw hardened even more.

"It's okay, Mama," Janie whispered, patting her mother's knee. "He already knows."

"Fine." The one word was all she was willing to give at this point. "So, what now?"

Talen cleared his throat. "I need a list of your relatives."

"Excuse me?"

"A list. You mentioned your sister—is she an empath, too?"

Hell no. None of his freaking business. "No."

His massive shoulders straightened, and he leaned forward to grab her hand. "I'll take that as a 'yes.' If the Kurjans are after you, they'll search for your sister, too. Where is she?"

Raw and hot terror sped through Cara's veins. She searched his face, seeking truth. "You'll help her?"

He gave a short nod. "Yes. I'll send someone immediately."

The moment mattered. Trust hurt. Cara gulped in air and gave Emma's work and home address. So close to her own house. God, please let Emma be all right.

Talen nodded and grabbed a cell phone from his back pocket, using speed dial before barking out orders. Soldiers would retrieve Emma the next day. He clicked it shut. "Any other relatives?"

Retrieve Emma? Boy, her sister wasn't going to like that. "Not that I know of." Her mother had been an only child and who the hell knew about the bastard that had been her father. Who the hell cared? "What is really going on here?"

The director eyed the door. "Mr. Kayrs can explain the whole situation to you while Janie and I hunt up more doughnuts." He stood.

"No, wait," Cara grabbed for Janie's hand.

"Cara," Talen's deep voice thickened. "We need to talk. Alone."

Janie leaned forward. "It's okay, Mama. I've dreamed about Talen. He's okay. I know it."

Cara shook her head, dread pooling in her stomach as Janie left with the director. A slow anger began to burn away the dread. She glared at Talen. "So talk."

He took a deep breath. "The discovery of your daughter has ended nearly three centuries of peace between my people and the Kurjans."

"Janie? What people?"

Talen pursed his lips, a frown settling between his eyes. Shrugging, he yanked a brown contact out of one eye, then the other.

"What the—" she gasped. Luminescent gold eyes glowed like molten lava. She pushed away from the table only to have Talen grab her wrist, flattening her hand under his.

"Stay. There's a lot more." He smirked and rolled her chair closer.

"This is a trick." She glared at the impossible golden hue, the heat of his hand overpowering the coolness of the table beneath her own.

"No trick, Cara. I am a protector of the Sanguisuga race."

"Sanguisuga? Isn't that Latin?" She'd taken only two semesters of the language in college.

"Yes."

"For what?"

His grip tightened on her wrist. "Vampire."

Cara coughed out a laugh. "You're a vampire?" Her gaze swung to the door. Where was Janie?

Issuing another of the deep sighs she was starting to equate with him, he smiled. Two sharp canines instantly emerged.

"Oh God." Cara struggled to yank back her hand.

"Do I need to bite you for you to believe me?" Interest and something darker wove through him, into her. She fought to block herself from his emotions.

"No. No biting." Her mind reeled while reality spun away. "This can't be true." She shook her head. "But you were out in the sun. It was early, but the sun was out." This wasn't happening.

"The sun only bothers the Kurjans, Cara. We're fine with a day at the beach."

"They're vampires, too?"

Talen shrugged. "No. They're monsters." His canines retracted.

"But they have fangs and drink blood?"

"Yes."

"And you drink blood?"

"Only in extreme situations."

"Extreme?" This couldn't be happening.

"During a fight or sex." His voice lowered to the growl he'd uttered just before deepening their earlier kiss. Something skittered through her belly in response.

"Oh." Her mind flashed, unbidden, to his fangs. And sex. Her heart thumped once. Hard. "Why?" She stopped fighting. For the moment.

"Why what?" His thumb traced heated circles on the pulse point of her wrist, his golden gaze dropping to her neck.

"Why Janie? Why do they want women with odd abilities?"

Talen ran a hand over his jaw, his eyes returning to her face. "Janie's special. You know that. Her psychic abilities are the strongest we've ever seen."

Cara straightened her spine. As fear cascaded down it. "But how do you know? How did they find her?"

Talen scowled. "Both races can sense such abilities in humans, but we need to be in close proximity to do so. We don't know how they found Janie. It could've been a fluke, but I doubt it."

"How did you find us?"

"We have sources in the Meridoze gang; we heard about the extraction plan just in time."

Cara stamped down on the panic fighting to rise. "Your peace has ended?"

"Yes. We were at war for hundreds of years until we both suffered too many losses. A treaty was signed prohibiting any contact with humans." Talen shrugged. "Peace lasted much longer than anyone predicted."

Cara narrowed her eyes. "You don't sound sorry peace is over."

Deceptively normal canines flashed in a grin. "We were made to fight. Plus, living among you, yet having no contact, has been difficult. We need humans." Golden heat ran over her face.

"For blood." Nausea rose within her.

"That too." His voice lowered.

Everything in her stilled, and even her heart may have stopped for a second. She lacked the focus to block the feelings coming from him now. "What else?" Her voice cracked.

"Both races are born male. Only. Our mates are human. And Cara"—his voice dropped to a rumble—"you're mine."

Chapter 3

This time Talen let her go.

Cara jumped up, knocking over the narrow chair. "Not a chance in hell." She didn't recognize the snarl echoing in her own voice. She was in a safe building protected by the U.S. Marshal's service, for goodness' sake—she had nothing to fear here.

Slowly, Talen pushed to his feet and strolled across the conference room.

Cara took a step back, her breath hitching.

Smiling, he leaned against the closed door.

She'd need to go through him to get out. God, he was huge. Even if she had known how to fight, she doubted she'd stand a chance when faced with such size and obvious strength. A feminine fear and a flutter she refused to identify whispered through her.

"I won't hurt you." His voice lowered, deepening to a tone that increased her flutter. He relaxed his stance against the door, his muscled arms crossing. "I won't let anyone harm either of you. Ever."

Okay. Fine. He was too big for her to fight, but she did have a brain. "Listen, Talen," she kept her voice soft, soothing. "It's great your dating pool just opened up and all, but I'm not looking for—"

A dimple winked in his cheek, stopping her words. She fought to keep her tone mild. "Am I amusing you?" Her chin lifted.

"Yes."

"Why?" She could even feel his amusement in the air, damn it.

"Your people. I've never understood why you ignore fate. She has her own plans."

"Fate?" He was throwing destiny at her? Come on.

He nodded. "Fate."

"Wow. That's poetic, Talen." Sarcasm replaced the softness. "But there's no way fate is involved here."

"You're wrong."

"Prove it."

"Okay." He lifted his right hand, palm out. A crest, an intricate one, spread across his calloused skin. Thick and black, a webbing of arcs together formed a knot with what might be an elaborate K in the middle.

"A tattoo?" She quirked an eyebrow, wondering if he had other tats on that magnificent body.

"No. A brand of sorts. It appeared earlier after I took your arm."

"A brand?" She snorted. "Bullshit."

Talen shrugged. "It's true, Cara. The mark usually doesn't appear until the mating act, but there are exceptions." Golden eyes pinned her. "Our bond must be strong."

"No."

Talen lifted a shoulder.

Her mind rebelled at the physical evidence before her eyes. "I said, no. I choose to ignore your fate." How could the mark have appeared? Conviction sat easily upon his face and her stomach rolled at the question of how far he'd go to follow his fate.

"That is your choice," he agreed.

"Damn straight." She searched his face for a trick, determination tightening her own jaw. A raised eyebrow met her glare. "But, you don't know anything about me. I could be married."

"You're not."

"How do you know?"

He shrugged. "My brother Dage shot your file to my smart phone."

Smart phone? Vampires used smart phones? Come on. "Where were you?" Damn her curiosity.

"In a meeting with my other brother, Conn."

Geez. Sounded like a family-oriented creature of the night. Or day. Or whatever. She tried another tack. "Besides, I have a date tonight."

She wasn't sure what her goal was, but she didn't reach it. A genuine smile played across his lips, and he uncrossed his arms. "You're not going to make it."

She inhaled the thick sweetness of the impatiens, trying to calm her nerves. Trying to clear her head. Most men relaxed when they smiled, became more approachable. With Talen, a showing of teeth seemed like a warning. His gaze ran over her face and her skin flushed in response. Enough. A creeping anger started to burn in her belly. "Get out of my way so I can get my daughter."

A slow shake of his head skittered unease down her spine. "While you may choose to ignore fate, the outcome of this day is inevitable."

"Outcome?" She hated the quiver in her voice.

"We will be married before leaving this building and mated before another dawn emerges."

"I. Said. No." She fought the urge to grab the chair off the floor and chuck it at his stubborn head.

"You may choose to ignore fate, and you may choose to ignore your own abilities, your own intuition that would tell you this is right, but"—angry green flecks swirled through the molten gold of his eyes—"you have no choice when it comes to the safety of your daughter. It is paramount. As her mother, you know that."

She stumbled back a step, fury slamming through her. "You're threatening my daughter?" Panic warred with her rational mind, and her breath caught. She needed to get to Janie. Now.

Talen straightened to his full height. "Hell, no. The most sacred duty I'll ever have is protecting that child." The green flecks in those eyes overtook the gold. "And any others we may have."

"I don't understand." Chaos and pure denial swirled through her brain.

"That's because you're not being rational."

"Rational?" Her voice rose to an uncomfortable shriek. She wasn't a woman who shrieked, damn it.

"Yes. Stop for a moment and think. The treaty's over. You and Janie have been discovered. You are a potential mate, one the Kurjans will do anything to acquire. You don't want that, Cara."

"I can keep my daughter safe." Her eyes widened as he laughed. He actually laughed.

"I took you in less than three minutes, and that was with keeping you from harm. With not scaring Janie. You can't protect her. Hell, your government can't protect her. Face it Cara, I'm all you've got." He straightened his stance.

She took another step back. "If our government isn't helpful, why are we here? Why are we meeting with them?"

"I didn't say they weren't helpful. I said they can't protect you. They do come in handy for a good cover story, which you'll need. Since you just disappeared."

Disappeared? Oh God. A sob rose in her throat, and she stamped down on the fear. Who was going to water her plants? She scrambled to reason with him. "I'll hire you."

"I don't need money." He pushed away from the door.

Toward her.

"If what you say is true, and I'm not saying I believe it, but, even so, if I marry you, the Kurjans would still want me."

"No. You only get one mate, darlin'. You'll be safe as soon as tomorrow. They won't be able to touch you. Literally." Two slow strides and he stood less than a foot away.

She lifted her head to meet his eyes, refusing to retreat another step. "Why?"

Talen pushed a curl off her cheek. "Chemicals. Something exchanged during the mating act." Another step and his energy swam over her, through her. The scent of man and purpose mingled with spiced pine to dance over her skin.

The gold of his eyes held her in place. Her heart started to thrum. His hand cradled her chin and those eyes dared her to stop him. Tension threaded through the room, and a buzzing began between her ears. She opened her mouth to say something, anything.

He lowered his head. Then, fire.

Firm lips heated hers, taking her under. His other hand moved to the small of her back. He pressed her closer. Into impossible hardness. Lava washed through her and she slammed shields into place, but this passion was her own. She couldn't shield herself from within.

He bent her to fit him, his mouth taking hers with a hunger barely checked. She forgot where she was. Hell, she forgot who she was. She returned his kiss, whimpered deep within, and pressed into pure strength. Her body softened as his hardened.

Still, he went deeper.

His growl echoed in the blood racing through her veins. He pivoted, lifting her onto the table. Her butt slapped hard wood as he stepped into her, one hand fisted in her hair, the other holding her upright. Her knees clenched his hips, and his tongue took hers, fiercely and without question.

He lifted his head, and she could only stare, bemused. The green dominated the gold in his eyes. How was that possible? A dark flush worked its way across his high cheekbones, and his canines dropped low and sharp.

Alarm cut through her desire, her body froze, preparing to flee. Her heart galloped into a run, and her mouth went dry. "Wait." She started to struggle.

Talen lifted his head toward the door like a wolf catching a scent. He released her and stepped away. "They're returning." His canines retracted again.

Cara jumped off the table to straighten her hair and clothing. What in the hell had just happened? Good God, she'd kissed him like the truth to the universe existed on his tonsils. Her breasts still ached heavy and full—for him. A deadly stranger with fangs—one who could probably kill her without breaking a sweat—and she'd kissed him like he was hers. She needed a shrink.

"Still questioning our bond?"

She concentrated on the closed door, refusing to look at him. "We don't need to get married."

"Yes, we do."

"You believe in marriage?"

"No. Our mating rituals predate your marriage. But I find I want your vows." He watched the door as well. "Since I can hear our minister with the director, you might want to accept that fact now."

"Talen—" There had to be some way to reason with him.

"Janie isn't safe until we reach my headquarters. Only mates are allowed to know its location, and we're not leaving until you give those vows, Cara."

Her mind scrambled for some way out of this mess. There was nothing but the need to keep Janie safe. "Fine," she spat, "but my taking vows doesn't mean anything else, Talen." The walls closed in on her, and she stifled the urge to scream her head off. Like a mouse in a maze, her gaze darted around the room searching for a way out.

"You think you'll say no, darlin'? After that kiss?" His deep chuckle sent her temper spinning.

"What kiss?" she retorted.

His second chuckle echoed louder than the first.

A small beep made her glance toward Talan's watch where he pressed a button. "My brother has arrived to pick us up. Are you ready to get married?" The deep hue of his eyes met hers in challenge. The door opened, and Janie skipped in before the director and a round man in black robes.

Cara's heart stuttered and then melted as Janie ran into her arms. Instinct and love washed over her—she'd do anything to keep her daughter safe. Even marry a vampire.

"I'm ready."

Less than an hour later, Cara signed the license for the minister wondering if the document would be recorded. Anywhere. The marriage ceremony had taken place quickly in the small conference room. Talen uttered his vows in a deep, sure voice while holding her hand in a large, gentle grip. Janie had all but danced with glee at her side. Then Talen wrapped a warm metal cuff around her left wrist. She attempted to study the intricate pattern inlaid on the thick copper but had been interrupted when the justice told Talen he could kiss his bride.

He gripped her chin with one warm hand, his eyes darkening to burnt gold as he leaned down, pressing her lips with his. It was a hard, quick claim; a promise of more to come, sending a rush of heat through Cara which nearly doubled her over. She was so damn unprepared for this.

"Very well folks," Director McKay brought Cara out of her reverie. "Talen, I need you to finish signing the new agreement in my office and Cara you need to sign your program papers with Marshal Nelson." The director nodded toward a wiry marshal, who had arrived at the conference room in a bustle of papers.

Cara's mind refused to focus. "Program papers?"

"Yes. We need to put you formally into WITSEC before we lose your file. That way we can explain to any family and friends that you saw a gang hit go down and needed to be relocated." The director rehashed the cover story they had invented for her earlier. He scrutinized his watch. Probably wishing this day was over.

"All right, come on Janie." Cara turned to go, forming a plan for their escape—after they left the secured government building. They'd take the elevator to the bottom floor and steal a car. Talen was wrong. She could keep Janie safe. They only had to get to her sister Emma.

"No. I want to go with Talen." Janie screwed her face up in an expression promising a fight. Cara sighed. Her daughter needed a nap.

"She can come with me." He moved forward and took Cara's arm. "You stay with Nelson, and I'll meet you in his office in a few minutes." She tried to jerk her arm away, but Talen's grip tightened on her as his eyes focused on her face. "I'm serious, Cara. From here to Nelson's office only. The Kurjans have allies all around you."

"Fine." She needed to get the formalities over with so she could make a break for it. Talen released her arm. Her small daughter skipped forward and took Talen's hand to lead him out the door behind the director. Talen shortened his strides to match Janie's. At the end of the hall, Talen turned, giving Nelson a hard warning look before following Janie into the room.

Panic filled her at being separated from Janie. She soothed herself with the instinctive knowledge that Talen wouldn't let anything hurt her daughter. However, she was no longer certain of her own safety with the man.

"This way, Ms. Paulsen." Nelson swallowed and gestured her toward the elevator. "I mean, Mrs. Kayrs."

Irritation jumped under her skin, and she yanked shields back in place. "Is there something you'd like to say, Marshal Nelson?"

"Oh, well, no." He punched in a lower floor number, something near his left foot capturing his muddy brown gaze. "It's just, well, they're such *barbarians*. I mean, they *kidnapped* the director three years ago, call all the shots, and won't even tell us where they live. They're cavemen with superior technology. They won't even share that technology with us!" Nelson took a breath to continue his rant and then slammed his lips together when the doors opened. Two large marshals entered the elevator, crowding the small space.

As the car descended, one of the men smiled at Cara with a perfect row of even, white teeth. She automatically returned the smile until she met his eyes. An uneasy warning trilled in the back of her mind. The feelings swirling through him contained a darkness she'd never encountered. Her shields slammed up.

She swiveled to warn Nelson just as the other marshal pivoted, shoving him against the side wall, injecting him with a small needle. She started to scream as Nelson fell to the floor and then, with a quick pinch to her neck, there was nothing.

Chapter 4

Groaning, Talen finished signing the last of the legal papers while Janie happily colored pictures of ponies beside him. His brother Dage owed him big time for appointing him liaison to this agency. The metal building housing the secret U.S. Marshal base hoarded heat like a miser with gold, and he wanted out. The third floor was even more stifling than the lower ones with the sparse conference room. He was anxious to get his new family home and claim his mate.

Suddenly, his watch blinked an insistent green. He pushed a small button on the side.

"Why the hell do we have you traveling away from the pick-up spot at a quick rate?" Although he phrased it as a question, his brother's deep voice sounded more irritated than curious.

"What?" Talen's heart thumped.

"We. Have. You. Moving. Away." Dage's voice went from irritated to pissed in a heartbeat. He was well known for disliking surprises.

"Fuck." Talen jumped to his feet and picked up a startled Janie, running for the elevator. The door slid open, and he wasn't surprised to see Nelson unconscious on the floor. Talen dodged inside as the director swiped a card over a small window before leaning down to make sure Nelson was still breathing.

Talen didn't spare a glance at the fallen man. An odd clenching of his gut caused his breath to hitch and a ringing sound to fill his ears. Fear? Brittle pine filled his nostrils, and his eyes started to burn.

"Are you on the tarmac?" he asked his brother, a rage building in his gut.

"Of course," Dage growled. "Where the fuck are you?"

"In the elevator, heading down. I'm not wearing my cuff; my wife has it on." Talen held Janie close as the car moved slowly—too damn slowly—down several floors. He should've taken the stairs.

There was a silent pause, then, "Wife?"

"Yeah, wife," Talen confirmed as he ran from the elevator, straight at his brother in the secured landing site, the small child held safely in his arms. He passed Dage, jumping aboard the open side hatch of the sleek blue vessel. His brother pivoted and followed, setting himself in the pilot's seat next to Talen, punching buttons before he even sat down.

"Ready for takeoff," Dage said while the engine quietly roared to life. The military vessel had been tweaked a bit by their brother Conn.

"What the hell?" Dage muttered at him while expertly maneuvering the small craft into the air. Talen had never appreciated his brother's ability to jump into action as much as he did right now. Or his brother Conn's ability to take any vehicle and alter it to fit their needs.

"Here she is." Talen's mind focused into the cold state of killing as a small blip moved over the radar. Janie's quiet sob against his chest had him schooling his face into a bland expression. He lifted her chin with one gentle finger, smiling at her tear-filled blue eyes.

"It's all right, sweetheart. We're going to get your mama back." The wide eyes on his held a humbling amount of both fear and trust. Talen felt an age-old male instinct to draw blood. Someone had taken what was his. He pushed any thought of Cara being hurt to the back of his mind and started to coldly plan for her abductors to die.

Dage nodded at Janie. "This must be the child you were to acquire?"

"Hi." Janie snuggled closer to Talen's chest. "You've been in my dreams."

Dage turned his full attention on the little girl, his grin of recognition matching hers. "You've been in mine, too."

"'Cept for your eyes, you look a lot like Talen," she said shyly.

"Nah." Dage focused his silver eyes and flashed twin dimples at the little girl. "I'm a lot better looking."

"My daughter, Janie." Talen wasn't surprised his new daughter apparently understood the private joke Dage shared with fate. "Janie, this is your Uncle Dage."

Dage's metallic eyes met Talen's before he looked back at the small, fragile female. "My niece," he said solemnly and with acceptance, as if only he heard the sound of fate clicking into place. Talen thought it was loud enough even humans could decipher its tenor.

Dage turned a full smile on him. "You were only gone for a day."

"I know."

"So, brother, I never said you had to marry the female." Dage lifted a brow.

"Someone had to." Talen's jaw firmed. "You know it was the only way to keep her safe."

"Yeah, but why you?" Dage challenged as his fingers moved deftly over the control panel.

"Because, she's mine," Talen answered with a finality that had Dage grinning in acceptance. Then he flipped over his palm to reveal the intricate design.

Dage's eyes widened. "The marking."

"Yep," Talen said smugly. "Definitely mine."

"Congratulations." Dage ran a hand over his face. "I'd begun to wonder if Conn's marking was a fluke, if the legends of the natural marking were true. If it could happen without an arrangement and the vow."

"I think it's supposed to happen that way," Talen said. "The brand formed the second I touched Cara's arm. And it hurt like hell for a moment."

Dage grinned. "I'd wondered about that as well. Conn said his hand felt as if a burning spear pierced right through it." He punched a couple of buttons on the consol. "I'd hoped a couple of us would naturally find our mates."

"We all should, Dage. Living with mate arranged via contract is no way to spend eternity, brother." Talen's hand started to throb the closer they came to the vehicle holding his mate. "Plus, you wouldn't have been dreaming about the same woman for centuries if fate didn't have a plan for you."

"Maybe," Dage allowed. "Did you tell your mate everything?"

"Of course not."

"How did you lose her?" The life scan attached to the life-cuff was strong and steady as it moved to the northwest. Dage's grin disappeared as Talen caught him up on recent events. "We should both go."

"No." Talen snarled. "My wife. My fight. Plus, you must keep Janie safe."

"I'm coming with you." The little girl sat up with a haughty glare. "My mama. My fight."

Both men stifled chuckles as their eyes met over Janie's head. Dage's gaze cleared like it did when a window to the future opened in his mind—his eyes narrowed and he cocked his head, listening to something only he could hear. Fucking psychic. He'd better predict good news this time.

Suddenly, a voice came in over the radio. "Dage, come in please." Strain hummed through the male's voice.

"Dage here, Chalton. What's up?"

"There's a rapid smattering of activity over the com-lines. A contingent of Kurjans is moving toward our base in DC. They know we've acquired the females."

"Shit," Dage muttered under his breath as they caught up with a black SUV flinging clumps of dirt high into the air as it maneuvered between masses of tall pine trees. "Send reinforcements to DC. I'll arrive at headquarters within the day. Dage, out."

He turned to Talen. "Her life signs look good—can you sense anything from her?"

"No. I haven't mated her, yet." Talen spied the SUV below them. "Pull back a bit so they don't see us."

With a nod, Dage eased the controls up as Janie tapped on the display. "Is my mama in there?"

Talen hugged her close, the scent of powder and innocence surrounding him. "Yes. She's fine, Janie."

"I've scanned them." Dage pulled away a safe distance and Talen turned his attention to the onboard scanner. "A driver, three passengers, and a fifth person prone in the rear of the SUV."

Talen's blood boiled at the image of his wife on her side, her hands tied before her. He quickly brought up an electronic map of the entire area. "The road leads here." He pointed to a deep, forested area about fifty miles to the north. He punched a few more buttons until a small lake with a few sparse cabins came into view.

"They have to be heading to one of these cabins. This one is the largest, probably their destination. There's a clearing." He pointed to a dubious clearing about a mile from the largest cabin. "Let me out here; I can make it to the cabin before they do."

"All right." Dage increased their speed, and they veered sharply to the left toward the small clearing. "We can wait for an hour."

Talen frowned. "Too risky. Get Janie to safety and I'll head to Jordan's. We'll get transport there."

When his brother landed, Talen buckled Janie into the seat before he jumped out and grabbed a duffel bag. He donned a dark vest, inserted knives of various widths and lengths, then tucked his gun in the back of his dark jeans. Finally, he secured his thick hair with a rubber band.

He leaned forward, giving Janie his most reassuring smile. "It'll be all right, Janie. I'll bring your mom to you as soon as you and Dage take care of business."

The little girl threw both arms around his neck and effectively sliced his heart in two as she whispered, "Be careful, Daddy. I've been waiting a long time for you."

Talen rose, a lump in his throat as he handed his little girl over to his brother. "My child," he said, and with a nod, Dage responded, "My life." The vow was as old as their earliest ancestors, yet it was the first time one of the five brothers had cause to give it.

Talen felt the future rushing in as his child placed her small hand in Dage's.

He turned away from his family, all semblance of the civilized man he'd been wearing disappearing. His eyes heated to a fierce lava, his savage features warning nearby wildlife a true predator was in their midst. As a light rain started to fall, he ran toward the cabin to reclaim his mate.

Chapter 5

Cara stifled a groan as the SUV hit yet another pothole, and sharp rays of pain shot through her foggy head. How the hell was she going to get out of this? She held back a sob. Thank God Janie had gone with Talen.

"Mino said the buyer doesn't want her damaged," a low voice with a thick Spanish accent hissed from the front seat. "She and the girl are worth five million. Suckers."

"But, we didn't get the daughter," a voice closer to her spat out.

"Yeah, but this one's gotta be worth at least half," came the sharp retort from the first man.

"Who the hell would pay that for a couple of chicks?" someone else sneered.

"Mino wouldn't say. Probably someone the bitch pissed off."

"Well, can we at least have some fun while we're waiting?" A nasal voice this time, causing chills to creep up her spine.

"No. She is to be unharmed."

The hungry desire to cause pain radiating from the front of the car made Cara's shoulders tense and then shake. Her stomach clenched. She fought to slam her mental and emotion shields into place—maybe her father had been right about empaths being touched by the devil. God wouldn't hurt her like this.

She swallowed another sob, pretending to be unconscious. She had to think of a way out of this so she could get back to her baby. The moldy smell of old carpet tickled her nose, and she stamped down on a sneeze before it could erupt.

The car slowed until it came to a stop. Four doors opened and slammed shut. Seconds later, the back hatch opened and the man from the elevator reached in and yanked Cara out by her bound hands. Her head clunked against the hatch before she stumbled against him and then found her footing on the wet leaves, several feet down. They'd lifted the vehicle to a ridiculous height.

He squeezed her arm, his breath hot against her temple. "You should be awake by now, bitch."

She yanked to the side, her head throbbing. She kicked out against his shin to escape the pain at her arm while bile rose in her throat.

"Oh, we have a fighter." He laughed hard and coarse while he released her abused flesh. "This might be fun." His laugh carried images of dark pain, and she fought to block her mind. The slipping of her empathic shields ripped a raw fear through her that even his threats failed to reach. He dragged her toward a large cabin.

Trees surrounded them, pure safety waiting for her. If she could break his hold, she could run for the forest. She tracked the nearest trail through her peripheral vision. If she escaped that way, she'd veer into the bushes and they'd lose her.

She stumbled and fell to one knee. He yanked her to her feet and backhanded her across the face. Her head flew to the side. Apparently "unharmed" meant something different to him than it did to her. She flashed her teeth. Her daddy'd hit harder even after a three-day bender. The bastard holding her smacked her again, and while she stayed on her feet, the blow scattered her senses and the mental shields slipped away. Oh God.

A roar cascaded from the surrounding forest, and an anger

not her own slammed into her with the strength of a title weight punch. Her fear morphed into pure terror.

What was coming?

The man holding her froze, scanning the thick trees. Without warning, a large blur of dark motion launched itself past her to take the prick to the ground. Blood sprayed in a graceful arc across Cara's lower legs and adrenaline spiked her blood with a clawing need to flee. Rusty copper mixed with the clean scent of rain, and her feet refused to move.

"Talen," she said, barely able to breathe as he rose to his full height. Blood splattered across his brutal features and over his hands, his eyes a primal gold in the strengthening rain. She gaped at the sharp fangs protruding from his mouth. They ran red. Then, the rapid sound of gunfire filled the air. Talen tackled her and she screamed. He shielded her with his body and rolled them under the car to the other side, where wet leaves crackled with their musty scent beneath them.

Protected by the SUV, Talen leapt to his feet. In a smooth, fluid motion, he threw a double-edged knife through the air. Cara shifted to peer under the carriage of the vehicle. A man collapsed to the ground with a gurgle of pain, his hand on the weapon that was buried to the hilt in his neck.

Pulling herself away from under the carriage, Cara grabbed the door handle and hauled herself to her feet, determined to flee if necessary. The safety of the forest beckoned her.

The remaining two men scrambled toward the haven. With an animalistic bellow, Talen leapt over the SUV and took the first kidnapper down with a flying tackle onto the wet leaves. His bare hands crushed the man's neck with a loud crunch. With a final snap of Talen's wrist, he rose and faced the remaining man, who backed up toward Cara, praying in Spanish.

Talen's oddly glowing eyes showed no mercy as he stalked the horrified man.

"Please, don't kill me," the man begged as he continued to stumble backward.

"You touched what's mine." Talen's voice was unnaturally guttural as he reached the man.

"No, no I didn't," the man protested, making the sign of the cross in the air. "I never touched her."

"All right," Talen said agreeably, "then you die quickly." With one quick slice of his arm, the man's head tumbled to the ground. Then, Talen turned toward Cara. The knife's blade glinted silver in the emerging moonlight, its point dripping red life onto the wet earth. Blood splattered his clothes and covered his hands. Savagery was stamped into every line of his face. His fangs glistened sharp and deadly in the dusky light.

Cara's eyes rolled back into her head, and with a small groan, she collapsed to the wet leaves.

Chapter 6

Cara regained consciousness with a scream as Talen hefted her from the passenger seat of the SUV. He silenced her with a quick squeeze.

"Where are your fangs?" she asked groggily.

He chuckled and carried her into a small summer cabin, easily kicking the door open with one foot. He held her away from the blood coating his clothing. She looked around, struggling with reality as the lingering scent of lemon cleanser filled her nose. What had she seen? Her heart pounded while her back muscles softened in exhaustion. The conflict warring within her threatened to shut her down completely.

The living area contained a couch and huge hearth. To the left, the kitchen held avocado-colored appliances and a large, quilt-covered bed sat in the far corner. The rain continued to drum outside as Talen placed Cara on the dark leather sofa and grabbed an old towel to wipe the blood off his face.

He lit a fire, and once the logs crackled, he crouched down to her eye level and stroked the hair away from her face. "Stay here and warm up, baby. I'll be back shortly." Spicy pine and the dark, earthy scent of man washed over her.

"Wait." Cara clutched his arm, her gaze on the now calm features of his face.

His eyes gentled. "I need to take the SUV back to the

cabin. They'll send reinforcements when the kidnappers don't check in. While I've already left a few surprises for them, I'll add a couple more on the car. Don't worry, I'll be back soon."

"Where's Janie?" She was almost afraid to ask.

"With my brother, Dage. She's safe."

"Wait. Shouldn't we keep the SUV, just in case?" She couldn't outrun him if necessary, she needed a vehicle.

Talen shook his head. "No. They'll have GPS and the last thing we need is for them to track us if we run." And, with a final kiss to her brow, he disappeared into the drilling rain.

Cara sat up wearily, her gaze on the fire. Talen had saved her life, without question—even as he sprayed blood, she'd been thankful he'd come for her. But his eyes burned brighter with brutality when he killed, which he did without a second thought, without hesitation. The last man begged for his life. Part of her wanted to run, but Talen, whatever or whoever he was, had her daughter, and she had no choice but to stay until she had Janie back.

Then she could run.

She looked around the cabin. The quaint space was entirely too secluded and with the rain drumming outside, it was entirely too intimate. Since it was late fall, there was no chance anyone else would be around. She had to find safety.

She moved toward the window, peering into the drizzly grey. The rain peppered the front porch, and a tiny green pot sitting on the railing caught her eye. Sucking in air, she threw open the door and lunged across the wooden planks to grab the plant. An ox-eyed daisy. Left outside to survive when his owners had left for the season. Ass hats.

"It's okay," she crooned, carrying the plant inside the now warm cabin. The daisy hadn't flowered and its dark leaves drooped, but the nights hadn't been cold enough yet to do any real damage. "I'll call you Henry." She grinned, putting the plant in the center of the table.

Her stomach rumbled. When had she last eaten? What

time was it now? How she could be hungry? To get away from Talen and find Janie, she needed her strength. She began pulling open cupboards to search for food.

As Talen returned, she stirred an aromatic stew on the old stove. Maybe she wouldn't have to kill him. He did save her after all. He walked in, and she turned from the stove, taking in his size, the raw strength swirling around him. She'd never be able to kill him—not a chance in hell. Realization settled like a boulder in her stomach, and she clenched her hands together. What should she do?

He sniffed the savory air and then grinned. "Yes, mate?" he asked with a raised eyebrow as he closed the door behind him, muffling the sound of pelting rain.

"Mate? Sounds different than wife."

"Both apply to you, darlin'." He removed his vest and placed his weapons on the mantel above the hearth.

"You washed the blood off," she murmured, her spine straightening, her stance challenging. This man had her child. Did that make them allies or enemies? Either way she had to get Janie as far away from him as possible.

"The rain did that." His eyes flared in response as he squeezed water out of his dark hair.

"Are you hungry?" She retreated from the battle, trying to add some normalcy to the situation.

"Starving." His eyes flashed fire as they ran over her, claimed her.

"Sit." Cara ignored his double meaning, gesturing him to the table, and ladled out two bowls of stew from a can left by the owner. "Um, how do we know more of those guys aren't coming? Do we even have time to eat?"

He nodded. "I just talked to Dage and had him pull up a satellite for the area. No one is within hundreds of miles. We're also monitoring enemy camps—we'll hear when they're informed about the failed kidnapping." Talen dropped into a chair, which squeaked against his weight. "We'll leave when dawn lights, so no worries."

She sat across from him and unfolded her napkin on her lap, relaxing her shoulders now that she was safe. For the night at least.

He raised an eyebrow. "Where'd you get the sad plant?"

Really. "He's not sad. He just needed some warmth."

"He?"

"Yes, he," she said, tossing her head. "So, you're really a vampire?" Damn. She had meant to ease into the discussion.

Talen's chuckle relieved some of the tension in the room. "Not like you think."

"What does that mean?"

"You've seen my fangs. Sometimes I take in blood." He took a bite of the stew and closed his eyes, his pleasure dancing along her own skin until she pulled mental shields into place. "But only in extreme situations like during battle or sex. We don't drink blood to survive, and we don't melt in the sun. A wooden stake through the heart would kill anybody but us."

"You're faster and stronger than most men I've known. And I've never seen metallic eyes before." Plus, he'd killed four dangerous men without breaking a sweat, without receiving one tiny scratch in return.

"Yeah, I assume that's just a difference in our races." He shrugged, shoveling in another mouthful of the fragrant stew.

"But"—Cara sat back as the thoughts raced through her mind—"don't you think it's odd we have these legends about vampires and it turns out you actually exist?"

"No. Like I said, our mates have always been human." His emphasis on the word *mate* brought a flush to her skin and a tingle to her belly.

"Why?" she asked, focusing on his words and not her internal reaction.

Talen shrugged. "Basic genetics. Human females have two X chromosomes and males have an X and a Y, right?"

Cara nodded.

"In humans, the woman always passes an X chromosome, and if the man passes an X, you create a girl, XX. If he passes a Y, you get a baby boy, XY." Talen took another bite. "Chromosome-wise, vampires have a V and an X."

"You have a different chromosome?" Cara thought for a moment. "So a human female will pass on an X chromosome to a baby, and you either pass a V or an X?"

"No. We can only pass on a V, thus creating an XV baby, which is a male vampire. Nobody knows why."

"Never, in all of your history, have you created a female vampire?"

"Never."

Wow. Emma was the geneticist in the family—she'd be fascinated by this. "So, somehow the word got out. About you guys, I mean." Someone somewhere had to have noticed their odd eyes and fangs.

A dull flush worked its way over his face. "There was another reason." Talen spooned himself more stew from the pot in the middle of the table. "About a century and a half ago, we had a group of nut jobs who thought they lived to suck blood. You'd call them a cult. They interacted with your people and acted like the vampires of your legends. We took care of them. But, we're not proud of it."

"My people? You mean the United States or all humans?" Cara asked. "And why didn't you reach out to us before? I mean, if you are so advanced and everything, why didn't you become allies with us earlier? Let all of us know about you?"

"You hadn't advanced to a point that made you beneficial to us, so we protected you from afar."

"Beneficial? Weapon-wise?"

"No. Science-wise."

"You need our scientists?"

Talen took another bite of stew before shaking his head. "We don't. The Kurjans do."

"So you saw no reason to interact with us before now." Truly, it was a bit insulting.

"Nope." He shrugged. "Individual contact was one thing, but as a race, you didn't have anything we wanted. Until now." His gaze raked over her face, and she squirmed in her seat.

A braver woman might have asked what he wanted now. Cara accepted that she wasn't as brave as she hoped. "Amazing." She shook her head as the world changed around her. "Wait a minute. My daughter is with vampires? Right now?" Her gaze darted to the door, nerve endings flaring to life along her skin.

"She's safe, Cara. My brother will protect her with his life."

She didn't think so, and her mind scrambled to keep up. "The Kurjans, evil vampires from somewhere I've never heard of, want my daughter." A red haze wavered across her vision. "Does that fucking sum it up? Vampire?"

"Pretty damn close." His eyes narrowed. "Though you probably *have* heard of it. They're based in Minnesota."

"Minnesota?" She breathed out in almost a laugh. This couldn't be happening.

"Yeah."

"How long have they been based there?" Her mind reeled.

"I think they moved there maybe three hundred years ago," he said, as if discussing simple historical facts.

"Oh." Sarcasm came easy to her now. "And we humans didn't notice?"

"Nope. You humans don't notice anything you don't want to, Cara." He took another bite of stew.

She asked her questions in rapid fire. "How have vampires lived among us for three centuries? Do they kill? Do I know any vampires? Do they pay taxes like everyone else?"

After she calmed down, Talen answered. "We've lived among you to protect you from the Kurjus nation. Our treaty has protected you."

"And now they've broken it?"

"Yes and they kill, or used to before the treaty. You might

know vampires, but definitely not the Kurjans. They don't look like us and can't go out in the sun, which is where your science is coming in. And of course, everybody pays taxes. You don't mess with the IRS, no matter which race you belong to." He gave a wry grin.

"How many people know you exist?"

"Not many. A couple of key people in your government, that's all."

"Are you immortal?"

"Close enough." He sat back and studied her. "I've lived long enough to have lost loved ones." Rubbing a hand across his chin, he cleared his throat. "Your file mentioned Janie's father—I'm sorry you lost Simon. Is the wound still fresh?"

Cara's breath caught in her throat, and she shrugged. "I miss him. We were good friends, and I think Janie would've loved him."

Talen cocked his head to the side. "You were mere friends?"

Smoothing her napkin on her lap, Cara nodded. "Yes. We dated for a bit, but I never expected love or marriage in my life." Her mind scrambled for anything else to talk about. "You said earlier you were a protector for your kind."

"I am. As are my brothers." Talen crossed his arms across his chest, a thoughtful expression sliding across the strong planes of his face.

"What does that mean?" She needed to find Janie.

"I guess you'd call us the ruling family. My eldest brother Dage would be considered a king in many civilizations."

"If you're in the so-called royal family, how are you a protector?" She placed her napkin on her bowl. "I mean, if your title means what it implies?"

"It does. Even when protecting impossible humans." Talen snorted in amusement. "But as the royal family, we're the first to fight when necessary. The five of us have trained since childhood. It's our duty as the royal family to be the first to defend. The first to die, if need be."

Cara took in his solemn gaze with a puzzled frown.

"I know." Talen agreed with her look. "Your people wouldn't fight with each other so often if the ones deciding to fight were the first ones to bleed. Your society has a ways to go, if you don't blow yourselves up first."

The superior look on his face rankled her temper. Her baby was with the protectors. The first to die, if necessary. It was unacceptable. "And where are you based?"

"You'll learn all about our home when we get there, Cara."

"Oh, I don't think so." The absurd reality hit her like a wrecking ball. The man before her was pure danger and every survival instinct she had screeched for her to run. "Get my daughter here, now." She rose to her feet, her eyes darting to the knife block on the counter and back.

Chapter 7

"Try it." His voice softened dangerously as he relaxed back in his chair. The rain beat a soft hum against the cozy cabin in direct opposition to the now tense energy swirling around.

She thought about it, she really did—the image of the blade piercing his immortal chest, the absolute surprise on his face as one of his prey plunged the knife deep, wiping that infuriating arrogance away. But the man still had Janie.

Cara took a full breath and used her most reasonable tone. "This isn't going to work, Talen. I've changed my mind. Janie and I will be fine on our own."

"We're married, Cara. You and Janie will never be on your own again." He spoke slowly, as if making sure she heard and understood each word.

"We'll get unmarried, Talen. I'm not joking. Even your barbaric race must have some sort of annulment process. I want one."

"Barbaric?" Talen raised an eyebrow and shrugged. "Maybe. But only those who haven't mated are granted what you'd call an annulment, Cara."

"Good. We haven't mated." She blushed until her cheeks ached.

"We will mate tonight, wife." His eyes flared hot and golden.

"No." She lifted her chin and ignored the skittering in her lower stomach.

"Cara," he leaned forward in his chair, "before this night has ended you will have no doubt you've been mated." Intent surrounded him. Then it slammed into her. Damn those faulty empathic shields—maybe she should've been working on the damn skill instead of pretending it didn't exist.

"Not a chance." Her body hummed to agree while her mind screamed run. "Besides, you said *you bite* during battle or sex. You don't mean you would, I mean—"

"Oh yeah, darlin'." Glowing golden eyes met hers. "I will bite you. And you'll like it."

"No." Cara tried to shove force into the words even as need scampered through her stomach and danced up her spine. "None of that's going to happen, Talen." A longing tingled inside her veins and called her a liar.

An arched eyebrow met her earnest gaze. "We're married, Cara. Soon we'll be mated. 'No' isn't an option for you."

"Bullshit." Cara may not know the man very well, but he would never force himself on her.

"I should probably tell you now to watch your language." Talen's face settled into set lines, his eyes direct, his jaw firm.

"Fuck you."

His teeth flashed and he stood to his full height. "Damn if you aren't perfect." He rubbed his chin, his gaze dropping to her breasts. "And don't think for a second you won't pay for your defiance."

The rumble of his voice issuing the sexual threat soaked her panties. Plain and simple. She searched for another tact. "You promised you wouldn't hurt me."

Talen's gaze traveled to her eyes, and his lips tipped in almost a grin. "I won't."

She slammed her hands on her hips and wondered if a decent sidekick could take out his knee. "I don't want to be mated."

"You will."

Cara opened her mouth to respond just as he gave an annoyed snort and yanked his shirt over his head. Her gaze caught on a smooth, perfectly muscled chest before moving to the side. A bloody hole covered his upper arm. She gulped. Crimson wove through the outline of muscles. "You were shot," she said slowly.

"Yeah, looks like it." He shrugged. "I think one bullet hit me, but it went right through." He poked at the round dark hole. "I should probably put something on this now, though."

The room spun around her, and she grabbed the counter for support. "You sat through dinner with a bullet wound?"

Talen raised an eyebrow in surprise. "I said it went all the way through. It's not a big deal, Cara." He reached over and grabbed a kitchen towel to press against the wound. "Check under the sink for a first-aid kit, will you?"

Cara looked under the sink before darting into the bathroom to find a kit in the medicine cabinet. She concentrated on not throwing up as she wiped the wound clean, amazement pooling in her stomach as the bullet hole closed and pinkened into healthy flesh once she'd removed the clotted blood. She worked with plants for a reason. It didn't help that Talen's gaze heated on her as her hands touched his flesh. Then he emitted a low growl from his throat.

Cara cleared her own throat. He was the only access to her daughter, and she had to bide her time. She stepped back after taping the bandage to his large bicep and wiped a hand across her forehead. She studiously refused to look at his strong, very bare chest and moved so the table sat between them.

A flash of lightning caused her to jump. The storm outside broke with the fury of a long-ago battle, and Talen's gaze remained hot and still on her within the tiny confines of the cabin.

"Stop staring at me," she snapped, facing him squarely.

She shivered as the storm outside brought an uncomfortable stillness to the small space.

"Stop running from me," came his arrogant reply. He crossed his arms, his eyes darkly golden in the dusky light, his stance deceptively calm.

Cara stared at the intimidating warrior only a few feet from her. Arousal warmed through her like a fine wine. His long dark hair lay in thick, wet tendrils around a face carved from stone. His eyes sparked as wild as the land around them, his body forged from steel. He was every dark fantasy she'd ever had—she ached in undiscovered places. Her muscles clenched in the need to break something.

There was no way she'd give herself over to an arrogant, dominating alpha male she just met. A vampire, no less. A tiny voice reminded her he had hunted for her, he had killed for her. His actions had consequences she might not be able to put into words, but she felt them to her bones. Without even touching her, he had made her his. His primal gaze told her so.

Her nipples hardened at the thought, and she shook her head against his claim.

Talen's eyes narrowed as the air vibrated around him. "You'll not shake your head at me." His command was quiet compared to the drumming rain outside, yet held more danger.

Her pulse quickened. "I'll do what I damn well please, Talen." She welcomed the onslaught of her rushing temper as a relief from the unfulfilled aching in her lower body. "We may be temporarily married, but I'm not one of your people, and I don't take orders from you."

He stilled, his unique eyes sharpening to burnt gold. Absent of even a hint of mercy, they captured hers.

"I had hoped to wait until we were home before taming that temper of yours, *mate*." Talen's voice softened in warning, a predatory light enhancing the green flecks in his eyes. "But I'm all right with taking care of it now, if you so wish."

Cara could only stare at the large man before her. A rushing desire warred with her hefty temper. Danger swirled around her. This shouldn't turn her on, damn it. She bypassed the nearest movable object, an old cast-iron pot, and went for the knife block instead.

Talen moved faster than possible. His much larger body pinned her against the lower cupboards, one hand tangled in her hair, the other around her small waist. She never even touched a knife handle. He easily picked her up with one arm and plopped her on the counter. His hips forced her knees apart. With a twist of his wrist, he tugged her head back to stare down into her eyes.

"You're not the only one with a temper, mate." Churned gravel coated his voice. He lowered his chiseled face to within an inch of hers, and his hardened groin pressed firmly against her softness. "You'd best remember that."

The rush of heat was unwelcome, and she struggled furiously in his firm grip. Her hands pushed uselessly against his rock-hard chest. Her breasts thrust out as he held her head still. "Stop calling me 'mate,' and let me go." She stifled a groan against the desire pooling between her thighs.

His lips tickled hers before he spoke. "You are my mate," he brushed her lips again, "and there's no fucking way in hell I'm letting you go." With a groan, he took her mouth, his lips firm and unrelenting. He delved deep into the warm recesses of her mouth, the arm around her waist pulling her against his straining erection. There was no issue of Cara refusing him. He didn't ask. He took.

She froze against the demanding heat of his mouth, fighting the liquid fire rushing through her. He angled her head, delved deeper than before, taking exactly what he wanted, and apparently what she wanted as well. The rain and wind clamored outside while the erotic savagery of his kiss ruthlessly conquered any remaining resistance.

With a whimper, she stopped trying to wrestle control over her new reality and gave herself up to the fire rising fast and burning hot inside her. What could one kiss hurt? The scent of man filled her head and suddenly, she *craved*. She returned his kiss with all the passion she had kept at bay for years. The amazing strength of him, the sheer maleness of him, overwhelmed her. Her palm splayed against the solid granite of his chest, and she moaned deep inside her throat.

Heat filled her. He began to draw away, and she nipped at his bottom lip, wanting more. His eyes darkened to molten fire. The hand in her hair tightened and his wrist twisted again, exposing the graceful column of her neck. He lifted her off the counter by her buttocks. She ran wet as he easily balanced her against him with one hand, her knees clasping the sides of his hips. Giving a smart shake of her head, she waited until he relaxed his hold and pressed her mouth to his neck. Salt and spice exploded across her taste buds.

Moaning, she reached down to his abs, tracing hard muscle with her hands. Perfect. Male. Strong. She leaned forward, swirling her tongue around one nipple, and fought a smile as he trembled.

"Cara?" The hand in her hair tugged until her slumbering gaze met pure liquid gold.

"Hmm?" She reached for his belt buckle, sliding the clasp free. She'd never felt such arousal. It may be temporary, but she wasn't going to miss out on this.

"Cara." He tightened his hold, sending erotic pain down her scalp. "I need to know, darlin'."

"Know what?" She yanked his belt free and dropped it to the ground, trying to press her aching core harder against him. She was ready, damn it—and now he wanted to talk?

He leaned closer, his breath brushing her skin, his gaze boring into hers. "That you accept me, that you accept us. That you want this."

Warmth spread through her heart to match that in her loins. "I want this."

He grinned, the hand in her hair sliding to cup her scalp. "And?"

She inhaled his spicy scent and her mind spun. "I accept you right now—the rest we'll have to see." Man, if she didn't get him naked soon she'd die. Or he would.

"Good enough," he said.

Then the world shifted as he tugged her head back, lowering his mouth to her vulnerable neck. "Did I tell you my people mark our mates?" His hot breath feathered over the soft skin, his hand kneading the supple flesh of her rear.

"Um," Cara could feel only the delicious friction as he rubbed her core against his.

The hand in her hair tightened in warning as he stilled their movements, "I asked you a question, Cara." He raised his head to pin her with a look that dared her to lose focus again.

"Um . . ." She struggled to find his words in her mind. "Wait. Did you say you mark your mates?" She stopped moving.

"Yes." Satisfied, he started to again lower his mouth to her neck.

"Wait." She struggled for release. "No. Wait, Talen. No marking."

Talen easily held her in place as he raised his head to within an inch of hers. "Oh, there will be a marking, Cara."

"You'll not mark my neck," she hissed, even as she pulsed against him.

"Who said anything about your neck?" With his dark question, he took her mouth with a flash of heat. He turned toward the bed, his strong hands cupping her rear, the sound of thunder directly overhead.

Fire licked underneath her skin as her knees clasped Talen's narrow waist, his hands on her, his mouth on her, demanding more. She whimpered deep in her throat. "Hurry up," she moaned, her entire being on fire.

A strong arm swept her shirt off her body in one fluid motion, baring her breasts to his flaring eyes. He growled and then, with a mere step forward, she was on her back, and he was on her. With his mouth hot and insistent on hers, he leaned down and ripped her jeans and panties from her body and threw off his own.

Cara gasped in shock as he penetrated her to the hilt, no preliminaries, no easing, just pure, primitive possession. He instantly moved in and out. Strong fingers dug into her hips, moving her to meet his thrusts. Good God. What had she agreed to? Her body wet and willing, she fought to adjust to his penetration, her breath catching painfully in her throat as he plundered to untouched depths. The orgasm had a life of its own, mercilessly, fiercely bearing down on her and ripping through her entire system. His name filled her head and then there was silence around them when she cried out and stars exploded behind her eyes.

Still, he thrust. "You okay, darlin'?" His voice rumbled to a tone deep enough to echo along her every nerve ending.

"Yes." She pushed up into the hard planes of his amazing body. "Do it again."

He may have chuckled, tightening his hold, somehow increasing his speed.

She could do nothing but hold on for dear life, her legs wrapped around Talen's solid hips. A painfully sharp desire washed through her again. The wide girth of him filled her to the point of pain, his mouth hot on her neck. She had no control over the pace, no control over her own body as the next orgasm slammed as suddenly as the first. She bit into the hard flesh of his chest as she rode out the waves. She wouldn't have missed this for the world.

Talen growled when her teeth penetrated his flesh. When the waves stopped tearing through her, he reared up and flipped her over onto her hands and knees, pumping his hips the entire time. His thrusts increased in speed and strength and her last image of his strong face burned into her memory—the sharp angles set into brutal lines of desire, his thick, dark hair wild around his shoulders.

She groaned as he pushed her shoulders to the bed, one

hand moving up to tangle in her hair, the other clenching her hip as he rode her. Burying her face in the soft quilt, she sobbed his name. A stirring started deep within. It spiraled out into a sensation that stole any breath she might have kept. It strengthened to a pinpoint sharpness. She teetered on a fine edge, fighting against falling over, fighting against the unknown, when, with a fierce twist of his hips, he forced her over. She gave a sharp, keening cry as her pleasure spiraled higher and hotter until her world exploded. She could only open her mouth in a silent scream. Intense waves of ecstasy rippled through her.

She came down with a whimper, her eyes shut tight, her body slowing relaxing. He continued to pump in and out. His roar filled her head when a nearly painful release tore through him, echoing throughout her own body, her empathic shields in tatters.

He remained full and hard inside her. A strong hand gripped her shoulder to guide her limp body upright while his other hand burned like hot coal on the front of her hipbone. He held her before him on her knees, her back to his damp chest. He clasped long fingers through her hair, pulled her head to the side, exposed her neck and growled, "Mine."

With a quick strike, he bit.

Chapter 8

The large screen fizzled from deep black to static grey in front of Dage's eyes. Sometimes the reception in his underground headquarters left something to be desired, though the pure oxygen that flowed through the well-lit caverns and reinforcements to the granite walls ensured not even a quake from Mother Earth herself would harm the inhabitants here. Several meters under the surface, where heat-seeking missiles or scopes would never penetrate, he let the pure scent of earth and rock ground him.

His shoulders had been in a relaxed state since Talen's check-in the previous night—he and his new mate were safe. Dage figured it'd taken his brother less than an hour yesterday to reclaim and protect the woman. Pride filled the king.

Dage focused, and the picture cleared to reveal furious activity surrounding the nearest Kurjus camp.

"Sir." Chalton, his computer expert, looked over his shoulder. "They want to talk."

Dage straightened in his chair and punched a series of buttons on the control panel to his left. A large image immediately filled the screen.

"Kayrs." The figure moved closer to the screen and coal black eyes hardened. "It has been awhile."

"Not long enough." Dage acknowledged the current Kurjan ruler with a bored nod. "Sorry to hear of Lance's death."

He studied the iron ore and taconite making up the blank rock wall behind Lorcan. The headquarters could be anywhere from Russia to Brazil. Though his money was still on Minnesota, and when his intuition whispered, Dage listened.

"Yes, well." Lorcan had pulled his bloodred hair back from his pale face, showcasing the blackness of his eyes. "Accidents do happen." He shrugged and gestured with a slash of sharpened nails. "I was named Ruler last week. Things are about to change, Kayrs."

"Really?' Dage asked as another Kurjan moved into view to whisper something inaudible to Lorcan. "I don't think so."

Lorcan nodded at his subordinate and lifted his head, his dark eyes gleaming. "You have the child."

"What child?" Dage kept his voice neutral as Chalton ran fast fingers across the keyboard to gain information. He better not have a security leak. Though chances were the Merodize gang had already reported back to Lorcan.

"You know what child," Lorcan hissed, his naturally red lips contrasting with the pasty whiteness of his skin. "Our Oracles have seen her destiny. You must turn her over to me now."

"No transmissions in or out the last day," Chalton mouthed silently, his hands tapping across the control panel. "No breach on our end."

"There's no child here, Lorcan. You might want to reevaluate your informants." Dage's bored façade remained in place. "Plus, what could you possibly want with some human child? Are you starting a school for humans?"

"Funny. This girl is special. She has the gift of sight we've been waiting for and is to be mated on her twentieth birthday to my eldest son, Kalin. The Oracles have declared the future that must happen, if any of us are to survive what's coming." Lorcan's eyes gleamed to rusted purple. "And the mother is mine."

Dage lifted an eyebrow at his brother's certain response to

that claim. "Really? Something's coming, huh? You know, I've always wondered why each Kurjan successor is just a bit nuttier than the one before. Is there some sort of lunatic criteria you guys try to meet?" And God help them all if that nut job Kalin ever took office. Dage hadn't met him personally, but his nightmares told of a possible fate none of them would survive.

"Silence!" The force of Lorcan's bellow sent his subordinates scurrying back a foot or two, and Dage watched impassively as Lorcan's eyes morphed to a pinkish purple. "You will not mock the Oracles. They have seen the future to arrive. For even your people, the shifters will end us all." Lorcan visibly struggled to control himself, his canines grinding like a rock crusher. "Turn the child and mother over now, and you will avoid the war you've run from the last three centuries. Last chance."

Dage smiled the predatory grin he was known across the Realm for. "Fuck you." He nodded to Chalton to arm the weapons stored deep below the earth's surface.

Lorcan failed to hide an uneasy swallow. "Fine." He moved back from the screen, apparently not willing to start his war at this time. "But you won't be able to concentrate on human women for long, Kayrs. In fact"—Lorcan's yellow teeth gleamed in the semi-darkness—"I think you'll be occupied with more important matters. Soon." With the last word, the screen went black.

"Damn it Chalton!" Dage keyed several commands into the console at his fingertips. "Contact our scouts and find out what the hell is going on."

"Yes, sir," Chalton replied absently, his gaze on the computers.

Dage sent out a message for his brothers to contact him. Jesus. Kane was across the ocean, Talen raced through the U.S. with a mate in tow, *a mate.* And Conn. Man, Conn had to get his life in order—distraction rode him hard these days. They all knew that red-headed distraction practiced powerful magic in the land of the faeries, magic they might all need soon.

Rubbing his hand across his eyes, Dage sighed. He couldn't order Conn to reacquire his mate, especially since they'd probably have to go to war for Moira ever to leave the green isle. He grinned. He'd liked that spunky witch from the get-go.

A request sounded through his earpiece, and he pushed a button to let the door slide open. Janie bounded inside and hopped to perch on his lap. "Hi, Uncle Dage."

He settled her safely into place. "Hi, sweet girl." Determination flowed through him to protect the perfect child. Her blue eyes gazed with adoration as she showed him the drawing she carried. "I made a monkey."

Well, maybe. Or a dog with long arms. "It's perfect."

She grinned, giving a happy squirm. "Whatcha doin'?" Her world had apparently righted itself last night when he'd informed her that Talen and Cara were safe.

"Working." He glanced around the rock wall surrounding the quiet cavern—only Chalton worked busily on his computer, his blond hair tied at the nape and out of the way.

"This is almost an empty room," Janie said, grinning at Chalton. She gave him a tiny finger wave that pretty much ensured an excellent Christmas present from the computer expert. He gave her a half smile and mock salute before turning back to the console. Did Chalton just smile? Dage hadn't known the guy had teeth.

Dage tweaked Janie's pert nose. "Yeah. We just use this room for teleconferences." Maybe the chamber was too stark for a little girl. He didn't want anything to scare her. Ever.

"What's a telie, a teliconf . . ." She pursed her tiny mouth in question.

He grinned. "It's like a telephone but with a screen."

"Like TV?"

"Yeah." Except the monsters on television weren't real.

He fought the frown that wanted loose. Janie needed to believe in the security and safety of her world.

"Are you worried about the war?" she asked, her small hands clasping together.

The frown won. "The war? It's over, sweetheart."

"No." She shook her head, patting her prized picture. "Not that one. The one that's coming."

Awareness and something close to dread slid through his body. His muscles tensed. "You know about that one?"

"Yeah." She frowned, her pretty blue eyes darkening as she met his gaze.

Regret filled him now. "I'm trying to keep it from happening."

A wise smile much too old for her young face slid across it. "I know. But, it's gonna happen and we need to fight."

He shook his head. "I'll fight, sweetheart. You won't need to."

She put both of her warm hands against his face, effectively immobilizing the ruler of the most powerful beings in existence. "I will need to. You know that, Uncle Dage. You do."

God. Not while he drew breath. Fate was in for a beatdown in this case, and he needed to get back to work. Punching a code on his earpiece, he waited. "Jase? Meet me in the rec room, we need to plan." Who would've thought his youngest, wildest brother would become the most dependable—at the moment at least. What the hell was his world coming to?

Several states away, Lorcan nodded to a subordinate to flip off the screen. Long nails clicked against the keyboard until only overhead fluorescents lit the underground control room. A black screen covered the rock on one entire wall with two consoles on either side—sterile and giving no clue as to his whereabouts. The thick Minnesota mountains provided safety from interlopers, enemies, and the sun.

He turned toward the door and swept into a long hallway furnished with priceless Picassos the world didn't know about. Fucking Kayrs. The bastard was only fifty years older than Lorcan's three hundred, yet an ancient wisdom rested in the king of the Realm. Bastard.

The plush white carpet muffled Lorcan's heavy footsteps, and he inhaled the pure lilac scent he had infused into the air each morning. Almost as good as being aboveground or even outside. Almost.

Kayrs had no right for such superiority—most of the non-human creatures alive today were about the same age. Their ancestors had procreated quickly during the war, knowing that death was likely and a possible treaty prohibiting contact with humans on the horizon. Prohibiting contact with potential mates. Human ones, anyway.

Lorcan grinned as he opened the door to his private office. Not that he'd adhered to the treaty. Proof of his defiance lounged in a thick leather chair watching an ultimate fighting championship.

His son flipped off the television and turned to face him, deep purple eyes anything but interested. "You wanted to see me?" Boredom and just a hint of insolence coated the words.

Lorcan straightened his spine, shutting the door. He walked around his massive onyx desk, putting himself in the position of power with his chair raised. "Yes." The bubbling of his six-foot long tropical fish tank failed to provide its usual distraction from its place against the side wall. "I understand you nearly killed Jastin during training yesterday."

Kalin shrugged a large shoulder. "So." He rested one broad hand on the arm of the leather chair, relaxed.

The casualness sent a shaft of irritation through Lorcan. Damn kid could at least pretend to be in fear of his father. His ruler. Lorcan studied his young son, noticing the way the black jeans and white shirt gave him an older, more dangerous aura than a fifteen-year-old should have. He'd tied his thick black-red hair off his neck, throwing the sharp white planes of his face into prominence. His coloring was muted, more subtle than most. Lorcan tried to hide all emotion from the boy, knowing any weakness would be instantly exploited.

Kalin rolled his eyes. "He's weak."

Lorcan fought a chill at the nearly blank look in those unusual purple eyes. Most of his people had purple eyes, but Kalin's were a purple almost mixed with green. Unnerving. Eyes should be purple, red, or black. Not the color of the hottest of fires, the green at the bottom of a polluted lake. "True. But, you're going to lead him someday."

"Then he should learn to fear me now." Not by one decibel did the inflection change.

Lorcan cleared his throat. "Also true." He reached forward and shuffled some papers on the desk. "I also wanted to discuss the fact that another woman has gone missing from St. Paul."

"Really?" Black eyebrows lifted. "St. Paul's a big city, father."

Damn if pride didn't infuse him with his siring of the little sociopath. "Yes. But we need to keep a low profile for a while. Not that I'm accusing you, son. But—"

"Accusing me of what, father?" Kalin leaned forward, his deep maroon lips creasing in a smile. "Of taking that woman off her back porch and carrying her into the forest? Of laying her down and stripping those silly yoga clothes off her lush body?" Sharp canines flashed in what could never be considered a smile.

Lorcan fought to keep his face calm, his eyes amused. He had hoped Kalin limited his rage to the training field—for now at least. He really didn't want to have to relocate—he liked the weather and overcast skies in Minnesota. And if Kalin persisted in his escapades, the human authorities might become a bother.

Kalin hissed out a breath. "She shouldn't have taken that dog out once darkness fell. Would you like to know how it felt to sink my teeth into her thigh?" A dark flush covered the natural white of his cheeks. "Of how I took her body, her soul, and ultimately her blood as she begged? As she promised anything to live?"

"Kalin—"

"They'll never find her body, father. I promise you that." Kalin smirked, and Lorcan fought the urge to roll his own eyes. Taking such pride in killing a defenseless human female—the boy had maturing to do.

A knock on the door ended their discussion. "Enter."

A tiny blond human shuffled inside carrying a Belleek tray set with two cups. "Morning tea, your lordship." She kept her gaze down, focusing on the steaming shamrock teapot, each step carefully placed until she reached his desk.

"Orange zing?" Lorcan asked.

"Yes, sir," the woman answered, her fingers trembling so the cup she extended rattled against the saucer. A sour milk scent mixed with the fragrant orange spice tea. Damn it. The woman's fear would ruin his tea time.

"Lila?" Kalin asked, his voice dropping to silk from behind her. "Are you with child yet?"

She jumped, clanking the teapot down that she'd just picked up. Lucky for her not a drop spilled onto his thick desk. "Er, no Master Kalin, not yet." Her gaze stayed on the pot even as her shoulders stiffened to rock.

Lorcan frowned. Damn. Blythe had mated her nearly a year ago—what was the problem? The clairvoyant woman had made a deal with the devil, and she'd better keep up her end. She was what, a starving homeless artist when they found her? The gods certainly had a sense of humor requiring his superior race to mate with their own prey.

"Hm. Pity that. Well, we could always use you for the experiments." Leather protested as Kalin shifted his weight. "Or I could knock you up. Blythe need never know."

Her gasp preluded the sharp smell of sulfur that accompanied raw terror.

Lorcan rolled his eyes. "You're dismissed. I'll pour my

own tea." Now the little shit was offering to procreate with the mates of his soldiers. What was next?

Her muffled "Yes, sir," barely made sound as she all but ran out the door.

"Jesus, Kalin. She almost spilled on my desk." Lorcan leaned forward and poured tea into his cup, raising his eyebrow at his son.

"No, thanks. Tea's not my thing," Kalin said, his gaze on the door.

A warning tingle wandered down Lorcan's spine. "She's a mate, Kalin. You leave Lila alone." That's all he needed—a war among his own people. Killing was a fine sport, but as a future leader, Kalin needed to learn diplomacy. Strategy. "Plus, the mating allergy might kill you at your age."

Kalin shrugged, settling back into the chair. "No worries. She's not my type."

"You're fifteen. You have a type?"

"Yeah. Fighting mad and desperate. I'd be bored in two minutes with that bitch. We should use her for the experiments." Kalin flashed his canines again. "Speaking of challenges, how did the conversation go with the king? I take it they have our females?"

Fury danced along Lorcan's spine. "Yes."

"Hmm. Well, we'd better get going on the experiments. You know one of the Kayrs will mate the mother."

Bastards. "I know. We'll get to her before that." Lorcan took a sip of the tea, and orange spice exploded across his taste buds.

"Maybe." Kalin rubbed his chin. "I've always wondered why they only get one mate. I mean, if one of ours dies, we can just get another to give birth."

Lorcan shrugged. "I don't know. It's their biggest weakness."

"Or, their biggest strength," Kalin said, pursing his lips.

Perhaps. Lorcan took another gulp. "Though, we have had Kurjans mate for life."

"But you didn't." The purple in Kalin's eyes swirled with the green. "With my mother, I mean."

"No," Lorcan agreed, a pit lodging in his stomach. "Though I didn't kill her, Kalin." He wondered if Kalin would've engaged in his extracurricular activities if his mother had lived. Had shown him the love of a female, if the worthless bitch had been capable of it. Not that Lorcan gave a shit. But, if the hunt, if the killing, overshadowed the war at hand, then Kalin must stop.

"I know. She killed herself the day after birthing me." No emotion showed on the young man's face. Maybe he had no real emotions.

"Yes, Kalin." And it worked out—now Lorcan could mate the Paulsen woman. "Your mother was a whore I took off the streets of Dublin." But a gifted one and not just with her mouth. "How are your psychic abilities coming along?"

Kalin shrugged. "Well enough to know that my young mate won't be captured."

That was unacceptable. Kayrs couldn't hide the child forever. "You're wrong; we'll acquire your mate."

Kalin hissed out a breath. "I already told you—I don't want her acquired yet."

Shaking his head, Lorcan sipped more tea. "Of course you do. If we get the child now, you'll have time to train her—to teach her our ways."

Standing and heading toward the door, Kalin turned. "I don't want her trained, father."

Lorcan paused with the cup halfway to his mouth. "That's ridiculous. Why in the world would you want her to grow up with the vampires, rebellious and independent?"

"So I can break her."

Chapter 9

The rain drummed an idle pattern on the roof while Talen tangled his fingers in his wife's silky hair, the scent of lilacs surrounding him. *His wife.* He had always figured he'd be the last of the brothers to mate, not the first. Or rather, the second. He rarely remembered that Conn had mated nearly a century ago, since the dumbass hadn't seen the woman in that long. Talen stretched in surprising contentment and wondered at the gift he held. He was no stranger to sex, but never had he felt the merging and pure searing pleasure of the night before. He had told her in temper he would never let her go. He now knew that to be the full and absolute truth. "Mine," he whispered quietly into the cozy cabin.

A distant explosion rent the air, and Cara awoke with a soft cry. She found herself curled on her side against Talen's large and warm body, her hand flat over his heart while his fingers moved softly through her hair.

"It's all right," Talen's sleep roughened voice whispered above her, and she lifted her head. God. He looked even more like an ancient warrior with a day's growth of dark beard and golden eyes mellowed with sleep. The breath caught in her throat as her body came alive. Then his eyes deepened to liquid gold, and she exhaled on a gasp.

He leaned down and gently pressed his mouth against hers before lifting to study her face. "Are you all right?"

Heat spread over her cheekbones, and her lids closed to cover her eyes. "Yes, er, I'm fine."

"Open your eyes, Cara."

She looked up into deep gold. "I'm fine, really." She ran a hand down her arm and pulled at the metal cuff still attached to her wrist. A burnished gold, it wrapped twice around like an ancient Egyptian armband she had once worn with her Cleopatra costume during Halloween. "I can't take this off."

Talen grinned. "I know. It's my cuff. Only I can remove it."

Seriously? Good thing it wasn't a chastity belt, for Christ's sake. "Is it gold?" She pulled at the warmed metal, frowning when it didn't budge.

"There's gold in it. A Shaman Alchemist created them for us brothers centuries ago as a gift to my mother. He figured she'd need help tracking the five of us." Talen shifted onto his back and tugged her into his side, running a hand down her arm to clasp the cuff. "We can track each other anywhere in the world with it."

"Can you put it on anybody?"

"Nope. The cuff goes on us or a mate." His hand wrapped around her wrist, the gentle motion in such a strong man making her breath catch in her throat. "Or, in Conn's case, it's thrown in a drawer somewhere."

"Conn's a brother?" She shifted against Talen's side, warmth pooling in her abdomen from his heat.

"Yep. He's the fourth—pure soldier. My older brother, Dage, is always on Conn to wear it, but it's a sticky subject, so . . ."

Cara tilted her head back to meet Talen's golden gaze. "Why?"

Talen grimaced. "Conn accidentally mated the youngest daughter of an Irish Witchcraft High Priest about a century ago. The cuff belongs on her."

Accidentally? How in the hell . . . "Oh." Cara snorted. "You mean he had a one-night stand and ended up mated?"

Not that she believed in this mating crap, but still. Served him right.

Talen's full lips tipped up. "Close enough. Though, I do believe he's given her enough time to come to grips with the situation." Thunder bellowed in the distance, and a slight pattering sounded from the roof.

"Ah, a witch? Like a real witch?" Curiosity battled with Cara's scientist's mind.

"Yep. You'll probably meet her soon. I wouldn't be surprised if you had a sister-in-law to gripe with sometime soon."

Unease swept through Cara. "Um, Talen. We should probably talk about this whole thing. I mean, it's temporary, you know?" One just didn't get married and mated after a couple hours of knowing somebody.

"Temporary, it is not," he said, dropping his head to place a smart kiss on her mouth. Thunder now pounded directly overhead. His eyes narrowed, and he rolled out of the bed, apparently unconcerned with his nudity. She couldn't blame him. He was all smooth skin and hard packed muscle. Good God, a bite marked his left pec—one that matched her teeth. She fought a blush as he quickly donned his clothing and weapons from the previous day.

"Stay here, darlin'. I'm going to check out the cabin and make sure my surprises for the human gang-members finished the job." He leaned over and gave her a hard kiss before heading for the door.

Cara waited until the door closed behind him before stretching in the big bed with a soft groan. She was tender *everywhere*. Her mind played scenes from the previous night like an old movie projector. Talen had alternated between wild sex and gentle seduction, leaving her relaxed and loose in the morning. And sore.

She had never considered herself a passionate woman. Her father had taught her early on that men weren't to be trusted—the bigger they were, the harder they hit. She graduated high school a year early and immediately headed into college and graduate school. After losing her parents, she had thrown herself into her studies and concentrated on plants, not people; resulting in her being shy and a bit awkward. Her one sexual experience had been more of an experiment with her good friend and associate lab geek, Simon, who died in a car accident a mere month later, leaving her with the wonderful gift of Janie. Between motherhood and work, there had been nothing left. She smiled softly about her newfound knowledge—she could be a very passionate woman.

Cara lost her smile as she ran a finger over the already healing puncture wounds in her neck. His unique scent of spiced pine clung to her skin. She barely knew Talen; well, maybe she knew him quite a bit better than she had the previous night, but still, they weren't even of the same species. He had claimed her on a primitive level she didn't know how to define; she didn't know how to protect herself from him. Even more, she knew he wouldn't allow her to.

And that scared the hell out of her.

A crash of thunder outside made her jump and propel herself out of the bed to grab her clothing off the hardwood floor. She needed to be dressed when Talen returned. She paused in pulling on her underwear. "What the . . ." She twisted her torso to stare at her right hip. Her skin held the full imprint of fingers from a man's hand. A large hand. She swiveled to see the connected palm on the backside of her hip with the intricate black crest settled in the middle. Was that a K? It was the perfect imprint of Talen's hand as he had held her when he had bitten her. A marking on her ass.

"How?" she hissed as she poked at the imprint. It didn't hurt. So it couldn't be a burn. But she remembered how hot his hand had been, though her focus had admittedly been elsewhere.

The front door crashed open, and her mouth opened in shock at Talen.

"You *branded* me?" Fury greater than she would have

thought possible swept through her and made her voice hoarse. Rage quickened her breath and sprang the nerves along her skin to life.

She was going to kill him.

Talen paused as the wind threw hard pebbles of rain inside the cabin before he stalked inside and slammed the door shut. "Not now darlin'. Get dressed, quickly. We have a problem." He turned to peer outside the window, pushing a button on his watch.

"Dage, come in." His voice was low and controlled, but the sense of urgency in the air had Cara throwing on her clothing. She'd kill him later.

"Dage here." Tension crackled across the line.

"Are you at headquarters?" Talen peered into the drizzly grey day as Cara stared at his back.

"For a few more minutes. They've hit us in Texas, Canada, and Spain."

"Shit. We're at war." Disgust coated Talen's voice. "I need you to pull up satellite for my location and tell me how many Kurjans are in the area."

"It's daytime. There shouldn't be any," Dage said as the sound of typing came across the line.

"Tell that to the one I just killed," Talen retorted. "Plus, it's raining. No sun in sight."

"Crap. A squad of five is about two miles southeast of your location."

Talen nodded. "I killed the scout."

Jesus. How many people had he killed? How often did he kill? Fear slumbered down Cara's spine to settle below her ribs.

"I'll send someone to you," Dage responded.

"No need. We'll head your way. You take care of Texas."

Cara moved toward him with a soft sound of distress. Talen turned narrowed eyes on her. "Dage? How's my daughter?" His eyes held her wide ones captive.

A male snort echoed over the line. "She's now the proud

owner of seven ponies. Though, she liked the one I gave her the most." Pleased pride came clearly across the miles. "Tell your mate Janie's safety is our highest priority. I'm leaving Jase and Brack with her while I'm in Texas."

Talen's brow furrowed in concern. "Brack? He'll protect Janie with his life, but looking at him could give a sweet child like her nightmares for years."

Dage chuckled. "Yes. *Uncle* Brack is currently learning how to make sprinkled iced cupcakes with your bewitching daughter."

"Cupcakes? He's the deadliest soldier I've trained—his frown is rumored to bring the devil."

"She even has him wearing an apron."

"What?" Talen grinned at Cara.

"It's blue with white flowers," Dage laughed out loud. "I'll be in touch from Texas." The line went dead.

Talen turned amused eyes on Cara. "Apparently our daughter has enthralled our soldiers."

Cara's eyes filled with tears. "We've never been apart, Talen."

Talen's gaze softened on his wife. "Then let's get to her, darlin'." He opened the door for her. A beat-up brown Chevy pickup with its engine running waited in the pelting rain.

After grabbing the plant, Cara ran through the deluge and jumped inside the truck to settle on a rough thunderbird blanket. She buckled her seat belt as Talen settled his large bulk and starting driving across the bumpy road toward the north. "We'll keep heading northwest to meet some friends," he murmured as the windshield wipers worked at top speed to clear the window.

"What about the Kurjans?" Cara scrutinized the trees before peering out the back.

Talen shrugged. "They're a couple of miles behind us and at some point we should hit sunshine." He turned toward her. "Can you sense them?"

"Of course not." What was he talking about?

"I think you can, Cara."

"That's ridiculous." She ignored the big rock in her stomach as she protested. "Whose truck is this?"

"I borrowed it from a neighbor."

"Ah." Cara's mind reeled. "Who are Brack and Jase?"

"Jase is my youngest brother, and Brack is one of our soldiers. Janie couldn't be any safer than she is right now." He swore under his breath as he dodged falling branches from the pine trees surrounding them. "You can't ignore your abilities forever, mate."

Cara again ignored the subject. "You called her 'our daughter,' " she said softly, her eyes on the muddying road as lightning lit the sky before them.

"Of course," Talen said in surprise. "I meant what I said, Cara."

"Where is she?" The softness had steel beneath it.

"She's at our headquarters."

Cara let out an irritated hiss of breath. "Where, Talen?"

He was quiet for a moment. "In the mountains around Boulder."

"Boulder? Colorado?" She turned in surprise to his profile as a fierce wind beat against her window.

Talen nodded. "Yes. We like the mountains and the amount of sunshine ensures the Kurjans don't visit."

Cara thought a moment. "Boulder?" Her voice rose as fury slammed into her. "You couldn't just take us there—I mean, without the ceremony?"

"You were mine the second I saw you." His eyes didn't leave the road.

"You didn't need to marry me." Her eyes searched for something to belt him with.

"I did. Besides, only mates may know the location of our headquarters—it was necessary to keep you safe." He expertly maneuvered the large truck around a fallen tree, and its branches scraped the brown paint off with a shriek.

Anger caused her entire body to tremble. "How long will

your damn handprint stay on my hip?" She needed to get her daughter the hell away from the vampires.

Talen turned surprised golden eyes her way. "I marked you, Cara. I told you I would."

"How long, Talen?" she asked through clenched teeth. How could he sound so calm when every cell in her body burst with fury?

Talen shook his head, turning back toward the road and clenching his jaw. "It's a marking, Cara. It's permanent."

"You son of a bitch." She needed a weapon.

Talen wrenched the truck to the side before snapping it into neutral, and her heart surged to her throat. Silence echoed like thunder. He smoothly, deliberately shifted to face her. His eyes glowed a livid topaz in the dusky light, and the predator inside revealed himself.

Chapter 10

Mother Nature beat her fury against the rapidly fogging windows. Cara's mouth turned to sawdust as Talen's eyes blazed hot green sparks through dangerous gold. She reminded herself that she was right. And that he didn't scare her.

Yet she almost yelped when he reached out and deftly unsnapped her seat belt. Reason gave way to survival as she grabbed the truck's door handle with both hands and lifted up with all of her might. She didn't make it. Two hands grasped her arms and hauled her across the seat to perch on his firm lap. The marking on one palm heated her arm. She slammed her own palms against his chest. He lowered his furious face to within an inch of hers.

"Apologize, wife." His voice was low and controlled as were the hands gripping her arms. He wasn't hurting her, and yet the rapid pounding of her heartbeat echoed in her head. Spicy pine and male musk filled the air.

"You apologize," she challenged, forcing herself to meet his eyes and not gulp when the green overtook the gold, as she was learning often happened when strong emotions hit him. Oh God, what was she doing?

His face lowered even more. Several beats passed before he huffed out a sigh. "I'm sorry I didn't explain the situation better to you."

She gaped at his apology. She hadn't expected it. "I'm sorry I called you that name," she said grudgingly. "Why didn't you tell me everything?"

He raised an eyebrow at her.

Cara rolled her eyes. He was probably right. She would have run screaming in the other direction. "Does the handprint really stay forever?"

Talen nodded. "Yes. I marked you—changed you. It was necessary for your protection."

As the warmth drained from her face, she gasped and began to struggle in his arms. "You *changed* me? Oh my God. Am I a vampire?"

Talen started and then threw back his head and laughed. Even so, he kept her in place. "Of course not." He grinned at her before placing a quick kiss on her lips. "Vampires are born, not made." The wind beat harder against the windows as lightning flashed again outside.

She stopped struggling and frowned. "Oh. But . . ."

Talen took a deep breath. "The mating process involves the marking, the biting, and an exchange of fluids. Besides the mark, your DNA has been altered to match mine."

"Altered?" Panic rose again in her.

Talen gave her a quick nod. "Yes, altered. My antibodies are now yours. You'll age at the same rate as me and should be protected from all human diseases." He turned serious. "And no other male can touch you intimately without having an adverse reaction."

"Seriously?" Cara frowned in disbelief.

"Really," Talen confirmed. "My brother Jase tried to sleep with a mated woman a century ago and within a minute of light kissing, he had a reaction akin to the worse allergy you could imagine. He said it was beyond excruciating." Talen grinned in remembrance.

"A century ago?" She frowned. "Exactly how old are you?"

"About three hundred and fifty years." He peered outside as the storm swirled around the truck.

Cara was quiet for a moment as she took it all in. "How many women through the centuries have held your handprint, Talen?" The jealousy surprised her. So did the ding to her heart.

Talen turned back, his eyes softening on hers. "We claim one mate, Cara. You're mine."

"Oh." The pleasure swamping her surprised her even more than the jealousy. "So, er, um, it's not like you were a . . ." Hmm. There's no way.

"A what?"

"Um, I mean, you've had, um . . ." Geez, could this be any more awkward?

Talen grinned. "I've had sex before, darlin'."

Yeah, she figured that. "So, how? I mean, why me?"

"Because you're my mate. We get just one, and when we find her, fate takes over. Or, if it makes you feel better, biology takes over."

Oh, well, okay. Biology, she could understand. "Always?"

Talen shrugged. "Well, maybe not. There was a time when we had arranged matings involving a ceremony and vows—the brand appeared and those couples seemed as happy as the rest. Just like arranged marriages of your people, I guess."

Cara frowned. "But we didn't do an ancient ceremony or vows." The marking on her hip warmed. The permanent marking.

"I know. Like I said, fate." Smugness coated his voice.

Her hip began to throb with his words. "So now the Kurjans won't want me."

Talen shook his head. "They're still after you, Cara. They just can't mate you now."

She frowned. "You should have explained all of this to me, Talen."

"Maybe," he allowed as he gently placed her back into the passenger seat and buckled the seat belt around her. "But it wouldn't have changed the outcome."

"You're awfully arrogant, aren't you?"

"Don't make me bite you again." He flashed a careless grin as he put the truck into drive and maneuvered the vehicle onto the pothole riddled road. Her breasts tingled in response.

"Is there anything else you haven't told me?" she asked.

"Probably."

"About the biting . . ." Her voice trailed off when he shifted to face her.

"You bit me too, darlin'." His smile was pure sin in a face carved by gods.

Desire loped through her lower stomach as he turned back to the road. How could he affect her with just a look? Cara turned her troubled gaze to the blustering storm outside as she tried to control her libido. Control had been an illusion since she met this man.

Her mind tried to organize and make sense of the changes in her life. She had been married, mated, and marked. She knew deep in her heart the safest path for Janie was with Talen and his family, but she was a woman who had always lived in her head, and Talen wanted that same heart. Had she given it to him last night? At one point she would've given him anything, even her soul. Maybe she had.

"You're thinking awfully hard," he mused as he upped the speed of the windshield wipers with a flick of his wrist.

"It's a lot to take in, Talen."

"It'd be easier if you just accepted it, Cara."

"You want all of me."

"Yes." He tensed as he held up a hand for quiet.

"What?" she whispered while searching the surrounding forest. "Is it the Kurjans?"

"No. They're about a mile behind us."

"How do you know?"

"I can sense them."

"Then what?"

Talen parked the truck into a small clearing between the

trees before shutting off the ignition. "I'm sorry darlin', you're going to get wet." Unbuckling her belt, he helped her across the seat, and she grabbed the plant, then followed him out of the truck and into the rain.

The smell of wet pine assailed her as Talen grasped her arm and led her through trees and high brush. The truck faded behind them. The wind beat against their wet faces. She stumbled through the drenched weeds, trying to keep up. He halted, and she collided with his strong back while he closed his eyes and lifted his face to the breeze. Then he grabbed her arm and hurried her toward an outcropping of rocks set into the base of a tall hill.

She kept quiet as the rain plastered her long hair to her face. Talen leaned in close to her ear. "Just over that hill at least six men are waiting to ambush the truck. They're well armed."

"Men or Kurjans?" she whispered back.

"Men. The Kurjans are coming from the south; if we stayed on the road we'd be trapped between the two."

"How do you know there are six men?" She shivered in the wet cold.

"I can smell them. And hear them." He lifted his face to the air again. "So could you if you'd stop being so stubborn." He pulled her toward an opening in the rocks and reached into his waistband to take out an odd-looking green gun, which he put into her hands. "Crouch in there and shoot anyone that's not me." He leaned down and gave her a hard kiss on the lips. "I'll be right back."

He faded into the forest.

Cara crouched between the large rocks with her back against crusty weeds, placing the plant safely on the ground behind her. Nature surrounded her, grass, bushes, and trees. Safety.

The rain beat down. Tall pine trees slammed bristled cones to the ground around her. She tried to focus her thoughts, but fear made everything cloudy and the cold hacking into her bones didn't help. The boom of an explosion sounded from the north, and she jumped in fear—only to freeze in place as the wild roar of an animal filled the air.

The scene came into sharp focus as a cacophony of howls blended with the crashing thunder across the dark sky. The scientist within her knew this sudden clarity was the adrenaline plowing through her veins. The woman inside her wished for the cloudiness to return.

A blur of fur leapt over her and landed with a light thud in the wheat-colored weeds. She muffled a shriek. The animal turned and she was face-to-face with the largest mountain lion imaginable.

Wide blue eyes met golden brown as they both froze in place while the rain pelted without distinction on their heads. Cara's hand tightened on the gun in her lap as she studied the creature. Her instincts warned her not to make any sudden movements. The massive multicolored animal was more than seven feet long, weighed at least several hundred pounds, and had a graceful black-tipped tail resting on the ground. Its colored pelt rapidly darkened from a burnished gold to a wet red in the rain. Its eyes focused on her and its whiskers twitched across a soft white patch of fur spread over its face. Sharp fangs protruded from the corners of its mouth.

Intelligent tawny eyes held hers for a moment. The cougar lowered its head in an exaggerated movement to focus on the gun in her hand. Fur flew as the animal's head shook from side to side. Then it straightened up to search her face.

Okay. That did not just happen. "You don't want me to shoot you?" Her hoarse voice barely carried through the storm.

The massive cat shook its head again and waited for her response.

Her mind reeled. She figured they had traveled from DC into the mountains of West Virginia. She was pretty sure mountain lions weren't indigenous to the area. Even more bizarre, she was communicating with the wild cat. "Okay. I won't shoot you if you don't try to eat me." Her calm voice belied her racing heart. And her disbelieving mind.

A sharp nod came from the cat before it gave two abrupt growls. A higher pitched snarl erupted behind Cara before a smaller lion joined the first. This one was more white than red and obviously a female. She moved even closer to Cara and sniffed the air before lifting her ears in interest toward the male, who appeared to almost grin in response. The two turned and took up what could only be described as defensive positions between Cara and the forest.

She stared in bewilderment at their straight backs while the animals peered into the forest. A series of howls and gunfire erupted from the north, and all three whirled toward the sounds. With a cry, Cara started to her feet to help Talen; she did have the gun after all. A growl from the male lion stopped her as his large head swung around to zero in on her. Startled, Cara sat back down and the lion returned his focus to the forest.

Clarity came with a sudden snap. "I have a brain tumor." She ignored the loud snort from the male lion. It really was the only explanation. She must be in a hospital in a coma somewhere. She sniffed and wiped the imaginary rain off her face, hoping Emma was taking good care of Janie.

Both lions tensed and sprang to all fours with warning growls from deep in their throats. She forgot her tumor. Cara peered into the forest for what alerted them, but only dripping branches and large pines filled her view. Two figures stepped out from the trees, and the neurons in her brain stopped firing. Fear could freeze the thought processes as a means of protection—her mind refused to believe her eyes. With a mental shake, she forced herself to accept.

They were tall, well over six feet, with long black-tipped red hair and parchment white skin. Razor sharp fangs protruded between crimson lips as they strolled forward. They were dressed armed for battle in all black that matched their fathomless eyes, and besides walking upright, they weren't anything close to human.

The one in the lead focused on Cara and sniffed the air before peeling its lips back to further reveal its fangs. Then it started forward.

With a bone chilling howl that must have carried for miles, the male lion charged.

Chapter 11

Growls ripped through the air as the male latched onto the neck of the closest monster. A Kurjan—had to be. The monster bellowed in pain before stabbing its long claws into the pelt of the lion's fur. Cara gasped in shock as the female lion growled low and leapt straight for the throat of the other Kurjan, which pivoted and threw the lioness to the wet ground. The feline bounded to her feet and sunk sharp fangs into the knee of her enemy, forcing it to fall. She descended upon its neck and blood sprayed.

Cara's stomach revolted as the coppery smell of blood mixed with fresh earth. The male lion turned and flung a Kurjan's head into the darkness of the forest, leaving its decapitated body lying uselessly on the ground. Blood covered the cat's thick pelt and whiskers as he lifted his head and howled in fury. Then he turned toward the female just as three more Kurjans leapt out of the forest. He instantly pivoted to charge at the two nearest his position.

The female was absorbed in wrenching the head from her opponent and didn't see the knife thrown at her from the fifth Kurjan. She went down to the ground with a yelp of pain—the handle protruding from her side. With a fierce grin of yellow, the Kurjan soldier advanced upon her.

Cara cried out and jumped to her feet while pointing the

gun at him. She pulled the trigger. The impact of the odd green bursts of light threw the monster back several feet. She instinctively rushed forward to put herself between the downed lioness and the Kurjan, the gun pointed at the threat.

The lioness snarled in protest behind her.

"You're welcome," Cara hissed through the rain, her hand trembling around the gun. The Kurjan's eyes had shifted from black to a deep swirling purple. What the hell? He issued a high-pitched trill as he moved forward in an image reminding her of a horror novel she'd read as a teenager. How could this be happening?

She fired again, and he went down on one knee. With a sob, she kept firing and then gasped as he tensed and sprang toward her. She cried out and braced herself for impact. But a dark blur leapt over her from behind and collided with the Kurjan.

"Talen," she breathed in relief as he forced the Kurjan to the ground. With an inhuman burst of power, he twisted his body to plunge a large knife into its throat. He ripped the knife through cartilage and bone like it was silk, effectively decapitating the monster. His face hard, cold, and merciless, he remained focused as blood sprayed. How could he be the same man who had held her so carefully that morning? But she was grateful to her toes he had arrived to defend her.

More lions darted from the trees to join in the fray.

Cara turned to help the lioness, only to gasp in shock at the small woman lying naked on the ground. Blood flowed from the knife still embedded in her side. Cara fell to her knees at the young woman's side and pushed honey blond hair off a wet face. Brown eyes met hers.

With a groan, the woman reached around and grabbed a hold of the knife handle.

"Wait," Cara said urgently. "I think you're supposed to leave it in until you're at the hospital." She ignored the sounds of growls, hisses, and shouts of agony behind them.

The young woman rolled her eyes. "I don't need a hospital." She tugged the knife out with a small yelp of pain before dropping the red-tinted blade onto the wet ground.

Talen heard the sound of pain but didn't turn as he kept himself planted between his mate and the Kurjan soldier stepping over his fallen comrade. It gave an evil grin of sharp yellow fangs while yanking a sleek gun from its back. Talen returned the grin before concentrating on the creature's central nervous system and freezing it. He needed very little energy to manipulate the young and inexperienced Kurjan. Its purple eyes widened on Talen as he rendered it motionless with a mere thought.

"Yeah, those aren't rumors," Talen confirmed, reaching out to run his knife through the enemy's throat. Making a quick kill and showing mercy where none would have been shown his mate. With clean, logical precision, he decapitated the soldier before facing the remaining threat.

Blood scented the air around Talen, dark and oily from his recent kill, pure and slightly sweet from behind him. The image of his mate standing before the Kurjan soldier firing that gun would haunt him for the rest of his life. He needed to get her to safety. But first, he needed to end the white-faced monster advancing upon him.

It flashed deep yellow fangs, its eyes glowing to the red of hell. "Kayrs."

Talen lifted an eyebrow. "I don't know your name, asshole." Neither did he care. But, he did wonder why a simple foot soldier would know him on sight.

"Everyone will know my name after I kill you, then your king." The Kurjan pulled a double-edged blade out of his back pocket and straightened to his full height of about seven feet.

"My king could make your brain ooze out of your head with the blink of one eye," Talen answered as if they discussed the weather. Then the satisfied roar of a lion commingled with a Kurjan shriek of pain to his left and he grinned. "Sounds like the shifters have taken care of your buddies."

The monster shrugged as the rain turned his hair to the color of dried blood. "No matter. You die, too." He lunged forward, his knife aiming for Talen's throat.

Talen shifted to the side, catching the Kurjan in the gut with a solid punch. He could end it quickly, freeze the soldier's nervous system, but the need to spill blood pulsed through his veins. The Kurjan doubled over and Talen clasped his hands together, slamming them down on his enemy's neck. The wounded soldier fell to his knees, head bowed, hissing in anger.

Talen yanked his own knife out of his vest, slicing first one then the other ear off his enemy. He shrieked in pain, rolled and bounded to his feet.

A wave of terror slammed into Talen, and he realized it came from his mate. Damn it, this would be frightening to her.

With almost a sigh of regret, he jerked his head and froze the oncoming Kurjan in place. "Sorry to end this so quickly, but my mate requires my assistance." He plunged his knife into the enemy's jugular, forcing the Kurjan back to his knees. Talen ripped the blade to the side, stopping only when the Kurjan's head rolled off its body, which then fell to the ground.

Pleasure filled him—it was a good fight.

Cara ignored the sounds of battle around her as blood began pouring out of the woman's wound. She ripped off her wet sweatshirt and pushed it against the woman's ribs. "We need to get you to a doctor." She shivered as the malicious rain drenched her plain white bra.

"Nope. We heal pretty fast, Talen's mate." The brown eyes filled with pain and a trembling smile curved her full lips. Even as a human, the woman had sharp feline features with dark lashes framing amber eyes over high cheekbones. Not even one freckle blemished her deep cream-colored skin.

"My name's Cara." She pushed the cloth firmer against

the still bleeding wound, looking frantically around at the wild brush surrounding them.

"I'm Katie." She grimaced at the surprise on Cara's face before groaning in pain. "What? Were you expecting Sheena or Shayla or Lyonina?"

"Something like that." Spotting a clump of tiny white flowers with yellow middles, Cara leaned forward and yanked.

"What are you doing?" Katie asked, her eyes fluttering closed.

"It's *Achillea millefolium*," Cara said, pulling the small flowers off the stem, filling the air with the scent of sage.

"What?" Katie groaned.

"Yarrow. It's an herb used for wounds, cuts, and abrasions." Cara kept twisting, wanting the smallest pieces possible. "Achilles carried it with him into battle to help treat his soldiers when necessary."

"Oh, well that's handy." Katie blew out a deep breath, her muscles visibly relaxing. "The pain is receding, thank God."

Sudden silence filled the air and Cara turned.

The battle was over and not a Kurjan remained standing. Talen and five lions all covered in various amounts of blood tossed pieces of the Kurjan soldiers into a large pile at the edge of the forest. Two black off-road trucks pulled into the small clearing. Talen turned and purposefully started making his way toward her, his eyes golden and serious.

Katie sighed. "Do you have any idea how much crap I'm going to get for being stabbed?"

Cara didn't answer as Talen held her gaze. A cut above his left eye bled freely, and a dark purple bruise bloomed under his right eye. Deep scratches slashed down his strong neck. She froze in place while every instinct yelled for her to run. Toward or away from him, she wasn't sure. His eyes roamed over her as she crouched next to Katie, and the rain finally stopped falling.

Two men jumped out of the SUVs, and one held a can of what looked like lighter fluid.

"You are unharmed?" Talen asked as he pushed wet hair off her face while kneeling down. He ripped off his T-shirt and yanked it over her head, scattering the smashed flowers across the ground.

"Yes. But Katie was stabbed," Cara said urgently, pressing her hands against Katie's wound again, her gaze traveling along his tanned chest.

Talen shifted his gaze to Katie and gently placed his hand on her cheek. "Hi, Brat."

"Hi, Jackass," Katie retorted with a snort before leaning up and pulling Cara's hands away from the sweatshirt. She removed the cloth and Cara stared in surprise at the already healing wound. It had stopped bleeding.

"How did you get here so quickly?" Talen peered closer to examine the wound.

"Pure luck." Katie poked at her side. "Man, that hurt. My first battle injury."

"Your first injury, period." Talen sighed. "What are you doing here, Kate?"

Katie sighed. "We were hunting in the area and scented the Kurjan soldiers. Jordan sent me home and headed this way."

"You didn't go home," Talen said with a shake of his head.

Just then a large form behind Talen swooped down and covered Katie with a blanket before lifting her in his arms. Feral tawny eyes met Cara's as Talen helped her to stand. The large man was shirtless and had obviously donned a pair of faded jeans that he hadn't bothered to zip before heading their way.

"You're the male lion," Cara uttered as she stared at the hard planes of his face and long dark blond hair. She ignored the wide expanse of muscled chest holding Katie.

"Thanks for not shooting me," came the wry response as

he easily shifted Katie so he could reach out a hand to shake. "I'm Jordan."

"Cara." They shook. Cara shivered in the cold and Talen instantly pulled her back against his bare chest to rub warmth into her arms, the brand on his hand rough along her skin. The heat from his body slowly seeped past the wet shirt.

"I saw you put yourself between Katie and the Kurjan. Thank you." Jordan's serious gaze focused on her face.

Cara shrugged. "I had the gun."

"Um, Jordan," Katie started to speak and then stopped as Jordan lowered his gaze and his jaw snapped shut with an angry click. Cara would have taken a step back from the violence in his eyes had Talen not stood right behind her.

"Not a word. We'll deal with the fact you followed me against orders after I've made sure you're all right." Jordan turned his attention to Talen. "Come back to the ranch for the night and we'll talk."

Talen grinned and they followed Jordan to the first SUV. Behind them, a massive fire erupted on the pile and deep black smoke drifted into the sky.

Chapter 12

For the first time that day, the water cascading over her body soothed rather than beat into her bones. Several showerheads emerged from dark granite tiles and sprayed warm water along her skin. Cara groaned and closed her eyes in bliss. Jordan's sprawling home set on fifty acres of West Virginia mountainous land provided a welcome relief from the drilling rain.

She'd wasted no time jumping into the shower attached to the comfortable guestroom. Shrugging her shoulders, she allowed the hot water to pound into sore muscles. Then two broad hands flipped her around and she gasped. She hadn't heard him enter the spacious shower.

"You were very brave with the gun today, mate." Talen's deep voice echoed through the steam as he poured shampoo into his hands before lathering it into her hair.

"You don't sound happy about that." She closed her eyes again as his long fingers massaged her scalp. Tingles and a different sort of warmth cascaded down her spine.

He was quiet for a moment. "I'd prefer you safely ensconced somewhere not being threatened by predators or pneumonia."

"Hmm," she might have agreed as he pulled her so they almost touched. The heat off his body rivaled the spray behind her, and she lifted her head to open drowsy eyes on his.

His eyes were anything but sleepy. As his soapy hands moved from her hair to cup her breasts, a sharp tug made itself known in her lower belly. One callused thumb swept lightly across an already hardened nipple as his gaze held hers. A finger joined in and he rolled the peak. She gasped. Talen lowered his mouth to run his tongue along her bottom lip and a whole lot of heat rushed south. He pressed her back against the smooth tiles while his hand continued to play. The imprint on her hip began to burn like a fresh brand.

"Talen?" She breathed, not sure what she asked.

He answered by tracing a path south and cupping her pubic bone with his other hand. One finger moved and her eyes nearly crossed.

"What?" His eyes heated on her.

She stood in the steamy shower with golden eyes on her, with one of his warm hands covering her heart and the other cupping her core. She forgot how to think. He was big and dark and most definitely dangerous. Defined strength showed in the tight muscles and light smattering of dark hair across his chest, as well as in the set of his jaw and focus of his gaze. The hard planes of his face flushed over deepened hollows, stamping him with a predatory look that lived naturally on him.

And he wanted her.

She was a woman who lived in her head but now her body spoke louder. Hell, it screamed. She took the smallest step forward and reached up with both hands to tangle her fingers in his thick hair. She tugged his head down and took his mouth with feminine demand.

He may have growled as she plunged in deep, this time demanding everything from him. He was the most amazing male she could imagine.

And he wanted *her.*

He couldn't take that back. Broad hands curved around her body and lifted her by the buttocks. She didn't break the kiss as her thighs clasped his hips and pressed even closer to his hardness. Then, with a sharp nip to his bottom lip, she leaned until her head rested against the wall and demanded, "Now. Now. Talen."

He obliged. One powerful shift and he thrust into her. She cried out against his corded neck. They both stopped moving for a second to regain their breath. He moved one hand up to tangle in her wet locks and pull her head to the side, while the other held her tight.

Green sparks shot from his amazing eyes as he captured her widened ones with a fierce gaze. Ah, the green overtook the gold again. A wicked smile flashed across his face, and he started to move. He started to move faster. Then he started to pound, and Cara saw stars.

"I had thought slow and gentle this time, mate." He finished rinsing the soap out of her hair a second time.

She giggled. "Maybe next time, Talen."

"Maybe." But he sounded doubtful. He turned her to face him and placed a gentle kiss on her mouth. "I love your body."

She smiled against his mouth and was startled as he leaned back to stare at her.

"But I will demand your heart, Cara."

She didn't have an answer as he grabbed a thick white towel and dried her hair. They stepped out of the bathroom to find clothing laid out on the massive king-size bed. Cara shrugged into jeans and a long sleeved blue shirt while Talen followed suit in the spacious guest suite. The room was comfortable with maple dressers, wildlife oils, and a wide screened door leading to an inviting deck. Henry the plant had taken up residence on one side of the large dresser. The rain had started to fall again with dusk.

"So, how long have you known Jordan?" She did her best to finger-comb her hair into obedience.

Talen shrugged a large shoulder. "A few hundred years."

Cara stopped in shock. "Really?"

"Yes. Their clan has been an ally of ours for as long as I can remember."

"And they change into mountain lions—cougars?" It was almost too much to take in.

"Yes. Shape-shifters are predestined in their animal form, Jordan's is a mountain lion. Same thing as a western coug."

"Predestined form?" How cool would it be to change into a wild animal—to be that free, if only for a short time? She squeezed extra water out of her hair.

"Yes. Shifters are either feline, canine, or multi." Talen brushed his own thick hair back from his face with two broad hands.

"What does multi mean?"

He stretched his neck one way and then the other. "Multis can usually take whatever form they wish, except for feline or canine."

Fascinating. The genetics involved with a multi would keep her sister Emma intrigued for decades. "Jordan is the leader of the cougars?"

"Definitely." Talen rubbed his chin. "Jordan became leader of the Pride around the same time Dage became king."

"Really?"

"Yes." Talen's eyes darkened, and a thick green swirled through the gold. "We'd been at war with the Kurjus and its allies for nearly two centuries and a summit was called. Leaders from all over made efforts to attend, but it was a trick."

"The Kurjans have allies?" Cara asked, her heart speeding up in relation to the clenching of Talen's jaw.

"Yes. The Kurjans, leopard shifters, dark shamans, to name a few. We thought a treaty was likely as we'd all suffered many losses." He took a deep breath. "The Kurjus struck as leaders traveled and killed my parents. As well as Jordan's."

Cara's gut clenched as if someone had punched her. "I'm sorry, Talen. How old were you?"

He shrugged. "Twenty. Dage was twenty-five; Kane eighteen, Conn sixteen, and Jase only fifteen."

"Dage became king at twenty-five? And brokered a treaty?" Wow, unthinkable.

Giving a sharp shake of his head, Talen focused his gaze somewhere in the past. "He became king, and we went to war, creating a bloody battlefield the earth had never seen." A muscle ticked in Talen's jaw and his spine straightened. "Until blood and death overshadowed life and air."

Palpable pain emanated from the immortal man holding her hand, and Cara sought a way to soothe. She snuggled closer. "What then?"

"Then Dage brokered the treaty." Finality coated Talen's words. "It was either that, or end life for everybody on this planet."

Cara ran a gentle finger down his strong face. "What were your parents like?"

Talen's lips tipped up, and a light twinkle lit his eyes. "My mother was Irish, temper and all. Black hair, blue eyes, and she ruled the world."

"Your father?" Was the former king a good man? Had Talen been lucky enough to know love from a father, rather than pain?

"A soldier and a diplomat. He was a large man with a bigger laugh." A full smile illuminated Talen's face for a moment. "He worshipped the very air my mother breathed."

Ah. Lucky woman. "So, you've known Jordan through war and peaceful times?"

Talen gave a short nod.

"And Katie is his mate?"

Talen flashed white teeth against tanned skin in an amused grin. "Oh yeah. But neither of them has a clue yet."

Cara smiled in response. "It's obvious, isn't it?"

His gaze warmed on hers. "Always." He held out a hand for her and tugged her to sit on the big bed. "Close your eyes."

"Why?" she asked as she complied, the marking on his palm pulsing with heat against her own.

"I want you to tell me where Jordan and Katie are in the house right now."

Cara's eyes flew open in alarm as she tried to tug her hand from his and stand up. "I can't do that."

"Yes, you can," he countered, his hand tightening on hers.

"No, really, that's ridiculous." She breathed out as anxiety started to pool like glue in her stomach. She tried to yank her hand from Talen's while he kept her on the bed.

"It's easy." His voice was low, soothing. "Just pinpoint them by their emotions. I can tell you can feel them."

"You can tell?" she asked, confused.

"Yes. We're mated, Cara. I can feel what you feel. Now your abilities should strengthen."

"No." Her jaw set as she shifted away from him. One firm hand on her chin turned her to face him, his golden eyes soft and thoughtful.

"Why not?"

"Because I can't." The last was said with frustration. Sometimes she couldn't help feeling along with other people, but she certainly couldn't make herself do so.

"Why not?"

"It's not natural," she whispered, her eyes almost tearing up.

Talen's gaze hardened. "Who hurt you, Cara?"

"Nobody," she closed her eyes against his questions. "Please, Talen . . ."

Chapter 13

Something shifted inside him. His courageous, stubborn, sweet wife was afraid. He liked her temper, and he liked her firm chin when she challenged him. He didn't like her uncertainty or her fear. He glanced around the spacious bedroom of Jordan's ranch. "Open your eyes."

Wariness filled them. He leaned in and placed a gentle kiss on her soft mouth. "I won't let anyone hurt you Cara, ever." He stroked one finger down the smoothness of her face. "You are exactly who you are supposed to be and your gifts are a part of you, mate. It doesn't get more natural than that."

Damn, something in his chest ached for her. It couldn't be his heart, he'd lost that during those bloody years after his parents had been murdered. But he liked his little mate; he'd like her even more if she allowed herself to love him. She was a female, she was a mate. Love was her calling.

He may not be able to feel love in return, but he sure as hell could give her safety and peace. Making sure she smiled and laughed, well, that was his calling now.

He rolled to his feet and pulled her along with him. "Come on, I have a surprise for you."

Her hand clasped his warmer one, and she let him pull her from the room. Talen glanced in appreciation at the antiques and genuine western oils on the dark walls as he led his mate across the spacious main room of the ranch house to a home office with an impressive view of white-covered mountains in the distance.

He crossed around a wide burnished oak desk and punched in a couple of keys on a large computer before gesturing Cara to the desk chair. She walked toward him and then gasped as Janie's small face filled the computer screen.

"Hey Mama. How cool is this?" Janie grinned and his mate gasped again.

"You lost a tooth." Cara's voice lowered with the sound of tears.

"Yep." The grin widened. "Can you believe it? And the tooth fairy gives a lot more here than at home."

"Really?" Cara sat heavily in a padded leather chair as Talen wrapped a reassuring hand around the back of her neck. He hoped this was a good idea. "How much does she give for a tooth there?"

Janie leaned forward conspiratorially. "*Fifty* dollars, a new pocket game, and three dolls." Talen wondered if that was too much. Maybe he should talk to his brothers.

"Geez," Cara coughed out with an answering grin. "That's a lot."

Janie's blue eyes all but glowed with happiness as she held a doll in one hand, though the several braids woven through her hair were lopsided and mismatched. "Um, honey, who has been doing your hair?"

Janie rolled her eyes. "First Uncle Jase but then he got frustrated cause his hands are too big and then Uncle Brack, but he can't get them even. Uncle Dage did them the first day before he had to go and those were the best. Today Uncle Conn tried really hard but it was double damn hard for him." She shook her braids sadly.

An embarrassed cough sounded as a broad face leaned into camera range. "Sorry about that. I'll er, watch the language from now on."

Cara nodded as Talen scowled at his brother. Conn's metallic green eyes smiled his apology as he grinned at Cara.

"I'm Conn. Welcome to the family." Then he dodged out of range.

Janie smiled in adoration off camera before turning back to her mother. "When will you be here?"

"Soon as I can," Cara said softly. "Are you having fun?"

"Oh yeah. It's really fun here in . . ." A large masculine hand over the microphone muffled the rest of her statement. Janie grinned. "Oops, I forgot I wasn't supposed to say where we are. Anyway . . ." she rolled her eyes toward Conn, "I'm having lots of fun but miss you."

"I miss you, too. Aren't there any other kids around?"

Janie shook her head. "No."

"Really?" Cara wondered. Janie nodded in affirmation before looking quizzically around Cara.

Talen leaned down so he could be seen by Janie. "Hi, sweetheart."

"Hi." The little girl smiled, her eyes lighting up even more. "I met all your brothers 'cept for Kane cause he's across the ocean somewhere but I talked to him on the phone this morning, and they all said it was okay you're my dad now."

Talen grinned. "Thought they might."

"Yeah." Janie bounced happily. "And Uncle Conn even said you deserved me."

"Did he now?"

"Yep. Somethin' about wild days, whatever that means."

"It means my perspective toward beautiful women has changed."

"Why?" she asked with a wrinkled brow.

Talen shook his head. "Hard to explain, sweetheart."

Now Cara rolled her eyes next to him. Talen gave her a few more minutes to talk to Janie before he said they had to wrap it up. As the screen went blank, Cara lifted watery eyes.

"We'll get there as soon as we can, Cara."

"I know." She clasped his hand as they left the room. "When?"

"Soon." He led her past the formidable stone fireplace of the great room and into a wide, expansive kitchen where Jordan stirred something in a large Crock-Pot.

Cara sighed. She guessed "soon" would have to be good enough. Then her stomach growled as the scent of fresh stew assaulted her senses.

"Stop messing with it," Katie said from the nearby table with a glare.

"You always burn it," came the dry reply. Then Jordan turned flecked brown eyes their way. "Your call was successful?"

"Yes, thank you," Cara replied warmly as she moved to join Katie at the table. The young woman had showered and changed into faded jeans and a red shirt. "How's your side?"

"Healed." The grin was pure imp.

"Thanks for the clothes."

"No problem." Katie looked up as Jordan began dishing out fragrant bowls of stew before the men joined them at the table. Cara couldn't help but notice that even in human form, a sense of wild danger clung to Jordan. No wonder he and Talen seemed such good friends.

They dug in as if starved.

Halfway through the meal Jordan excused himself to take a phone call, only to return to the comfortable kitchen with a serious expression on his hard face. "We go in thirty minutes."

Talen's eyes narrowed. "I thought the raid was set for tomorrow night."

"It was. We've lost contact with Dr. Bigsby. We can't take the chance they're preparing for us."

Talen nodded and pushed to his feet.

"Wait a minute." Cara put out a hand in protest. "What raid? Who's Bigsby?"

"I'll give you a minute," Jordan said to Talen as he turned from the room.

"Wait, Jordan," Katie called after him as she jumped up and hurried from the room. Cara couldn't hear what Katie said, but she did hear Jordan's sharp reply of, "Absolutely no fucking way," as their footsteps retreated through the great room.

She turned inquisitive eyes on Talen as he sat at the round oak table. His burnished eyes shone a serious pure gold with no green. "I'm not sure where to start. The Realm was at war with the Kurjus for several hundreds of years until we both suffered so many losses we created a treaty to protect us and the humans—about three hundred years ago."

"The Realm?"

"Oh, yeah." Talen frowned. "That's us. It's like your United Nations; there's us, several shape shifting clans, friendly wiccans, and some others."

"No faeries?" Cara asked dryly.

Talen shrugged. "They don't align with anybody. We've fought with them, against them, you never really quite know."

"Seriously?" Cara had been joking.

"Oh yeah. The faeries are kind of like Switzerland with a big stick." He gave an exaggerated shudder with a grin.

Cara shook her head in amazement. "So the Kurjans have broken the treaty by coming after Janie and me?"

"Yes. Plus, they violated the agreement by conducting research at various facilities to alter their DNA so they can withstand sunlight. We've had allies in different places around the world to keep an eye on things."

The scientist in her took notice. "How is it possible to alter DNA?"

Talen shrugged. "Believe me, I am not the scientific one in my family." He grinned. "I guess you are."

"I'd love to see the research," she said thoughtfully.

"You will. We're raiding one of their Springfield facilities in about fifteen minutes. I'll bring you what I can."

"Maybe I should come. I'd know better what to look for." Her mind spun with the scientific results that could be reached. If such an alteration of DNA were really possible, most human genetic diseases could be cured before they started. Her mind boggled.

"No." Green flecks appeared throughout the gold in his eyes.

"But Talen, this could be bigger than any of us."

"I said no, Cara."

Her temper rankled. "I don't think that's your call, Talen."

His flash of teeth was anything but a smile as he ran a finger along the twin puncture marks on her pale neck. "I disagree."

"Then we're at an impasse."

This time he chuckled. "Not really. We're going on foot, it's much faster than using vehicles. Even as stubborn as you are, there's no way you'd keep up."

Cara let out an irritated huff. He was right. His speed matched that of the lions, and even on her best day she wasn't very fast, even for a human. "This sucks."

Talen stood from the table. "Look at the bright side. At least I don't have to tie you to the bed to ensure you stay here."

"Funny."

"I'm not joking." His face showed he wasn't.

"Humph." It wasn't the most intelligent response but it would have to do.

He rolled his eyes before stalking from the room, and she barely repressed the urge to stick her tongue out at his retreating back. Huffing with irritation, she focused back on her dinner, no longer hungry. Maybe she'd just do the dishes.

She just about had the kitchen spotless when he returned dressed in black cargo pants, shirt, vest, and flack boots. All soldier, all purpose. All pure, hot male. Her body responded instantly, her nipples pebbling and a slow skittering sliding through her belly.

Talen sniffed the air and gave her a grin. "I won't be gone long, mate."

Ass. She threw the dish towel into the sink. "Be careful." The words rose unbidden from somewhere she refused to acknowledge.

In response, he grasped her arm and tugged her closer, lowering his mouth. He took his time, tasting her, tempting her with raw heat and dangerous promise. She moaned and pressed into him, her hands splaying out against the rough material of the vest covering his broad chest.

The marking on her hip began to burn.

Jordan cleared his throat from the doorway, and Cara jumped back. What the heck was she thinking? She pushed her hair off her face and ignored the lion's smirk, as well as Talen's chuckle. He gave her a quick peck on the forehead, then they were gone.

She finished the kitchen and told Katie she wanted to get some rest. The young woman nodded, fully engrossed in shoe shopping on the Internet.

Once in her room, Cara locked the door. Taking a deep breath for courage, she sat on the bed, grabbed the phone, and dialed the right number. Her sister answered before the first ring had finished.

"Cara?"

"Em!" She should've known Emma would be prepared for the call. Breath she hadn't realized she'd held whooshed out in relief.

"Where are you? Are you okay? Where's Janie?" Footsteps pattered together across the line, as if Emma were rushing toward the door.

"We're both fine." Cara sighed. "I just needed to make sure you were keeping this low key." She plucked at a loose thread on the luxurious comforter.

"Low key!" Emma's voice rose to the point that Cara winced. "Are you kidding me? Some freaking marshal tells me you've been relocated because of some gang hit? What the hell's going on?"

Cara ran a trembling hand through her hair. "Okay, just calm down." Yeah right. "Janie and I are safe for now—and you can't make waves. Just for a bit, Emma. Or we'll all be in danger."

"But—"

"Emma! Do you trust me?" Cara waited after playing the trump card. She had to keep Em safe, it was her turn.

"Yes."

"Then, listen to me. We're safe. For now, if you don't make waves." She hoped. The last thing she needed was Emma making enough of a ruckus to alert the Kurjans. If they found out how gifted she was . . .

"No, you don't understand. God. You need to trust me. We're all in danger, and it's my fault." Emma's voice lowered. "Where are you? We need to run."

Run? "Emma. What—"

"The marshals can't keep us safe from these guys, Cara. Now where the hell are you?" The echo of a door slamming shut pounded over the line. "I'm in my car. I have a safe place to hide." The ignition flared to life across the phone.

Cara froze, goose bumps ripping through her skin to cause a shiver. "These guys? You mean the Kurjans?" How in the hell did Emma know about the devils?

Dead silence slid across the line for a moment before Emma spoke. "You know about the Kurjans? Tell me you're not with them."

That answered that. Dread began to slither below Cara's skin. "We're not with them. Um, do you know about the vampires?"

"You're with the *vampires*?" Tires squealed across the line.

"Yes. Tell me they're the good guys, Em." Considering one had just branded Cara's ass.

"Well, they're not the bad guys, anyway." Emma exhaled on a loud sigh. "I don't think so—I mean, I just found out about them yesterday. Okay. You're relatively safe for now. Probably."

Probably? Crap. "We need to meet up." Her sister would probably try to take the Kurjans down all by herself. Fear exploded through Cara's mind.

"We will. I've been working in one of the Kurjan research facilities—"

"What?" Cara gasped.

"I didn't know it was owned by them. Anyway, I found out what was going on and hid some of my data—I need to retrieve it, then I'll contact you." A horn blared loud and clear. "Damn it. Where do these people learn to drive?" Another horn blasted. "Okay. I have to toss this phone. You need to find out if the phone you're calling from is secured, which I'm assuming it is."

Secured? Holy crap. She may have just led the Kurjans to Jordan's ranch. What was this, a spy movie?

"I'm sure you're fine, Cara. Also, I set up new e-mail accounts with an online provider using false names, so it can't be traced. Check yours every few days, and I'll try to keep in touch. You're hotdixie@yaddah.com. I love you."

"I love you too."

The line went dead.

Several states away Janie snuggled down in her girly bed with Uncle Jase relaxing on the couch outside her room watching basketball on TV. She knew she was safe, and her Mama would be here soon. Cuddling her blankie and Mr. Mullet closer, she slid into the murky world between dreams and reality and sighed as she looked around for her friend.

"Hi, Zane," she smiled and flashed the dimples she knew he liked. Her dream world was her favorite place to be.

"Hi, Janie Belle." Zane emerged from the mist with a smile

on his broad face, the sharp angles already hinting at the warrior he would become. He had given her the nickname the first time she had invaded his dreams, declaring Janet Isabella too grown up for her. "Are you somewhere safe now?"

"Yes," Janie said with a smile. "I'm finally with my new family, so stop worrying."

"Good. My father received word last night of your safety, so I stopped my preparations to come after you."

"You were coming after me?" Her four-year-old heart warmed at the thought. The transformers were cool, but Zane was a real-life hero. Hers.

"Of course." Although she was six years younger, she was Zane's best friend. And even in his youth, he would die to protect her. In fact, he knew deep down someday he would be called upon to do so, which was the reason he trained longer and harder than any other. His father proudly thought Zane prepared to take his place someday as their leader, which in a sense he guessed he was. But the fight to come would be for Janie. And he intended to win.

They played for a while with Janie showing him mental pictures of her new ponies. An awareness tickled along the back of his neck, and he glanced toward the tree line.

"What?" Janie asked, changing the leaves from green to white and the sky to yellow.

Zane shrugged. "Dunno. I felt something."

She followed his gaze. "I can keep the bad guys out, Zane. It's my dream."

Flashing green eyes shifted to her. "Bad guys? You feel something?"

Janie copied his shrug.

"Janie?" Zane's jaw tightened.

She fought the urge to stomp her foot. When was everybody going to learn she was strong? "Yeah. I can feel something, somebody wanting in. He's tried it before." And she didn't let him. It was her dream. Well, their dreams, anyway.

Zane stood. So much taller than her. He moved toward the trees.

She sighed, dropping her pictures to the now peach-colored ground. "He's not in the trees, Zane. He's outside the dream."

Zane stopped with his back to her, the new muscles in his arms bunching. She liked that he'd grown his black hair out to his shoulders. "*He?*"

She waited until Zane turned back to face her. "Yeah. I think so. It feels like a he."

Putting his hands on his hips, Zane frowned. "Why didn't you tell me?"

Darn it. She didn't want Zane mad at her, and she didn't want his feelings hurt. "I didn't want you to go."

"You're in my dream—how could I go?"

She shrugged. "You could. We both have our dreams, and we opened them to each other." He didn't know he could close his dreams to her. If Zane left her she'd never talk to him again. Never-ever.

"So," he rubbed his chin, "someone else is dreaming? Someone else is trying to get in our dreams?"

Janie nodded. "I think so. But if we don't let him in, he can't get in." Right now, anyway. She'd learned that practice always helped with stuff like this.

Zane took a deep breath and focused. "Do you know anything about him, Janie? I get the sense he's not one of us."

Janie shook her head, even as a name whispered across her mind. *Kalin.* She wasn't going to tell Zane anything else. He'd go for sure.

Then, peace settled across the tiny meadow. "He's gone," Janie said with a smile.

Zane raised an eyebrow, reminding her of Talen. "Promise me you won't keep any more secrets like this from me."

She thought about it. "Okay, Zane." There weren't many secrets like this, really.

"Okay. I'll see you soon." He gave her the smile that always warmed her heart.

"Do you have to go already?" she asked, almost whining.

"I do." His dark green eyes turned serious. "I have training with my brothers in half an hour. You know how important that is."

"I know. Do you think we'll always be friends, Zane?" Sadness swept through her with the thought of life without him.

"Of course." He winked at her before turning to go. "Always, Janie Belle."

Janie giggled at the nickname before falling deeper into a calm sleep.

Chapter 14

Dressed in her new yoga outfit, Cara hit the mat with a slap and rolled to her knees, pushing curls out of her face. "Nice move." She rubbed her arms, thankful for the thick pads covering Jordan's basement gym. As well as for the new clothes—she and Katie had done some serious shopping a couple of weeks previous.

"Thanks." Katie grinned, her tennis shoes dancing happily on the blue cushions. "You forgot to block again."

No shit. She should've listened to Emma and taken those damn self-defense classes. "Yeah, but you've been training since you turned four years old." Cara staggered to her feet, her hands going to her knees, the yoga pants loose and comfortable. She'd been training with Katie every evening, something to do while the guys either prepared to raid, raided, or recuperated from raiding.

"You'd think in these three weeks of training you'd know how to counter my one good move," Katie smirked. "You've spent too much time deciphering all the information the guys have retrieved from the raids and not training with me."

True. Every time the guys raided a facility, they discovered two more places to raid. "I sure wish we could find your Dr. Bigsby, though," Cara said.

Katie nodded. "Me too. So, how did your talk with Janie go earlier?" Her gaze slid to Cara's knees.

"Great." Cara readied her stance, happy to have discovered that not only was Jordan's phone secure, so was his computer. "She really enjoyed that bedtime story you told her last night about the lost lion girl in the woods."

Katie grinned. "Yeah, some of that was true—especially the part about the handsome lion king who rescued her."

Nodding, Cara gave a snort. "I thought so."

"Did she like it as much as the one Talen told her about the vampire princess?"

Cara rolled her eyes. "Janie thinks Talen hung the moon and the stars. I wouldn't even try to compete." She could attest to seeing stars every night clasped in Talen's arms. There were times she actually thought she might belong there. In fact, her husband showed her a side of herself she'd never dreamed existed; although she worried her heart was mistaking passion for love on this vacation from reality. She pointedly ignored that tiny voice in her head whispering that maybe it was love.

"Don't blame her." Katie lunged, knocking Cara to the ground, who rolled to pin the lioness to the thick mat.

Katie tapped out. "Nice job!" Jumping to her feet, she stretched her arms behind her head. "I knew you could do that—you work out regularly and have decent muscle tone." She shifted in her purple workout clothes, dropping into a crouch. "And, since you've mated, you should be seeing physical results as well."

Heat flooded Cara's face and she settled into a defensive crouch, inhaling the scent of lemon cleanser.

Katie laughed out loud. "I didn't mean *those kind* of physical results."

Rolling her eyes, Cara moved in with another tackle, knocking the lioness to the ground again. This time Katie pushed Cara to the side, flipping her legs over her head to backflip onto her feet. "Much better. Your strength has improved like crazy the last few nights."

Cara rolled to her own feet. "Yeah, weird, huh?" It was almost as if Talen's blood pumped through her veins with ancient strength. "I feel stronger, tougher." She giggled. "When I was sixteen, my sister Emma took a karate class and within a month, she said she felt like a major bad-ass."

Katie snorted. "Was she?"

"No. But she sure felt like one." Cara stretched her hands over her head. "I wonder if I feel so tough just because I think I have Talen's strength now." Who could know? She then lifted an eyebrow at her new friend. "What about you? You already have the strength of a cougar; will you become even stronger once you mate?"

Katie shrugged, grabbing a towel off the ground. "Depends who my mate is."

Cara grinned. "Right. Well, hypothetically speaking, what if your mate is the leader of a mountain lion pride? Just out of curiosity, of course."

Throwing the towel at Cara, Katie huffed out a breath. "Considering I'll probably go absolutely freaking crazy waiting for that to happen, I don't think we need to worry about it."

"What if?"

Katie shrugged again. "Then yeah, I'd gain strength. And he'd gain my instinctive ability." She dropped to the mat to stretch. "Though he'll always see me as that cub he saved from those rotten foster parents."

"They freaked when you shifted, huh?"

"That's an understatement. I ran, and old Jim Bob chased me with a shotgun. It was pure luck Jordan hunted nearby." Kate rolled her neck one way and then the other.

Man, Cara wished she could've seen the girl's face when she shifted for the first time. "You had no idea you could shift?"

"Nope. My dad left the Pride to settle in the city with my mom, who was human. They died in a train wreck, and I was put into the system." Katie shrugged. "I don't know what would've happened had Jordan not been hunting in the woods that day."

"So Jordan raised you?" Okay, that may be kind of weird.

Katie giggled. "No, thank God. He paid off the foster assholes, and my mum adopted me. She was widowed with no kids and really wanted me." Pride and love flowed through each word, and Katie smiled. "Though Jordan was always nearby, especially when I got into trouble."

Cara grinned back. "Figures. Where's your mom now?"

Katie snorted. "She's on a two-month mahjong cruise with a bunch of friends—they love that game." She lifted an eyebrow. "What was your first husband like?"

Cara sat and stretched her legs out before herself. "Simon and I weren't married."

"Oh." Katie pulled one arm across her chest. "What was Simon like?"

"Nice. He was a good friend. We worked together in the lab with plant viruses." Tall, serious, clumsy as hell, the guy had a heart of gold. "He approached me one day, all serious, and proposed we date." Cara smiled. "I figured it a rational, well thought-out plan for some companionship." No passion, no fear usually associated with being around men. She reminded herself that unlike her father, most men didn't hit.

Katie giggled. "I see. Sounds different than Talen."

"Oh yeah. No question there." Her heart had never been in any danger from Simon. "He died in a car accident, not even knowing about Janie." If he'd lived, they'd have worked out sensible arrangements regarding their daughter.

"Would you have married him?"

Would she have? "No. I never intended to get married."

"So, Talen changed your mind?"

"You could say that." She grinned at her friend, the marking on her hip starting to throb just before Talen poked his head inside the door.

"More female bonding?" he asked, pushing at a dark purple bruise under his left eye, crossing to where she lounged.

Cara stretched her back and groaned. "If you consider me getting my butt kicked bonding."

Talen pulled her to him, scraping his teeth down her damp neck. "Why don't you let me train you?"

Heat slammed into her loins. Giving him a two-handed push that failed to move him an inch, Cara sighed. "Because I want to learn to fight, not . . ." Her face heated as she realized Katie was still in the room.

The young woman cleared her throat, making a beeline for the door. "I'll go check on Jordan. Later."

Talen chuckled against the rapidly beating pulse in Cara's neck. "Smart girl." He nipped at her collarbone. "You were saying?"

She lifted her head, studying the bruise. "What happened? I thought you guys were making dinner."

He flashed sharp canines at her. "We disagreed about the amount of hot sauce for the chili and took the argument outside."

Cara huffed out a laugh. "You got into a fight over hot sauce?"

Talen shrugged. "Consider it training without the mats." The purple bruise shifted to green then yellow.

"Who won?"

He raised an eyebrow. "It was pretty close, then Baye shouted out the window that he added jalapeños instead."

"Ah. Baye's the mediator, huh?" As one of Jordan's enforcers, he looked more like an assassin to her.

"Nah. He just likes jalapeños." Talen grinned, his hands lowering to cup her ass. "So, have you learned anything?"

Her body instinctively pressed into his. "I've learned that fighting isn't one of my talents." She reached up to trace his chest through the thick cotton. "And I've learned I'm glad to have Katie as a friend."

He traced Cara's ear with his tongue and lowered his voice. "Do you have many friends?"

"No." Her eyes rolled back into her head. "I haven't really

gotten too close to people before." Talen drew her earlobe into his mouth and she moaned. "I have acquaintances at work, but no real friends like Katie." She figured the lack of childhood friends had something to do with her father being a complete bastard and her not wanting to bring other kids over to see him, but she didn't feel like going into past hurts at the moment. Especially with Talen's hot mouth on her skin.

Talen lifted his head, green shards emerging from the gold in his eyes. "Have you checked your e-mail account for a return message from Emma today?"

"Yes. She hasn't replied yet." Her sister refused to use the computer at whatever safe house she'd set up, instead taking the laptop to public places. Somewhere. "But she's only checked in twice. Have you heard anything?"

"No. Our contacts inform us that the Kurjans haven't found her but are actively searching." The hand on her butt began to knead.

They wouldn't find Emma. "My sister's probably one of the smartest people on the planet, Talen. And apparently she has some work to do before trusting your people." Pure pride had Cara lifting her chin even as desire began to speed up her heart rate.

"I think you have a skewed opinion of your superhero older sister."

Perhaps. Cara had survived childhood because of Emma, no doubt about it. "Maybe. But then again, only a superhero could elude the Kurjans for three weeks."

Talen nodded, one lip tipping up. "I'm not surprised the Kurjans haven't found her, but the fact that our scouts have been running in circles alarms me a bit."

Cara lifted a shoulder, fighting a smile. "Maybe you're all out of practice. Peace can lead to laziness." If Emma didn't want to be found, nobody would find her.

His grin turned his eyes into the color of fresh sunshine. "Laziness. Hmm." Lowering his mouth to run along Cara's jaw, his hand roamed around her hip to brush across her core.

Only his other arm around her waist kept her knees from buckling her to the mat. "Talen—" Wasn't there something they should be doing? White static filled her mind while her body took over.

Just then Katie called down the stairs, "Dinner's ready."

Oh yeah. Dinner. With a sigh of regret, Cara stepped back. "Saved by the chili."

"Slight reprieve, mate. Very slight." Talen took her hand and led her to the door as the bruise faded completely from his face.

Chapter 15

Cara stretched against Talen's hard body later that night while grimacing and throwing off the heavy comforter. "You let off a lot of heat," she murmured, her body liquid putty after several hours of her husband showing her just how much heat he was capable of.

As an answer he tugged her closer into his embrace and ran a thoughtful chin across her forehead. "Cara, it's time to stop running."

"Running? From what?" She yawned and burrowed down.

"From yourself."

She stilled as her heartbeat picked up. "I don't know what you mean."

"Yes, you do."

"I'm tired, Talen." She snapped her eyes closed.

"Good. The time between wakefulness and pure sleep is the best time to reach out with your mind. Now, tell me how I'm feeling."

"Content," Cara countered.

"You don't need special abilities to make that determination, mate." He chuckled against her hair. "Now, tell me what Katie is feeling."

"I don't even know where she is, Talen." She tried to control her anxious breathing.

"Yes, you do. Tell me where."

"No." Her breathing turned choppy as she tried to pull away from his inflexible body. He easily held her in place.

"Why are you about to have an anxiety attack?" He did nothing to hide the firmness beneath the concern.

"I don't know."

"Don't lie to me, mate." The firmness turned to stone.

"I'm not," she breathed out and started to struggle against his hold. He smoothly, almost casually, rolled until she lay trapped beneath him. His heavy weight pushed her into the mattress, his eyes direct on hers. Two strong hands pinned hers on either side of her head, his brand rough against her skin. Even on edge, a thrill of desire rushed through her.

"Tell me what Katie is feeling." He clearly emphasized each word.

"She's probably asleep, Talen," Cara said in exasperation. The desire waned.

"We both know she isn't," he countered.

"How?" Cara couldn't help but ask.

"Because those of us not denying our natural abilities can all but feel her frustration and need to hit something."

"Men do that to us," Cara said, disgruntled. She pressed up into the solid body above her and hid a satisfied smile as he hardened. She did it again. His eyes narrowed on hers as green started to slide through the gold.

"Don't distract me, mate."

For answer, she arched up again. She nipped his collarbone before wrapping both legs around his muscled hips. "What do you mean . . . mate?" Her breath hitched for an entirely different reason as a dark flush worked its way across his sharp face.

His eyes dropped to her mouth. She ran her wet tongue along her bottom lip.

"You don't know what you're inviting, Cara."

"Don't I?" She challenged, tightening her thighs around him, her blue eyes filling with dare.

The growl low in his belly vibrated against her and sent liquid heat spilling from her. His heat melted through her pores as her legs surrounded him. With a wicked grin, he placed both of her hands in one of his and stretched her arms above her head. She was trapped, helpless. He tugged and her breasts flattened against his hard chest. His other hand ran down her length to firmly grasp her bottom and lift it off the mattress.

"Talen?" she asked, uncertain.

He didn't answer as he drove inside her with one powerful stroke. Even as ready as she had been, he startled her and she cried out. He filled her past what she had thought possible. She lost her ability to think. His mouth lowered to brush across her pebbled nipples. He slowly moved in and out of her raging body before he took one pink berry in his mouth and suckled. Hard.

She moaned against him as he tortured first one then the other breast while he continued to glide through her softness. His mouth wandered up her neck to kiss her eyes, cheeks, and finally her mouth. Her body was on fire and she wanted more.

"I get lost in your scent, your passion," Talen's breath brushed her neck. "There's no sweeter taste in the entire history of the world than your skin on fire. For me." He growled low and deep as he withdrew from her body before plunging in again. "I want all of you, mate. And I'll get it."

Her mind reeled at the claim. A hint of threat wove beneath the words but she couldn't focus on it. For seconds, for minutes, he moved within her—around her. A gentle kiss, a tweak to her nipple that had her seeing stars, then he'd increase his depth, increase his speed until she was so close . . . Then he'd slow down again. Damn it.

She lost track of time, of how long he had been inside her as he continued his assault. His movements were too slow, too controlled.

Finally, her mind mush, her body vibrating like a plucked

guitar string, Cara gave a frustrated sigh and clenched her thighs against his hips. "Move faster." She didn't recognize her own voice with its low, desperate edge.

"No." He continued to take his time, driving her nearly to madness. His mouth took hers in a brutal kiss that shot her blood like electricity through her veins. Then, he quickened his strokes and started to pound. Just as her internal muscles started to clench, he slowed down.

"Talen," she drew out his name on a moan, her thighs gripping him with a strength that impressed them both.

"What?" He chuckled against the soft spot behind her ear.

"Stop teasing me."

He lifted his head with a satisfied male grin at her bruised mouth, bemused expression, and flushed skin. "You don't get what you want until I get what I want, mate."

"Wh . . . at?" she asked in confusion, moving against him again. "What do you want?" Jesus. She'd give him anything at this point.

"Open yourself up, Cara."

"Talen. I'm as open as a girl can get." She moaned the jest as her hands started to struggle in his.

He chuckled against her mouth. "That's not what I mean. We'll start slow. Forget about other people, just concentrate on me."

"I am," she hissed in frustration.

He nipped her bottom lip before laving the small wound with his tongue. "I mean, feel what I'm feeling."

"I am feeling you, damn it."

He shook his head above her, only the fine dotting of sweat on his brow showing what his control cost him. "No, you're not. You're feeling from within your own skin. You don't get what you want until you feel from inside my skin." He leaned down to punish her with a hard kiss. "I promise you'll like it."

"I can't." She moaned in frustration as she writhed against him.

Talen stilled, his body trapping her while his eyes held hers captive. "You can. And you will."

Cara ached. Hell, she hurt. The need for release clawed through her with animalistic demand and became sharper, stronger than any anxiety she may have held. Nothing in the world mattered more than giving her body the exploding release it so desperately craved. With a shudder, she gave in. She opened her mind and sought the connection she already had with him. Instantly, strength and power slammed into her. Along with incensed desire and need. He finally started to move. To hammer into her as he felt her within him.

Cara's eyes flew sightlessly open as her body sailed. As the feelings between them rose, she could no longer tell which feelings, which compulsions, were hers. She couldn't have imagined the fire welling within him. The blinding need to take, to claim. The basic, primal urge that drove him to assert his dominance—to imprint his very soul on her. In her. She had been blissfully unaware of the incredible strength he had shown in his restraint thus far. In his control.

As she accepted him, it shattered.

His teeth latched onto her neck as he slammed harder, farther into her. Spicy sweet blood teased her own taste buds as he drank. She could feel the strength and light that filled him as he lusted for her blood. As he let it fill him. As she filled him.

With a carnal growl, he twisted his hips and sent her careening somewhere she hadn't been. Somewhere she couldn't have imagined. She exploded into a million pieces without a coherent thought of protection, of staying attached to her world. There was only him. And he followed her with a hoarse shout.

Then, as she saw blackness, sleep claimed her with soft arms.

* * *

The comfort of a mindless sleep was hers only for a short while. Her mind, maybe her soul, wouldn't let her off that easy. She had changed something. She had finally accepted a part of herself, and her conscience had a price to pay. Like a gambler paying his bookie, relief could only be found in the repayment.

The dream started hazy like a southern summer day. She walked in a pretty blue flowered dress, her small brown Bible clutched in her tiny hands as the faded screen door clanged shut behind her. Orange blossoms perfumed the air. "It's okay, Mama. Don't be upset," she said softly to her mother as she bounded down the steps.

"I'm not upset." Her mother looked back with bruised blue eyes, a concerned furrow between her brows.

"Yes, you are, I can feel it," she had said. With certainty.

She hadn't seen him standing to the side of the house. She wouldn't have spoken otherwise. The backhand caught her by surprise, and she cried out as she hit the hard dirt ground. "The devil's in you as much as your sister." Daddy had shouted, his ruddy cheeks puffed in a round indignant face. "If I could beat Satan out of her, I can beat him out of you." His large shadow fell across the sun as he walked closer.

Crying out with alarm, she awoke to find herself clasped against a firm chest. Heat and spiced pine coated her skin, providing warmth through muscle, bone, and heart to her soul.

"I'm sorry," Talen murmured against her forehead, having walked in her dream with her. "Let it out, darlin'."

She shook her head even as the tears started to fall. He held her, whispering comforting words in languages she'd never heard before. But felt to her bones. Finally, when she was finished, he brushed her hair off her forehead. "I'd kill him if he wasn't already dead." The softness of Talen's voice failed to conceal the rage vibrating through his body.

She burrowed into his warmth. Into safety. "I didn't mind when my father died. But I do wish Mama could have lived. Safe and happy instead of dying with him."

"I know, baby." He settled the covers more securely around them. "Go to sleep, Cara. I can protect you in your dreams now. Trust me."

Amazingly enough, she did. Sleep was a comfort this time.

Chapter 16

Cara placed the popcorn bowl on the sturdy table next to the leather couch and yawned at the late hour. "That was the dumbest werewolf movie I have ever seen." She fought the urge to whisper in Jordan's silent ranch house, even though she and Katie were the only occupants.

Katie giggled as she snapped the disc back into its holder. "Yeah. I make Jordan watch it when I'm really irritated at him."

Cara rolled her eyes. "I know—I thought we had them convinced this time to let us go on the raid." She'd been on the ranch for five weeks now, and it was time to go home. Although she had enjoyed forming her friendship with Katie, her daughter needed her. She'd tell Talen the second he returned.

"I wish. I'm going freaking stir crazy here," Katie groaned.

Cara smiled as curiosity got the better of her. "How long have you lived with Jordan?"

"I don't live with him," Katie sighed. "I have my own place. I'm just staying here until we figure out what the Kurjans are up to."

"Oh." Cara nodded. "So, if you don't mind my asking, exactly how old are you?"

Katie grinned. "Exactly twenty-four."

"Really?"

"Yeah. I'm the only member of our clan less than a hundred years old. Sometimes it really sucks."

"Wow. Will you keep aging?"

Katie shook her head. "No. I'm probably about done."

"Why aren't there more of you?"

"Most of the Realm creatures have a difficult time reproducing. Babies are rather rare, even with mates bound for centuries." Katie wrinkled her nose. "Probably fate's way of ensuring we don't mass produce and take over the world."

"Lucky humans," Cara said wryly.

Katie nodded seriously. "Yeah. Your sheer numbers balance the scales a bit."

Cara opened her mouth with another question just as the phone rang.

"Hello?" Katie froze in place. "Wait a minute. Wait a minute. Calm down, Dr. Bigsby, I can't understand you. Where? When? No, he's not here." She lifted concerned brown eyes to Cara as she listened. "No, I don't know when he'll be back." She listened more. "Are you sure? How many?" Her eyes turned desperate. "Samples? Where are you now? Yes. Stay inside with other people. We'll get there as soon as we can." She hung up the phone.

"Bigsby has been on the run and is at a truck stop outside of Martzaville." Katie ran a frustrated hand through her blond hair.

"Is there any way to get in contact with Jordan?"

Katie blew out air. "They could be gone all night. And Bigsby said he thinks a couple of Kurjans are waiting outside the diner for him."

"Did you say samples?" Cara's mind sharpened.

"Yes. He took samples and much of his data."

"Can you tell if he's lying?"

"He's not. He's worked with us too long. And besides, I can tell if someone is lying. The timber of their voice changes just a bit. He's terrified. And telling the truth."

"We need to go get him." Cara jumped to her feet.

"Geez, Cara. You know it's a trap, right?"

"You said he's telling the truth."

"He is. But the scientist isn't quite the covert operator you'd think," Katie said wryly. "If he was allowed to make it to the diner and call us, the Kurjans allowed him to do so. It's a trap."

"Oh." Cara thought for a moment. "But they'll be expecting Jordan, right?"

Katie pursed her lips. "Yeah, I see where you're going."

"And they won't wait forever to make their move, will they?"

Katie ran two hands through her thick hair, biting her bottom lip. They were silent in the late hour as they looked at each other across the comfortable family room. Finally, Katie nodded. "All right, come on." She moved toward the home office to push a button and reveal a hidden room filled with a myriad of weapons. She dodged inside, grabbed guns and several knives before handing two guns to Cara, who shrugged and put one in the back of her waistband while keeping the other in her hand. Just as cold, green, and heavy as she remembered.

"Why are the guns green?" she asked.

Katie reached low and grabbed an ordinary looking cell phone out of a box. "They emit special hard-energy bullets that impact the Kurjans. And vamps and shifters." She turned and pushed the button again so the panel closed. "So don't accidentally shoot me."

"I'll do my best," Cara replied, forcing her mind to accept she was going out to rescue a scientist with two guns in her possession. It was a good thing they were point and shoot, because her one experience with a weapon was when she'd protected Katie from the Kurjan soldier. Man, if Emma could see her now. "What's up with the phone?"

"It's a disposable. In case we need to call back here or Bigsby."

She and Katie headed out in Jordan's beefed-up Dodge Ram SRT-10 with Viper power and sped along at a rate that couldn't be safe. Even she had heard of the faster than fast truck. Cara buckled her seat belt and then gulped as Katie followed suit.

"What do you think they'll do when they get our note?" Cara asked nervously.

"Come after us," came her tense reply.

"How mad do you think they'll be?"

"I don't think we should think about that."

Cara nodded. "I like that plan. No thinking."

"Plus," Katie put her foot harder to the floor and dark trees illuminated by a half moon blended together outside, "we only have about an hour to think of a good plan."

Cara nodded. "We should get there about midnight, so unfortunately the truck stop won't be busy. Are you going to turn into a lion?"

"Only as a last resort. The Kurjans don't know about me, and I'm under pretty strict orders to keep it that way. But"—Katie turned serious eyes on Cara—"if I do start to shift, stay out of the way. The energy released could break every bone you have."

Cara hoped it wouldn't come to that. "You know, it seems like the more people at the truck stop, the better off we'll be."

Katie nodded in agreement.

"I take it the disposable phone is true to its name? I mean we'll ditch it if we use it?"

"Yes."

"So let's use it."

"What do you mean?"

"I mean, let's call in a bomb threat. Or an anthrax threat. Or some type of big threat that will get either the police or military or both to the truck stop."

Katie thought for a moment. "That's a good idea. But

we'll need to remove the battery and damage the phone the second we're done so it can't be traced. And then we won't have a phone."

Cara shrugged, not seeing an alternative. "How fast will the authorities in that area respond to a threat?"

"Ten, fifteen minutes."

"Okay. Let me know when we're ten minutes away."

Before Cara knew it, it was time to make the call. Katie pulled the truck over and they stood outside with crickets chirping in the now dry night as Cara dialed 911 with the report of having seen a bomb in the back of one of the trucks at the stop. They had decided an anthrax or biological threat created more of a diversion than they wanted. After giving the information, Cara slammed the phone shut and handed it to Katie, who ripped off the battery and tore the remainder apart before tossing the pieces into the woods. They jumped back into the truck and sped off toward the truck stop.

The only spot of life along dark Highway 35, the truck stop illuminated the night for miles. As Katie maneuvered into the bright parking lot, a strong male voice sounded with a resounding "*Stop— Get back to the ranch!*" in Cara's head. She blanched and grabbed her head with both hands. "Ow."

"What?" Katie turned in concern.

"I could swear Talen just yelled at me in my head." She turned incredulous eyes on her friend as her heart sped up even more.

"Oh," Katie wrinkled her nose. "Crap. I guess they know where we are."

"What?"

"Man. He really didn't explain this whole mating stuff to you, did he?" Katie pulled closer to the long diner that threw light out of rectangular windows along its red and yellow side.

"No." Cara lowered her hands. "Are you telling me he can read my mind?"

"Oh, no way. He can just track you and apparently send

you a strong message or two." Katie peered outside before turning toward Cara. "I think you can do the same thing. Close your eyes and find out if they're at the ranch or still at the facility."

Cara shook her head in disbelief before closing her eyes and concentrating on Talen. Nothing came to mind. She cleared her thoughts and tried again. A blurry image of a big white building came into focus, and she opened surprised eyes on her friend. "They're not at the ranch."

Katie tapped the steering wheel. "That's what I figured. We don't have time to wait for them. Did the voice in your head sound mad?"

"Oh yeah."

"Crap. Oh well, we've come this far. I'll pull right next to the door, when I stop, we run."

Cara yanked her shirt out to cover both guns and nodded. Katie pulled the truck to a stop, and they both jumped out and ran for the door.

Cara breathed a sigh of relief as the door closed behind them. The interior was bright and warm with orange Formica tables and thick blue booths along the window. Greasy cooked bacon scented the air. Several male gazes turned in surprise to watch the women make their way past the booths to sit at one across from an older man in a beige cardigan. He trembled as he clutched a notebook in his hands.

"Katie? Where's Jordan?" Concerned brown eyes peered through thick glasses under wiry grey hair standing on end.

Katie shrugged. "At the facility. Dr. Bigsby, this is Cara."

Cara nodded. "Do you have the samples?"

Bigsby patted a large leather briefcase sitting on the bench next to him. "Yes, and all of my data. But I saw at least one Kurjan out earlier tonight." He shrugged bony shoulders in defeat. "I don't know how they found me."

Katie's eyes met Cara's. The doctor had probably been herded to the remote area. "Dr. Bigsby, we think this is probably a trap. You need to be ready to run, all right?"

"Trap? Run to where?" The doctor's voice rose in pitch.

"To the black truck parked outside," Cara answered, reaching out to pat his gnarled hand.

Just then, police vehicles came to a screeching stop outside. Blue and red lights flashed eerily around the diner as several officers jumped from their vehicles and headed over to the trucks parked across the lot. Two fire trucks, an ambulance, and a large vehicle marked BOMB SQUAD rolled to quick stops.

A heavyset woman in a brown sheriff's uniform strode into the diner and raised a hand. "Folks, I need you to make your way to the nearest exit as soon as possible, please." Her short cap of black hair bounced as she nodded. Utensils clacked against the plates as people stood up from their meals.

Cara stood and whispered for Bigsby to follow them. They walked behind several truckers in flannels into the damp night and to their truck. Bigsby climbed in the back with his briefcase clutched next to him on the seat. Cara and Katie climbed in front, and Katie slowly pulled out of the lot.

"Can you sense any Kurjans around us?" Bigsby hissed.

Katie shook her head. "They must've taken off when the cops arrived." She turned a relieved grin at Cara as they sped into the darkness. "Nice plan."

Cara swallowed as the soft moonlight played across their faces. They weren't home yet, and the biggest threat most likely would be meeting her there. "Yeah," she agreed somberly.

Katie shrugged. "I had hoped we'd make it home before they did, but I forgot Talen could track you. How mad can they be? We got Bigsby and didn't fire a shot."

"Are you trying to convince me or yourself?" Cara asked wryly.

"Both of us," Katie answered quietly.

They rode for several miles in silence, all lost in their own thoughts. As they turned from the highway onto the smaller country road, Katie tensed.

"What?" Cara asked, peering outside.

Katie was quiet for a moment; her head lifted as she thought. "Nothing, I guess." She shrugged. "Wild imagination."

Cara relaxed back in her seat as the blur of trees flashed by outside. "It has been a crazy night."

Katie nodded and then cried out as an explosion ripped through the air. The truck veered to the left with a high-pitched squeal. She struggled and righted the large vehicle only to have three more explosions impact the tires in rapid succession. The truck careened wildly until slamming head-first into an ancient pine tree.

Cara screamed as she was thrown into her seat belt before the airbag slammed her back against the seat, knocking the breath out of her lungs. The bag deflated with a dusty cough. An odd tingeing of branches dropping onto metal filled the air.

She turned wide eyes on Katie, whose mouth formed a perfect O. "The trap wasn't at the diner."

Chapter 17

Quiet pressed in on the truck with a dangerous beat. Her breath panting out, Cara peered into the barely illuminated light for any sign of movement. All was still on the deserted roadway.

"I can sense them." Katie ripped off her seat belt. "There are at least five."

"Damn it." Cara removed her belt and grabbed both of her guns before turning to check on Bigsby.

"I'm fine," the doctor said wearily as he too undid his seat belt. After a thoughtful moment, Cara handed him one of her guns. He nodded in response and turned toward the night. Terror and determination flowed from him in strong waves, and she concentrated on blocking both.

"So, we weren't so clever, huh?" Cara asked softly.

"Nope." Katie's eyes swirled to a lighter brown. "I'm stronger if I change."

"But they'll know about you." Thoughts zinged through Cara's brain. "Let's use the guns, then if you need, you can shift and—"

A figure appeared outside the vehicle and ripped her door off the hinges. She cried out and reached for Katie, but rough hands ripped her from the car. Her scream turned silent as she looked into evil purple eyes. Raw, dark rage emanated from him, and she struggled to yank shields into place.

Yellow teeth gleamed as the Kurjan dragged her onto the road before leaning in to sniff her neck. "She's mated," he growled over his shoulder at the Kurjan dragging Katie and the doctor toward them. Cara started to struggle against the strong hands holding her. She had dropped the gun when he'd pulled her from the truck, and her mind worked furiously to come up with an escape.

The Kurjan soldier gave her a sharp shake. "Stop."

Cara looked in desperation at Katie, who stood with one Kurjan while the other held the doctor. The moon shone down on a quiet scene made for love—not blood. Dressed in all black from their boots to thick vests, the Kurjans had various weapons tucked throughout. Their thick hair glowed an unearthly red in the soft light.

Another Kurjan strolled out of the forest to stop before Cara. He stood taller, broader than the others, and two metallic red bars decorated his shoulders. He shot out a sharp nail against her chin and tugged her head up to face him.

"I'm Lorcan." His voice resonated through the night, and Cara struggled not to cringe away. "You were to be my mate, Cara."

She stared in surprise at his use of her name, and then fury washed over her. "I guess you're too late, asshole."

The claw under her neck sliced the delicate skin. Sharp pain lanced through her followed by pure terror. He forced her face farther up, and she bit her lip to keep from crying out.

"Not necessarily, human. Our scientists have been working on more than our aversion to the sun." He stepped back and put his red finger into his mouth. "Delicious."

Cara's stomach revolted. Strong hunger, dark and evil, slammed against her shields, staining her. She stamped down the bile rising in her throat.

"Where's your daughter?" He stepped closer and almost gently scraped the same overly long fingernail down the side of her face. The Kurjan behind her prevented her from backing up, so Cara could only stand there and glare.

Bigsby began to struggle and the soldier holding him brought an elbow down on his neck, sending the scientist sprawling to the ground. Unconscious.

Cara peered at Bigsby, sighing in relief when the man's chest moved as he breathed. He was still alive. "You'll never find my daughter." Out of the corner of her eye, she could see Katie pivoting to stand between two of the Kurjan soldiers.

Lorcan smiled sharp yellowed teeth at her. "We'll see about that. The lives of our oracles depend on their being correct about the future. They always are."

Cara kept her face calm as Katie gave a signal and tossed a green gun her way. Then the air started to shimmer around the young woman.

"Fuck," the nearest Kurjan bellowed as a force of air blew him back several feet. He landed with a sharp thud on the dark asphalt. The other Kurjan went down to all fours as a mountain lion stood over shredded clothes where Katie had been. She wasted no time in going for his throat.

Cara caught the gun and fired into Lorcan's chest, throwing him back several feet. She turned to run, only to have the Kurjan behind her wrap both arms around her, effectively immobilizing her. She kept her wide gaze on Lorcan as he struggled to regain his balance, which happened sooner than she would have liked. With a fierce roar that raised the hair on the back of her neck, he rushed forward and wrapped one bony hand around her throat. He squeezed, cutting off her air supply. Her eyes watered and her lungs clenched. He nodded to the monster holding her. "Go take care of the shifter."

Cara's arms fell uselessly at her side. Her vision going grey, she swayed toward her enemy. Lorcan lowered his face to an inch of hers, his foul breath washing over her mouth as he spoke, "Breaking you shall be enjoyable."

A sharp feline yelp pierced the night followed by a furious howl miles away.

Awareness hit her as she realized she still held the gun. She lifted and pulled the trigger. Lorcan released her and fell back two steps. The air started burning down her throat to her screaming lungs and she gulped it in. A murky haze still clouded her vision, but her hand kept firing at the monster in front of her.

Lorcan fell back with a shrill howl. Then he leapt to the left and lifted Bigsby's limp body off the ground to use as a shield. With a sob of fury, Cara stopped firing and searched for a way out. Katie lay unconscious in naked human form with a decapitated Kurjan next to her. The Kurjan soldier thrown by the blast still lay prone several yards up the road. He slowly climbed to his feet and started prowling toward them.

The one who had bound Cara stood over Katie and deliberately placed his booted foot on the back of her neck, pressing her face into the rough asphalt.

Lorcan gave a high-pitched hiss. "Drop the gun, or I'll have him crush her neck. Even a male shifter wouldn't heal from that, Cara." He continued to hold an unconscious Bigsby in front of him.

With one last desperate look around, Cara dropped the gun at her feet.

"Kick it over to me." Lorcan's fangs flashed bright and dangerous.

Shivering in the damp night, Cara kicked him the gun.

"Cara," Lorcan spoke softly, "watch what happens when you challenge me." With a dark gleam, he lifted Bigsby's body a foot off the ground, latched his fangs into the doctor's neck, and began to drink with sharp pulls. His eyes darkened to black, then swirled to red.

"No," Cara cried as she started forward, only to have the returning Kurjan grab her by the hair and tug her back. She struggled as Bigsby's color turned from a healthy flush to pasty white. Until his blood was drained. His eyes remained shut until Lorcan gave an unconcerned shrug and dropped him to the ground. Lorcan shot his tongue out to lick the red liquid off his stained lips.

He took a step toward her. "You tasted better."

A grey fog descended across her vision, and she began to sway. A roar sounded, the Kurjan holding her was ripped away and the ground rose up to meet her. The last thing she saw before succumbing to blackness was Talen, his eyes a wild green, his face a feral mask, and his fangs covered in blood.

Talen hadn't truly felt fear in centuries and thought furiously that he didn't like it. He swiftly ripped the head off the Kurjan who had dared to touch his mate. Then he lunged toward Lorcan, taking the leader to the ground in a crunch of bone. Blood splayed by his hand before two soldiers tore him away.

Throwing elbows, he knocked them back and turned. They both jumped for him. He stopped the younger one in midflight with a mere thought. But he allowed the second one to tackle him to the ground. So he could feel the warm blood of his enemy. He vaguely heard Jordan roar into the clearing.

His knife flashed out, sharp and wicked. Deep red blood coated the asphalt while the Kurjan's head rolled away from its body. Talen rose, his gaze on Lorcan, his canines elongating until the animal within hungered.

The one he'd froze broke loose with a shrill shriek of anger and rushed him in a crushing tackle. They hit the road, leaving a bowl-shaped dent in the hard surface. Talen shot an elbow into the soldier's windpipe and rolled until he straddled the struggling enemy. One swift slice through the neck and the struggles stopped.

Talen stood, fury filling his pores at the now empty roadway. Lorcan had disappeared. The strong urge to hunt warred with the need to take his mate to safety. As always would be the case, his mate came first.

Chapter 18

The last woman hadn't died easy. Kalin wasn't sure why, but he liked that about her. Nothing special, no extra abilities, surely not someone he could take back to camp. Yet, she fought death like an animal.

Yet in the end, she'd taken her last breath. Even her God wouldn't save her, further proof of the damnation of this silly, easy prey. The thick trees had provided canopy from the bright moon in the quiet forest, with no life shuffling around. Nothing in the wild was as deadly as him.

He wondered when the sport would become exciting again. When the thrill would return. Possibly not for decades, when he finally met *her*. Janie. So far away, yet a blink of an eye to his people.

The fall Minnesota nights had cooled to a comfortable temperature. He buried the shovel with his latest prey, kicking the remaining foot of dirt around. Rolling his neck, he surveyed the area, making sure he'd cleaned up. Then, with a glance at the waning moon, he began to jog for home, his thoughts on his future mate. He'd tried repeatedly to enter Janie's dreams but bounced against something strong each time; somebody else was there, somebody who probably didn't even know they blocked him.

Kalin had little interest in the young Janie at this time, but the other presence, a dangerous, still developing presence, well that was interesting.

Still wondering about the new player, Kalin scaled the rock wall and dodged inside the obscured cave entrance before pressing his palm against speckled rock. The wall slid open, revealing a large elevator which he rode down into the earth. He ignored the sentries posted on either side as he emerged and strolled across plush carpet to his father's quarters.

Three human women exited just as he reached the door. Pale, trembling, reeking of sulfuric fear, they kept their eyes lowered while passing him. He inhaled deep, swiveling to spot the red oozing out of one thin neck. Copper and sweet temptation filled his nostrils. His father had been feeding.

Grinning, Kalin strutted through the door. Muted light, ivory carpet, and thick oak paneling showed class and elegance while stark black, red, and white paintings adorned the walls. Scenes of blood and twisted death. If nothing else, his father truly had excellent taste in art.

"Father?" he called, moving toward the small kitchen to the left.

"Here," Lorcan returned in a low growl.

Kalin stopped short at the sight of his father bleeding over the oak table. "I take it the plan did not go well?" They should've let him go.

Lorcan hissed, pressing a blood-soaked towel to his neck. "No. Bastard damn near ripped out my jugular and the helicopter ride home took forever. It's taking me forever to heal." He ran appraising reddish-purple eyes over his son. "Where the hell have you been?"

Kalin shrugged, reaching for the tin of cookies in the cupboard, specially made in London. "Out."

Throwing the drenched towel into the sink, Lorcan ripped off the remainder of a tattered sleeve, revealing several breaks in his left arm. "I can't wait until you finish with puberty; this is getting tiresome." His eyelids closed, and he took a deep breath, the bones snapping back into place with a sharp crack. His eyes swirled purple through the red when he reopened them. "Did you cover your tracks?"

"Of course." His father's failure irritated Kalin. He'd looked forward to meeting Janie's mother, maybe of having her. "I take it one of the Kayrs showed up?"

"Yes. Talen Kayrs. Along with a clan of shifters." Lorcan rubbed his chin. "I can only hope cousin Franco doesn't hear of the disaster."

"You think he'll challenge you for the throne?" Kalin munched on a cookie, wondering if he'd be the one to eventually kill his father for the title.

"Yes. I'd thought to get my sotie in place and with child before Franco becomes too tempted. I'd hate to have to kill one of our best fighters on the eve of another war with the vampires."

Kalin shrugged. "I say we take him out now."

His father sighed. "Kalin, you need to understand strategy. Right now, we need Franco and his force to battle the Realm. Starting our own internal war would lead to disaster for us. And your future mating is imperative."

"Do you understand why?" Kalin tossed the tin back inside and shut the thick oak cupboard. "What is so special about this human girl?" He wondered what the oracles had revealed.

Loran speared him with a sharp gaze. "No. I'd thought you'd have an idea, considering the psychic skills of your mother."

Kalin lifted an eyebrow, lying easily. "I have no idea. Maybe your sotie didn't pass on enough of the psychic ability to me." Knowledge was power, and he intended to gather the most. "Well, father, I'll let you rest. See you in the morning." He turned, wondering if tonight would be the night he finally broke into Janie's dreams. He had a feeling that his biggest adversary, whoever that presence was, would be waiting for him there.

Kalin's fangs elongated, his heart sped up, and he smiled.

Chapter 19

Cara woke up well rested and stretched, thankful to be alive. Talen and Jordan had taken care of the Kurjan soldiers while Lorcan had escaped. She shuddered in the warm bed at the thought. Katie had only been knocked out and had returned to consciousness on the ride home after one of Jordan's men had retrieved them, and Bigsby's body had been buried by the same man later that night. While she and Katie had gone to bed, the men had moved on to an additional research facility they'd discovered from files taken in the earlier raid. Talen had warned her that several guards were positioned around the ranch, and she was to stay put.

The sound of the shower made her jump from the bed. Talen was back. He had informed her the night before that they'd discuss her activities when he returned and she'd had a good night's sleep.

With a grimace, she threw on her clothes and all but ran out of the room and to the quiet kitchen. It was empty. It was too early to be out of bed. She looked at a full basket of apples on the counter and her stomach swayed. She wasn't hungry.

"Hello, mate. Running, are we?" His voice was a deep growl.

Startled, she flipped around with her back to the granite

counter, knocking over the basket of apples. "Talen, you scared the heck out of me," she hissed on a breath.

"I believe I told you to stop and return to the ranch last night." His silky voice awoke the butterflies in her stomach as he advanced into the kitchen to halt a few feet from her.

She took a good look at the man before her. The extremely pissed off, pure dominant form of a male. "Um," she started as the tension began to surround her, fill her. "We had to go after Bigsby, you know that." Then, as she realized her vulnerability in answering to a man, especially this man, she lifted her chin.

Dark golden eyes narrowed in a strong face. The wet hair curling at his nape did nothing to soften him. He raised an eyebrow at her slight show of defiance, and his muscles rippled much like a Doberman controlling itself before receiving the attack command. "After Bigsby? Knowing full well the Kurjans waited for you?" The very air vibrated around him as he moved, his voice dangerously soft.

He stalked another step closer.

She suppressed a shiver at the tension. At the danger swirling around her. She noticed belatedly that her thong was getting wet. Danger shouldn't turn her on, she mused, as her wide pupils tracked the threat before her. This shouldn't turn her on.

He'd dressed in all black, a tight T-shirt emphasizing the sheer strength and muscle of his torso. As did his crossed arms with steel biceps. A muscle ticked in his inflexible jaw as he checked her over, head to toe, much like a predator examining prey, ensuring himself of her safety.

Man, he looked pissed, and a shiver ran down her back. Her panties got even wetter. She tried to cover the telltale shiver, but his amused smile showed he saw. Not just the shiver, but his effect on her. And that ticked her off. She welcomed the arrival of her temper as a relief from this other, desperate feeling. In fact she clung to it.

Her chin lifted higher, and she met his steely stare head on. "Yeah. It was the right thing to do. And you know it." Her cheeks flushed as she spoke in the face of danger. But her eyes remained steady on his, even as her body tensed to flee.

He stilled. Completely. His eyes changed into something predatory, something intense. He cocked his head to one side and his voice, when he spoke, was dark, silky, and dangerous.

"You want a taming, little one?" He moved a step closer, a bare foot of tension-filled air remaining between them.

Unwelcomed heat rushed through her body and nearly doubled her over. Temper and desire warred throughout. He wasn't playing games. She didn't need to read him to know he meant his words. Her eyes darted around the large kitchen, searching for escape from the intimidating alpha male before her. There was none.

She had no words to combat this effect on her senses—to combat him. Defiance was her only defense, so she tilted her lips in a small smile that was part sweet and pure sass.

"So be it," he growled in immediate reaction. One long step closed the distance between them before he ducked and tossed her over a broad male shoulder. The jarring impact took her breath as he spun around and headed down the hall. Her breath came back in a rush as she struggled over his shoulder, her clenched hands beating on the wide expanse of his hard back.

"Knock it off." A large male hand smacked her rear. Hard.

Her cry of outrage and increase in struggles had no effect on him. He stalked through the bedroom door and banged it closed with one thick boot. He easily controlled her struggling body, swinging her around to cradle in his arms. "A taming it is." His eyes showed no mercy as one hand ripped off her jeans and thong before flipping her to the bed onto her hands and knees.

The sheer strength of his movements made her catch her breath as she found herself facing the headboard, fully exposed to this being stronger than any human man. She tried to move forward as a strong arm banded around her waist. His hand slid up her torso to wrap around the front of her neck. Desire controlled her as he pulled her to her knees, his fierce erection digging into her back, her ability to breathe commanded by one broad hand.

She gasped as his other hand swiped the soft top and bra over her head. Her bare back met his thick T-shirt. The brand on her hip started to burn. She stifled a moan of desire and tried to bring common sense back into the situation.

"Talen, please," she breathed as his left hand tangled in her hair and pulled to the side. He dipped his head to run a sharp fang from her exposed ear to the hollow of her vulnerable neck.

"No, baby," his coarse voice was pure sin in her ear as he held her where he wanted her. "I'll tell you when to beg." He bit down.

The bite sent a direct line from her neck to her core. An oncoming orgasm hinted through her. Desperate, reduced to feelings, she pushed against the hardness behind her, searching for release. "No," the fierceness of the voice in her ear made her pause. "I control that, too. You'll come when I say." He pushed her forward again onto her hands and knees.

Startled, out of her element with her body vibrating for release, she stayed put as his belt rasped when pulled through his pants. The harsh sound filtered around the silent room, and she stifled a moan as it hit the floor. A rustle of clothing and his shirt followed the belt. Then, the rasp of a zipper made her shudder before he kicked his jeans out of the way. He spoke, his voice low and harsh. "And, I've had enough of you denying your natural abilities. They're likely to save your stubborn ass if you'd let them."

She jolted when two large hands grasped her hips. One hand caressed around to her rear and then farther down along her crease. She gasped as finally, he touched her where she needed it the most. "Ah, fuck," his voice was harsh in the darkness. He cupped her with one large hand. She thought she would faint as he inserted one finger in her, then two. "God, you're tight," he leaned over her back—his fingers working inside her—and gently kissed the bite mark on her neck.

She whimpered as she started to move in time with his fingers, his heat surrounding her. "You need to come for me, baby," he rasped in her ear, his fingers working inside her as his palm shifted and ground against the hidden bundle of nerves. "Now." The orgasm hit with a ferocity that stole her breath as waves of pleasure coursed through her.

His expert fingers drew out the orgasm until finally, she shuddered and fell forward onto bent arms. Her body began to relax until he rolled her onto her back. Then she got a good look at the fully aroused male before her.

She began to edge backward toward the headboard. He snaked out a hand and grabbed her ankle, pulling her back into place. "Oh God," she moaned, her eyes trapped by the dark promise in his golden eyes.

"Too late to pray, sweetheart." His voice was amused, aroused, as he put one hand on either side of her body and moved up until they were nose to nose, skin to skin. His erection, long and hard, pulsed against her stomach. Then he didn't move. Just lay against her, muscles bunched and tense, watching the play of moonlight against her pale skin. "God, you're beautiful," he murmured as he levered himself up on one elbow and devoured her face with his gaze.

Blue eyes, filled with confusion and awareness, opened at his words. Talen smiled. Truth be told, he didn't mind seeing either. He liked her off balance. And he demanded control. She was smart to be aware of him. Especially if it made her think twice next time before throwing herself into danger.

He traced the contours of her face, gentling her, watching as desire replaced awareness in her eyes. The confusion remained as the intensity of the night was out of her experience. Frankly, it was out of his, as well. He had never wanted to possess a woman like this. She was his and had been from the second her helpless government handed him her picture.

A possessive intensity rocked out of him into her. He made sure of it. They were connected, and it was damn well time she realized that. In response, adrenaline jumped her into flight mode, and her eyes filled with the need for escape.

"You've nowhere to flee," he murmured against her lips, reading her correctly, his large body all but surrounding her much smaller one. "Mine," he growled as he took her mouth with possession, demanding surrender as his tongue swept inside and dueled with hers.

He knotted one hand in her hair to angle her head more to his liking. He fought a groan as her sweet body arched up into the hard planes of his. He could even feel the heat from the brand at her hip. It shot straight to his heart.

Almost panting, he broke their kiss, staring in male satisfaction at her bemused gaze and swollen lips. He had wanted this since the first time he saw her pretty blue eyes challenging him.

The arrogance on his face brought Cara back to reality, or partially back, anyway. Her shields were useless against him. Damn it. She was out of her element, desperately turned on, and her heart was vulnerable. And vulnerable in a way she arrogantly thought she'd be able to avoid. The last frightened her, and fear slid into anger. She moved against him, tried to keep her eyes from falling back in her head, and rebelled. "So"—her voice aimed for sarcastic but the breathiness probably ruined it—"am I tamed yet?"

His short bark of laughter was unexpected, and she widened her eyes at the sound. Dominance chased the arrogance off his face. Her womb clenched as the hand in her hair tightened and pulled, exposing her jugular to him. She tried to toss her head to dislodge his hand and succeeded in drawing tears to her eyes as her hair was pulled by her own action. Her head remained where he wanted it.

"No. But you will be." It was a vow. He leaned down with

quiet purpose and enveloped her throbbing jugular with his lips, his tongue rough against the pounding vein, his fangs a mere hint of his power. She stilled at the implication and edged closer to another orgasm.

He stayed motionless a moment, letting her feel his strength and her vulnerability. He held her life in his hands. Or rather, his mouth. She tested the strength of his shoulders with a shove. He was rock hard and immovable.

He lifted his head and pinned her wide-eyed gaze with golden heat.

"Put your hands above your head." It was a command. She searched his eyes for softness or quarter. She found none. With a soft sigh, she stretched her arms above her head. He flashed his teeth at her obedience and started to penetrate her.

She struggled against the feelings rushing through her. The physical response to him, she welcomed—she clung to it. If he stopped, she'd freaking kill him. But the emotional demands of her own heart, of his, she couldn't block anymore. And he knew it. He allowed no compromise as he nipped her on the neck and slowly, firmly began filling her even more. "Relax," he purred in her ear, and amazingly enough, she did. He kept up his steady pace, and soon enough, he was completely inside her. She felt stuffed to the point of pain and took a deep breath to relax her body. Then he moved.

"Oh God," she moaned as he caressed nerves she didn't know she had. He partially withdrew, then pushed back in to the hilt, his desires commingling with hers. She sobbed at the exquisite pleasure. She had had no idea.

He began to drive in and out of her, keeping it slow and gentle until suddenly, filled beyond passion, she reared up and bit him above his heart. She felt the change within him before he did.

He roughly grabbed her thighs and pushed her knees to her chest as he pounded in and out, pushing her up the bed as he did so. Cara dug her nails into his back as he rode her, another orgasm threatening.

She looked up into his eyes and was nearly conquered with the intensity reflected in their metallic depths. He was primal, his focus on making her his. It was too much. She shut her eyes with a moan as he increased the strength of his thrusts past what she'd have thought possible, his hands on her thighs keeping her open, exposed for him.

"Open your eyes, Cara," he commanded, pushing her legs even farther against her chest.

Overcome, she obeyed and focused on the dark eyes claiming her. Her acquiesce fueled something in him that had him increasing the speed of his thrusts. Suddenly, deep within, an orgasm hit with an intensity that had her whole body jerking in response. She cried out. Her orgasm triggered his, and he threw his head back with a hoarse shout. Then he dropped to latch onto her neck. The bite prolonged her orgasm until she collapsed in exhaustion. Talen released her legs, and she fell asleep within seconds.

Chapter 20

Cara awoke for the second time that morning and grimaced as intimate muscles yelped in protest. The ache in her heart outdid them all. She covered her face in denial of the raw vulnerability rippling through her. Her mind, impressive as it might be, was no match for the combination of her heart and body and their willingness to give everything she had, everything she was, to another being. To Talen.

A sly voice in the back of her head whispered she should accept fate's offering. As if it were safe to do so. Her ability to blindly trust had been ripped away during her childhood, and the instinct to protect herself couldn't be denied. The same voice reminded her that neither could Talen.

A knock on the door brought her out of her internal debate. Katie poked her head inside the warm guestroom. "Are you awake?"

Cara nodded and sat up in the big bed. "Come on in."

Katie smiled and jumped onto the bed to peer at Cara's chin. "Your cut from that jerk Lorcan healed pretty quick."

Cara nodded. "I guess I have Talen's healing ability now. Pretty handy."

"You don't seem too happy about it."

Cara shrugged and sighed.

"He loves you, you know."

"It's scary." The words were inadequate.

"Yeah, I know. But at least he's willing to take the chance." Katie picked at the comforter.

Cara smiled at her friend. "It's obvious Jordan has feelings for you, Katie."

Hope filled Katie's eyes before she frowned. "Yeah, but not enough. I'll always be the brat who followed him around when I was a kid."

Cara shrugged. "So show him you're all grown up now."

"How?"

Cara was quiet for a moment. "I have absolutely no idea." She grinned and then giggled as her friend joined in. "Where are the banes of our existence?"

"They're in the kitchen looking through Bigsby's research. They'd like some help, if you're ready to get up."

"I'll jump in the shower and be right out." Cara smiled. "Um, exactly how mad was Jordan last night?"

Katie raised two eyebrows. "Let's just say I had to whimper and pretend my headache was horrible just so he'd let me get to bed. He's beyond furious the Kurjans know about me now."

"So you haven't really dealt with it yet."

"I'm not thinking about that."

"I don't blame you." Cara headed for the shower.

She emerged and changed into yet another pair of jeans and a deep green sweater before heading through the spacious house to the kitchen. Talen studied a mass of papers spread across the large oak table. Jordan leaned against the granite counter, reading a printout into the phone while Katie typed furiously on a laptop perched on the granite center island.

Talen glanced up as she entered, his burnished eyes running her length from head to toe. It was impossible for her to stop the warm flush that crept from her chest to her face in reaction. Talen grinned. "I checked your e-mail account and printed out the latest message from your errant sister." His voice held grudging admiration for the fragile human evading his troops.

With an eye roll, Cara walked forward and sat next to him at the table before leaning over and peering with interest at the paper. *"Hey sis. I'm on to something, no worries. These yokos can't find me. Run into the sun, dear one. Em."*

Cara fought a smile. Run into the sun. Apparently her sister knew all about the Kurjans. She turned toward her husband, telling herself he didn't look amazing in a deep brown graphic T-shirt and jeans. The voice in her head warned her to stop lying to herself, that it wasn't healthy.

He handed her a stack of research documentation. "We'll go through these papers this morning and take copies with us when we fly home." Talen ran a gentle hand down her hair, turning back to his reading.

"Home? Soon?" Cara turned her gaze to him, wondering if he had any idea how often he caressed her. A pat on the hand, a tug on her hair, often a gentle glide down her back. He'd probably face the demons of hell before admitting it, but her mate was touchy-feely.

He nodded with a grin at his papers.

Cara relaxed into her seat. She'd see her baby soon. Then her gaze focused on the paper in front of her. "Wow."

Talen nodded. "Yeah. They took the results of the Human Genome Project and are trying to apply either genetic engineering or gene therapy to the Kurjans."

"Hmm. Whereas humans have twenty-three pairs of chromosomes, the Kurjans have thirty." She read farther down. "As do the vampires." She read for a while. "And it looks like they've isolated the pair carrying the 'no sunlight gene' for the Kurjans."

Talen leaned forward and handed her a piece of paper. "Decipher that, would you?"

Cara nodded and read for several moments. "They've been attempting germline engineering to genes in eggs, sperm, or very early embryos." She leaned back to look at Talen as Jordan hung up the phone and sat at the table across from them. "This means they have been trying to manipulate the germinal cells, or rather, the egg and the sperm. In practice today that means altering the fertilized egg." She leaned forward, interest swirling through her mind. "The first cell in the embryo is the fertilized egg, and if you change that, all of the changes will be copied into every single other cell. The interesting thing about this type of manipulation is that it would be inheritable by all succeeding generations."

"How close are they?" Jordan asked in concern.

Cara shook her head. "First they used healthy vampire DNA and inserted different viruses into what they thought were the appropriate Kurjan cells, but so far they haven't seen any success with the method." She rifled through the papers and sat back with the one she sought. "But then they attempted to create an artificial Kurjan chromosome and add it to the thirty existing. Their research is impressive, but so far they've met with little success."

"And from what I've read," Katie piped up from across the kitchen, "it looks like they're still working on overcoming the mating 'allergy,' for lack of a better word."

Cara nodded in agreement. "It's only a matter of time until we can manipulate genes, but since we're not even sure which genes do what, the risk far outweighs any possible benefit." She pursed her lips. "They've looked at everything from plant photosynthesis to light aversion therapy to virus manipulation."

She reached for the next stack of papers as the telephone rang next to Jordan.

"Pride here," he answered. He listened before sitting back in his chair. "Hello, Detective. Yes, the Dodge truck is mine. I was at the truck stop last night." Talen looked up from his reading and his eyes narrowed. Katie sprang from her chair, and Jordan shook his head at her to be quiet before talking to the caller.

"No, I was just walking in when all the excitement started, and a police officer suggested we move away from the building. So, I headed home." Jordan listened for a moment. "I wish I could help identify the others in the restaurant, but as I've said, I didn't go inside. Of course. If there's anything I can do to help, please call me." He clicked the phone shut with a direct look at Talen.

"We should be getting out of town," Talen said.

Jordan nodded. "They won't be able to identify Cara or probably Bigsby, and we'll keep Katie under wraps for a while. I have my men preparing the Blackhawk to take you home. We'll leave in an hour."

Cara shuffled her papers. "Isn't that a military helicopter?"

Jordan flashed sharp white teeth. "It was until it was modified. You'll be home in no time."

The morning flew by and soon Cara said an almost tearful good-bye with Katie. She promised to stay in touch and hoped the young woman could visit Colorado sometime soon. Jordan piloted them for several hours west until the Colorado mountains came into view. The wild lands suited her new husband. Both were fierce in their beauty and well able to withstand the dangerous forces around them.

The sharp white peaks against the pure cloudless sky provided a stunning welcome to the higher elevation as the sprawling town of Boulder flew by beneath them.

Jordan piloted the craft low through several mountains until he landed in a small clearing with deep green grass blowing in the wind. Talen jumped out of the front and reached in to help her. She climbed into the cool air and followed Talen across the meadow to a large pine tree. They waved and watched Jordan rise into the sky. He gave a nod and then the sky was silent.

Birds chirped happily in the trees. The smell of pine and something sweeter from the myriad of purple and yellow wild flowers surrounding them wafted through the air. In the distance echoed the whinny of a stallion. Monstrous trees just losing their fall fir surrounded the clearing, and the scamper of small animals living their days sounded softly.

Talen grinned. "Welcome home, mate."

Cara turned in confusion. "Home?" Healthy trees and wild flowers ruffled in the breeze. "There's nothing here."

Talen took her hand. "There will be." He walked around the tree and Cara followed—they dodged and wove through the forest, carefully stepping over fallen branches and uncut brush. The thick trees repelled the sunlight, and Talen kept her close to lead her through the darkness. Finally, they came to a broken ridge covered in a ragged exposure of rock. Talen walked up and placed his palm to the right of the smooth surface, and Cara took a step back as the dark glade slid to the left, revealing a small square room.

She froze in place. "Oh my God. You actually do live underneath the ground."

He laughed. "No, I live right outside of Boulder on the lake. This is our main headquarters and our safe house when necessary." He gently tugged her inside. "And it's where your daughter is waiting for you."

Cara clasped cold fingers around his warm hand as the wall shut, leaving them in the darkness. She jumped when the room filled with light and a deep voice asked, "Identify?"

"Kayrs 23416," Talen replied.

"Welcome home, bro." The voice held a smile and the elevator began to descend.

Cara turned toward her husband. "They didn't know it was us until you identified yourself?"

Talen shook his head. "They knew it was us the second we flew into range. The code was to make sure all was well—that nothing unexpected was going on."

"Good security," Cara said thoughtfully.

"You have no idea," Talen grinned.

"Well, you have had centuries."

Before she knew it the lift came to a stop, and the same

door opened to reveal a wide room carved from metamorphic rock and granite. Two soldiers stood guard on either side of a massive rock door. They were large, armed, and unsmiling. Cara moved closer to Talen.

He tugged her across the expansive floor and stopped with a grin. "Max, Jones, this is my wife, Cara."

The change in the men was immediate and a bit astonishing. Broad smiles covered predatory faces as they took turns shaking her hand, being very careful not to crush her.

"Hi, ma'am. Janie is so excited to see you she can't keep still." The one dubbed Max turned and punched in a code to open the door behind them. "Please tell her she owes me a rematch on Old Maid."

Cara stumbled behind Talen as he pulled her through the door and it slid shut. Large arms grabbed her and yanked her into a hard chest, squeezing her in what could only be called a bear hug. "Welcome home, little sister," a deep voice boomed in her ear as she was put back on her feet. Familiar green eyes twinkled down at her.

"Thanks, Conn." She grinned as she regained her equilibrium. The brothers were matched in height and size but Conn had lighter brown hair cut short and silver flecks throughout his mossy eyes. The strong shape of his face resembled Talen's, and a large dimple winked to the right of his generous mouth.

The large room looked like an ordinary conference room. If one could call granite walls, a huge dark granite table, and a myriad of mounted plasma screens ordinary.

"This is the first gathering room where we sometimes invite allies to meet." Talen gestured her forward to another deep door set into the rock.

Her feet echoed dully on the hard surface. "Where's Janie?"

"The family safe quarters are toward the center of the mountain. She wouldn't be anywhere near this close to the perimeter or entrance," Conn said as he placed a hand on the wall next to his head, leaned forward and peered into a small screen that shot out a green beam across his eyes. The door clicked open.

Conn led them into a wide rock hallway that wound past several closed doors until they finally stopped at one layered with sedimentary rock. His palm print opened the door, and Talen gently pushed Cara inside.

Chapter 21

"Mama!" Janie yelped and jumped for her mother.

Cara laughed as she swung her daughter into her arms and held. Tight. She burrowed her face into her daughter's soft neck and smelled the scent of powder and child. Her world finally righted itself.

She knelt on one knee with her arms still around Janie and shifted back to take a good look at her baby. Janie had on new jeans and a dark blue shirt and her braids were an odd mess of starts, stops, and wraparounds. Blue eyes sparkled and her hands clapped together in glee—blue, green, and pink fingernail polish decorated each nail and some of her fingers.

"I've missed you," Cara whispered.

Janie smiled and threw her arms back around her mother's neck. "I missed you too." She leaned back with her hands still on Cara's shoulders. "We're in the middle of a mountain, close to the earth. She likes us here." Janie showed her gapped tooth.

"She does?"

"Yeah. And it's easier to talk to her this close."

"To the Earth?" Cara asked.

Janie rolled her eyes. "Who else?"

"Don't I get a hug?" A deep voice asked from behind Cara.

Janie gave a happy gurgle and released her mother to hurdle herself at Talen, confident he would catch her.

He did and then swung her high off the ground in a gentle hug. "Did you know we were coming today?"

Janie nodded. "Yep. The Earth told me."

"Thought she might. Rumor has it you owe Max a rematch on Old Maid."

Janie shook her head as she put both small hands on Talen's cheeks. "He's really not very good at cards." She shut her eyes for a moment. "Watch behind you, Daddy."

Talen narrowed his eyes. "What do you mean?"

Janie shrugged. "The Earth told me to tell you. Don't forget."

"I won't." He promised. "What else has she told you?"

Janie was quiet for a moment before shrugging. "I'm going to have a baby brother." Cara coughed in surprise as Janie grinned mischievously. "But I don't know when."

Talen chuckled and placed his daughter back on the ground.

Cara nodded at the two soldiers on either side of the small entry room, and they smiled at her in welcome. One turned and palmed the wall behind him to have a smooth door roll open. The security in the place was beyond obsessive.

"Talen," Conn murmured, "Dage is back with some information. Jase is meeting us in the control room in a minute and Kane is joining in virtually—there's some kind of problem. We need to go now."

Talen nodded and leaned down to place a soft kiss on Cara's lips before leading her and Janie through the door. "Stay in the family quarters and have Janie show you around. I'll be back as soon as I can."

Cara gulped in air with a nervous glance around. "I left my plant at Katie's."

Talen frowned. "I'm sure she'll take good care of it, Cara."

"I know." Cara's heart sped up. "It's just that plants provide oxygen and comfort. They can't live under the ground." Man, she needed nature, not pure rock surrounding her. The walls began to close in.

Talen ran a comforting hand down her back. "It's all right, sweetheart. I promise we have plenty of oxygen pumped in." He gave her a gentle push. "Now go explore with your daughter."

She took Janie's hand in hers and the stone door silently closed behind them. Janie tugged her along the hallway brightened with landscape oils until turning into a large, comfortable family room with a big screen plasma television mounted into the wall and two plush brown leather couches before an oak coffee table. The plasma showcased a peaceful mountain scene viewed out of a framed window. A small open kitchen with a round table sat to the left.

"This is the fun room," Janie said as she maneuvered her mother around a couch to enter a narrow hallway opposite the kitchen. Three doors stood open down the granite hall. "This is your room"—Janie pointed into a large bedroom with king-size bed covered in pale blue silk before she nodded toward the end of the hall—"a bathroom, and"—she tugged Cara into the third doorway—"my room."

Wow. The bright pink room held a twin bed covered in a purple flowered comforter, a light white dresser and a huge dollhouse in the corner. A cheerful lime green rug shaped like a flower spread from one end to the other, and a mounted plasma screen showed pretty ponies running through a river.

"Amazing," Cara said.

"Yeah," Janie agreed. "I got to pick this stuff out the first day on the computer, and then everything showed up the next morning. Can you believe it?"

Cara shook her head. "Have you been staying here by yourself?"

Janie nodded. "But Jase or Conn sleep on the couch every

night. Or they work with the TV on. I don't think they sleep as much as us."

"Oh," Cara said lamely as she noticed the sheer amount of little girl clothes in the opened closet.

"I told them they could sleep in your bedroom, but they liked the couch." Janie shrugged.

Their position kept them directly between any threat and her daughter. The vampires might be a scary race, but they'd sure done everything possible to protect her baby.

"So Mom," Janie turned hopeful eyes on her, "will you fix my braids?"

Cara giggled and nodded before getting to work.

They had just settled into the warm leather sofa to watch a movie about princesses and ponies when Talen stalked into the room with Max right behind him.

Cara turned curious eyes their way. She had only been apart from Talen for less than an hour and yet butterflies fluttered in her stomach. His thick black hair was tied back in a band, throwing the hard angles of his face into focus while green flecks danced through his golden eyes. Danger, or maybe even violence, percolated just under his skin. The gold warmed to gilt as his gaze swept her.

Then her heart thumped at what he carried in his hands. Set into a deep white cleaning bucket sat a young *Pseudotsuga menziesii.* "You brought me a small Douglas fir tree?" she asked, turning and rising from the sofa.

Talen shuffled his feet and cleared his throat. "Yeah." The fir stood about two feet, the soft green needles faded to brown, drooping toward the earth. "It was in the shade of several larger trees not getting any sun. I figured we'd replant it at home."

Her eyes filled with tears. He'd brought her a tree. The scent of rich earth and pine filled the air, and she took a deep breath, settling herself.

Talen turned and placed the fledgling tree on the table.

"It's okay. I tore it out by the roots, so it'll be easy to plant." He frowned at his offering.

She crossed to him, reaching up with both hands to cup his face. "Thank you."

He grinned, his arms going to the small of her back. "You're welcome. I figure he'll bring enough oxygen to the space to make you happy."

Peace and warmth flushed through her. She leaned up and placed her mouth against his.

Max cleared his throat, shoving a coffee cup filled with a mountain dandelion between them. "I brought you this." He was as tall as Talen but not quite as broad across the chest; long light brown hair illustrated a sharp face with light blue eyes.

Cara took the cup, stepping back and giving Max a big smile. "Thank you, Max."

He shrugged, a small blush coloring his high cheekbones. "Talen said you liked plants and stuff around, so I thought this one was pretty." His gravelly voice lowered, and he tucked his chin to his shoulder.

"It's beautiful," Cara agreed, fighting a giggle. The big, dangerous vampire was shy.

He turned toward Janie sitting on the couch and tugged a deck of cards out of his pocket.

"I'm here for my rematch." Max tossed the deck into the air to catch in his other hand. His smile at Janie was genuine.

"All right," Janie piped up, "but the loser has to paint their fingernails pink this time."

Max balked for a moment before shrugging and stepping toward the couch.

"Cara"—Talen shook his head in amusement at his friend—"Kane is sending some information from a lab in Canada, and we thought your knowledge of plant viruses and gene manipulation would come in handy. Do you mind?"

Cara frowned, glancing at her daughter.

"It's okay, Mom." The little girl grinned impishly. "Max will be pretty with pink nails."

"Oh, I brought my A-game," the vampire snorted as he sat on the other couch.

"Bout time," Janie retorted.

Cara nodded and, with one last look at her child watching Max shuffle the cards, followed Talen from the room. Once in the hall his strong body turned and pinned her against the wall before he lowered his mouth and entrapped hers. The kiss was hot, deep, and insistent. Cara moaned in the back of her throat. When Talen stepped back, his grin was easy but his eyes swirled green through the gold. "I missed you, mate."

The hunger emanating from him stole her breath. The ache in her own lower body wanted relief, now, and she shook her head for clarity.

Talen grasped her chin before running a thumb over her swollen bottom lip. His eyes heated even more as her tongue reached out and connected with his thumb—then he stepped back and dropped his hand. "They're waiting for us, mate. Two more seconds and we're not going to make it."

Cara clasped her hands together in an effort to control raging hormones.

Talen grinned again. "I wouldn't mind, but my asshole brothers would come searching for us, trust me."

"Oh," Cara said with a grimace. That was the last thing she wanted.

"Come on." Talen put a heavy arm around her shoulders and propelled her through the winding hallway until he stopped and placed his palm against the stone wall next to a large granite door. It slid open.

Cara stepped inside a spacious round room cut into the rock with an enormous plasma screen mounted on the opposite wall. Several computers sat directly ahead and to the right perched a large rock table where Conn and two other men peered at an array of printouts.

Conn gave her a wave as the other two men jumped to their feet. The first was well over six feet with copper eyes flecked with dark zinc; he was a bit thinner than Talen but the resemblance with the long black hair and deep grin was obvious. "I'm Jase, the smart brother," he said as he shook her hand before returning to his spot at the table.

The other man was bigger than the rest and appeared a bit older. Not in the face, but his eyes spoke of a long life. He studied her with an intent that almost made her uncomfortable.

"Dage?" Talen asked.

Dage cleared his throat before stepping forward to take her hand in a gentle grip. "Sorry," his husky voice rumbled with an ancient power. "You resemble somebody."

"Who?" Cara asked, bemused.

Dage grinned and shrugged. "I don't know her name."

Cara smiled and tipped her head way back to take in the leader of the Realm. Deep silver eyes shone out of a hard face only softened by his full mouth. He gently tugged her forward to the table to sit next to Jase. Talen sat on her other side, and they all faced the large screen. Giants surrounded her.

Conn punched in a couple of keys and the face of another brother filled the screen.

Intelligent metallic violet eyes scanned the room before they rested on her. "You must be Talen's mate." The grin was one she'd already seen in his brothers. "I have to tell you blue eyes, you could've done better."

Talen scoffed next to her. "You wish." He threw an arm around her shoulders. "Before we get started here, will you be returning for the colloquium next weekend?"

Kane nodded. "Yes. Well, at least for the second day, I may miss the ball."

Jase snorted from down the way. "You *always* miss the ball."

Cara turned her head. "What's the colloquium?"

Talen grinned. "Every ten years the Realm has a symposium or convention of sorts that begins with a ball. One Kane somehow manages to miss every decade."

"A ball? But . . ." The protest died in her throat.

Talen leaned in, his breath stirring her hair. "Don't worry. Full wardrobes are provided for all of us." Grinning, he settled back into place.

Cara rolled her eyes. Okay, that's what she was going to say, but still. It's not like she had ballroom dresses just hanging in her closet, for pete's sake.

Dage cleared his throat, obviously ready to get down to business. "Kane, do you have the newest feed?"

Kane nodded, his eyes turning serious. "It's coming in now. I'll relay the information to you, and we can figure it out together." He looked down and the sound of typing could be heard. "We just cracked the encryption on these files—we took them from a research lab in Paris last night."

Dage tensed on the other side of Conn.

"What?" Talen asked, his eyes still on the screen.

Dage shrugged. "Bad feeling."

The level of tension in the room rose, and Cara shifted in her seat. Apparently Dage's feelings carried some weight with his brothers. Conn typed some more and the screen split into two, so Kane remained on one side and a series of images came up on the other. Cara studied the images for a moment. A graphic of a spiraled helix of acids chained together swirled in a multitude of colors. "There are twenty-three pairs of chromosomes—that's human DNA, not plant."

Talen nodded as a second image came up next to the first. Cara gasped as she counted thirty chromosomal pairs on the second chain. "That's vampire DNA," Talen confirmed quietly.

Cara peered with interest at the third colorful chain of DNA spiraling together next to the others. She counted the pairs. Then she counted them again. "There are twenty-seven chromosomal pairs." She turned inquisitive eyes on Talen. "Who has twenty-seven?"

Talen shrugged. "Dunno. Shifters have twenty-eight." They all studied the different images for several moments as Kane worked furiously to decode more of the file.

Cara slowly pursed her mouth in understanding. "Conn? Would you put the unknown strand of DNA in the middle?"

Conn nodded and switched the images on the screen.

"Now put the unknown over the human." He did so and twenty-three pairs of human DNA lined up exactly with the unknown, leaving four left over from the unknown DNA sample.

"Now over the vampire." This time twenty-seven pairs of vampire DNA lined up perfectly with the unknown sample, leaving three vampire DNA pairs left over.

Simultaneous sharp intakes of breath erupted around her when the men saw it.

"The unknown is combined DNA." She turned surprised eyes on Talen, whose jaw had hardened to match his eyes. "A combination of human and vampire. You said you changed me. It's probably my DNA."

Chapter 22

Cara studied the screen as angry tension chiseled through the silence in the underground conference room. "Or it's the DNA of any mate, I guess." She thought for a moment. "Maybe this has something to do with the allergic reaction you get with someone else's mate."

"Maybe." Talen didn't conceal the raw anger riding through his voice.

The giants sitting at the table kept their gaze on the large screen.

"Oh, shit," Kane said through the monitor as he sent additional images to replace the strands of DNA.

A healthy cell came onto the screen before a prickly round blue blob attached itself to the cell and wormed its way inside. "It's a virus," Jase said somberly.

Cara nodded and her heart started to stutter as the blob infected and changed the cell. "They've created a virus that attacks the mates of vampires?" A dull ache pounded in her stomach. "If the cells are from the vampire mate, why wouldn't the virus attack vampires, too?"

"Maybe the three extra pairs of chromosomes we don't pass on protect us and the Kurjans from the virus," Talen said, fury riding his words.

That actually made sense. Cara shifted in her seat.

Kane watched something off camera for a moment before

turning back to the group, his eyes narrowing as he spoke. "Talen, you might want to take your mate back to your quarters."

"No," Cara protested. "Whatever it is, I want to know."

Talen looked her over for a moment before giving his brother a short nod.

Kane shook his head and punched in a button. A small woman pacing a cold square cell came into focus. She had dark blond hair, light blue eyes, and milky pale skin—Cara guessed her age at about twenty-five.

"Who is she?" Dage asked quietly.

"She was a Kurjan sotie," Kane answered after reading something off the screen.

"What's a sotie?" Cara asked.

"A mate." Jase answered.

"Why would anybody mate a Kurjan?" Cara wondered out loud.

Talen cleared his throat. "Mating doesn't have to be done willingly."

Her stomach dropped. She wished she'd gone back to their quarters.

"The woman was injected with the virus less than an hour before this recording was made," Kane said quietly, shuffling a stack of papers.

The woman paced the cell before starting to talk rapidly to herself, the words incoherent and full of pain. She slapped one hand against the stone wall and then punched the unforgiving surface several times in quick succession; blood sprayed from torn knuckles as she started to scream in agony. Cara jumped in surprise.

The woman's hands went to her head with a resounding clap as screaming turned to moaning and then back to screaming before she began to rip blond hair out of her head in thick chunks that soon matted the cement floor. Her eyes wild, her body contorting, the screaming stopped as madness overcame her, and she began slamming herself against the steel bars. The shrill snapping of bones echoed through the camera. Cara's own bones ached in response but she refused to turn away. She somehow couldn't leave the woman alone in her misery, even if it had already passed. Dizziness swamped her, and she whimpered in sympathy as the caged woman tried to claw her jugular out with one hand.

"Enough," Talen growled at his brother.

Kane nodded and the screen went blank. "She broke her own neck against the bars exactly two hours after being injected with the virus."

"Oh my God," Cara breathed, taking deep breaths to keep from throwing up. She really didn't understand. "Why create a virus you have to inject to kill mates? Why not just shoot them?" The scientist in her came awake. "Oh. It's just the first step. If they evolve the virus until it is airborne, they wouldn't have to know where vampire mates were located. They could just set the virus free."

Talen jumped to his feet, his body all but vibrating with violence. "They won't let it free until they have an antidote or immunization for their own mates."

Dage shrugged before standing and walking behind them to a computer keyboard and punching in some information. "Maybe. Maybe not. To my knowledge, the Kurjans have never valued their mates to any great degree."

Cara spoke up softly. "We need a geneticist on this. I'm not experienced with human genetics."

Kane nodded through the screen. "We're working on that." He rustled papers. "In fact, we're going to need to divert some funds into scientific research—I have a proposal to present when I return home." He forced a grin. "In time for the colloquium, of course."

Nodding, Talen leaned back against the wall. "Apparently while we have been modifying weapons the last century, the Kurjans have turned to science." The anger burning in his belly gave his words a guttural sound. A virus had been specifically engineered to injure or kill his mate, and his need to protect lengthened the sharp incisors in his mouth without conscious thought on his part.

Cara thought fleetingly of her sister Emma, who was at the head of her field in genetic engineering. She also shared Janie's odd ability to see the future. Cara struggled with her need to solve the crisis and protect her sister.

"Cara?" Moving into her line of vision, Dage's eyes deepened to zinc. A base intent cascaded out of him and a tingle tickled Cara's mind. Like spider legs tiptoeing across her skull. She mentally shoved him back.

She shook her head as Talen placed both hands on her shoulders from behind. He squeezed and then moved to block her from his brother.

Dage closed his eyes for a moment before they flashed open in a blaze of silver light. "Your sister is more than a geneticist, isn't she?" His gaze roamed the angles of her face. "She's a psychic."

Talen froze in his tracks. Cara didn't answer, her gaze wary on Dage. How did he do that?

"She is?" Talen asked in surprise before staring at Dage. "It makes sense, but that wasn't in the Intel I received. And stay the fuck out of my wife's head."

Cara started. "You received Intel on me?" She turned to face him.

Talen nodded. "Of course. I told you Dage sent information to my smart phone." He looked to his brother in question.

"There wasn't time." Dage ran a frustrated hand through his thick black hair. "We heard about the order to acquire them just in time to intercept, and we've been dealing with the Kurjan research facilities since. We haven't done a complete background check yet." He sighed. "I apologize for invading your thoughts."

She ignored the apology—she'd deal with the king later. "You already know the Kurjans are chasing Emma for her genetic research."

"Cara." Talen swiveled her chair around and crouched down to her eye level. "They're not chasing her for the research. They're chasing her because she's psychic and therefore a potential mate."

"Oh God," Cara whispered, blue eyes filling with tears. "Emma."

"And apparently good at hiding," Dage said grimly as he read the information flashing across the computer screen before a picture of Emma smiling in a lab coat filled the space. He stilled, every muscle in his impressive body tightening before Cara's eyes.

"What?" Fear chilled her blood and she shivered.

His head swiveled toward her as if in slow motion. "She looks a lot like you, Cara." Shards of navy pierced the silver in his eyes, swirling to a color not even close to human.

The emotions coming from the king were too strong for her to block. Anger. Determination. Impatience. "So?"

"So we need to find her before the Kurjans do. It's just a matter of time." Dage typed a series of commands into the computer. "I'm sending everybody we have—and I'll join them tomorrow." His jaw hardened to granite.

Talen stepped up to the computer, typing in her e-mail account, then her password, which she'd shared long ago. A message from fleeingfanny@yaddah.com came up on screen. Cara lurched forward to read.

Hey sis—I had to move. I'm safe, no worries. Love to the kiddo. E

Cara sighed. If Emma said she was safe, then Cara could believe it. She stepped back from Talen as fury swept through her. "I don't understand. Why the heck is it so important to find women with enhanced traits?"

A startled cough came from Jase, and the rest of the Kayrs men remained silent as several pairs of eyes turned to look at Talen. He opened his mouth to answer just as Kane came back on the screen.

"I don't mean to interrupt, but we just decoded ten more

discs labeled with different female names we need to view." His voice was an angry growl.

Cara's knees knocked together as she turned back toward her seat. "Okay. I'm ready." The Intel they'd taken from the Kurjan facilities was the best chance they had in ending all of this so her sister could stop hiding.

Talen lifted her off the ground and into his arms where she gave a startled yelp. "You're going back with Janie, Cara."

"No, I'm not," she protested as he pivoted around and headed for the door, his strong face determined, his jaw set hard. "I can help, Talen."

"There's no need for you to see the tapes. If we discover anything dealing with either genetics or information regarding your sister through the viewings, I promise I'll retrieve you."

Now in the hall, she started to struggle in his arms. He tightened honed muscles, effectively stilling her movements. "Don't argue with me, mate." His voice held no quarter.

With an irritated huff, Cara allowed him to pull her closer into his chest. "What if the Kurjans find her first?" Cara stifled a sob.

"Then we'll deal with it." He dropped a gentle kiss on her head. "But she's hidden successfully not only from the Kurjans but from us. Chances are she's safe."

If anyone could do it, her big sister could. She thought for a moment as Talen's sure steps echoed on the rough stone floor. "Talen? Does Dage read minds?"

Talen sighed. "He has the ability but he's promised to stay out of our heads. Usually, he does."

"Humph." She'd have to learn to block him. Another thought occurred to her. "How many vampire mates are there?"

Talen shrugged. "I don't know. We're spread across the world, I don't know an actual count."

She shook her head. "But there can't be that many. It seems like a waste of resources for the Kurjans to spend so much time on a virus to kill us."

Talen's grip hardened. "Who knows why the Kurjans do anything." He put her outside the door to their quarters before placing his palm against the rock. "However, they are well aware that our mates are our lives—take ours and you pretty much destroy us." The door opened to reveal Janie gleefully putting the finishing touches of the bright pink polish on Max's hands.

"Nice timing," the soldier said with a grimace.

Talen snorted. "You're relieved, in case you need to powder your cheeks."

"Funny." The soldier tweaked Janie's nose as he stood and ambled for the door.

Talen gave Cara a kiss on the cheek before turning to follow Max. "I'll be back when I can."

Cara walked into the room to plop with a sigh next to her daughter who looked at her with wise eyes. Too wise. "Everything is going to be all right, Mama."

Cara straightened and searched her daughter's face. "Are you sure?"

"I promise." Janie reached over and grabbed a remote control. "Let's watch the pony movie, you'll like it."

Talen returned several hours later when Cara was making a big pot of macaroni and cheese in the tiny but well appointed kitchen. The appliances were stainless steel and top of the line.

"Smells good," he said as she turned to study his face. Sharp lines cut through his cheeks, his eyes hardened to dented metal and a pulse pounded in his jaw. The tension vibrating through his shoulders set her teeth on edge, and she wondered what he had seen in those tapes.

"Bad?" She ran a gentle finger down his enduring face.

He briefly closed his eyes. "Yes." He looked around. "Where's Janie?"

"Napping."

He pulled Cara to him and touched his lips to hers before

diving deep with a groan. She responded as if she hadn't seen him in days. Her hands reached up to clench in his hair while his hands wrapped around her buttocks to yank her into his erection. They both panted for breath when he lifted his head. The imprint on her hip pulsed in demand.

The anger still blistering in his eyes made her take a step back.

"What?" She turned to stir the noodles.

"The virus isn't meant to kill," he said soberly.

Cara turned around in surprise. "Not meant to kill? How?"

"Seven of the eleven women killed themselves to escape the agony of the virus." Talen dropped into a thick wooden chair at the round granite table. "The others survived it."

Cara sat down across from him. "They survived being infected? I don't understand."

"The purpose of the virus isn't to kill—it's to change the mate back to human form." His eyes were metallic flints of rage.

"Oh. Why?"

Talen took a deep breath. "So they can be mated to a Kurjan."

Cara wrinkled her forehead. "They created an entire virus just to steal your mates?" She gave a disbelieving laugh. "There aren't enough human women in the world to go around?"

Talen remained silent, his gaze serious on her as she caught up.

"There aren't enough women," she murmured as realization dawned. She jumped to her feet. "Don't tell me. Only those with the stupid enhanced abilities are able to mate with you."

"And bear our children," Talen snapped back.

"Oh God. How rare are we?" Fear for her daughter overrode all else.

"Extremely," Talen confirmed, his eyes narrowing.

She took a step back from the table. "You knew. You knew that when you mated me."

Talen unfolded to his feet. "I knew you were *my mate* when I mated you."

A small voice made them both turn. "Mama?" Janie rubbed twin fists in her eyes. "I'm hungry."

With one last glare at Talen, Cara hurried over and picked Janie up. "I made your favorite sweetheart—come and sit down." She carried her daughter to the table and placed her gently on a chair.

"This discussion is tabled, not finished, wife," Talen said in a deep growl as he flipped open his buzzing cell phone and read the text message. "I need to go. The most recent information revealed another lab in southern California, and we need to raid it tonight." He snaked out a hand to tangle in her hair before lowering his head for a quick kiss.

"Emma?" she asked softly as he stepped away.

Talen shook his head. "The lab looks like a research facility, but we should gain more information from the raid. I'll keep an eye out, Cara."

"Do you have to go?" She felt safer with him; besides she wanted to finish this fight and see where they stood.

He nodded. "Yes. I'm the head of security for the Realm."

Cara shook her head in surprise at this new information. "There's so much we don't know about each other, Talen." She stepped back.

Golden eyes narrowed. "Then it's a good thing we have centuries, isn't it mate?" With a small kiss to Janie's head, he was gone.

The rest of the night was spent playing Old Maid, watching movies, and finally tossing in bed for several hours. When Cara was able to sleep, she dreamt of pale white monsters with blood red teeth laughing as they buried her in a coffin made of granite.

Chapter 23

Cara awoke in the sprawling bed with a cry, only to have a strong male arm wrap around her and drag her into his body, spoon style. "Go back to sleep, it's early," Talen murmured drowsily in her ear.

Her body melted back into his warmth, and she tamped down on the instant stutter of her heart. "Did you raid the facility?"

"Yes. We'll go through the data later. We found much of the same information as the place in West Virginia." His hair roughened leg caressed her own smooth one.

"No mates?" Her voice caught on the last word.

"No." His breathing deepened and his body relaxed into sleep. The warmth surrounding her lulled her into comforting dreams this time.

She awoke alone in the big blue bed. She leaned up to see a full basket of clothes on the granite floor—her clothes. Her heart jumped a bit that Talen had her clothes brought to Colorado, but that voice in her head reminded her about her doubts. The doubts screaming Talen wouldn't have married her without some strange gene she'd inherited that gave her not only enhanced gifts but the ability to breed a vampire child. Duty to his people rode him hard.

With a shrug, she took a quick shower in the attached bath before donning jeans and a blue sweater and heading into the hall. She followed muted voices to the kitchen where Janie and Talen ate scrambled eggs and discussed the best colors of the rainbow.

"No way," Talen said with a grin. "Golden yellow is the best."

Janie shook her head sadly. "Grown-ups are so blind." Her hair fell in perfect braids on either side of her head when she refocused on her breakfast.

"Who did your hair?" Cara asked.

Janie smiled in delight at Talen, who gave her a smug grin. "He did." Then she started bouncing on the chair. "Guess what? We get to go to our new house today."

Cara frowned. "Is it safe?"

Talen nodded. "Yeah. I have men sweeping the house and grounds—the Kurjans have no idea where we are—even if they had time to mount a raid. We've hit too many of their facilities this last week, and they're scrambling to protect themselves."

Cara ran a hand down Janie's hair before taking a seat at the table.

"What about all my stuff?" Janie asked before shoveling in a bite of eggs.

"Just bring your clothes and dolls, Janie. I have duplicates of everything else already at the house," Talen said.

"Dupl . . . duplicates?"

"Um, the same. You have the same bed, dollhouse, and rug at the house."

"Cool."

Talen's phone buzzed, and he flipped the top open to read the text before standing. "Our allies raided another facility in eastern Europe—no mates found but a lot of information." His gaze pinned Cara's. "I'll go meet with Dage while you two pack Janie's stuff. Be ready to go in an hour." His expression told her louder than words their discussion from the previous night remained on the table. She frowned in response.

Cara bypassed breakfast to help Janie pack her things. They had just finished piling everything into the myriad of laundry baskets delivered by Max when Talen returned to take them home. Several soldiers followed to help carry the baskets.

Just as they passed the control room, Janie balked. "Wait a minute. I forgot my picture from Uncle Dage."

"There wasn't a picture left in your room," Cara answered.

"It was still in his room, Mama. He promised. He drew a pink pony, and he said I could take her home. Please?"

Cara turned in exasperation to Talen, who chuckled and walked several doors down to place his hand against the rock near a big granite door. The door opened, revealing quarters similar to the one they'd vacated, except this one had two laptops and bunches of paper scattered across the table. Several empty grape energy drink cans littered the area as well.

Rushing forward with a happy cry, Janie flipped open a large sketch pad sitting haphazardly among the mess. A pretty pink pony smiled up at them.

Janie gingerly grabbed the paper by the corner and lifted it, pausing only when Cara gasped and moved forward. Cara reached out and lifted an intricate charcoal drawing of a face she knew almost as well as her own. Narrowing her eyes, she flipped page after page detailing her sister with different expressions in different settings. Dage had perfectly captured Emma's intelligent almond-shaped eyes, pert nose, and tiny dimple to the right of her full mouth. Emma's hair was piled high on her head in the last portrait, and her dark eyes smoldered with an expression Cara had never seen.

She turned in shock as Dage entered the room behind Talen, his silver eyes serious on hers. Talen moved to her side, his curious gaze on his brother.

"I don't understand," she murmured, ready and willing to put herself between Emma and any threat.

Dage remained silent.

"Why do you have so many drawings of my sister?"

Dage didn't look surprised but Talen gave a sigh of understanding next to her.

"Why, Dage?" Her voice firmed in annoyance.

Dage flashed a grin. "I've dreamt of that woman for two hundred years, Cara."

"Oh." She wasn't sure what to say. "Dage, Emma's not, I mean, she's not exactly . . ." She might not know Dage well, but she knew her sister like a book. And her sister would never put up with a dominant alpha male type of guy, which Dage screamed in spades.

"Not to worry little Cara," Dage said with an arrogant nod. "Fate wants what she wants. I won't hurt your sister."

Cara shook her head. "I wasn't worried about *her*."

"Humph," came the response as he gestured them out of his quarters.

It was a two-hour drive in an enforced black Hummer from the headquarters to the sprawling ranch house overlooking Great Bear Lake. Cara didn't miss the large gate or multitude of mounted cameras on several lodgepole pines as they wove through the trees until the asphalt driveway circled in front of a deep wooden house with a large wraparound porch. The door was a forest green enforced steel and looked like it could withstand a nuclear blast while somehow keeping its quaint and woodsy character.

Quiet and solitude surrounded her as she stepped from the vehicle and fought the feeling she had finally come home. The smell of pine filled the air, and birds chirped from high above. Then she yelped as Talen swung her up in his arms and crossed the thick wooden porch before kicking the door open with one strong boot and ushering her across sparkling granite tiles to the living room.

He gently placed her on the hard oak floor before dodging outside and carrying a giggling Janie over the threshold.

"Wow," Cara said as she stared at the floor-to-ceiling windows showcasing the calm lake surrounded by trees and mountains. She walked right past the tall stone fireplace, comfortable black couches, and stunning oil paintings to stand at the windows and just look. She turned around to find Talen staring at her, an unfathomable expression in his unearthly eyes.

"It's beautiful," she whispered, almost afraid to break the silence.

"Stunning," he agreed, his eyes caressing her face, the potted Douglas fir in his hands.

Janie broke the mood. "Where's my room?"

Chuckling, Talen lowered the tree to a spot near the door and held out a hand, which Janie took with a happy hop. Cara followed them down a carpeted hall to a pretty room in familiar pink. Besides the bed, dresser, and dollhouse, this room had a light white desk, walk-in closet, and attached bath.

"Awesome," Janie breathed before running and jumping on the bed.

Pictures of Janie, Cara, and Emma lined the dresser, and warmth flooded Cara as she turned toward Talen. "These are from our house in Massachusetts."

He nodded. "And the garage is full of boxes that need to be unpacked."

Cara smiled. "You had all of our things moved for us?"

Talen grinned back. "You can thank me properly later."

Hm. Maybe she just would. Talen showed them the remainder of the house; the huge kitchen had dark granite countertops, deep cherry cabinets, and all stainless steel appliances. The center island had plenty of room for someone who enjoyed cooking, which Cara did.

Talen soon disappeared into his office to plot strategy for the Realm while Cara and Janie set to work unpacking their boxes. A desire to create a life with her husband teased her while fear whispered that their marriage was merely convenient. She had the right gene and was in the right place at the right time. Or the wrong. It wasn't like he'd proclaimed any great love for her. If anything, he had treated her as a possession. One to be guarded, true, but Cara's plans had always been to enjoy a nice, mellow, and solitary life.

Talen was anything but nice or mellow, and there was nothing lonely about the feelings he inspired in her.

After dinner Talen put Janie to bed while Cara tackled her new closet. She'd finished lining up her shoes when Talen moved toward the open drawer at her side of the bed and removed her silver nine millimeter gun.

"Can you shoot?" Talen took the weapon and checked the empty clip.

"Um, no," Cara confirmed. "The gun is Emma's and she wanted me to have it when there were some break-ins in the neighborhood."

"It isn't loaded."

"I didn't feel safe with it having bullets, but I promised Emma, so . . ."

"I'll teach you how to use it, Cara." He placed the gun inside the drawer and pulled out a dog-eared book.

She shrugged and then flushed scarlet as she saw what Talen held in one hand. She struggled to stand.

"Bound Hearts?" Talen's voice deepened as he scanned the back cover. "Well, well, well, Cara. Nice reading material." He looked up from the book, and his eyes flashed liquid gold as they trailed over her burning face.

"It's just a book, Talen. Not a big deal and definitely none of your business." Cara willed the heat from her face, with no luck. For pete's sake, everyone read a bit of erotica once in a while, though she should've tossed the book after unpacking the box from her bedroom at home.

"I'm not so sure about that." Talen's voice was almost hoarse now. "You ever been spanked, darlin'?"

Cara caught her breath at the dark intent in his eyes, and her behind actually clenched in protest. "Um, well no," she blushed even more. "It's just a book, Talen. That's all."

"I don't think so." Masculine power flowed strong in his

husky voice. "I think you'd like it." His gaze kept hers as he replaced the book and closed the drawer. Cara took one step back and stopped herself from taking another when his eyes flared as he recognized her retreat for what it was.

The silence blanketed heavy as they stared at each other across the blue-covered bed, Talen's watchful eyes holding her wide ones captive. "Run."

With an instinctive yelp, Cara turned and did just that. She ran down the hall, through the living room and into the dining room, seeking safety. She felt, rather than heard, the hunter on her heels as she skidded to a stop around the large cherrywood table.

"Now, Talen," she held up one hand to placate him as she gulped in huge gusts of air.

He raised an eyebrow and stood deceptively calm inside the wide French doors, not panting in the least.

"This room is full of pretties—lots of china and breakables." Cara's eyes darted for an escape as she tried to catch her breath on a nervous giggle. Unfortunately, she was trapped. "We don't want to break anything," she continued with another stuttering chortle. "Let's stop this silly game and maybe watch a movie or something."

"But Cara"—Talen moved gracefully to the left, his voice low and soothing—"I want to play." He stopped moving as she inched in the other direction, her eyes tracking him. Even playful, Talen was as intimidating as hell.

Yeah," Cara retorted with a snort, "like a lion plays with a gazelle. Before he eats her."

A slow, lazy smile crossed his face and she gulped, realizing what she'd said. Her blood started to thrum with the thrill of the chase, with the thrill of what he'd do to her if he caught her.

"It looks like you're trapped, little gazelle." He moved a bit farther to the left. "Now I get to eat you." With the last, he lunged across the table in a formidable display of power and speed.

Cara shrieked in feminine panic and darted in the other direction, barely escaping his outstretched arm. She flew out the wide doorway, Talen's masculine chuckle echoing behind her, letting her know she was free simply because he hadn't finished playing. Only the thought of waking Janie kept her from shrieking again during the chase.

Cara's bare feet slapped against the thick tiles in the entryway as she darted past the front door into the safe haven of the kitchen. She skirted the dark, granite-covered island and backed up to the counter, her eyes wide on the entryway, and her elbow hit the huge basket of deep red apples.

The hurled red apple hit Talen on the chest as he stalked into the kitchen. He caught the second sailing apple an inch from his nose as Cara raised a third to throw.

His "I wouldn't" made Cara pause, hand cocked, ready to throw, the breath heaving in and out of her chest. He moved forward much like the time he'd stalked her in Jordan's kitchen, and Cara stifled a whimper.

His answering smile was more predatory than mischievous as he started around the island, holding her eyes captive. Cara froze as the sharp edge of desire warred to reconcile the predator with the fun she was having. Talen stepped up to her still form and gently took the apple from her hand.

One finger lifted her chin to meet his strong face. "Such a temptation." His voice sounded like gravel and sent desire rushing to her core. "Adam didn't stand a fucking chance in hell." Talen slowly ran the smooth skin of the apple down the side of her face. He lowered his lips to hers.

Cara melted into him as he deepened the kiss, his tongue dueling with hers, desire raging to the hint of pain throughout her body. Suddenly, she was lifted off the ground and deposited on the cool granite counter, her skirt pushed up and her knees spread wide on either side of his masculine hips. She felt small and feminine compared to the powerful male trapping her on the counter, and damn if that didn't turn her on.

He'd told her to run. He'd chased her around the house while she fought the need to giggle like a teenager. Pure instinct had her fingers digging into his ribs.

"Hey." Talen moved back, his hands clasping her arms. "Knock it off."

No way. No way! She dug in harder, pressing between his ribs and squeezing.

"Stop," he chuckled out, grabbing her hands, trapping them in his.

She grinned, her knees clasping strong hips. "I had no idea big, bad vampires were ticklish, Talen." How freaking cute was that?

He grinned in response, and her heart tumbled in slow motion without a net. "Hmm. Well, let's see." He released her hands to go for her waist. And he pressed.

The shriek she gave as his massive hands tickled her sides should've raised the dead. "No, no, nooooo," she cried, struggling to get away, giggling as she returned the favor, pushing her knees against his front to escape. Good thing Janie was a sound sleeper.

Talen shifted to the side, tangled a large hand in her thick hair and tugged not too gently to one side, exposing the graceful column of her neck to his mouth. His lips traced a path from her ear, down her cheek to the hollow between her neck and shoulder where he nipped. The imprint on her hip burned for him. "How about we call a truce?"

Hmm. A truce sounded good. She'd worry about her heart later. It was one thing to want the man, quite another to genuinely like him. The fun side of the dangerous leader was almost too much to resist. Then his sharp teeth nipped again, reminding her that his true idea of fun held a hint of genuine danger.

Cara's knees clenched his hips as she pressed her aching core against his jean-covered erection. One strong arm around her backside pulled her even closer as he continued his exploration down her body. He murmured in appreciation as his lips found the swell of her left breast above her rounded neckline. Releasing her hair, he inserted one finger in her cleavage and tugged her T-shirt down to expose one hardened pink nipple, which he immediately covered with his mouth, his eyes closing in pleasure.

His pleasure fueled hers and she opened herself to the sensations rioting through him—maybe being an empath wasn't so bad. She closed her eyes and leaned her shoulders back against the smooth cupboards as he rolled her nipple in his mouth, her pelvis pressed flush against his. She moaned and tangled both hands in his thick hair, pulling him even closer to her throbbing flesh. Her body screamed for her to give him whatever he wanted while her mind sought reason.

Her heart should remain her own.

Talen raised his head, gave her a hard kiss on the lips, and ripped her T-shirt down the middle with two strong hands. "I'll buy you a new one," he promised as he turned his attention to her other breast. Cara could only gasp as the sharp pulls on her breast coupled with Talen's covered erection pressing into her damp panties sent her spiraling into a sharp orgasm.

She buried her head in his salty neck to keep from crying out too loud. The ripples tore through her, and her every muscle tightened with the effort to keep quiet.

Talen gentled her with soft kisses along the undersides of both breasts as she clung weakly to him, her hands now limp in his hair. She stopped trembling, and Talen lifted his head to again claim her mouth, his hands spanning her waist. Lost in his kiss, Cara instinctively wrapped her legs around his hips and her arms around his neck as he lifted her off the counter and deserted the kitchen.

Talen strode across the house, nudging his bedroom door open with one foot, his mouth claiming hers. He deposited her on the bed before yanking his T-shirt over his head. His belt and jeans followed his shirt to the floor, revealing his warrior's body. Desire clawed through her again as she took in the hard muscles and sheer strength of the inhuman male. He placed one hand across her upper chest and pushed her onto her back.

"My turn to eat, little gazelle," he murmured, eyes intent on the scrap of lace before him. He knelt on the ground. Two strong hands reached out and pulled her closer to the edge of the bed, his breath hot through her soaked panties. He leaned down and clasped the elastic waist with sharp teeth, tugging. The panties refused to move, so with a growl Talen ripped them in two with desperate hands. "I'll buy you new ones," he repeated as he lowered his mouth to now bare flesh, his hands cupping her thighs.

She arched into his mouth with a soft cry. Her mind shut down as sensation took over.

"So sweet. So spicy," Talen declared against her, the vibrations making Cara clench her thighs against his hands. He licked her from one end to the other, releasing a thigh to insert one, then two fingers into her. He stretched her wide and spoke against her, "Truly succulent, Cara." With a growl, Talen nipped at her, throwing her into the crashing wave of another orgasm. She clenched the sheets with white knuckles as he plundered her, prolonging wave after wave until she shuddered with a final sigh of release.

Then she exploded again when twin fangs pierced her thigh and he drank.

Talen kissed the puncture wound and then slowly crawled up her body until they were groin to groin, his erection nestled impatiently against her core. His mouth mastered hers without leniency. The kiss was dark and dominant; Cara tasted herself on Talen's tongue while he began to slowly possess her. Then, with a growl and powerful thrust, he buried himself in her warmth. His mouth claimed her startled cry.

Cara was stretched wide as Talen began to drive in and out of her, his mouth delving deeper with a commanding kiss, his hand twisted in her hair. She couldn't fight her reaction to him—even if she wanted to. Why the fuck would she want to? She'd worry about that later. She moaned as he increased his thrusts and the friction created a wondrous series of electrical explosions deep within her womb—she opened her mind, her heart as much as she could. Powerful energy slammed into her from within him—claiming, striking at nerves, at emotions she hadn't known she had. In fact, she wasn't sure they were her emotions. Maybe they were his.

They shattered at the same time. Cara didn't know if it was her release or his that had her seeing stars. Perhaps it was the combination of both.

Chapter 24

The phone shrilled Talen awake as dawn began to cling to the horizon. He snatched up the receiver, instantly alert. "What?" He sat up in bed and switched on the light. "When?" He pulled Cara closer to him, and her blue eyes widened. He shook his head at Jordan's words. "She can't go on the raid, Jordan. I know . . ." He wiped a frustrated hand across his eyes. "All right. We'll see you in a half an hour." He hung up the phone before facing his mate.

"Is it Emma?" Her voice whispered with fear.

Talen shook his head. "No. The Kurjans have kidnapped Katie."

"Katie?" Cara sat up with a gasp. "No! Why?"

Talen shrugged. "I don't know. Could be any number of reasons." He jumped out of bed. "Jordan tracked them to eastern Oregon; he thinks he knows where she is being kept." He threw on jeans and a dark long-sleeved shirt.

"Why does he want me on the raid, Talen?"

"It doesn't matter." He may not yet own her full empathic abilities, but her determination slapped him with impressive strength.

"It does," she countered as she threw on jeans and a sweater and faced him across the bed.

Talen looked Cara over carefully. "She's in a large private

hospital, and Jordan doesn't know where she is. He thinks you can sense her if you are close enough."

"I probably can."

"No."

"Talen, you can't push me to accept this ability and then not let me use it. Especially when a friend needs me." Her voice stayed low, direct. Impressive, that. "You didn't see how she fought when Lorcan had me, or how she shifted into a lion to protect me when she knew it would expose her to the Kurjans. I owe her."

Talen gave a low growl from deep in his throat and strode out of the room. Cara had a point, and he didn't like it. He'd pushed her from day one to embrace her empathic abilities, so how could he refuse her need to use them? Every instinct he had bellowed for him to lock her in a closet until he dealt with the threat. He had not counted on this fucking turmoil when he'd pictured his life with a mate.

He sighed. She wasn't just *a mate*. She was his. The little smart-mouthed scientist held his heart in her hands. He'd kill her if she let anything happen to herself.

Once in his office he lifted the phone and started barking orders. His mate may still need to learn her place in his life, but the rest of the fucking Realm would do as he ordered.

He had just clicked off when she entered the room dressed in faded jeans and a navy sweater that emphasized pert breasts and fragile shoulders. Her skin pale over delicate cheekbones, she'd set her soft mouth in a hard line. Eyes the color of heavens late in the day flashed blue sparks at him, and only the child on her heels kept him from answering her challenge and taking her to the floor right then and there.

His gut clenched as he realized his anger lay with himself. He loved her.

Then Janie gave him a tiny smile, her pretty hair in little braids with pink ribbons. His heart tripped. Jesus. They were his life. Fear and a fierce resolve to keep them safe nearly knocked him off his feet, and the marking on his palm burned right to his heart.

Cara opened her mouth to speak. Hell, to argue probably.

He raised a hand. "Jordan's picking us up in fifteen minutes. We'll drop Janie off at headquarters and get reinforcements before heading to Oregon."

"We?" Hope flashed across Cara's face.

He took a deep breath, fighting every impulse he had to shield her. "Yes. You were right. There's no sense having your abilities if you don't use them. But, mate"—his voice lowered and he sent out an emotional wave as a threat—see her block that, damn it—"you follow orders. You remain in the background until we clear the facility and if I tell you to do something, you damn well do it." If she gave him one hint that she'd put herself in danger, he'd leave her here.

"I will," she promised, her sexy voice low and breathy.

Talen shook his head as unease swept through him while he fought his gut. Every instinct he had bellowed for him to keep his mate safely away from the Kurjans and the raid—hell, away from any hint of danger. The sound of blades slashing through the air caught his attention. "Jordan's here."

She nodded as she took Janie's hand, and they headed out the front door to watch the massive helicopter land on the grassy lawn.

"Duck your heads," Talen yelled as they ran forward and jumped into the sleek vehicle. With a quick nod at them, Jordan lifted the Blackhawk into the sky.

Deep in the Kayrs underground headquarters sat a room with an impressive array of computers and technology that was at least as advanced as anything owned by Cara's government, maybe even more so. Data scrolled across screens in flashes of green, black, and yellow, reminding Cara of a science fiction movie she'd seen as a teenager.

The Kayrs men stood shoulder to shoulder with the four

towering shape shifters. Talen brought a holographic image of a private hospital in downtown Portland up on the large center screen. “The primary objective here is to rescue Katie and any other captives, per Realm Operating Directive 25.”

Jordan slammed a knife into his vest. “Are we expecting other captives?”

Talen shrugged. “It’s possible. Second objective is retrieving information, grab any computers or files you see. The final objective is killing Kurjans.” He shook his head. “This new Kurjan policy of hiding in plain sight concerns me. A hospital, for God’s sake. We’ll need to alter our battle strategy as well as our training scenarios.”

A momentary thought whispered across Cara’s subconscious—how in the world had Jordan tracked Katie to Portland? Realization slammed home. Oh. No. He. Did. Not. She shook her head. Katie would be furious. “When did you put the tracker on Katie, Jordan?”

His tawny gaze met hers before he gave a shrug. “What tracker?”

Jase snorted next to him.

Talen cleared his throat. “The data we’ve collected shows the facility is fairly new and probably not fully secured yet. Even so, they’ll know we’re coming, so the plan is shock and awe. We hit fast, and we hit hard, flying the two Blackhawks in together.”

Once everyone had their orders straight, Talen led them into another secured room stocked with every weapon imaginable, including guns, swords, knives, cannons, and rockets.

“Wow,” Cara said, scanning the abundant weapons. Her breath hitched in her throat.

Talen was all business as he dropped a lightweight black vest over her head and secured it at the sides.

“Bulletproof?” she asked. Her mind flashed to her child. Janie needed a mother. Fear and guilt swept down Cara’s spine.

"Yes. The vest will protect you even from our bullets," Talen said soberly as he pulled a similar vest over his own head. He lifted his gaze. "Are you sure you want to go?"

No, she wasn't. But Katie needed her. "Yes, I'm sure."

His jaw hardened, and he stepped back to prepare for battle. The weapons room suited him as the head of security for the entire Realm. The vest fit snug over his black shirt, clearly emphasizing the breadth of his chest and the muscled strength of his arms. He'd pulled his dark hair back into an efficient band, and his face set hard in lines of concentration as he checked each weapon before handing it to the waiting warriors. The very air around him vibrating with purpose, his unearthly golden eyes glowed with intent.

But it wasn't just the dangerous color of his eyes; it was the sheer intelligence and basic power shining out of them. His ability to strategize and create the battle plan to ensure their success impressed her while creating a yearning deep within she couldn't quell. Damn it.

She pressed her back against the wall, seeking a moment of calmness in her own thoughts. Dage, Conn, and Jase were all quiet business as they placed weapons within easy reach before double checking each other's vests and donning dark sweatshirts. She recognized the shifters with Jordan from her time on his ranch—the three brothers, Mac, Noah, and Baye, were his top Enforcers and they looked it. The three were tall and muscular with deep blond hair streaked with a myriad of darker colors—had she not known they were lions, she would've wondered at the coloring.

Mac winked a dark chocolate eye at her and nodded for her to double-check her earpiece. Cara complied, noting she was the only person in the room under six and a half feet tall. She was also the only woman, and the testosterone swirling around made her light-headed.

"Keep this with you and shoot anyone you don't know." Talen brought her out of her silent thoughts as he secured a glowing green gun to the side of her vest before covering her in a dark sweatshirt and zipping it up. "The gun is point and shoot—you've used one before."

"It'll be all right, Talen." She rubbed his thick forearm as he inserted his own earpiece.

"It had better be, mate." He swooped down and placed a hard kiss on her lips before taking her hand and leading her from the room through several corridors until they reached an elevator that took them outside. Jordan and his men jumped in one Blackhawk, and Cara snuggled between Talen and Jase in the back of the one piloted by Dage. Conn punched in buttons from the co-pilot's seat.

"Cara, I hope you don't get motion sickness," Dage said dryly through her earpiece as he powered up the impressive vehicle.

"I don't think so," she replied, dread pooling in her stomach.

"We'll find out," Jase noted from next to her with a slight grin.

"We're going to fly close to the earth so they don't spot us, mate. The ride will be fast, twisty and turny. Are you sure you don't want to stay here?" Talen's smooth voice shot through her ears and straight to her core. How did he do that to her?

Cara shook her head as Dage pulled a lever and the ground dropped away faster than she would have thought possible; then the world spun by below her in a blur of green and brown. She almost giggled at the exhilaration. Apparently she wasn't prone to motion sickness. Even when Dage dropped so close to the ground tree branches scraped the belly of the helicopter, she enjoyed the feeling of winging through the air. While Jase shook his head in amusement at her wide-eyed delight, Talen stared at the flashing clouds, his mind clearly on the battle to come.

The touchdown was quick and unexpected. They landed on the roof of the building figuring the Kurjans would have been more prepared for a frontal assault. She jumped out of the helicopter behind Jase and followed him to the metal door set into red brick with Talen right behind her. She shifted as the other six soldiers swung over the sides on thick ropes attached to the Blackhawks; seconds later glass shattered with a large boom.

"Fire in the hole," Jase yelled.

Talen yanked her around the side and covered her head with his body. An explosion rent the air. He stepped back and she followed Jase through the smoke-filled doorway—the metal door sat wrinkled and smashed to the side. Two Kurjan soldiers came into view and she screamed at the guns trained at her chest, then shock filled her as the enemy froze in place, both obviously trying to move toward her but acting as though they waded through concrete.

Sweat beaded on Talen's upper lip. "These are older and fairly well-trained," he hissed to Jase. Then his head slammed back and he grimaced.

"What?" Cara asked.

Talen shook his head. Jase instantly fired two shots and dodged forward to slice the head off one Kurjan while Talen dispatched the other.

"Come on," Talen growled as he grabbed Cara by the arm to run down the cement stairs behind Jase. They descended the four flights to land at the first floor doorway. He turned to her. "Shut your eyes. Do you sense Katie?"

Cara closed her eyes, her heart pounding in her chest. God, please let this work. Nothing. With a hiss, she concentrated on her friend's face, her smile, her impish grin. A shiver of awareness started to hum in the back of her head. She concentrated harder and her eyes flew open. "She's here. She's really mad and trying not to be afraid."

"Where is she?" Jordan's growling voice through her earpiece made Cara jump.

Cara shook her head and turned anxious eyes on Talen. "I don't know. It's like she's muted." Cara closed her eyes and concentrated even harder. "Like something heavy is between us."

"She's underground," Talen muttered.

"Fourth floor is secured," Mac said clearly through the earpieces. "This place is actually a hospital, and we just scared the crap out of a bunch of patients. We cut the communications and declared a military situation, so they can't call out."

"Status?" Talen asked as he placed one hand on the tan metal door and closed his eyes to concentrate.

"Third floor secured," Conn affirmed. "Nurses and patients, no Kurjans."

"Same with second floor." Baye's low voice came across clearly.

"First floor secured, no Kurjans," Noah reported.

"We found the entrance to the basement in a closet, north corner of the first floor," Dage said quietly. "Jordan and I are going in."

"Wait," Cara said as more whispers went through her mind. "She's not alone. There's someone else with her, another woman. Feminine. Hurt."

"Another captive?" Talen turned from the door.

Cara shrugged, her eyes wide on him. "I don't know. She's kind of blank. Like merely an essence is there." The breath in her throat turned to ice. "I also sense a darkness, maybe an evil surrounding them."

"Yeah, I sense that too," Talen said dryly. "I sense five Kurjans below." He nodded at Jase. "Everyone hold their positions. Jase, Cara, and I will head for the north corner, and when I give the signal, everyone evacuate for the roof." He gave a short nod to Jase, who yanked open the door. "Act casual," Talen murmured under his breath as he pulled her into a standard hospital waiting room with fabric chairs and patterned linoleum. It was empty save for Noah standing next to a forty-something blonde at the admittance counter. The heavyset woman blushed a soft pink, trying to smooth down her fluffy hair.

"Colonel, Nurse Reed and I have secured the first floor," Noah said solemnly to Talen. "The doors are locked and the patients are all safe."

"Very good, Major," Talen said smoothly and turned a smile on the woman. "Your country thanks you, miss."

The nurse's thickly made-up eyes went wide and her mouth slack. She blushed even more, gasping as Jase moved into her view. The hand on her hair began to tremble.

"I believe this was a false alarm, but we need to check one more thing," Talen said as he walked past the desk with Cara and Jase on his heels. "Major, stay here with the nurse."

They jogged through the quiet hallways until coming to a janitor's closet at the northern corner. Conn's voice came through the line thick and amused. "You did not tell her that her country owes her."

Talen chuckled. "Too much?" He dodged inside and closed the door behind the three of them. A gaping hole in the far wall showed where Dage and Jordan had gone. They walked carefully down a flight of hard cement steps to a narrow hallway where two decapitated Kurjans lay.

"Damn it," Jordan's voice echoed through the earpiece. "Five Kurjans down, I don't sense any more."

"Me neither," Talen agreed as he started forward. "They certainly weren't expecting us."

"I'm sure they got the word out, though. We probably have ten minutes until reinforcements arrive," Dage said grimly with running steps sounding in the background.

Cara edged away from the hard stone walls, her boots sending up dust from the dirt floor. Mold scented the stale air.

"This place is a maze of twists and turns," Jordan hissed out through her earpiece as they turned a corner into a round room with four halls spreading out in different directions.

"It's almost like they just created the lab or just abandoned it. Where the hell is she?" Rage echoed throughout each word.

Cara came up short as Dage and Jordan emerged from one of the big tunnels. She closed her eyes and tried to relax. She pictured Katie smiling and turning into a lion. She focused as hard as she could, and giving a sharp cry, she turned and ran down the tunnel to the far left with Talen and Jordan on her heels.

Dirt pounded up from their feet as she passed closed door after closed door before emerging into another round room with tunnels veering off. She stopped and closed her eyes again. "This way," she said as she ran straight into the nearest tunnel. It was narrower than the others and industrial yellow lights cast eerie shadows across the pale rock. Finally, she halted in front of a narrow stone door and started to pound on the smooth surface. "Katie?" she yelled, pounding harder. A fierce softness vibrated at her from the other side—her friend was so close.

Talen pulled Cara away and gave a short nod to Jordan before both men threw massive shoulders into the hard stone. The door flew open with a loud crash, revealing a hospital room with two beds, monitors, and a myriad of medical equipment. Both beds were occupied.

"Katie," Jordan growled as he rushed forward and ripped the restraints off her wrists and ankles. "Are you okay?" His hands went to her shoulders to yank her against his chest. Cara's breath caught in her throat at the raw emotion etched into the shifter's face even as her shields moved to block the rage and relief rolling off him in deep waves.

"Yes," Katie said, pushing a shaking hand through her tousled hair and straightening her white hospital gown. "They injected me with something once, but I think it was just a sedative." She jumped off the bed and wobbled before Jordan scooped her up in his arms. "Help Maggie," she said almost on a sob.

"Why didn't you shift?" Jordan growled, moving toward the door.

"At first I couldn't, then I didn't want to hurt Maggie," Katie sighed.

The antiseptic smell of bleach slammed into Cara as she hurried to the other bed which held a small woman with dark brown eyes and thick black hair. The eyes widened in fright. Pure terror cascaded out of her very pores, and Cara instantly tried to soothe her with soft, nonsense words. She started to yank on the leather restraints only to have Talen push her gently aside and rip them apart.

"I told you they'd come," Katie said with almost a grin at the other woman, settling further into Jordan's broad chest.

Maggie nodded and tried to stand on her bare feet, only to sway to the left. Grabbing a worn blanket, Talen wrapped it around her and quickly picked her up and headed for the door. "Cara, stay between Jordan and me," he ordered as he moved into a jog. He handed Maggie over to Jase in the large round room and led the way down the final tunnel with Dage taking the rear position.

"Everyone evacuate." Talen gave the order as he ran up the steps into the janitor's closet. The sound of feet on concrete and doors bursting open filled their com-lines as everyone headed up to the Blackhawks. Within several heartbeats, Cara was again safely ensconced between Jase and Talen with the world spinning by below them.

Chapter 25

Cara jogged between Baye and Jase with Talen at her back through another deep haven carved in the earth. Dage led the way while Jordan and Mac carried Katie and Maggie behind them. Less than two hours had passed since they'd retrieved Katie from the Kurjan hospital, and Cara's limbs began to tire as the adrenaline subsided.

The underground rock outside of Seattle was a lighter, flecked color than the hard stone in Colorado. Dage turned into a wide room with several large tables surrounded by orange chairs. Antiseptic and bleach filled her nostrils. Two men dressed in white doctor smocks and wearing thick plastic gloves rushed forward.

"I'm Dr. Jones," the first said, his grey eyebrows lifting with each syllable. He motioned toward a table littered with medical supplies. "The medical facilities are still being set up—this will have to do for now."

Jordan placed Katie on a table with careful precision. "I guess you guys haven't worried about emergency medical facilities since the war ended."

Talen nodded. "Yeah. Sorry about this—we're scrambling a bit." He shifted to face the doctors as Mac sat Maggie next to Katie. "They were injected with something—we need to know what it is."

Cara's heart slammed twice against her rib cage. Katie looked so small and vulnerable in the hospital gown with her feet bare. What had the Kurjans injected her with?

Dr. Jones nodded and pulled out a syringe before inserting it in the young lioness's arm. The other doctor did the same with Maggie.

Talen took Cara's hand, the marking on his palm instantly warming against her skin.

"So, Katie. Want to explain how the Kurjans kidnapped you?" Anger Jordan did nothing to hide simmered just below the surface of his low voice, and Cara gave her friend a sympathetic smile.

"Well"—Katie grimaced as Dr. Jones removed the needle—"the sheriff called and asked me to come down and answer questions about the night at the truck stop."

"And you went?" Jordan asked incredulously. "Without telling any of us?"

"You weren't around," Katie all but hissed back. She began swinging her bare legs back and forth under the table. "He asked me to meet him at the truck stop, so I went."

"It wasn't the sheriff?" Cara guessed, swaying a bit in exhaustion.

"No." Katie frowned. "But I didn't get a sense he was lying on the phone. I just don't understand." Dr. Jones placed a blood pressure cuff around her arm and began to pump.

"Then what?" Talen asked quietly, releasing Cara's hand to pull her against his warmth.

"Well, when I got to the truck stop, I started to walk inside and this big white van pulled up, two Kurjans jumped out and grabbed me, and one stuck a needle in my arm before I could shift." Katie's voice rose in anxiety. "Whatever it was knocked me out, and I woke up in that room you saw." She looked around, stretching her arm as the doctor removed the cuff. "How long was I gone?"

"Five hours," Jordan snarled.

"Wow," Katie murmured. "How did you find me so fast?"

"Doesn't matter," came the reply. "It's just good that we did."

Katie stilled. "I think it does matter. How, Jordan?"

The leader of the lions shrugged, his strong jaw set. He leaned to the side to read the chart Dr. Jones was filling out.

Realization dawned across Katie's pale face. "You had a tracker on me?" She snapped her head up. "Where?"

"In your shoe," Jordan retorted, focusing back on her. "We tracked you to the facility, but they threw your shoes out. Cara found you from that point."

Katie bit her bottom lip until it turned white. "We'll discuss that tracker later, Jordan."

"You're damn right we will." His anger obviously outdid hers.

Katie ignored him and turned to Cara. "Thank you."

Cara nodded—she'd known her friend would be pissed. "Of course. What happened then?"

Katie shrugged. "I'm not sure. They were waiting for a doctor to come and inject me with something." Dr. Jones inserted a thermometer in her mouth and she shut her lips, her eyes still shooting sparks at Jordan.

"Dr. Jaylin," Maggie spoke up, her light skin paling even more as all eyes turned toward her. "He was supposed to be back tonight." The other doctor removed the cuff from her arm and moved to scribble notes in a file.

"Did they say anything about the injection?" Dage asked her quietly.

"No. Though I know I had several." Maggie glanced at the bruises inside her left elbow. "I don't know when, or how many times, either."

"You don't remember?" Cara asked, wondering if this was why she could only get a mild sense from the woman in front of her.

"No." Maggie shook her head, her brown eyes desperate. "I don't remember anything before yesterday. Dr. Jaylin said he'd explain it all, but I didn't believe him."

"He kept calling her Maggie, but we don't know if that's really her name," Katie explained.

"Yeah, I feel more like a 'Cassandra,'" Maggie said with a small grin.

"Or a Bernadette," Katie joined in. "We spent quite some time imagining possible names."

"Was Jaylin human?" Talen asked.

"No. White face, black eyes, really creepy," Maggie said with a shudder. "Yesterday I saw two others like him."

"Kurjans," Cara muttered as Katie nodded. She closed her eyes and concentrated as hard as she could on Maggie. Whispers of thoughts and feelings rushed through her.

"Can you feel if she was a mate?" Talen asked.

"No. But there's something there . . ." Cara focused again.

"What?" Maggie asked, her eyes filling with tears.

Cara opened her eyes and shrugged. "I don't know. There's an energy about you, kind of like the one from Katie. But different somehow."

"Maybe she's a shifter," Jordan spoke up.

"Maybe," Cara agreed.

"Shifter?" Maggie asked after a moment.

"Long story. We'll work on it after you recoup." Katie patted Maggie's hand. "Question. Why would the Kurjans want shifters? I thought they were after vampire mates."

Nobody had an answer for her.

Vampire mates? The clamoring in Maggie's head rose in volume. What the hell? Whispers of thought, spirals of color, hints of pain. Too much for one head, one skull to take.

Something pulsed through Maggie's blood, something the Kurjans had injected into her. Or had it been there before? She tried to concentrate on her new friend, tried to focus on the energy, mostly male, swirling around the room. The coppery taste of blood filled her mouth, she'd bitten her tongue to keep from crying out. Blood hit her stomach, and it growled. She hungered.

Crossing her legs, she shifted on the cold table. The sweet scent of her own blood filled her nostrils, and she fought the growl rising up from her soul. Hunger. Blood. Need.

She opened her mouth to speak, and a pitching growl emerged. Dead silence fell over the room, and all eyes turned toward her. Talen shifted his weight across from her, partially shielding Cara. Ah, yes. The most dangerous predator in the room, the one with something to protect. Then she caught Jordan moving toward her out of the corner of her eye.

Maybe not.

She shook her head. What was she thinking? These were her friends—her saviors. She turned toward Katie to say something just as a lightning bolt of pain exploded behind her eyes. The high-pitched scream assaulting her ears came from her own throat. She stopped, panting, her eyes going wide on Katie's frightened ones. Then as pain slashed through her skin, she opened her mouth to shriek again.

Her jaw kept opening with loud pops and sharp cracks, wider than humanly possible. The shriek emerging from her throat couldn't be human. Bones snapped in her jaw, in her neck, shifting, morphing, hurting.

Talen grabbed Cara and leapt over some chairs to head for the door. His brother Dage reached for a knife in his vest. "Is it a full moon?"

"Yes," Jordan said, grabbing Katie's arm and yanking her off the table to stand directly behind him. "Get your people out of here."

"But, wait," Cara protested from Talen's arms as they neared the door. "What about you?"

Jordan's gaze stayed on Maggie as he ground out, "Her shifting energy won't hurt us—we can absorb it." He pushed Katie back toward the wall, grabbing his communicator out of his pocket and inserting it in his ear. "Block the door. I'll call if we need backup."

The door clanged shut with an audible boom as rock met rock. Only Jordan's people and Maggie remained. She turned desperate eyes toward him. Eyes that now saw individual molecules in the air, a million more colors than she'd known existed. "What?" she growled out, nearly breathless from the pain.

He spoke low, calm. "I don't know. But you're going to be okay, Maggie." He settled himself into a readied stance. "Katie, Baye, and Mac—you shift. Noah and I will stay in human form for now."

Katie tried to move forward. "No, Jordan. I need to stay so she understands me."

Jordan blurred as tears gathered in Maggie's eyes.

"Shift or you're leaving," Jordan told Katie without moving his gaze a bit. His hands remained at his sides, not even inching toward the knife near his hip. Maggie could get to his hand, rip it off, taste that muscle and blood before he could move. Raw terror flushed through her at the very thought, even as her body craved the feeding.

An irritated sigh met his order before a shimmer of light surrounded Maggie's new friend, and then—

Three cougars prowled where people had just been. Oh God. Was she going to turn into a cougar?

Against her will, the fingers of her hands straightened and spread out. Bones popped and her skin flayed open as if raw shards of glass replaced her red blood cells. Pain from inside those cells, from a basic molecular level, skewered through her nerve endings. "Make it stop." Was that her voice? Low, guttural, inhuman?

"I can't," Jordan said, his tawny eyes sympathetic.

Her fingers curled, long yellow claws emerging. A coarse, rough sandy hair pierced through her skin, the bushels scraping and scratching on the way. A slight pain compared to the rest, yet the urge to cry nearly overwhelmed her.

"Fuck, she's a were," Noah said from his post near the door.

What the hell was a were? Werewolf? She was a *werewolf?* That didn't feel right. Growling, she kept her gaze on her hands, even as the bones in her legs began to throb and crack.

Nearly blind from the pain, shock swept through her as the hair on her hands changed into a dark brown, into something soft. Something familiar.

Jordan moved closer. "What the hell?"

Raw, blistering pain swept through her again, and the hair changed back to the coarse version. Gasping, she fell off the table onto all fours, emitting a wild howl and lifting her head. The cold stone floor soothed her rippling nerves.

The tension rose even more in the room.

Her face ached as it elongated and the sandpaper hair slid through her skin. Then it softened and her face narrowed, before changing back into the longer version.

Jordan dropped to one knee, his gaze on her now blurred eyes. "Fight it, Maggie. Fight the pain, search for the wolf."

Three cougars moved closer, flanking him, their intent to protect filling the air. The scent of cougar, of lion and earth teased her senses. Along with blood, flesh, and meat. Food. Friend. Foe.

Her spine straightened and she ripped out of the hospital gown, morphing into something hard, then something softer. Both wild, both crying to be free.

"Find the wolf, Maggie," Jordan crooned, his eyes flicking into a catlike phase. "Fight for the wolf. She needs you."

The wolf. The wolf needed her. Shutting her eyes, Maggie pushed against the pain. She wouldn't accept it, she wouldn't let it win. The wolf was there somewhere. The wolf needed her.

A jagged rip rent her heart, and she gave a piercing howl of agony. The shifters moved back. Where was the wolf? A whisper of thought, a voice. A plea. *Find the wolf, lass. She's mine, keep her safe for me.*

The voice, concentrate on the voice. Such strength, such purpose. The voice. With a snarl of fury, Maggie shoved the pain to hell and found the wolf. A soothing thrum just under her heart. A beat of nature, a whisper of truth. Easing into her skin, into the soft fur, into smooth muscle and bone. Home.

Settling into the familiar form, she shook her head, letting the soft wolf fur spread out. She gave a short whine and surveyed the room. She was surrounded by cats.

Well, crap.

Chapter 26

The Earth had her own presence underneath the ground where she hummed and echoed all round, vibrating with ancient wisdom and purpose. Still in the Washington state facility, Cara sat back in the chair and surveyed the small conference room, her belly happy and full. Dage might be the King of the Realm, an ancient vampire, but the guy made a mean omelet. Breakfast had been delicious.

They'd spent the night and awaited the test results on Katie and Maggie. Cara had been relieved to find an e-mail from Emma saying she was just fine, reaching the end of her research, and that they'd be together soon. Cara had also spoken with Janie—she missed her child and needed to feel the little girl in her arms.

Her gaze landed on Maggie, who sat pale and quiet across the marble conference table. The speckled beige rock surrounding them on all sides cast a sandy pall over her face. Less than fifteen hours had passed since Talen spirited Cara out of the meeting room when Maggie had started to shift. "How are you?" Cara asked.

Maggie shrugged, her deep brown eyes showing a weariness that matched her slumping shoulders. "I don't know. I mean, the wolf form felt right, it felt natural. Though I couldn't shift back until dawn broke, and that felt weird."

Jordan and Katie flanked Maggie at the table while Dage sat at the head.

Talen shifted his weight in his chair next to Cara, his hand warming hers under the table. He leaned forward. "So, let me get this straight. She changed into a wolf, into a were, and then back into a wolf?"

Jordan nodded. "Yeah, almost like the two forms fought each other to come out."

The door opened, and they all turned as a short man with bushy white hair stumbled inside, his hands full of papers. The scent of rubbing alcohol filled the air. Glancing around, he gave a nod and sat at the foot of the table.

Dage cleared this throat. "This is Dr. Miller, our chief scientist." Another human. Interesting that all three doctors were human.

The doctor nodded, spreading his papers on the hard surface. "Hi, er, yes hi." Pushing black-rimmed glasses up his bulbous nose, he took a deep breath. "I've never seen anything like it. Miss, ah, Miss Maggie is a wolf-shifter with the requisite twenty-eight chromosomes. However, she apparently was infected with a virus that attacked the shifting chromosome."

"Shifting chromosome?" Maggie asked, clasping her hands together on the table until they turned white.

"Er, yes. The twenty-seventh chromosomal pair marks shifters as type—canine, feline, or multi—much like the chromosome that determines eye color, you know, blue or brown," the doctor said. "Oddly enough, we believe the twenty-seventh chromosome of vampire mates holds the key to the so-called mating allergy." He yanked a handkerchief out of a breast pocket and blew loudly. "Some chromosomes are more powerful than others, and apparently the twenty-seventh is a doosie."

A doosie? Cara's mind reeled with the new information—man she wished Emma was here. "I see. And Maggie's chromosomes?"

The doctor tucked the hankie back in his jacket, facing Maggie. "You're a wolf shifter by nature, which is why the wolf came out last night."

Jordan sat back in his chair. "That's not all that came out last night."

"Yes, yes, well." The doctor's thick glasses enlarged his grey eyes until he almost appeared to be a cartoon character. "Isn't there a plant biologist here?"

Cara nodded. "I'm a plant physiologist."

"Er, good. Well, you know how your people are injecting viruses into plants, into crops for better yield?"

"Sure."

"Well, this is similar. The virus attacks the genetics of the shifter and mutates it." He pulled a paper off the bottom of the pile. "Into a werewolf."

Katie gasped and reached out to pat Maggie's hand. "It's okay, Maggie. We'll figure this out."

"Figure what out?" Maggie asked, tears filling her eyes. "It's obvious. I was a wolf-shifter, and now I'm turning into a werewolf. For some reason I can't remember, that's a bad thing."

Katie straightened. "You *are* a wolf-shifter. I saw your wolf form with my own eyes last night."

Cara cleared her throat. "What's the difference? I mean, between a wolf and a werewolf."

Releasing her hand, Talen brushed her hair off one shoulder. "Werewolves are pure animal, no reason, no intelligence. They're enslaved to a master with a simple spell, a master who has complete control over them."

That sucked. Cara's interest grew with the science involved. "But nobody triggered the change last night."

Jordan nodded. "True. But there was a full moon, and all weres change during the full phase—whether they want to or not."

This was unbelievable. "And when they're in human form? Do they live normal lives?" She again wished Emma was here—her sister would understand the genetics involved much better.

"No. The human becomes scattered, confused. Then after the third full moon, or the third change, the were form is permanent," Jordan said.

Wow. Urban legend was so wrong. "How does one normally become a were?"

Talen wrapped an arm around her shoulders. "The movies have that one right, mainly. If a human is either bitten or scratched by a werewolf, they'll change—then the spell, or curse, binds the beast to a master."

"And the Kurjans want to be the masters," Cara said. "So, not only are they using science to venture into the sun and steal mates, they are trying to make a slave class of werewolves from shifters." She drummed her fingers on the table for a moment, biting her lip. "But, I don't understand. If the Kurjans want a huge slave class, why not infect a bunch of humans? Why go to all the trouble of creating a virus to change shifters into werewolves?"

Jordan sat forward. "Because human werewolves live at the most one year. They're just too fragile to survive in animal form."

Wow, that did make sense. "So, changing shifters into werewolves might lead to longevity for a slave class," Cara mused.

Dage nodded. "It makes an odd sense and creates a twofold advantage. First, they end up with an immortal frontline army to do the dirty work, and second, they take out many of our allies. That is, if this virus actually works, and the Kurjans finds a way to mass contaminate." His silver gaze deepened, and he focused on the doctor. "Does the virus work? I mean, Maggie fought the change and shifted into a natural wolf form instead."

The doctor nodded, sniffing loudly. "Yes. Er, well, yes. I've never seen this before, and we don't know if the Kurjans perfected the process."

"So what happens now?" Maggie asked, her voice full of defeat.

The doctor shrugged bony shoulders. "I have no idea. Either the virus will run its course and you'll return to normal, or the virus will run its course and you'll end up a werewolf."

Geez. He could've sugarcoated that a bit more. Cara pursed her lips. "The curse or spell—how is it done?"

Talen rubbed gentle circles on her shoulder as he answered. "It's an incantation the master gives while the were is shackled in chains of silver before him."

"So they have to be in the same room?" Cara asked.

"Yes," Talen said.

Well, good. They'd keep Maggie safe until a cure or even treatment for the virus could be found. Cara smiled at her new friend, relieved when Maggie attempted a small smile in return.

The doctor cleared his throat. "I, er, ah, haven't notified the Banes Council yet."

Katie leapt to her feet, a red flush of fury sliding across her high cheekbones. "And you won't, damn it. She's not a werewolf."

Jordan tugged Katie back into her chair and the young woman grudgingly retook her seat, her gaze hot on the doctor. Jordan's eyes hardened to bronze as he focused on the man. "The statute dictates notification is only proper if a werewolf is found. Maggie is a wolf-shifter, not a werewolf."

The doctor leaned forward. "Yes, er, but the statute requires notification if someone suspects the presence of a werewolf." His eyes widened behind the ridiculous glasses, and his voice rose in pitch. "I suspect the presence of a were."

Next to her Talen straightened into readiness. What was going on? "What's the Banes Council?" Cara asked.

Turning beseeching eyes toward her, the doctor straightened his striped red bow tie. "The Council investigates, hunts, and terminates werewolves. We are bound by law to notify it."

She turned toward Dage. "You're the King of the Realm." At his nod, she continued, "Then can't you pardon a werewolf?"

Dage grinned, flashing even white teeth. "Pardon? No." He rested his hands on the spotless table. "We've sent out requests for information leading to a missing wolf-shifter and expect results soon. Also, since there was a full moon last night and Maggie turned into a wolf and not a werewolf, I believe she's not a werewolf." He pinned the doctor with a sharp silver gaze. "And thus the Council need not be notified at this time."

Man, Dage was smooth. A true diplomat who carried a big stick. Cara gave him a smile.

Jordan leaned forward and showed his own sharp teeth. "Maggie is under the protection of my Pride. Period."

Not so smooth, but just as effective. And deadly.

The doctor swallowed audibly, his adam's apple jogging up and down in his scrawny neck. "As you both wish." He stood, shuffling toward the door. "For now."

Several hours later, the earth pressed in and Cara pretended trees filled the room, their soft leaves cascading to fall around her as she lay in the huge bed. There was no real plant life in the Washington facility, damn it. She rolled onto her side, her imagination inhaling the fresh oxygen from the tall cottonwoods. Where was Talen? He said he'd be to bed soon.

They'd spent the day in the lab trying to decipher the lab results. No luck. Finally, after a late dinner of chicken casserole, she'd headed to bed while Talen remained to plot strategy with Dage. Several hours ago. He should be done by now.

She shifted onto her back. What the hell was going on?

Now she needed him next to her in order to sleep? That wouldn't do.

Yet she couldn't prevent her sigh of relief when he finally stalked into their room, dropping his clothes on the way to the bed. Heat and spicy pine enveloped her a second before his hard body wrapped around her.

"Why are you still awake?" he mumbled into her hair.

She shrugged, her shoulders bouncing off his chest. "Dunno." She yawned, her jaw cracking. "Maybe I'm worried about Maggie. What if she almost shifts into a were again tonight?" She hadn't thought about Maggie all night—she knew better than to lie to herself.

Talen placed a soft kiss on her ear. "No worries. Weres only shift on the one night of the full moon—the rest is urban legend." His arm banded around Cara's waist tugged her even closer. "Now go to sleep—you need rest."

"Why are we underground?" she asked as her eyes fluttered shut.

"For safety." His breath caressed her ear and she fought a shiver of awareness. Of need.

"But your sworn enemy can't venture into the sunlight. I'd think you'd live in glass houses in Florida." Geez—weren't vampires rational, or what?

He chuckled. "That was one consideration. But most of our enemies have powers that aren't obvious, teleporting, telekinesis, psychic abilities—the earth protects us from someone on the surface using those against us."

"But you can use those skills once you're underground against each other or anyone else down here."

"Sure. Now go to sleep."

She may have mumbled something, letting his warmth caress her into oblivion.

The dream claimed Cara easily after the exhausting day. Her father chased her throughout the forest near their home—he was really going to kill her this time. His large, stumbling footsteps hit the hard, packed earth on her trail, and even as drunk as he was, he would be able to catch her if he saw her.

"You little bitch," he screamed as thick boots destroyed low-laying branches. Ten-year-old Cara's scraped, dirty feet came to an abrupt stop as she turned to track his progress, hidden behind a thick blackberry bush as the full moon illuminated the brawny man coming after her. His buttoned shirt was torn across the big belly that had turned to fat, and his beefy hands clenched into hard fists as he scoured the trees with feverish eyes. His red bloated face contorted in rage. "I knew the devil had claimed you—just like your bitch of a sister."

Cara cringed as his harsh voice rang through the forest, trying to keep from shivering from the bite of the cool fall night. The trees stood eerily silent around her, all wildlife knowing to keep still. She watched warily as he turned and headed down a worn path, all the while screaming for her to show herself before he had to go back and kill her sister. Even in her terror, Cara smiled. She had given Emma plenty of time to get out of their beaten down house and to safety for the rest of the night, if they could just make it until he passed out from the booze, they'd live another day. They'd repeated the mantra to each other more than once. Her brow furrowed as she prayed Mama had let Emma lead her away this time. Otherwise, if he was still alert enough when he returned, he'd take it out on Mama.

The trees formed a thick canopy over her, and the bushes shielded her from view. The forest and plant life provided shelter and safety.

She lost track of time sitting on the cold earth. Soon her knees trembled and an ache rose through her skin. Finally, the birds started to chirp around her, proving the threat had ended, at least for the night. With a cry, she stumbled over to a large tree trunk and sank down to the packed forest floor before burying her face in her knees and letting the sobs come. Guilt, maybe shame, hurt worse than the fear.

She hadn't understood why Emma always seemed to make him mad. On purpose. She had thought he hit them because Emma made him angry. Tonight was the first time, with the wisdom of a ten-year-old, that she saw what Emma was doing. And why. Her older sister had been purposefully putting herself in the way of his beefy hands so he would hit her instead of Cara. Instead of Mama. She had cowered in the tiny kitchen corner as Daddy had advanced on Emma with a knife in his dangerous hand.

"If I kill you, little girl," her father had hissed at Emma, "then who will protect these other two? Hmm? Do you think I don't know why you're the first to jump in my path? Do you think I'm stupid?" he screamed and a vein stood out on his neck, his face flushed full with booze and rage.

"I know you're stupid," twelve-year-old Emma yelled back, wiping the blood from the corner of her mouth from his last hit as she steadied herself against the worn yellow cabinets. "And I also know the devil will be here for you soon."

Cara had no defense against the wave of rage that crashed from her father—she tried so hard to block his feelings, his demons, but sometimes they were too strong. Maybe he was right. Maybe the devil had infected her with the ability. Her eyes widened as he lumbered across the plain dirt floor, so big, so strong toward her sister, who was so small. And brave.

Emma's black hair curled disheveled around her pale face, a dark bruise already forming on her chin and deep blue eyes flashing with hate. And fear.

It was the fear that did it. Cara jumped from her crouch and collided with her father before sinking her teeth into the arm holding the knife. The knife clambered to the floor and with a bellow, he swung his arm, throwing her across the kitchen into the cabinets. Pain rocked through her shoulder up to her head, and she fought back a sob. She leapt to her feet. "She's right, Daddy. I had a vision. You're going to die and go to hell. Soon." Then, she ran out the kitchen door for the forest as the closest thing to the devil imaginable chased after her.

Finally, leaning against the hard bark, she sobbed as she fought to get rid of his rage that had filled her. It wasn't hers. She shouldn't have to feel the black hatred, she shouldn't have to feel the blinding urge to kill her own sister. It wasn't fair. And she wouldn't do it again. The sobs rose as her small shoulders shuddered with the pain.

Chapter 27

"Darlin', wake up," Talen's voice stayed low and soothing as his breath stirred her hair and his arms tightened around her in the big bed. "Wake up now, Cara." Well, this explained some things. Trees and plants had rescued her once, now she rescued them.

She jolted awake, freezing in place. Under his arm, her heart leapt into a rapid staccato and her fear slammed into him with icy fingers of pain. He pulled it in, refusing to even consider blocking her. It took her a moment, several actually, until her breath evened out. Then she buried her face in the tense column of his neck and keened.

Her pain was palpable even without their connection. He had to muster every ounce of strength in his formidable will to remain calm, to run his large hand down her shuddering back, to deny the anger, the need for violence vibrating for release beneath his skin. That beat with sharpened claws to get out. He felt each shudder of breath, each falling tear, as a physical slice through his own heart, bleeding frustration and anger into his very soul. There wasn't a monster alive he couldn't protect her from—nothing existed he wouldn't stand before and defeat to assure her safety. He was Talen Kayrs, the military leader of the most powerful beings in existence, and he had earned the title. Through wits, battle, and victory.

And now he was helpless.

He blocked his thoughts, his rage, as he comforted her, wincing at the delicacy of the fragile bones he caressed. The brand on his palm burned with a fury matched only in his soul. She was his mate and now gained strength from him. And power. But when she needed him, when she had neither strength nor power, he hadn't been there. He hadn't protected her. The failure suffocated him with a weight he hadn't thought possible.

"It wasn't your fault." Tear-filled blue eyes raised to his as her arms wrapped around his shoulders. "There was no way for you to have known, Talen." Now she rubbed soothing circles into his tense flesh.

He covered his surprise that she had maneuvered past his emotional block and dropped his forehead to hers while his eyes swam with emotion. "I'm sorry, mate."

Cara shook her head. "As powerful as you are, even you cannot control the entire universe and all its beings. I don't think you're supposed to."

"Sure I am." His arrogance brought the smile to her lips he needed so desperately to see. To feel.

"I'm so cold, Talen." She pressed further into him, one leg sliding between his and pressing up against his groin. He was naked and his reaction immediate as he hardened against her. "Warm me up." She leaned in and licked from his collar bone to the underside of his jaw while pressing herself harder into him.

His mind struggled for cohesion as his body heated and hardened. They needed to talk, and control was an illusion for them both right now. "Not a good idea, sweetheart. Your dream cut into us both." His emotions had reached a volatile level that he needed hours of rest to subdue. She couldn't have any idea of what she invited.

"Please Talen," her breathy voice whispered sweet air in his ear.

"Cara, for once heed my warning. Sleep now, we'll talk more tomorrow." A clamoring took up residence in his balls, and he considered a cold shower.

"No." She nipped his earlobe none too gently, and he was lost. With a swift movement he shifted and settled back while yanking her on top of him, and one hand ripped her shirt over her head. His movements threw her off balance and she gasped, gripping his hips with her thighs to right herself. Her smooth flesh around his own tempted him far more than he liked. She moved startled eyes to his as he casually, easily put one broad hand behind his head and relaxed back into the thick bed.

"Take what you want, mate," he dared her with a rough voice.

She licked her lips, and her eyes darted to his chest. He forced a calmness to his demeanor but feared she could feel the tumultuous emotions ripping through him.

Cara smiled. His control was impressive as hell. He dared her to make him lose it. And the girl who had been so paralyzed with fright a few minutes ago thrilled at the challenge, at the dare that she take his formidable power and make it hers. She lifted her lids in what could only be termed a sultry look that turned to triumph as he jerked against her in response. He leashed the growl low in his belly but she wasn't fooled.

"Just how long do you think you can restrain yourself?" she purred as her nails scored down his chest, over his dark nipples to pull on the trail of hair leading from his flat belly to heaven. Muscles clenched beneath her teasing hands. She pressed her core harder into the hard line of his erection, feeling safe with her cotton panties still in place.

"I could have them off you before you blinked." It was his turn to purr. And his turn for triumph as liquid heat spilled from her and warmed him even through the cloth as his words caressed her. She had forgotten he visited her head. He had warned her of his lack of control and something deep inside her, something feminine and powerful, wanted to destroy it completely.

"But then you'd lose," she reminded him as a heated flush rose from her chest into her neck, and her pelvis tilted against him with a mind of its own.

"Hardly," he retorted with an unreadable grin. "But since you wish to play, how about I promise I won't move my hands until you beg me to do so?"

Now arrogance flowed through her. "It's a bet." She ignored the flicker of warning whispering across her awareness that she had no idea what she unleashed. On purpose.

Talen shook his head, his eyes lightening to burnished teak. "Darlin', you should never underestimate me, a lesson I assume you'd have learned by now." His voice was calm but his body had begun to vibrate just enough to tempt her womb.

"Have I underestimated you, mate?" She rocked her hips against his fullness before running her own hands up her abdomen, over her breasts and through her hair.

Talen's blood leapt in response and the arm behind his head started to move before he furiously held himself in check. Her pink nipples pouted at him while nectar flowed unchecked from her; she was the most feminine creature he had ever imagined, and she tempted him.

Her laugh was a tactical error she would later regret. It awoke a dominance in him he had thought controlled, he had thought checked. She wasn't paying attention to his thoughts, to his drives, or she would have been cautioned. She would have regrouped. But she was busy playing, and the beast within him smiled. Then it set out to teach her a lesson.

Cara gasped as a warmth slammed into her at the base of her neck before flowing unchecked through her breasts, teasing, tightening them from within. Yet he hadn't moved a muscle. The unbearable ache hardened her nipples to diamond-sharp points. She needed something. Needed more. What was he doing to her? How?

Her eyes flew open on a startled gasp to see the green flecks light hard and flash full through the gold of his—his expression both merciless and promising. He watched her as the heat built in her chest before sliding, flowing south toward her core only to wrap around her to her backside and heat that as well.

With a cry, she pushed harder into his heated length as the fire moved around to pool in her womb while his eyes held hers. Kept hers. Taunting hers with what he did to her body. From within. Pure arrogance lit his features. His force, his power, caressed, teased, and tempted her from within her own skin, within her own heart.

"How?" She didn't recognize the sound of her own voice as her body heated past a point of pain where the promise of pleasure cut hard and deep.

His thoughts, his power, played her from within as he refused to answer. She furiously began to concentrate and force his power back into his own body, and the chuckle that came from his full lips increased her fury. She mentally pushed back as hard as she could only to have the heat swirl dangerously in her womb to pinpoint in one incredible spot with demanding need. Oh God.

She stifled a whimper as she tried to press against him; all feeling, all need. He stopped her. Not with his impressive strength. Or his large hands. With one thought. With one careless thought, he stopped her from moving.

Her eyes opened incredulously on his. Fear would come later, but now a blinding, animalistic need for release clawed through her. The painful heat demanded she move. "Talen."

He raised an eyebrow and determination settled hard on his face. "You opened the door, darlin.' Only I can close it."

What door? What freaking door? She moaned and tried again to move. A hidden force kept her limbs immobile even as it heated her blood.

"Talen . . ." she sighed.

"Not good enough." He shook his head and an orgasm hinted its presence deep within her abdomen. If he allowed it. She fought against his mental hold, anything to rub against him.

He flashed his teeth. "Say 'please.' You want me, you beg for me."

"Please."

The plea came unbidden from somewhere she never realized existed. A place she would have consciously denied.

His reaction was immediate. He snapped the sides of her panties and lifted her before slamming her down as he lunged upward. She threw her head back and keened a harsh cry. He filled her while she started to move at a speed and with a strength she hadn't known she possessed. She leaned forward to clutch his chest with sharp nails as she moved her hips in time with his thrusts, his hands clamping bruises into her hips as he drove up. His skin dampening beneath her hands, sweat flowed freely down her back.

She opened her eyes sightlessly and ruthlessly drove toward a spiraling feeling deep within that reached out with dangerous claws until, with a sharp cry, she careened into a million pieces; all thought, all identity, shattered. She vaguely heard his pained shout as he followed her. His burst of pleasure cascaded through her own chest as ecstasy conquered them both.

Her senses, the old familiar ones and the new frightening ones, all overloaded at once and her body slid into the security of blackness. She fell forward onto his heaving chest and sighed as unconsciousness blessed her.

Talen held his unmoving wife against his heart as remorse beat him. Oh God. What had he done? She was out cold. His need for her to acknowledge what was between them had overpowered any sense of caution he may have felt. He had always controlled the power within him and had never taken another's will unless in battle. A dense ego reminded him it had been battle, but his heart feared he had just sacrificed the war for its victory. He prayed the cost would not be so great as he closed his eyes and followed her into darkness.

Moments or maybe hours later, Cara awoke with the need to run slamming into her head. She remained still as awareness dawned, as she realized where she lay. And with whom. Deep under the earth's surface, in the very late hour he kept one heavy arm around her waist, his face turned into her shoulder, his heat keeping her warm. She opened wary eyes and shifted to study him, the small light in the corner of the room casting a soft glow over the bed. Even in sleep, the strength, power, and purpose stamped down hard on the sharp angles of his face, no sweet boyishness or innocence softened him while he rested, bold danger marked him even now.

She needed to run.

She wasn't capable of the trust required to balance the helplessness she had felt while he easily controlled her body. And her reactions. She ignored the sigh within her as her gaze roamed the ridiculously long dark lashes against his tanned skin, the full sensuous lips and firm jaw she itched to trace with one finger. She tensed to spring for safety and was stopped as those lids flew open and clear golden eyes pinned her in place. "No." His deep voice rumbled with determination.

Cara instinctively slammed down hard shields around her brain until they echoed throughout her head.

"Impressive," he murmured as the hand around her waist slowly, leisurely ran over her stomach and breasts, causing the skin to pucker and ache before he finally rested it against her neck. He left his hand around her throat against her rapidly beating pulse.

"Let me go." She meant more than the immediate moment, and they both knew it.

His eyes focused even harder on hers as he opened his mouth to speak, only to have a blaring alarm cut off his words. He rolled to the side and reached down to yank on faded jeans while grabbing his earpiece from the night table and shoving it into his ear.

"Status," he barked, nodding for her to get dressed, a red fury sweeping across his face.

Cara jumped from the bed and pulled on the jeans and shirt she'd dropped to the floor the previous night before turning back to Talen, whose fury had deepened to rage. She took a step backward. He reached into the table and drew out a green gun which he tossed to her before grabbing his two knives and tucking one in his back pocket. "Roll call," he muttered as he stalked across the room to the door where he waited a moment as he listened, then started barking orders. "They've only breached the first two levels—everyone head to the armory in section three—Jordan, do you know where that is? Good. Move now."

Yanking on boots, he turned toward her, his face cold and full of purpose, his chest bare and broad, an ancient warrior preparing for battle. "We're under attack and only have a skeleton crew here."

"How did they find us?" Cara whispered urgently as she moved toward him.

"I don't know. We'll worry about that later. Right now, we need to get to the armory."

Chapter 28

The alarm blared through the underground facility, and Cara rushed close enough to feel Talen's body heat. To sense his assurance; his strength of purpose.

"Stay behind me, mate. When I tell you to move, you do it." He slid open the door before looking first one way and then the other and escorting her into the hall, jogging down through several twists and turns until he halted and pressed her against the wall, shielding her from whatever threat he sensed, his entire body rigid and prepared. He relaxed as Jordan moved out of the shadows with Maggie right behind him, the young woman even more pale than the day before.

"Where's Katie?" Cara asked.

Jordan only growled. "Not where she should have been."

"She's with Jase—he called in saying they were playing pool in the rec room when the alarm hit," Talen answered her. Both he and Jordan stilled, lifting their heads and listening to their earpieces.

"Hit the lights, full power," Talen responded after a moment.

Cara winced and shut her eyes against the sudden glare all around them. The wattage of powerful white lights set hard into the stone ceiling was bright enough to be painful and had her squinting to see Talen's strong form before her.

"This should slow them down," Talen muttered as he

grabbed her hand and started down the hallway with Jordan and Maggie following. He stopped in front of a blank sheet of rock before placing his hand in the center and leaning forward to open both eyes. A hidden doorway opened to his left and he yanked her through to an ordinary looking stairwell made of cement lit hot and bright by the intruding lights, and they climbed down, their footsteps echoing rapidly on the hard steps.

They ran down two flights, and Talen did another scan before a door slid open and three mean looking guns instantly pointed at their heads. The guns dropped as Dage, Conn, and Noah recognized them and stepped back into a large control room with flickering monitors set into the wall showing different areas of the underground base. Two were blank.

Dage threw sunglasses at them and they donned them quickly. Cara sighed in relief.

A long counter holding a myriad of computer equipment ran the length of the room, and a large stone table covered in papers stood to the left and maps dotted the walls. An armory with its multitude of weapons showed through a door to the right.

"They cut the communications from sections one and two," Dage said grimly as he turned to a keyboard just as Mac and Baye exited the armory with vests and weapons at ready. "The doctors and their lab were in two—we have no contact with the guards at the front entrance or the three inside the first perimeter."

Jordan grabbed Maggie's arm and pulled her into the armory.

"Who else do we have?" Conn asked tersely as he typed into a different keyboard.

"That's it," Talen said. "We're spread thin after the recent attacks."

"Plus the fact that you folks haven't reproduced in a couple hundred years," Baye muttered as he checked his weapon.

"And you have, kitty?" Conn returned without looking up from his typing, missing the grin of appreciation Baye flashed back.

"It's time to remedy that," Dage mused, causing a chill to wind down Cara's spine. She was not put on the earth to breed soldiers to send to their deaths, damn it. The urge to run pounded hard and fast through her blood; in this, destiny was a complete bitch who wasn't going to get her way. She lifted her eyes to see Talen calmly waiting for her to focus.

"One thing at a time, mate."

She nodded in response and turned toward Dage as he spoke again.

"The Kurjan attack squad had twelve—seven made it through the first two entry points—they headed for the medical lab, then for the rec room." He shook his head in frustration. "We have four confirmed down. The cameras are useless." He looked toward Cara. "Can you sense Katie, Jase, or the doctors?"

Cara shut her eyes and tried to concentrate on Jase. An image of his grin, his delight with Janie and his strength filled her thoughts. She fell back with a cry as a rush of anger, of purpose hit her so hard she lost her balance and crashed into Talen, who righted her with gentle arms. "He's alive, preparing to fight . . ." She didn't finish the sentence as another wave of determination bordered with panic filled her. She had sensed Katie before and instantly knew her essence. "Katie's there, and I think she'd getting ready to shift."

"Back away, Cara," Talen said urgently into her ear. "Now."

She turned surprised eyes up at him even as she did as he ordered and let her connection with Katie's feelings subside. "Why?"

"She'll release an amazing amount of power, and you're not equipped to filter it yet, mate." He looked around. "Gear up. Dage, Jordan, Noah, and I will head for the rec room and the medical lab while Conn and Mac take Cara and Maggie through the tunnels out the east side. We'll meet you in Colorado."

"No, Talen," Cara said as she followed his long stride into the armory, "I want to stay here—I can sense Katie and Jase for you." She closed her eyes and reached for the doctors but only darkness swirled through her mind. "Though I can't sense your doctors." She opened her eyes as Jordan and Maggie, with protective vests and weapons, returned to the main room.

Talen yanked a vest over her head before donning his own. "No. We're outnumbered, and you need to get to safety. I promise I'll be there quickly." He checked his guns and knives and fastened his long dark hair in a band at the base of his neck.

"I'm staying, Talen," Cara muttered impatiently as she grabbed a knife off the stone wall.

He swooped in until his face was an inch from hers. "Don't argue, mate." His eyes narrowed implacably. "You will go with Conn, one way or the other."

"Really?" she sputtered back as anger filled her. How dare he? She'd done a great job on the last raid.

"Yes. I assure you, I can stop you from moving." He straightened to his full height, his eyes deadly serious. "But I guarantee you wouldn't like it. And I need to concentrate on other things." He waited for her reply.

"You wouldn't."

"I would." He actually meant it. He would take her freedom of movement away from her. It was unfathomable.

She turned on her heel and left the room without a backward glance. She had been helpless once before, and she'd be damned if she'd feel that way again. She understood that they were symbiotic, that they both had increased in strength and potential the second they'd mated, and she knew somehow, deep down, her power would someday match his. For now, she'd wait. And remember.

"*I heard that.*" Her husband chuckled in her head. Man. Now they could read each other's minds.

Her mental response was one she wouldn't have uttered out loud. He sent back a mental image of her over his knee, and she had to fight the answering grin in herself. Jackass. Then she sobered. Just because he had an ability, one he hadn't told her about, didn't mean he had to use it. He had no right to squire her to safety while others needed her help.

"*I have every fucking right.*" His chuckle was long gone and a brief image from her dream flashed through her head before he pushed it away. She stilled as she realized the dream had impacted him far more than she had thought. "*That's right, mate. You've been in danger before, and I wasn't there. I'm here now, and I vow you'll be safe.*"

"But, I went on the raid for Katie," she protested vehemently in her head as the men started to gather around her.

"*A mistake I will not repeat,*" came his firm response. His mental sigh whispered through her mind. "*Fight me another day, mate. Today this battle is over.*" He stalked into the room, armed with weapons as well as purpose, power all but gliding along his tanned skin above the dark vest.

Her eyes met his as she mentally asked her question. "Does everyone know about your ability?"

"*No. Just my brothers know I can manipulate movement, or rather, the desire to move.*"

"I hadn't noticed you use it before."

"*I didn't need it.*"

Dage cleared his throat while tucking another knife into his waistband. "If you two are done mentally whispering to each other, I thought we'd go and rescue our youngest brother."

Talen nodded and headed for the door.

Three stories up, Katie gulped in air as she and Jase took in the five Kurjan soldiers on the other side of the grand room, their smiles sharp and mean, their eyes hidden by dark sunglasses. The alarm abruptly cut off, leaving an odd ringing through the sudden silence.

Jase stood still as a statue to her side, the blue flecks in his eyes having taken over the copper as he'd killed the first two Kurjans to plow through the door before tackling her behind the pool table as a bomb destroyed half of the stone wall. A crumpled mess of arcade games, smashed dartboards, and a mangled flat-screen television splayed around the room while the neon light above the pool table swung back and forth, throwing sparks. The overly bright lights forced pure white pain into every corner.

"You'll have to shift," Jase muttered under his breath.

"No, Jase," Katie protested. "I could kill you."

"I'll be fine. You're too fragile as a human, Katie. You know it. If you're going to fight, you need to shift." He veered a bit to the left of the pool table, readying himself to charge.

He was right. She would be of little help against the monsters facing them in her current form. She hastened to the right, wanting to put as much space between them as possible. She stopped as the Kurjan soldier in the middle raised a large boned hand and smiled yellow teeth past crimson lips. "We don't want you, shifter. We just want the other one. Where is she?"

Katie cut her eyes to Jase, who studied all five soldiers with measured eyes. "I suppose you don't want me, either?" His voice was dry.

"On the contrary"—the rasp of the Kurjan's voice deepened—"killing a Kayrs will ensure my place in our military for all time. But, tell me where to find the other shifter, and I won't kill your friend here."

"Why do you want her?" Katie asked quietly.

The soldier shrugged his massive shoulders under his protective vest. "Irrelevant." He turned vicious eyes to Jase. "Well?"

Jase's grin was full of violence. "I decline your offer." He lunged for the head soldier while bellowing for Katie to shift.

Katie gathered her power, delving deep for the animal within her skin. Her spine tingled, an ache flashed along her skin, and her toes straightened out. Power flowed through her blood and with a simple command, she shifted from the delicate woman to a ferocious lioness, sending waves upon crashing waves of electric air slamming through the room. The electricity threw the two nearest Kurjans back into the jagged edges of the blasted rock walls to fall in heaps of muscle spouting blood while Jase was propelled against the opposite wall to land with a hard crash against several bar stools. With a fierce roar, he leapt to his feet, blood flowing freely down his face and from a wound in his side, charging to take a soldier to the ground with one strong hand around his neck. Katie lunged for the jugular of the nearest threat at the same time.

The leader turned to assist his subordinate with Jase just as the two injured Kurjans helped each other to their feet before rounding on the determined lioness with her jaws clamped into a Kurjan's neck. One raised a green gun and aimed for her shoulder.

The bullet impacted close to her neck and she screeched in pain before whipping around with a Kurjan's head in her jaws and tossing it at the soldier who had shot her. Damn it. They were healing quickly. It was four against two. And some of the blood scenting the air with copper wasn't Kurjan. It was vampire. She lunged at the soldier holding the gun without sparing a glance for Jase; he was a fighter and used to bleeding. The Kurjan cried out as she latched onto his leg and ripped his knee out of his skin, spitting it to the ground with a growl. She readied herself to pounce just as the shooter fired again, sending her to the hard stone floor with agony ricocheting through her body.

Excruciating pain lanced along her nervous system. She tried to regain her feet, only to tumble down again as the overly bright room spun around her. Her canines retracted, her fur disappeared, leaving her naked and vulnerable on the cold stone floor. The sweet smell of her own blood filled her nostrils. "Jordan," she whispered his name, wanting it to be the last thing she said before crossing over. Then, even in her pain, she rolled her eyes at herself.

Her heart thumped in tune with a fierce roar from deep in the earth before blackness claimed her, and her head rested against the cool stone of the floor.

Jase ripped the soldier's head off his shoulders with a shout of outrage before lunging for the next nearest target, fully aware Katie had gone down. He'd heard the shots and now smelled her blood. His mind reeled with pain as the soldier's fist plowed into the bleeding wound in his side before he pushed the pain back and went for the throat.

Picturing the combination of oxygen and water molecules in the air, he whipped up a swirling mass of debris to beat against his enemies. The elements belonged to him, air and water obeyed his commands. But the pain in his body persisted, and his concentration waned. He had to get to Katie to stem the blood flow—even now the air scented with coppery sweetness.

Jordan flew through the jagged hole in the wall, and Jase instantly allowed the air to drop her weapons. His hair a wild mass of color, his face chiseled into death, Jordan tackled the Kurjan still holding a gun on Katie and dug his fingers into the soldier's neck, his knees pressing into its chest. Odd that he hadn't shifted. Almost as if the need to kill with his bare hands rode him.

Jordan wrenched their enemy's head right off powerful shoulders, and deep, red blood scored across his chest and face. Livid topaz eyes sought and found Katie lying in a pool of blood across the way. With a deep roar, Jordan leapt toward her, sliding through red on his knees to reach her side.

Hmm. Jase had had no idea—the King of the Pride loved

the little lioness. Good thing he hadn't asked her out. Jase shook his head, darkness falling over his vision, his grip loosening on the enemy's jugular. Now was not the time to become philosophical. A humming took up in his ears. How much blood had he lost?

The Kurjan swiped sharp claws down Jase's face. Pain slashed right through to his skull. Jase tightened his grip on the neck, lacking the strength to rip the asshole's head off. This couldn't be good.

The air whispered in his ear that his brothers had arrived. About fucking time. Talen tackled the Kurjan currently trying to rip Jase's head off while Dage tossed the final one to the ground. An odd crunching sound filled the air as Dage went to work. Then blackness descended upon the youngest Kayrs brother, and there was no more pain.

Cara gasped as the helicopter veered to the right and changed course, the darkness outside providing no hint as to their new direction.

"We're heading for a safe hospital near Laird, Ontario," Conn answered her unspoken question through her earpiece. Wow. Now they headed into Canada? She reached out and clasped Maggie's hand as Conn continued, "Both Jase and Katie are injured, we'll be there in thirty minutes."

Cara leaned her head back against the vibrating seat and cleared her mind before seeking Talen. "How badly hurt are they?"

"Jase needs stitches, several, and Katie needs to have two bullets removed. They're both strong, mate."

"Are you all right?" An echoing pain lanced through his ribs, and her own ached in response.

"Fine."

Snorting in disbelief, she rolled her eyes. Tough guy. "What's wrong with your side?"

She could actually feel his surprise as he noticed for the

first time that his side hurt. "*Hmm. Three broken ribs, I guess. They'll heal by the time I see you.*" Then a sharp pain settled in his wrist and he swore.

"What's wrong?" she asked, her breath catching in her throat.

"*Fucking Jase is feeding on my wrist. His fangs have the subtlety of a Mac truck.*" Concern for his brother wove through the angry words. "*No wonder he can't get a date.*"

"How much blood did he lose?"

"*Not enough to take all of mine, mate. No worries—we'll both be close to fine when we see you.*" Now arrogance inflected his tone.

She shook her head. "Anybody else hurt?"

"*No. But Jordan is beyond pissed, as I would be if my mate found herself in danger instead of staying where I put her.*"

Cara bristled at the intentional warning. Then, remembering her instinctive response earlier, she reached out and slammed hard metal shields all around her brain. Silence echoed strong and sure, and she grinned in triumph at the blurring clouds outside.

Chapter 29

Cara had never been to Canada, yet the land welcomed her with open arms. Lush maple trees, their leaves brilliant in shades of orange, gold, and red, filled the landscape of the two hundred–acre private resort. Hospital actually, though only known by the creatures of the Realm. A dirt road led to a massive pine facility masquerading as a lodge, while worn trails meandered through the forest to rustic cabins. Rustic on the outside, anyway.

They'd arrived the night before and frightening dreams had plagued her, even while safely tucked into Talen's arms. With dawn arriving, they'd eaten breakfast in the lodge before visiting Katie and Jase in rooms more likely to be found in a bed and breakfast than a hospital. They'd both still been sleeping.

Finally, Talen escorted her down to the small gym located in the basement of the lodge. "I'll be back in an hour or so," he said, leaning down to trace her mouth with his own.

Warmth flooded her system and she pressed into him, parting her lips for a deeper kiss. Talen obliged her, slipping his tongue inside her mouth to taste. A low rumble echoed through his chest, and he lifted his head, golden eyes warm on hers. "Or, we could go back to our cabin."

Cara felt her own grin to her toes. "I thought you had to plot strategy with Conn and Jordan." The men had been furious to find a small transmitter inserted beneath Katie's left elbow which had allowed the Kurjans to follow them to the underground Washington facility. The doctors had quickly removed and destroyed the bug.

"Conn," Talen said, his gaze still on her mouth. "Just Conn. Jordan won't leave Katie's side until the doctor returns from rounds."

Yeah, Cara had noticed that earlier. "Hmm. Go plot, I really could use a run." She hadn't been on a treadmill since meeting Talen.

A sharp boom rent the air and she jumped, swiveling toward the corner of the sprawling space where Dage pummeled a purple punching bag hanging from the ceiling. Shirtless, the hard muscles of his back rippled beneath an intricate black tattoo. The design wove over his left shoulder, partially down his left arm and halfway down his back. Grunting, he slammed a ferocious fist into the center of the bag.

Talen raised an eyebrow, his gaze now on his brother. "Interesting. The king is pissed."

Cara gulped in air. Then she looked closer. "Hey. Isn't that the same design as on your hand?"

"Yep. It's the Kayrs marking," Talen said, rubbing his chin.

"Great. Your hand, Dage's back, and my ass. We match." That was a pisser, no question about it.

Talen grinned, swooping in for another kiss. "Yep." He turned to go.

"Wait, Talen," Cara said, holding her left wrist toward him. "I'm safe with Dage here. Take this off, I want it off in case I lift weights."

Drawing his eyebrows together, Talen studied the golden cuff. "Fine, but stay with Dage until I return." He placed his entire hand over the cuff and easily slid it off before wrapping it around his own wrist. "Have Dage spot you." With a grin, Talen sauntered away.

Arrogance. Pure and simple. Cara shook her head and jumped onto one of three treadmills, raising the incline to work her gluts. Sliding easily into a run, she unabashedly studied Dage as he pounded fist after fist into the bag, sweat flowing down his massive back.

Barefoot, he danced on the mat, his grey sweats molding to thick thighs and a hard ass. Not that she should be checking out her brother-in-law's ass, but anybody would appreciate the masculinity before her. It was like watching a thoroughbred race. Plus, there was no question Talen was the best looking out of all the brothers. Everyone knew that.

The other corner held benches and free weights lined against the wall, while treadmills, weight machines, and stationary bikes took up the rest of the space. The gym was empty save herself and the king.

Her mind wandered as her legs heated and her calves began to ache. She wondered about her experiments at work; had anybody taken them over? Had a stronger plant virus been created to increase crop yield of corn? The people, the nations, that such a result would help gave her hope. The world didn't have to be hungry.

With a beep, the treadmill ended the program and slowed so she could cool down. After five minutes of walking, Cara stepped off the machine, grabbing a towel to wipe her face. Stretching her calves as she moved, she placed twenty-pound weights on the barbell and lay down to do the bench press.

Dage instantly appeared above her head. "You need a spotter for the bench press, little sister." The scents of leather, amber, and sandalwood mixed through the air around him, creating the unique smell of power.

Cara gasped—the king moved fast. "I don't want to interrupt your imaginary fight." She reached for the metal bar and lifted up.

Dage grinned, his silver gaze on her arms. "Just a workout. Really."

Right. And she had a bridge she'd like to sell. "If you say

so." Damn, the bar was heavy. Pressing her head back into the padded bench, she lowered the bar to her chest, counting to five on the way down.

He retrieved her discarded towel and ran it across his sweaty face, his stance ready in case she needed help. "So, tell me about Emma."

Cara faltered and Dage grabbed the bar with one hand to balance her, his chiseled face frowning in concern as he gazed down at her.

"I got it," she said, regaining her balance, smiling at him when he released it. Tell him about Emma? Okay . . . "Um, well, she's the smartest person I've ever met, as well as the bravest." But she wouldn't take to the rules governing Dage's world, that much was certain. Cara continued raising and lowering the bar and finished the eighth repetition with a sigh of relief.

Dage nodded, taking the bar and replacing it in the stand. "Rest between sets."

Bossy. Correct, but bossy. "And she will never take orders from a man, even a king."

He flashed twin dimples. "What are you saying?"

Cara shrugged, sitting up. "You give orders all the time. Being autocratic is probably a job hazard with you, but Emma won't take it."

Dage chuckled low, handing her two blue hand weights from the stack and taking large silver ones for himself. He sat on the next bench, facing her. "Bicep curls?"

Cara nodded and settled into position. "Yours are bigger," she said, grinning.

"Just a bit." Dage's silver eyes twinkled at her as he curled his hand toward his shoulder, muscles bunching and flexing.

Cara grimaced. "But"—he really seemed a decent guy darn it—"she would like that you created a treaty and ended centuries of war."

Dage sighed, moving to his other arm. "I didn't create the treaty. Talen did." Shrugging, he put both massive weights together in one hand to continue. "Your mate ended the centuries of blood and death, Cara. I didn't."

Cara shifted one weight to her other arm, pleasure moving through her. "He did? Wow. Why?"

Dage jerked his head, raising an eyebrow. "Because of you, my sister. Peace ultimately happened because of you."

Intrigue caught her and she dropped the weights to rest between sets. "I don't understand."

Dage nodded, placing his own weights on the floor and stretching his legs toward her bench. "The first five years after our parents' death, blood ran thick along the ground. By my hand, by my brothers' hands. We killed." His voice lowered in remembrance. "Allies died, enemies died, too many humans died." The silver slid to coal as his gaze pinned her. "And I wanted more. More death. More blood."

Chilled fingers scratched down Cara's spine at the change in his eyes, the raw pain in his voice. "I'm sorry." The words weren't enough.

Dage nodded toward her weights and grabbed his own for the next set. "Talen came to me one day and dropped two stacks of paper on my desk." Grimacing, Dage focused on something above her shoulder. "On one stack, he placed his sword. Still red with blood which soaked into the paper and scented it with death. Talen nodded and told me that the battle plan to end our enemies lay beneath the blood; though most of humanity would die as well." Dage refocused on her. "I corrected him, said 'humankind,' not 'humanity,' and Talen, his young face so deadly serious, said, 'that too.'"

The vivid image filled Cara's mind and her heart ached for both brothers. "And the other stack of papers?" She shifted the weight to her other hand for a set.

"A pen. Talen threw our father's gold fountain pen on the other stack." Dage dropped his weights to the ground and grabbed for the towel to wipe his forehead. "The other stack comprised the treaty; the way we could all live in peace for a time." Clenching the towel with two broad hands, Dage continued, "I asked Talen why. Why the hell should we care about humans?"

Fury and self-disgust coated the king's words now, and Cara fought the urge to reach for his hand and provide comfort. "What did he say?"

"He said 'Because she's out there. My mate. And every time a Being dies, there's a chance she won't be born.'" Dage stood and stretched his neck, reaching for her weights. "Talen fought for peace so you could be born, Cara."

Did he? Was there only one mate for each? The thought filled parts of her with light, with hope. But doubt had a way of threading itself through faith. "So you chose the treaty?"

"Yes." Dage held out a hand to help her up. "The agreement took two years to broker and sign, but at the end of those years, we had the chance of peace." He gestured her toward the door. "Exhaustion rode me, and I told Talen he needed to ascend to the throne, so to speak—that I was finished."

Cara stumbled, turning back to face Dage as surprise clenched her stomach. "Really? You told Talen to be the king?" Wow. "What did he say?"

A full smile lit Dage's face. "Nothing. He broke my jaw." His hand going to rub that stubborn jaw, Dage shook his head. "My brother has a righteous left hook."

Oh. Cara frowned. "Then what?" Geez.

Dage shrugged. "I said 'I see,' Talen nodded, and that was the end of the discussion. Come on, Cara—I'll escort you to your mate."

She took his arm and stretched her calves with each step down the hallway, instinct whispering to her that she'd just been included in a very small club. "You don't normally open up to people, do you, Dage?"

He gave a short chuckle. "No. Being the king of a world ready to erupt doesn't lead to many confidences."

Warmth flushed through her, and she fought the urge to

skip. But she couldn't help the full smile spreading across her face.

"What?" Dage asked.

She shrugged. "There was this family in church where we grew up. They had about ten kids, often loud, usually fighting. But always together—especially if anyone threatened one of them. I was so jealous, wishing I belonged to a family like that."

The king took her arm and placed it through his. "Welcome to the family, little sister. You belong and we won't let anybody hurt you. Ever."

A family to keep Janie safe. What more could she want? "Emma doesn't trust men, Dage." Guilt filled her as she discussed her sister, but he needed to know. He needed to know Emma might act tough but had the kindest soul imaginable.

"Why not?" His entire body stiffened even as he slowed his stride to match her shorter one.

Cara shrugged, her gaze on the stunning colors outside the windows they passed. "Our father was a mean drunk."

A low growl rumbled in Dage's chest. "He hurt you?"

"Yes." Her voice lowered to a whisper. "He hurt Emma more."

"Is he still alive?" The muscles in Dage's arm bunched as if preparing to hit something. Hard.

"No." Cara patted his arm. "Emma put herself in his way every chance she got, so he'd hit her and not me or Mama. She was so brave, Dage."

Dage sighed. "Did she kill him?"

Cara started, her hand clenching on Dage. "No. He and Mama died in a car accident—they plunged down a cliff."

The king relaxed. "Good." At the door to Katie's room, he turned and touched her arm, his eyes shining a polished silver. "I'll protect your sister's heart, Cara. I promise." With a nod at Talen lounging in a thick orange chair, Dage gave Cara a little push inside before focusing on Katie. "Hi, Kate. How's the side?"

Katie rolled her eyes, sitting up in a plush hospital bed. "I'm fine, Dage. Talk to Jordan, would you?"

Dage grinned. "About what?"

"It's time for me to go home—my home. And he's pulling the 'I'm head of the Pride,' crap on me."

"He is head of the Pride."

"Yeah, but you're the king. You outrank him."

Dage shook his head. "Not true. I'm King of the Realm, but each species has its own leader, and they don't answer to me. We've all signed agreements to belong to the Realm."

Cara gasped as Talen yanked her down onto his lap. "So you're kind of like the United Nations?" she asked, settling herself more comfortably on hard thighs.

Dage nodded. "With a bit more teeth, though." Then he chuckled at his own joke before nodding and moving down the hall toward Jase's room.

Cara shifted toward Katie who had her tawny hair pulled into a band, showcasing her odd topaz eyes and flawless skin. "How are you?"

"Fine." Katie rolled her eyes. "Ready to get the heck out of here—I still need to find a dress for the ball coming up."

Talen snapped the golden cuff around Cara's wrist and she jumped. "Hey—"

"It's there or on an ankle, mate," Talen said, standing and placing her back on the chair. "I'm going to check on Jase—stay here until I return." He nodded toward Katie. "Jordan said he'd be back soon, so I'd stay in the bed if I were you." He whistled the Canadian national anthem as he strolled out of the room.

Cara twirled the cuff on her wrist and focused on her friend. "Men."

"Jackasses," Katie replied.

Chapter 30

The group flew en masse to the underground Colorado headquarters to stay onenight where Janie thoroughly enjoyed meeting the shifters. The idea of her new friends becoming mountain lions intrigued her, and she knew many of her future drawings would be of cougars and no longer of ponies.

She protested vehemently when it came time for bed, until Katie said she was going to bed as well. Janie figured if the way cool lioness went to bed at eight o'clock, then she could, too.

Her pink and white room surrounded her, and a butterfly night-light cast soft light into every corner. Mr. Mullet's blue hair tickled her nose until she tugged him closer into her chest. She closed her eyes to the smell of baby powder and before long wandered through a snowy forest full of tall trees.

"Zane?" she called, mentally throwing on thick furry boots and a blue coat. She didn't feel the cold, but wanted to pretend.

"Hi," he said, moving from behind a large brown tree trunk. "It looks like you're in my dream, now."

"Is this where you live?" she asked, leaning down to make a snowball.

"I live close," he answered, raising an eyebrow at the perfectly round weapon in her small hands. "From now on we meet somewhere other than where you live, okay?"

"But I want you to see where I'm living now." She patted the ball into a harder shape.

A thick grey coat suddenly covered Zane's black T-shirt. "No. We either meet here or in a make-believe place, Janie."

"Why?" She readied her stance to throw.

"Because we don't want whoever is trying to get into your dreams to know where you are." Zane grabbed a handful of snow and starting patting it into shape.

"You won't throw that at me," she said, pulling her arm back and letting the weapon fly. It smacked dead center in Zane's chest and snow exploded up to lodge in his dark hair. He turned twinkling green eyes on her and she giggled.

"Why do you say that?" he asked, winding up his arm.

Janie clapped her hands together. "Because you're too strong."

"Wrong," he said, and let loose.

She shrieked in delighted protest as the snowball careened past her left shoulder to collide with a thick tree. It protested and cold powder fell from high above to land all around them.

"I missed." Zane grinned even white teeth.

Janie rolled her eyes. She might only be four years old, but she wasn't *stupid*. "Whatever."

"So, Janie," Zane strolled closer, "can you feel someone trying to get inside our dreams right now?"

Janie lost her smile. "Yes."

Frowning, Zane reached her and tugged her collar up around her ears. "Can you tell who it is?"

She shook her head.

"Do you know anything about this person?" Zane focused eyes the color of Talen's lake on her, and Janie fought the urge to squirm. "Janie?"

She shrugged. "No. We could let him in and see." If she

told him the name, Zane would leave to figure it out himself. They needed to work together.

"No." Zane shook his head. "We never let him in. Okay?"

"Okay," she agreed, reaching down for another handful of snow.

Later that week Cara found herself snuggled in her new bed at Talen's home overlooking the large lake. The shifters remained at the underground headquarters, figuring they'd be back for the colloquium in a few days anyway. Dage had promised Katie he'd have an impressive selection of gowns delivered in order to get the young woman to agree to stay.

The last thing on Cara's mind was finding a dress. Her concern for Emma created deep holes of acid in her stomach, and she'd tried to open her mind to find her sister, but nothing.

She rolled over in bed, reliving her last visit to the headquarters. She'd packed Janie's clothing to take back to the ranch, thankful they'd be living aboveground for a bit. Before leaving, Cara had run to their small suite to retrieve Janie's sketch pad and on her way back had overheard an argument between Max and Brack as they played pool in the nearby rec room.

"Conn should get off his ass and go reclaim his mate," Max snapped. "You know we're all under orders to claim mates."

"We're not under orders," Brack had returned while leaning over to make a bank shot.

"Yes, we are. You know the Ruling council is as strong as the Kayrs family—the prophets still proclaim laws."

"Maybe," Brack had allowed.

"Yes. We can't wait any longer." Max took a shot. "I mean, I don't think we need to take mates right away. But the royal family does, just look at Talen."

Cara's heart dropped to her feet, and her skin started to ache.

"They fit, Max," Brack retorted.

"Yeah, they do. But you know Kayrs would've mated her regardless."

"I don't know."

With a soft sob, she had turned and ran as fast as she could for the elevator. God, was it true? Had he mated her because of orders? She had started to slide into love, but what if he married her out of duty? She had ignored his concerned glances on the ride home and turned immediately to bed after tucking Janie in.

Now here she sat in the dark, tossing and turning in a bed smelling of spice and man. But at least birds chirped outside and pinecones dropped to the ground periodically, reminding her nature kept watch over them all. She opened her mind again for Emma.

"Cara?" Talen asked, as he flipped up the comforter to slide into bed. "Why are you awake?" He lifted his head, as if scenting the air. "And why are you crying?"

She scrubbed her hands over her face, brushing away tears. "We still haven't found Emma, Talen. What if the Kurjans find her?"

Talen sighed and pulled Cara into his body. Warmth and instant comfort surrounded her. "She's tough, sweetheart. We have every ally out there looking for her, somebody's bound to have seen or heard something. So far she's been a master at hiding herself." He tucked himself more securely around Cara, and she sniffled.

"I know," she snuggled back into warmth. "But it's time to get her here safely. She's been on her own long enough." Damn it. Only Emma would believe she could save the world by herself.

Talen ran a hand down Cara's arm to settle around the golden cuff on her wrist. "We've gone through every bit of data from every raid, and we've contacted everyone. Don't worry, we'll know something soon. I don't think Dage has even slept since finally finding his mate."

Cara would worry about Emma's reaction to Dage later. Right now she was grateful to her very soul that the determined king was on the hunt. May God help him.

"Thank you for bringing my plants," she said softly. A row of lilies, impatiens, and irises now lined the dresser in pretty terra-cotta planters.

He nodded and his hand roamed to her hip. "Sure. Also, your house sold last week—the Marshal's service will send you a check for the money."

Money? She hadn't even thought about living expenses or such. "Oh, well, um . . . I guess put it with the rest." Frowning, she plucked at the comforter. "Do we need money?"

Talen chuckled against her. "No, darlin'—we're good. I've invested a bit through the centuries."

How odd. Centuries. The scientist rose within. "Centuries? What's the best thing invented during your lifetime?" Planes? Electricity? Her money was on the Internet.

Rubbing his chin along the top of her head, Talen gave her a quick kiss. "Frozen pizza."

She huffed out a laugh. "Seriously? Frozen pizza?"

"Yep. Dough, cheese, meat all in the icebox, and you just toss it in the oven. Heaven in every slice."

As if on cue, her stomach revolted and she groaned. Was she coming down with something?

He stiffened. "Are you feeling all right?"

Cara shook her head and forced nausea down. She wouldn't think about pizza for a bit. "No. Really Talen, I'm sleepy. We've had a pretty dramatic week." She scrambled. "So, what have you done during your centuries of peace besides eating pizza?"

He tucked her more securely into his large body. "Believe it or not, running the Realm is a full-time job. Just keeping our allies happy with each other can cause a headache." He shook his head against her hair. "Just wait until the ball tomorrow night."

Okay, maybe she should worry about a dress. "I can't go to a ball when my sister is on the run."

"Sure you can. It's part of the package, darlin.'" He tugged her hair up and kissed the nape of her neck. "Royalty has its price. Though, if you're not up to it, we certainly won't go. Now let's get some sleep."

With a sigh, Cara closed her eyes and let her husband's warmth provide comfort. Sleep claimed her with uneasy dreams.

She'd barely entered dreamland when small hands shook her awake. "Mama, wake up," Janie's face peered close to hers. "You've been sleeping forever. Wake up."

Cara came awake with a start and groaned as the room spun for a moment.

"Are you okay?" Janie sat back in concern.

"Yes. Just tired," Cara said while pushing thick hair away from her face. Her gaze caught on the pretty flowers lining the dresser in cheerful planters. Tears instantly filled her eyes, and she brushed them impatiently away.

"I had a dream about Aunt Emma last night," Janie said, her small face scrunching into a frown.

"Oh?" Cara sat up, trying to look unconcerned.

"Yeah. She was punching Uncle Dage in the nose." Blue eyes went wide with concern, and Janie bit her lip.

Cara rubbed her hand over her eyes. Unfortunately, the scenario was more than likely if Dage thought he could mate with her hot tempered sister, though it did give her hope the Kurjans hadn't captured Emma. "I'm sure they were just playing, sweetheart." Not a chance in hell.

Janie looked doubtful, but shrugged and turned as Talen strode through the doorway.

Cara raised an eyebrow at her mate. Black combat gear covered him from the flack boots to the bulletproof vest. Knives and guns hinted at war. With his dark hair tied at the nape, he looked like someone prepared to grant death. "Going somewhere?"

He gave a short nod. "We discovered two more facilities and need to raid now before the Kurjans move again." Stalking forward, he sat on the bed. "Janie, sweetheart, Max is waiting for you in the kitchen. He needs help finding the bagels."

With a happy hop in her step, Janie skipped out of the room.

Talen rubbed a hand over his shadowed jaw. "Ah, I need you to stay calm here."

Cara's heart sped up. "You found Emma?"

His eyes darkened and he pressed a warm palm against her arm. "We found where she's been hiding in North Dakota but she's no longer there."

North Dakota? Fear clutched Cara's heart into ice. "She's not?" Cara sat up, prepared to run.

Talen put both hands against her shoulders, holding her in place. "No. She'd rented a cabin at a private resort, but the cabin is empty now."

"Oh God." Cara pushed against him, determined to get out of bed. "We need to go."

He shook his head, his hands tightening. "No. You and Janie are staying here with Max."

"But, I can't—"

Golden eyes turned to sparks. "You can and you will. We don't know if the Kurjans have her. We'll find your sister, Cara. I promise."

Exhaustion swamped her for a moment. "But if they have, you'll need me to sense her."

"No. We're sending a team to raid a facility in western Nevada while my brothers and I fly to a hospital in Utah. If the Kurjans took her, Emma will be there. We'll find her, Cara."

Cara opened up every sense she had, praying to a universe that rarely listened. Nothing. She could sense nothing from Emma. Damn it. "I need to do something, Talen."

He stood. "Yes, you do. Stay here with Max, keep Janie

safe and trust me. While you're at it, there's more research data coming in on the computer, feel free to figure it out for me."

She sighed. He was right, the way she was feeling, she'd only slow him down. Fine. She held out her right arm. "I may do some yoga or even run—will you take the cuff off?" This asking permission to take off a bracelet was getting extremely tiresome. If they stayed together, they'd have to discuss this one.

He drew his eyebrows together.

Her temper began to inch toward boiling. "I am neither a dog nor a wild animal to be tagged, damn it. Now take it off."

He grinned. "It's not to tag you, darlin.' It's to locate you should something bad happen, like, I don't know, maybe a New York gang kidnapping you."

Cara rolled her eyes. "I think I'm safe from the gang here, Talen." She held out her wrist in a clear dare.

He pulled in a gust of air, removing the cuff. "There. But I think you should rest and not run." Placing the back of his hand against her forehead, he frowned again. "You don't have a fever, but you're pale. Max was going to take Janie fishing, but maybe they should stick close."

"No. Janie loves fishing. I'm all right, I just need some down time."

"Okay. I'll call as soon as I know anything." With one last concerned glance her way, he left.

Janie poked her head in a few minutes later, saying she and Max were going fishing and would bring back lunch. Cara sent her off with a wave.

She lay in bed for several moments and let the peaceful quiet of the home seep into and calm her. God, please let Emma be all right. With a groan, she maneuvered out of bed and headed for a hot shower. A breakfast of toast and tea had her feeling a bit better, so she went into Talen's office to continue deciphering the research they'd brought home. She also booted up his computer thinking she should at least check her e-mail. The computer gave a signal that it was updating and to be patient.

A chart on the printout next to her caught her eye and she scrambled in Talen's deep desk for a highlighter. Then she pawed through drawers to find some paper, and a file in the bottom drawer grabbed her attention.

With a sinking feeling, she pulled the file labeled "Directive" out and spread it open on the thick oak desk. A letter from the Prophet's Council directing the Kayrs brothers to seek mates of enhanced abilities. The letter dictated that the war with the Kurjus would gather force again, and it was time to shore up resources.

Cara read further, her stomach beginning to churn. Apparently, the marking on the palm of the hand could be forced, as had been done for centuries in order to procure mates. Arranged matings, sometimes marriages, were common and encouraged.

Once in the presence of an enhanced female, the vampire could will the brand to appear on his hand. It was simply a matter of mental energy.

She sat back and fought the nausea rising in her throat. Talen owned mental ability in spades. He'd said the brand naturally appeared on his palm, but had it? He'd meant to mark her—he told her he'd do so.

She flipped the page and her heart stopped as she read a copy of the letter sent by Talen in response wherein he agreed it was time to find mates. His bold signature sprawled across the bottom. He had *agreed.*

Cara slammed the file shut and sat back in the chair as if she'd been hit in the gut. Talen had married her to bear sons to train for battle. She was nothing more than a brood mare to him. She thought about the mark on her hip. He'd even branded her. Son of a bitch.

Here she'd begun to believe there might actually be love between them. Their passion ran through her head, fueling her anger like lighter fluid. That bastard. Fury made the room spin as a red haze covered her vision, and she replaced the file and shut the drawer with a sharp snap. She really was going to kill him.

Reason barely overcame anger, and she turned back to the papers in front of her. She needed to find a way to protect herself from the virus right now; she'd deal with Talen later.

Her mind continued to spin until a migraine loomed over her head. The computer finished updating with a sharp beep. Finally. She typed in her e-mail account, hoping Emma had fled and was checking in.

A familiar return address came up, and she gasped at the message sent the day before. Emma must be all right. She opened the message with bated breath, and her stomach hit the floor as a picture of her sister unfolded on the screen. Emma sat bound in a chair with a furious glare on her face and a bruise on her cheek.

A phone number scrolled under the photograph.

Cara's hands shook as she quickly dialed the number—with all of Talen's security, the phone lines must be secured. She hoped.

A deep voice answered the phone. "Hello, sotie."

Damn it. "I'm not your mate, Lorcan." Her heart started pounding.

"You will be." The sound of papers shuffling came across the line. "Thank you for calling."

"Where's my sister?"

"Ah, your sister. I have to tell you, I would've thought you were the pain in the ass sister after our last meeting, but I would've been wrong." A bone chilling laugh slithered across the line, and a hard fear took residence in her stomach. "I'm quite pleased I have the more mellow sister."

"Where is she?" Cara's knuckles turned white on the phone.

"She's perfectly fine, Cara. I have no desire to hurt the sister of my sotie and would very much like to let her go. Believe me." His voice intensified, apparently her sister was being difficult. "I will gladly trade her for you. As soon as possible."

Cara didn't need Janie's psychic abilities to know he lied. There was no way the Kurjans would let a woman with enhanced abilities go free—if Emma hadn't been mated yet, it was a matter of time. "Fine, Lorcan. Let me talk to my sister and ensure she's all right—if so, I'll trade myself for her."

A frustrated sigh came over the phone. "Very well."

Muted voices filled the silence, but Cara couldn't make out the individual words until a door opened. Then, "I'm not talking to anyone, you asshole," came clearly across the line.

"Emma?" Cara stood to her feet.

"Damn it. Cara? Whatever you do, *do not* listen to this prick. He's a fucking freak . . ." Her sister gave a muffled cry, and a door slammed.

"I swear on the prophets, I am going to kill that bitch if she stays here much longer." Lorcan's shrill voice sent chills down her spine.

"No, don't," Cara whispered, her heart thundering and her feet tingling with the need to run. God, she needed Talen. She may be seriously pissed at him, but there was no question she needed his help here.

"Only you can stop me, sotie. Our trace has revealed you're in the western United States, but, unfortunately, I can't pinpoint your location closer than that. Apparently the vampires have upped their technology as well. Where are you dear?"

She couldn't tell him. If the Kurjans had any idea where the vampires' headquarters were, they'd attack. Even for her sister she wouldn't do that, and her mind ran through the possibilities. "Where are you, Lorcan?"

"At one of my temporary strongholds in the west. We moved here as we tracked your movements."

Please let them be either in Utah or Nevada. The vampires should be at both facilities by now. "Good. I'll come to you. Just tell me where."

"I'd rather come and get you."

"I'm sure. But that isn't going to happen." She kept her voice calm and resolved even while her stomach clenched. "I will meet you anywhere you wish, but I will not tell you my location."

Silence filled the line for a moment. "You can't protect your former mate from me forever, Cara."

"Talen is more than capable of taking care of himself." Even she could hear the bitterness in her voice.

"Ah," Lorcan's satisfied tone nearly made her gag, "You have seen the true colors of the vampires, have you?"

"I am not having this discussion with you, Lorcan. Do you wish to meet up or not?" God, how was she going to save not only Emma but herself?

"Yes, I am in Wheatland, Cara. I'm warning you, should the vampires find me and attack, I will kill your sister—with great pain. And Cara, I'll enjoy myself."

She believed him. The truth echoed in his voice; he would sacrifice a potential mate in this instance. "Where the hell is Wheatland?"

He sighed. "The human educational system truly has failed you. Wheatland is in eastern Wyoming."

Damn it. The vampires were nowhere near. It would take them at least three hours to reach Wyoming. "I need some time."

"You have two hours. Then I start cutting pieces of this obnoxious bitch off."

So, she'd head north. She could stall Lorcan for the extra hour it took for the Kayrs brothers to show. "Fine. I'll call this number when I reach Wheatland. And I will speak to my sister before I tell you where I am."

"Of course. I look forward to seeing you again." He clicked off.

Chapter 31

Cara stood still for a moment, her mind reeling with the possibilities, her gaze flying around Talen's office. She had to save her sister, and she had to leave Janie to do so. Talen would make sure Janie was protected even if something happened to Cara. The bastard might have married Cara to breed her, but his affection for Janie was obvious. A deep voice wondered if the affection he showed for her was true as well. She told the voice to grow up, the files didn't lie.

The voice told her to grow a pair and fight for what she wanted. Fight for the man and stop being a chicken shit. Damn voice.

Punching keys on the computer, she found the most direct route to Wheatland. Basically, head north for about one hundred forty miles. She could do that.

She calmed herself with several deep breaths, her gaze calculating as she scanned Talen's office. She remembered the hidden room at Jordan's and wondered where Talen would keep his weapons. Somewhere safe. Somewhere away from Janie. She ignored the wall of windows and concentrated tapping on the side walls. They sounded alike. Not hollow. With a frustrated sigh, she sat back down and drafted a quick note to Max and a longer one to Janie.

Exhaling all her doubts, she opened her mind to Talen. "You there, mate?"

"*Yes. In the middle of something here, Cara.*" A mental sigh came over loud and clear. "*Emma's not here.*"

An image of a building nearly reduced to rubble filled her mind. "I know. I'm going to meet her in Wyoming."

"*No, you're not.*" Rage and fear edged each word.

He had the audacity to tell her what to do? Seriously? Fury had her shields slipping for just a moment. "I don't take orders from you, mate." She sneered the last word.

Silence. Then, "*I can explain the file, Cara.*"

"Meet me in Wheatland, Talen. I'll stall Lorcan until you get there." She slammed down hard mental shields before he could reply. Boy was he going to be pissed.

She wondered at her ability to do what she was about to do. The option remained for her to wait until Talen arrived, but Lorcan had sounded serious about hurting Emma. In fact, he'd seemed almost eager to do so.

Plus, her sister was an incredibly strong psychic—she'd be waiting for Cara, knowing of her plan.

Taking a determined breath, she ran into the kitchen and grabbed two knives off the counter, one she tucked into her right sock, the other she kept in her hand. With a quick prayer for help, she jogged to the garage which she opened with a punch of a button. She stared bemused at the black Hummer and a sleek two-seater sports car. Hmm. Well, in for a dollar . . .

Relief bombarded her as she found the keys in the ignition of the sports car, which purred to life like an awakened tiger, and she couldn't help but compare its muted roar with Talen—both sleek, hungry, and promising unimaginable power. She couldn't control either one of them.

She sped out of the garage, wondering how soon Talen could arrive in Wyoming. She punched her foot to the pedal and ignored her queasiness as the pretty pine trees blended into one long green blur outside. She reached Wheatland in just over two hours and wearily pulled into a Texaco outside of town to make her phone call. Her stomach revolted again, probably from fear they'd inject her with the virus as soon as possible. She wondered if she should've waited for backup.

With a sigh, she parked next to the light blue telephone booth and stepped out of the car into the mellow spring air. She grasped the side of the sports car as the world spun around her, and with a deep breath she centered herself before walking slowly, carefully into the booth. She ran her credit card through the slot and punched in the number before she could change her mind, knowing they'd be able to trace the phone call and seeing no reason to lie about her whereabouts.

"Hello, Cara." Lorcan's satisfied tone made her want to gag.

"Put my sister on." Her voice sounded calmer than she had hoped.

"Of course."

A shuffling came over the line, then "Tell me you did not come to Wyoming." Outrage rose her sister's voice an octave.

"Hi, Emma. Good to talk to you, too," Cara said wryly.

"Damn it—Cara, run! Now!" There was the sound of a scuffle, her sister swearing like a trucker, and then silence.

"As you could hear, your infuriating sister is just fine," Lorcan hissed.

"Yes." Cara agreed, a lump in her throat. How long Emma stayed fine was certainly up in the air.

"Where are you, Cara?"

"I'm at the Texaco east of town."

"Ah, good. I will send men to retrieve you. And, if you are not with them when they return . . ." He let the threat hang across the line.

"I will be, Lorcan." She had come this far, it was too late to back out.

"I look forward to starting our life together." His eerie voice almost had a calming quality. Almost.

"I don't suppose it matters that I don't want a life with you?" Maybe she had misread him.

"Not in the slightest." His laugh rivaled the scariest Halloween recording ever made. "But you should consider yourself lucky we can return you to human form and rid you of the vampire's taint. Otherwise, I would just have to kill you."

Cara's mind reeled for an appropriate response. There wasn't one. Dread pooled like dinosaur sludge in her gut as she thought of Talen, while he may have married her because she was a potential, he wouldn't have killed her if things hadn't worked out. There truly wasn't a question of who the good guys were here.

"My sister had better be in one piece when I arrive, Lorcan." She hung up the phone, grimacing at the pretty sports car. She'd better hide it before the Kurjans showed up.

Tucking the second knife into the small of her back, she sat on the yellow curb with her chin cradled in her hands when the shockingly white van pulled up. The gas station sprawled behind her with empty asphalted parking slots. There was little activity on the outskirts of town, and she figured she was on her own as she took in the silent vehicle. The windows were tinted almost black but she knew who, or rather what, lay inside waiting for her. Dread slid inside her stomach in even time with the van door opening; before she could peer into the darkened interior, the stench of evil rolled outside and her heart stopped. She stood and took one step forward.

She faltered on her next step as Talen's voice wove strong and sure through her conscious while she stared into the darkness. "*Do not get into that van.*"

"I don't have a choice," she thought back to him as strong as she could.

"*Run into the sun away from the van, mate.*" Anger thickened his voice, and her heart jumped to life in response.

She shook her head, her thoughts swirling. She had to save Emma. She tried to send back a plea for Talen to take care of Janie should she not survive this. She took another step toward the van just as a cascading wave of pure fury rolled through her brain to land in her heart, and with a cry, she saw blackness.

"Fuck. I think I short-circuited her brain," Talen growled in anger from his seat in the modified helicopter.

"Seriously?" Dage turned in astonishment. "Do you know how rare that kind of connection is?"

Talen cut golden eyes at his brother. "Who cares? Now she's out cold, and I can't tell where she's going." He turned back to watch the landscape below them flash by. "And she ran from me. What kind of connection is that?"

"She went to save her sister, Talen." Dage concentrated on flying the bird at a greater speed than he should. Jase and Conn muttered something to each other in the backseat.

"Well, that's my fucking job, isn't it Dage?" A fierce growl rode through the words.

"Actually, it's my fucking job, brother. And don't you forget it." Dage's tone matched Talen's.

Talen swung pained eyes at Dage. "Do you really think Emma's your mate?"

"I know it." An absolute tone echoed through the earpieces.

"Well good fucking luck."

"Thank you." Now the tenor was dry. "And frankly, you're more pissed at yourself than your mate."

"Excuse me?"

"You should've told her about that damn file, Talen. Also, leaving her access to the computer and that account? Of course they'd contact her."

"I was trying to keep her mind occupied while we searched for her sister." In truth, he hadn't been thinking. In fact, he hadn't thought straight since he'd met the little scientist. "And you're wrong." Talen's jaw snapped shut.

"About what?" Dage asked.

"I'm more pissed at my mate. A fact she will soon regret."

Dage shook his head. "I'm pretty sure you don't understand women."

Talen shrugged. "I don't care. But mine will understand me."

Dage checked several gages. "We're five minutes outside of Cheyenne. Has she regained consciousness?"

Talen closed his eyes to better concentrate before reopening them. "No. Not yet." He turned his anxious gaze out the window.

Cara came awake in strong arms with a cry, but the arms were wrong—too long, too cold, and too unwelcome. She looked up into swirling purple eyes and nausea slammed into her.

"Hello, Cara. Do you faint often?"

"No. Put me down." She peered around Lorcan at some type of dark tunnel with thick stone walls. Underground, again. His booted feet sounded softly on what must be a dirt floor, and his pasty white skin glowed above her face while he stopped before a rounded wooden door, kicking it open with one foot.

He put her on her feet and gave her a quick push inside. "I'll be back for you."

The door slammed shut, and a key scraped through a lock. She stared across a round underground room and blue eyes met identical blue eyes for a startled beat. "Emma," she breathed as she met her sister halfway, and they clasped each other tight.

"Cara," Emma said with a groan and stepped back. Her tired face scrutinized her younger sibling. "Holy crap. You're pregnant."

"What?" Cara said through tears as the room tilted dangerously.

"You. Are. Pregnant." Emma grabbed both her hands. "You didn't know?"

Cara shook her head. "No. I guess it makes sense, but . . .

I've been on birth control. I know it's never one hundred percent, but . . ." Her mind spun as Emma enfolded her in a gentle hug. "Are you sure, Emma?" She already knew the answer, even before her sister nodded. Emma's psychic abilities had never failed them. Of course, who the hell knew if birth control worked against vampire seed for God's sake?

Cara took a deep breath and studied her big sister. "You've looked better." Emma's dark hair lay tangled around her slender shoulders, a purple bruise marred light skin and covered one entire cheekbone, and dark marks of worry slashed under her eyes.

"Yeah, and you're knocked up," Emma retorted before moving toward the door and yanking a mangled lipstick tube out of the back pocket of her faded jeans. "The door is a thick wood, and I'm close to picking the lock. The walls are made of stone bricks, and we're under the ground somewhere, but I saw a map when I first got here and think I can figure the way out."

Cara raised an eyebrow. "You're picking the lock with your lipstick, Em?" Man, her sister had lost it.

Emma snorted. "It's a lock pick camouflaged as a lipstick, dummy. I've been on the run for two months—believe me, I've been preparing for this." She moved forward toward the door and inserted the pick into the old-fashioned lock before bending to one knee and starting to twist. "All those times Daddy locked us in the closet is actually coming in handy. Funny, huh?"

"Not really," Cara retorted. "He really was a bastard, wasn't he?"

"Yeah. Maybe he's enjoying hell right now."

"You think so?" Cara bent closer to watch her sister manipulate the lock.

"Yeah. I don't think you can use God to beat the heck out of people and then get away with it."

Her mind still reeling, Cara slid down to the hard dirt floor, not needing to check for the knife at her back—it was clearly gone. Dust and wet mold made her sneeze. She belatedly remembered the knife hidden in her sock before leaning down to pat her leg. Damn. Lorcan must have taken the weapon while she was unconscious. "So, where are we, Em?"

"Somewhere in Wyoming. At a new facility because something happened to their stronghold in Portland. The good news is that this place isn't fully staffed yet, and they brought me here only because they knew you were fairly close." Emma rubbed her hands on her jeans before returning her attention to the lock. "This is a temporary facility—I have a feeling their permanent one would be a lot harder to escape from."

"Yeah, we raided the place in Portland—though I don't think that one was fully staffed yet, either."

Emma turned surprised eyes her way. "You raided the place?"

"Uh, yeah. They kidnapped a friend of mine, and we had to go and get her."

"Who exactly is 'we'?" Emma turned back to the lock.

"Um, well, my husband, Talen, and his brothers."

"You're married?" Emma's voice rose to an odd pitch.

"And mated," Cara said quietly, wondering how much Emma knew. She had her answer when her sister swiveled around to face her and paled to near white.

"Not to a Kurjan?"

"No." Cara leaned forward to pat her sister on the arm. "To a vampire."

"What? You married one of the vampires?"

"Yeah. What do you know about them?" She chose not to mention Dage and his interest in Emma.

Emma shrugged. "They're mortal enemies of the Kurjans, look like us except for their eyes, and also need mates with enhanced abilities." She ran a rough hand through her rioting hair. "I guess your empathic abilities made you a potential." Her eyes focused in concern. "Where's Janie?"

"Safe."

"Thank God." Emma studied her closely. "Were you forced?"

"To mate?" Cara blushed to the roots of her hair.

"Yes."

"Um. No, not really."

"Not really?" Emma's gaze hardened.

"Not at all, actually," Cara sighed as she dropped her hands and blushed again under her sister's searching gaze.

"Where is he, Cara?"

"On his way," she said miserably.

"On his way?" Emma frowned, storm clouds brewing in her eyes.

"Um, yeah. They were at least three hours out and I could get here faster without waiting for them." Cara whispered the statement, a deep flush rising under her skin to pool in her face.

"Why didn't you wait for them?" Emma asked in astonishment. "Since neither of us are exactly strong fighters, a sworn enemy of the damn Kurjus would come in handy right now."

"I know." Cara sighed. "But Lorcan said he'd start cutting off your body parts if I didn't hurry."

"And?" Damn it. Her sister knew her too well.

"And I found a file in Talen's desk ordering for him to mate and bear sons." Cara avoided her sister's eyes by looking around the small, empty room, but only yellowed stone walls and a dirt floor were visible. She just couldn't go into the whole branding situation yet.

"Oh. So you were pissed?"

Cara nodded.

"And you were hurt?" Emma's voice softened.

Cara nodded again and blinked back tears.

"Okay, we'll figure all of that out later. Right now we need to get the heck out of here before some doctor arrives. If Lorcan knows you've mated, he'll try to use the virus on you."

"You know about it?"

"Yes. The lab I worked at helped develop it, but we thought we were curing genetic diseases. We had no clue the Kurjans even existed. When I found out, I tried to destroy the virus, but it was too late."

"And they came after you?"

Emma nodded. "Yeah. They knew about me from day one; it was always their plan to 'acquire me' after we developed the virus." She flushed. "And they checked into my background and found out about you and Janie. It's my fault you're here."

"It's their fault, Em." Cara closed her eyes and concentrated on reaching Talen. Only static filled her head, and she wondered if whatever had happened earlier had broken their connection. If so, she fervently prayed that the results were temporary.

"Cara, they showed me the tapes of what the virus does to mated women." Emma's eyes filled with concern for her sister. "We didn't know what we were developing."

"Is there any way to beat the infection?"

"No."

"What are we going to do?"

Emma didn't have a chance to answer before the lock clicked and the door shifted open. "Now we run," Emma said with determination as she rose to her feet and pulled Cara through.

Chapter 32

Cara followed as Emma took a sharp turn down the damp, empty tunnel before starting to jog through the barely lit area.

"Come on," Emma whispered. "We can't go back the way you came in—the Kurjans are setting up the main control room by the entrance, and I'm pretty sure I saw a back way out."

Cara shrugged and increased her pace to keep up, her feet pounding on dirt that swiftly turned to mud as they ventured farther into the dimness lit by faint industrial lights strung every ten feet. It seemed like she'd spent most of her life underground at this point.

She tried again to reach Talen with her mind and only ended up with a dull throb in her temples—damn it, what had he done? A guilty little voice in the back of her aching head whispered he had reacted to her running off to meet his mortal enemy, and his anger was probably justified. Maybe. But that was no reason to short-circuit her brain.

A voice in the darkness ahead froze them in place.

"Matre here, south tunnel is secure," a deep Kurjan voice wove through the space.

Cara pressed against the stone wall until water dripped down the back of her shirt. "Do you still have the lock pick?"

"Yes." Emma looked around furtively. "We'll have to take him out. There isn't time to get back to the room."

"I know. He's probably armed, if we could get him down, I could get the gun."

"You and *your baby* stay out of the way," Emma snapped back. "Duck down."

They both slipped into a crouch as muffled footsteps echoed through the underground space.

"Go for his neck with the pick." Cara leaned in close to her sister's ear. "You have to go for the jugular and decapitate him."

"I do not want to know how you know that," Emma replied just as softly.

Water dripping down stone to pool in dirt beat in time with the footsteps coming closer as the sisters crouched in the darkness like angry prey ready to spring. Determination flowed strong and sure between them as they both tensed—Cara saw his feet before Emma and kicked out her leg to trip the soldier who fell with a startled grunt into the mud. Emma leaped forward and plunged the slim metal into his neck just as Cara reached for his glowing green gun. Hissing, the soldier swept out a clawed hand to throw Emma into the nearest wall before bounding to his feet and yanking the bloody weapon out of his flesh.

His teeth glimmered sharp and deadly in the soft light as he moved toward Cara, and with an answering glare, she raised the gun and pulled the trigger, only to have the gun sputter in her hand. With a growl, she focused as hard as she could on an image of the Kurjan's heart and tried to seize the organ mentally, drawing on any power Talen may have passed to her. The soldier gasped and stumbled, his purple eyes widening on her as she stopped him in his tracks. Then, with a fierce shriek, he shook off her control and started forward again.

Crying out, Cara squeezed the trigger, and this time the weapon fired. The soldier gave a harsh screech as he was thrown back into the stone wall, and Cara kept firing straight at his neck, moving closer, her hands clenching the gun so hard her fingers fought numbness until the Kurjan dropped to the ground. Emma leapt across the tunnel in a blur of motion and grabbed the knife stuck in his belt, while Cara shifted her aim to his head and kept firing.

His flesh split and blood sprayed.

"Plunge the blade into his neck," she hissed as green fire continued to erupt from the gun.

With a harsh sob, Emma reached forward and stabbed the knife into the Kurjan's neck and then twisted her head to the side as blood sprayed toward her face. She looked back and tried to yank the knife but to no avail. Cara put the gun in the back of her pants and leaned down with both hands to help her sister, but the blade didn't move. "Talen made this look easy," she grunted as she pulled with all of her might. The knife sat immobile in the hard tissue of the soldier's neck.

"Yet another reason it'd be nice if he were here." Emma fell back onto her butt. She nodded to the fallen soldier. "Well, he's unconscious at least—let's get the hell out of here." She scrambled to her feet.

Cara nodded, yanked the soldier's earpiece out, and jumped up to follow her sister at a dead run—who knew how long it would take for the soldier to regain consciousness and pull the knife out of his throat? She tried to reach Talen in her mind as she ran through the now thick mud and dripping ceilings, but soft static crackled where his voice should be. Damn it, he probably couldn't track her, either.

She and Emma were truly on their own.

The light became even dimmer as they ran, and after a while her calves started to burn as the tunnel shot upward, the slushy mud camouflaging their footsteps until they came to a large stone door. They both reached forward to tug, and it opened with a harsh groan. Light made Cara blink against the pain. She hurried after Emma through the doorway, both of them pushing the door shut with their bodies before looking around a large cave with smooth walls.

Cara's heart dropped to her knees as she realized the distance to a hole in the roof that was letting in abundant light. "How in the hell . . ." she asked wearily as nausea sped through her. Gasping, she turned to the stone wall and lost the meager contents of her stomach. Emma rushed forward and held her hair out of her face. "I'm okay," Cara muttered as she wiped one dirty arm across her mouth.

"No, you're not," her sister retorted while looking anxiously about the small cavern. "There's a type of ladder carved into the rock," she mused while pointing across the small space.

"God Emma"—Cara breathed out while looking up into the now fading light—"that's at least fifty feet up."

"I know," Emma said as she hurried across the room and put her foot into the divot in the otherwise smooth rock. Cara's heart sped up as her sister reached with a soft grunt and pulled herself up before starting to climb awkwardly hand over foot. She paused about halfway up.

"Are you okay?" Cara called.

"Yeah, just taking a moment," Emma replied before starting to climb again.

Cara breathed a sigh of relief as Emma made it to the top and pulled herself outside the large hole. Dark hair flew around her bruised face as she peered down at Cara. "We're in the middle of a forested area—I don't see any rope or anything. You need to climb up, sis."

Cara nodded and took a deep breath before placing her foot in the lowest cut. Her hands trembled as she reached into other crevices to balance herself before starting to climb hand over foot up the wall. She ignored her lurching stomach and possible danger to her baby if she fell and concentrated on climbing steadily, calmly up. Before she knew it, Emma helped her into a small clearing surrounded by large pine trees. Thank God. Nature and oxygen. She lay on her back gasping air for a few precious moments until she noticed the thickening black clouds forming right above them, then she rolled to her feet.

Damn it. The Kurjans could venture outside with cloud cover like that. They needed to run.

"Which way do you think?" Emma asked anxiously.

"That way." Cara pointed to the opposite direction from the underground tunnels. Emma nodded and quickly led the way through two monstrous pines as thunder clapped with fury above them. Cara followed her sister through trees, over deep brush, and alongside rocky hills as lightning flashed bright around them and rain pelted their light shirts and jeans. She gasped and stumbled in the sudden darkness more than once. Finally, her foot caught on a low-lying branch and with a cry, she went sprawling onto her hands and knees on the pebbled earth.

"Cara!" Emma, her dark hair plastered to her wet face, instantly rushed to her side and pulled her to her feet. "Come on," she yelled over the driving rain and yanked Cara along the rock side to a small opening.

Cara looked around the secluded cave before sliding down one smooth rock wall to sit on the hard, packed dirt. The storm raged outside. She pulled her soaked hair out of her dripping face and shivered until Emma sat beside her and put a gentle arm around her shoulders.

"We'll ride out the storm and then keep running," Emma soothed.

"Good plan." Cara shivered again while her hands and knees ached worse than a compacted tooth. The sensation of huddling with her sister while a monster sought them brought a raw ache to her throat. They'd been here before. "I've never thanked you."

"Hmmm?" Emma murmured, rubbing Cara's shoulders to warm her up.

"Em. I've never thanked you—for saving me from Daddy. For getting hit so I wouldn't." She turned her gaze, now blurry with tears, toward her older sister.

Emma breathed out, her own eyes filling with tears. "We saved each other, Car. He would've killed me the night with the knife, if you hadn't charged him." She tilted her head to rest on Cara's shoulder. "We survived him—we can survive this."

They could, and they would. She wondered if she should warn Emma about Dage.

"So"—Emma lifted her head to lean back into the rock—"tell me about this husband of yours."

"Talen," the name was a sob on her lips. "He's big, strong, stubborn as hell . . ."

Emma laughed. "Sounds perfect for you."

"Humph."

"That's not a word. So, does he love you or not?"

Cara was quiet as she thought about it. As she fought it.

"Come on Cara. Even if we lie to ourselves, we don't lie to each other." Familiar blue eyes gave no quarter.

Cara sighed in defeat. "Yes, I think so."

"So, why did you run?"

"To rescue you," Cara huffed as she leaned into her sister, fighting a sneeze.

"Humph."

"That's not a word," Cara retorted.

"You ran because you love him, too." The words sunk in. "Dumbass."

Cara chuckled. "He's larger than life, you know? And besides that, he has this power. To manipulate or control the physical actions of other people. I won't be helpless again, Em."

Emma sighed deep. "No. You can't compare him to Daddy—he wasn't larger than life, Cara. He was small. A very small, mean, pathetic man." Emma tightened her hold. "It sounds like your Talen is nothing like our father."

The wind whistled a mournful plea, sending a chilled air inside the cave. "It's just," Cara struggled to explain, "he takes over everything, like Daddy did but in a different way, I guess."

"Is Talen mean?"

The image of Talen carrying a giggling Janie over the threshold of his house filled her mind. "No."

"Does he hurt you? Or Janie?"

"No."

Emma snorted. "Geez, Cara. Is Talen one of the good guys or not?"

Cara was silent for a moment. "Yes. He is definitely one of the good guys." She breathed out heavily. "Though he's going to be really pissed about this."

Emma shrugged. "Can't blame him too much for that."

"Hey. You're supposed to be on my side."

"Always." Emma was quiet for a moment. "You mentioned vampires have different eyes from us. How did you mean?"

"The color. Talen's are gold."

Emma tensed next to her. "Like a metallic gold?"

"Yeah. Why?"

"Have you met one with eyes that were, I don't know, like silver?" Emma's voice cracked on the end.

Oh crap. Emma knew about Dage. "Um, well, actually yes. A couple of his brothers have silver eyes."

"And they bite. Like vampires?" Emma turned breathless.

"Yes. I'm taking it you have dreamt of one? Maybe a big, rather dominant one named Dage?" Oh boy, was Em in for a rude awakening. Or Dage was. Maybe both.

"I don't know his name," Emma said.

She owed Emma the truth, if for nothing else so she could prepare herself. "Now you do. He thinks he's your mate."

"He's not." Stubborn pride lit her sister's face.

"I told him that." Not that he'd listened, of course.

"Thanks."

The rain slowed to a drizzle outside as the sisters sat, both lost in their own thoughts. Cara had the sudden need to find her mate. She had been so stupid. He filled her with power, and damn it, they belonged together. Fate or not.

"We'd better get going," Cara said as she stood to her feet and pulled Emma with her. They moved gingerly out of their safe haven to the now calm rain bathing the earth. Cara turned to her sister just as a strong arm enclosed her neck and lifted her off the ground. She threw her elbows and kicked back until she turned and saw Emma in a similar position, held by a Kurjan soldier off the ground with a glowing gun pressed against her temple, her eyes shooting furious blue sparks as she struggled.

"Hello, sotie," Lorcan's voice in her ear chilled her to the bone. "Stop struggling or I'll have my soldier shoot your sister." Cara stopped kicking and moved a hand toward her back. "No, no, no," Lorcan chuckled as he pulled the gun from her waistband and gave her a hard shake. "No more shooting Kurjans, Cara. You've shot your limit today." He leaned in closer to whisper in her ear. "If you fight me, I will give your sister to Matre; you remember the soldier you shot in the tunnel? He's itching for some payback." Cara stopped fighting and shook her head in warning at her sister before closing her eyes and trying to manipulate the Kurjan leader's nervous system. A rough chuckle sounded in her ear.

"You're not strong enough to influence me, sotie." With that, he slammed her focused thoughts back into her own head along with sharp spikes of pain. Cara clenched her eyes shut as the pain webbed through her whole system. Lorcan started running through the forest with her still in his arms while the other soldier carried Emma.

"*Cara? Keep your eyes open, mate. I need to see where you're going.*"

"Talen!" She shouted his name in her head, the trees flying by her. Her heart leapt as she realized she could hear him again, and she watched carefully as the forest blurred together until they emerged in a large field outside of an older white farmhouse. They had made it back to the entrance much faster than she and Emma had run away. She kept her eyes wide open as Lorcan walked inside and stomped down several stairs to a big stone door that he kicked open with one boot—then they were in tunnels again. He walked for a few moments before opening a door leading to a familiar room.

"We've taken your sister's lock clip," Lorcan hissed too close to her ear. "This time you stay put." He dropped her on her feet and pushed her inside with Emma. "Say your goodbyes." He slammed the door shut behind him.

Emma slid to the ground with her back against the wall and a sad look of defeat on her classic features. Cara hurried over to sit by her sister and place a comforting arm around her shoulders. "Don't worry, Emma, Talen and his brothers will be here soon."

"How do you know?" Emma whispered.

"Trust me, I know." She patted her sister. "He's in my head, we can communicate that way." She rolled her eyes. "Not to mention my hip is heating like crazy."

"Your hip?" Emma asked, turning to face her and raising an eyebrow.

Heat filled Cara's face. "Um, long story."

"I believe we have time." Emma's lips trembled in a parody of a smile. "What, is it something like old Ms. Tulley's arthritis—when it rained she could barely walk, remember? Do you have Talen arthritis near your ass?"

Cara snorted. How many times had her sister made her laugh while they huddled, praying for safety? A true gift, that was. "Okay, don't freak." The woman should be warned anyway. If Dage got his big old paw anywhere near Emma, her hip would probably ache, too.

Standing, Cara unsnapped her jeans, pushing them down enough to show the mark.

"What the heck?" Emma rose to her knees, poking the flesh. "A tattoo?"

"Um, kind of."

Emma prodded harder. "What does 'kind of' mean? What is this design?"

Cara studied the intricate design. "It's the Kayrs marking. The design appeared on his hand, then on my ass during, um, well . . ."

Falling back against the wall and sliding down, Emma gasped. "You let the man *brand* you?"

Cara yanked her jeans back up. "I didn't know about the branding until too late." She rolled her eyes, sitting near her sister. "I was otherwise occupied."

"Holy crap."

Yep, that about summed it up. "I know. Apparently vampire mating involves biology—the exchange of fluids, a marking, and now I have his defenses."

"Oh my God! Are you a vampire?" Emma's eyes went wide and blue.

Cara snorted. "Of course not. Vampires are born, not made."

Emma relaxed. "Will you age?"

Shrugging, Cara straightened her top. "Not very fast, if at all." She cleared her throat. "It's good you know, Em. I'm pretty sure Dage has plans for you to wear his mark." God help the king.

"Then he can plan to lose his balls."

Yep. The king had his work cut out for him. Cara sighed.

Time moved too quickly, and they both jumped to their feet as the door swung open and Lorcan filled the space. Both women moved to shield the other from the monster facing them with a mean looking gun in one hand. With a sigh, Emma won the battle and put Cara behind her, whispering, "Save my nephew."

Cara stumbled to a stop.

"Emma, come with me." Lorcan nodded at Cara over

Emma's head. "I promised you I'd let your sister go, sotie. She's free to go."

"I'd rather stay here," Emma said angrily, knowing as well as Cara that Lorcan had no intention of letting her go free.

"Too bad. Come with me now, or I'll shoot you both."

"You'd shoot your future mate?" Cara challenged.

"Yes. The gun is set to stun, but you never know what kind of damage a Kurjan weapon will have on a human."

Or an unborn child.

"We can't risk it," Emma muttered. She raised her voice, "Don't worry, Cara. I'm sure he has better plans for me than death."

"Of course." Lorcan gave up the pretense and gestured Emma forward. "You'll like my cousin Franco. You're a perfect match." He laughed at his own joke.

Emma turned and gave Cara a quick hug. "I'll see you soon." She turned and followed Lorcan out of the room.

Tears filled Cara's eyes as the lock slammed home. She closed her eyes on a sob as she leaned against the far wall and slid to the floor.

"*It's all right mate, I'm coming.*"

Chapter 33

"I'm scared," Cara whispered into the empty underground room. The Kurjan facility even smelled of brimstone and decay—pure evil.

"*I know.*" How in the world could they communicate like this? It didn't matter—thank God they could talk again. She would discuss the fact that he had short-circuited her communication skills with him later.

Cara closed her eyes and leaned back against the stone wall before placing both hands against her stomach. How could she not have known? It was so obvious. What would the Kurjan virus do to the baby? She shielded her thoughts about the baby from Talen before she reached out again. "How close are you?"

"*Five minutes*," came back clearly. Concern and anger rode through the words.

God, she hoped she had five minutes until they injected her with the virus. She bit her lip to keep from sobbing and tried not to wonder what was happening to Emma. She reached out with her thoughts, with her heart, and found nothing. Where was Emma?

Talen would arrive in time. She was so stupid—why hadn't she turned to him for help in the first place? They should've made a plan together.

The silence hung thick and heavy in the room as she waited.

For what, she couldn't be sure. Emma would stall Lorcan as long as possible to keep him from injecting Cara with the virus, and she hoped her sister didn't get herself killed in trying to protect her.

She concentrated again on Talen and saw Dage, Conn, and Jase running away from a black helicopter toward a small farmhouse surrounded by fields. With a start, she realized she saw through Talen's eyes. He was coming.

She refused to just sit and wait to be rescued. So, she jumped up and headed for the door with determination—a quick twist of the knob confirmed it was locked. She searched for something to pick the lock, but only dirt and stone walls stared back at her. With a sigh, she returned to her former seat and shut her eyes to concentrate on Talen.

Her eyes slammed open with the door. Lorcan stood in the opening with three bloody red scratches slashed down one side of his inhumanly pale face, his eyes the color of dark death.

"It looks like my sister kicked your ass," Cara said smugly from her seat.

"She got in one while I got in several," Lorcan retorted, yellow fangs flashing in the muted light.

"Where is she?" Cara still didn't move, dread pooling in her stomach.

"On her way to meet her destiny. Franco has very specific desires in a sotie, and believe me, killing her would have been kinder."

"You know at some point I am going to kill you, right?" Cara asked, tilting her head to the side.

Lorcan's laugh crawled over her skin like the legs of a centipede. "You are welcome to try, sotie. But as I expect you to be pregnant within the first couple of months, I assume you'll have your hands full."

Cara struggled to contain herself. What would he do when he discovered she was already pregnant? Assuming the baby survived the virus. Oh God, where was Talen?

Lorcan's boots made a dull thud against the earth when he stalked forward and yanked her to her feet. His claws dug deep into her arm. She pulled back only to have him force her across the room and into the tunnel where he tugged her behind him for several moments before stopping in front of another small wooden door. He pushed it open to reveal a hospital type room with bed, monitors, and a tray holding two syringes filled with amber liquid. She stumbled as she noticed the restraints attached to the bed.

Lorcan tracked her gaze. "So you don't harm yourself as the virus takes hold."

Fear rushed through her, and she tried to yank her arm away. "Let me go."

"Don't be silly," Lorcan said congenially. He pulled her farther into the room and lifted her almost gently onto the table.

Cara kicked out hard with both feet and connected with his legs. With a growl, he backhanded her across the face, throwing her on the big bed and quickly securing one of her hands in the thick leather restraint. Raw pain echoed through her face, and she shrieked as he pinched the skin on her wrist. She struck out with her free hand and scratched her nails down the already healing marks on his face, whipping her body in protest as Lorcan grasped her wrist in a painful grip to secure the other restraint. Cara struggled uselessly against the hard mattress for a moment before searing him with her gaze.

"You are such a complete prick," she said with feeling, her wrist and face smarting. The smell of bleach and antiseptic swirled around and threatened her stomach. Bile rose from her belly.

Gingerly touching the fresh marks scoring his face, Lorcan flashed sharp yellow teeth. "And you're an undisciplined bitch who should know better." He reached out one razor sharp nail and ripped her T-shirt down the middle. "Hmm. Maybe we'll get to know each other before you're injected with the virus. Though, I prefer red lace to white cotton, sotie." His gaze deepened to purplish red as he leaned down and grasped one breast through her bra in his clawlike hand.

Pain bloomed through her chest. Cara cried out Talen's name as fear almost choked her, whether out loud or in her head she wasn't sure.

"*I'm coming, mate.*" He sounded cold, determined, lethal.

Cara drew strength from his voice and started to struggle just as Lorcan hissed and yanked back his hand as if burned. He took a surprised step away from the bed and put both hands to his head as if in agony.

"That mating allergy is a bitch, isn't it Lorcan?" Cara said triumphantly, pulling against the restraints, blocking his pain with tattered shields.

"I had wondered if it were true," Lorcan muttered as he dropped his hands. His eyes sharpened to red. "Well, I guess we will have to wait until the virus takes its course, Cara." He nodded at the two shots with large needles on the tray next to her head. "Our physician will be here shortly to administer one—I'd do it myself but I keep forgetting the correct order of the injections. We wouldn't want you to turn into an orangutan, now would we?" He laughed at his own joke.

"Fuck you," Cara said with a mean grin.

Lorcan stepped closer to the bed, his face turning livid.

"Go ahead," Cara taunted softly. "Touch me. Try it."

His eyes raked her but he didn't move closer. "Oh I will, don't you doubt it."

Then a shrill alarm sounded throughout the underground tunnel, and he jerked a phone receiver off the wall. "How many?" His face tightened as he listened. "No, I sent four with Franco's mate." He growled low. "Take care of them."

He replaced the receiver before rounding on Cara. "We checked you—there are no tracking devices on you. How did they find you?"

Cara widened her eyes on his swirling purple ones. He

didn't know about the ability to track mates? She shrugged. She sure as hell wasn't going to tell him.

Lorcan looked at her a moment before lifting one of the syringes and moving it into her line of vision. "You know, if these are injected in the wrong order or even at the same time, the human system pretty much shuts down. With unimaginable pain."

Cara struggled to contain her fear and keep her face calm while lying on the white bed. "I've seen the tapes, Lorcan."

"I see." He smiled. "Well, that was before we learned to give the injections a day apart—there's a less likely chance of death."

"Death would be preferable to staying with you, Lorcan."

He pushed reddish black hair over his shoulder and gave a deep sigh. "I plan to guarantee that, Cara." He again flashed yellowed incisors. "You will beg for death by the time I'm through with you."

"Seriously?" Cara forced out a laugh. "That's the best you've got?" Her voice lowered into an eerie imitation of a movie monster, "You will beg for death, my pretty . . ."

"Silence!" His shout echoed inside the small room as he leaned over her and pressed the needle to her neck. She glared mutely up at him while the alarm screamed through the underground hell.

Lorcan swore and reached for the phone again. "Do you have them?" He swore again. "Why the hell not?" He slammed the receiver down, turning to her. "You've become quite the pain in the ass, Cara. It's a good thing your daughter is prophesized, or it'd be easier just to kill you."

"You'll never get my daughter." Pure conviction rang through every word.

Sharp canines flashed. "Oh, I wouldn't be too sure. You haven't met her mate, my son Kalin. The boy is truly focused, truly gifted." Pride slithered through Lorcan's purple eyes, along with just a hint of fear. What kind of evil would this monster fear?

A chill skittered down Cara's spine followed by pure rage. Her baby would never end up in the hands of monsters. Then a boiling wave of heated fury reached her from the tunnel.

The door burst open with a bang and before Lorcan could turn, large hands grabbed him by the neck and threw him across the room to land with a loud thud against the opposite wall. Talen's gaze raked her and then hardened at her ripped shirt and bruised face.

"I'm all right," she said softly, trying not to be frightened by the desire to kill dancing in his topaz eyes. The sound of battle could be heard in the tunnel outside where eerie cries of pain echoed. Talen swiftly reached down and sliced through both restraints before turning to face Lorcan, who slowly rose to his feet.

"You'll never get her out of here alive." Lorcan wiped blood from the corner of his mouth with a fast swipe.

"Think not?" Talen's voice was unrecognizable. It was animalistic, guttural, and promised pain. Cara gulped as she scrambled to sit up on the bed.

Lorcan took a slow step toward the door.

"You won't make it." The words were barely out of Talen's mouth when Lorcan lunged for him and the two hit the tray, knocking the shots to the ground before crashing into the wall. Talen grabbed the phone receiver and viciously wrapped the cord around Lorcan's neck before yanking from both sides. Lorcan connected an elbow to Talen's face, knocking his head back into the wall, before clawing through the phone cord and jumping for the door.

Talen was on him before he cleared the doorway, and the two went down to the ground with fierce growls and struggling limbs. Cara cried out as Lorcan threw Talen over his head to land with a crash against the tunnel wall. Rocks rained down upon them all.

Talen flipped to his feet, bunched and tackled Lorcan to the ground with a blood curdling roar, landing a foot from where Cara still sat on the table. She tracked the furious flurry of punches between the two by counting the sound of bones breaking and skin flaying open. Blood flew in wide arcs to decorate the stone walls and soak into the dirt floor until Lorcan connected with a solid crack to Talen's wrist. The knife went spinning, throwing up wisps of dirt as it went.

Cara instinctively jumped off the table and dove for the knife while the two beings grappled ferociously on the dirt floor. She grasped the handle and pivoted as a crunch accompanied Talen throwing his elbow into Lorcan's nose. The monster screeched in pain. Clutching the knife against her chest, she inched along the wall, looking for an opening in the thrashing bodies.

"Stay back," Talen growled as he plunged his fist into Lorcan's face.

She froze against the wall, ready to jump in and defend her mate. The instinct to do so was so overwhelming she nearly ignored the slight warning flowing through her brain. Janie's voice, echoing with an ancient pulse, threaded throughout her consciousness. But the words eluded her.

Her mind reeled. What did Janie want her to know? What had she said? Cara's thoughts scrambled through the last month to finally land on the first day they'd been at headquarters. Janie had given a warning from the Earth. What was it? She gasped, remembering and turning just in time to turn to see a Kurjan soldier appear at the doorway clutching a long bladed knife. Talen crouched over Lorcan with his hands in a vice grip around the Kurjan's throat, slowly choking the life out of the monster—with his back to the door.

"Watch your back!" She screamed Janie's warning at Talen before throwing the knife with all of her might. The blade landed with a sharp thud in the Kurjan's throat. The Kurjan soldier turned incredulous reddish-purple eyes on her, reaching up with both hands to yank the weapon out of his throat with a bloody gurgle. Her ten years of playing softball had finally come in handy. Thick red blood flowed down his chest as he smiled sharp canines, twirled the knife around to clasp the handle, and started toward her.

Talen was on his feet and had Lorcan in a headlock before Cara could blink—his swirling golden eyes focused on the new threat. The soldier took a half-step forward and froze in place, his face transforming from excitement to horror. Then, with a ferocious twist of Talen's arms, Lorcan's neck broke with a loud snap.

Talen let Lorcan's body fall to the floor with an unconcerned air as he advanced on the still frozen enemy. He kicked an impressive boot into the side of the Kurjan soldier, who went down to the ground with the sound of thunder. Lacking even a hint of mercy, Talen yanked the knife out of his hand, plunged it into his throat, and ripped his head off. Blood sprayed toward all four walls. Cara couldn't look away as Talen turned, tipped Lorcan's head back, and slashed from side to side.

Lorcan's head dropped to the ground and rolled to the far wall. Cara bit her lip, bile rising in her throat, the room beginning to spin. She tried to focus her thoughts, control her reactions. Grey fuzziness edged into her vision, and she swayed until darkness kissed her and she was out.

Talen gave Lorcan's head a swift kick as he stood to his feet to see his wife passed out on the hospital bed, the vicious purple bruise all but spreading across her delicate cheekbone. He swore and then leaned down to lift her in his arms as Conn ran into the room, a thick cut marring his jaw.

"Is she okay?" Conn asked with concern as he reached down and grabbed the still full shots to place them gingerly in a leather bag.

"Yes," Talen said abruptly as a blood-covered Jase appeared at the door.

"Come on, they've sent for reinforcements," Jase said urgently, wiping red off his face with his saturated sleeve. "Not my blood," he answered his brother's unasked question.

Talen nodded and followed Jase through the tunnel with

his mate in his arms and Conn at his back. Silence reigned around them—he was fairly sure they'd dispatched every Kurjan still at the facility to hell. Except for the one currently being interrogated by Dage. That Kurjan's screams echoed high-pitched and loud through the tunnels as they ran for the exit—then silence. Dage must have retrieved the information.

Chapter 34

Cara jostled awake safe and secure in Talen's arms as he ran out of the farmhouse into the sun. She breathed a sigh of relief, realizing the clouds had burned off in the early afternoon hour. The Kurjans couldn't come outside now.

Dage waited by a large black helicopter while Jase and Conn jumped into the front. "Where's Emma?" she asked Dage.

His eyes narrowed to silver daggers on her. "Gone. They flew her out of here earlier headed for Franco's headquarters up in Nunavut." He tossed his gun to Talen, his hands going to the fasteners on his dark vest.

Cara gasped and tried to struggle out of her husband's arms. "Where is that? We have to find her."

"Nunavut is in northern Canada—sparse and cold. And don't worry, Cara, I will find your sister. I promise you." Shrugging out of his vest, he threw it into the back of the helicopter. He turned to his brothers. "Talen, secure Colorado—Jase, Alaska, and Conn, Texas. I'll be in touch." He unclasped his cuff and handed it to Conn. With a nod to them all, he disappeared. One second he stood in front of them, the next he was just gone.

"What the heck?" Cara asked numbly.

"He can transport, mate." Talen settled into the backseat of the helicopter. "It's one of Dage's gifts. Jase can teleport as well."

"Why did he give you his cuff?" Nausea welled up from her stomach.

"For some reason metal can't transport with him. We've never figured out why." Talen reached out one broad hand and yanked the door closed.

"Can you teleport?"

"Unfortunately not, darlin'." The words were an endearment but the tension in the rough muscles holding her told another story. He was livid. She had to gather her courage to glance up into his face. Stone cold, his eyes sharp flecks of gold, the hard planes of his face settled into fierce and unforgiving lines. Even his generous mouth clenched tight, and his jaw made granite seem soft.

"So, you're pretty pissed, huh?" she whispered as dread filled her lungs like poisoned air. She struggled against the urge to cough it out.

His eyes glowed to topaz as his arms tightened around her. "We shall discuss that later, mate." One swift movement and her gold cuff was wrapped around her wrist again.

She chose not to object, and yet couldn't stop the chill his words sent winging through her chest. The innocuous words held more threat than she had imagined. The shrill motor cut the silence like a blade through flesh, and she leaned back into Talen in exhaustion, sleep claiming her before they even left the ground.

Talen let Cara sleep for several hours after they returned to the ranch. Like a predator on a hunt, he watched her move slowly, purposefully into their comfortable living room as the fading sun cast a mellow pink light across the hard planks of the floor. She had dressed in faded jeans and a pretty white knit tank that hugged her full breasts—the decorative Celtic knots winding along the neckline whispered of feminine secrets and allure. Her unbound hair flaunted oak sparks as the sun danced across porcelain skin. She was so beautiful his chest ached. Yet her stunning blue eyes were determined, her slim shoulders back, her chin lifted—she looked ready for a good fight. The ache receded as desire clawed with sharp talons through his blood to strike at his groin.

He'd oblige her with the fight.

The touch of his eyes on Cara was more a lash than a caress, and she had to concentrate not to stumble as she skirted the couch to stand at its edge. He stood next to the rumbling fire in the massive stone fireplace, one masculine arm resting negligently on the mantle, his hand swirling golden liquid in a tumbler. He had changed into faded jeans and a deep bronze shirt that had to be silk and turned his eyes to the topaz of a night predator. They fit perfectly in a face stamped with a dangerous display of hardness and hollows. A muscle ticked in his rugged jaw, and the shadow he unintentionally cast from the firelight hinted of breadth and strength.

Fear fought with desire through her veins.

"Where is Janie?" She had looked into the little pink room on her way to the living area to find it empty.

"She's still at headquarters with Jase." The underlying reason slid like a whispered threat over her skin.

"Why?" She was stalling, and she knew it.

"We needed privacy." His golden eyes revealed nothing as he continued to swirl the liquid—ice cubes clanked against the crystal, and the chill tickled down her spine.

She didn't have a reply as they stared at each other across the wooden coffee table. The large imprint on her hip started to burn.

He broke the silence first. "Franco's helicopter didn't make it to his headquarters—I think Dage has Emma now. Jase and Conn are en route to pick them up."

Relief filled Cara for a moment, even with the tension infusing the room. "Thank God."

Golden eyes hardened to ancient copper. "Are you well rested?"

"Yes." Her stomach lurched as she fought to remain calm. She knew him, didn't she? He wouldn't hurt her. "I don't want to fight with you." The words surprised her—she hadn't meant to say them.

His raised eyebrow showed his surprise as well. "Don't you, now?"

"No." Her eyes narrowed in anger, and she fought the urge to stamp her foot. "Of course not."

He took a sip of the liquid, his eyes both hard and thoughtful over the rim. "I believe I have been less than clear as to the rules governing our marriage."

"Rules?" Anger wove through her words as her spine straightened one vertebra at a time. How dare he?

"Yes." His face gave no quarter.

"I'm sorry to tell you this, Talen, but if you wanted a mindless, obedient wife, you should have found one during the last century. I'm sure you had your chances." She welcomed the anger, so much easier to deal with than the fear.

In the way of wild animals from wolves to men, Talen showed his teeth—the beast within him rearing with a vengeance demanding to take. To dominate. He had almost lost her today, and yet here she stood challenging him. "There isn't anything I wouldn't do to keep you safe, mate."

The possessive tone of his voice slid south of Cara's stomach as an unwanted desire pooled fast and hard between her thighs. "Meaning what?" It came out as a husky whisper.

"Meaning that reality is something you will come to grips with, and you'll do so now."

"I don't understand."

"Don't you?" he asked silkily as he took another drink of scotch. "I think you do, Cara. I think you do understand that the freedom you've enjoyed, the freedom you've abused," his voice hardened on the last, "is one I've allowed."

"Allowed?" She choked on the word as a fine red haze covered her vision. If it were possible for her head to spin around and explode, it would have just happened. Boy, this was one vampire who needed a good lesson in modern relationships. "You picked the wrong girl to dominate, Dracula."

His broad hand slapped the glass onto the mantle with a harsh snap as he turned to face her. Desire clawed through him with sharp blades as he took in her flushed face, clenched fists, and the sheer daring it had taken to call him by that ridiculous name. Yet his voice when he spoke was silky, dark. "Have I, mate?" He took a step forward, and his eyes flashed to the hard pebbles of her nipples through the light cotton.

She resisted the urge to cross her arms over her traitorous breasts while her thighs softened even more in response. This was getting out of hand—she needed to bring some reason into the conversation. Even worse, she knew she had been wrong before. It would about kill her, but fairness demanded the truth—she would deal with his idiotic proclamation about rules later.

She shifted her feet. "I'm sorry I went to Wyoming without you."

At the very least she expected a graceful acknowledgment, even an acceptance of her apology. What she got, however, was an arrogant smile. "Do you think so?"

She blinked in confusion. "Do I think so what?"

"Do you think you're sorry?"

"I just said I was."

"No." The arrogance remained.

"No, what?" Cara asked in exasperation.

"You're not sorry. Not yet anyway." His stalking step forward was as graceful as any jungle cat hunting its prey. Spiced pine tickled her nose.

It was either stomp her foot in frustration or take a step backward in retreat. The wooden floor vibrated as she took the first option. "Stop threatening me."

The harsh caress of his eyes over her aching nipples made her shiver in response. Hard gold lifted to meet her gaze, and she shivered again. Desire, want, and need all blended through her blood. "That was a statement, not a threat." Another step closer. Less than a foot of tension-filled air remained between them.

"You're the one who lied," she snapped back, remembering suddenly why she had been so angry.

A superior eyebrow lifted. "I didn't lie."

"Yes, you did. You married me because some damn high prophet said you had to." Her temper gathered like a winter storm through her veins.

"Bullshit."

She gasped and a haze of fury crossed her vision. "I saw the damn letter, Talen."

"I know that, mate. What I don't know, what I don't understand, is why you didn't ask me about the letter." His temper rose to match hers. "In fact, I believe I do understand it. You weren't running from me, Cara. You were running from yourself." Rage flashed across his face as he remembered the danger she had put herself in. "Do you truly believe that I would let anyone *order* me to mate?"

"Well you did," she retorted, fighting the urge to retreat. "I saw your return letter."

"Did you see the dates of either letter?" His voice lowered.

She tilted her chin. Not exactly.

"I didn't think so. The letters were copies of those sent over a century ago, mate. The originals are in a safe at headquarters."

"You still agreed." Her voice trailed off at the end—maybe she should've looked at the date.

"I mated you because you're mine, Cara. And you damn well know it." At her stubborn silence, a dangerous glint entered his eyes. "And you're going to admit it, darlin'."

The claim hung in the tense air between them for several beats. "I'm not going to run," she murmured, unsure whether she warned herself or the warrior closing in on her.

"Running would prove fruitless," he agreed, reaching out to run one finger over a cloth-covered nipple.

She bit her lip to keep from moaning and then gasped as he pinched her. "No more holding back, mate," he issued a quiet warning before soothing her abused flesh with one broad hand. Flesh that was all but begging for more, damn it. She gave a negligent shrug and moved to step back, only to have his other palm grasp her hip and hold her in place. He flexed his hand on her waist and sent fingers of anticipation through her abdomen; she quickly stifled the whimper that wanted loose. The hand on her hip slid around and smacked her backside in retaliation.

"Hey," she protested, raising both hands to push against his chest. Liquid heat spilled from her, readying her body for him with gleeful abandonment.

"I said no more holding back, Cara." The hand reached up to tangle in her hair and tug, forcing her eyes to meet his deadly serious ones. "Every cry, every moan, every whimper is mine. You will give them to me, mate."

"They aren't yours." She wasn't even sure what they were talking about but knew she needed to protest. Though her body was all but begging to get him naked.

He reacted with the speed of a striking cobra. With a twist of his wrist he exposed her neck—and instantly dipped to sink razor sharp teeth into tender flesh. She couldn't hold back the cry that escaped her this time, and there was no doubt it was a sound of ecstasy and not of pain. As he drank from her with sharp pulls, she wondered why it didn't hurt. Shouldn't it hurt? Instead, fire spiraled first to the imprint on her hip and then lower to the apex between her legs. She moved into him with a soft whimper and groaned as he slid one muscled thigh between her legs to press. Hard. Somehow, with another cry, she shattered.

When she came back to earth, she focused on his eyes right above her. With a fierce grin he leaned down and spoke heatedly against her mouth. "They are mine. As are your blood, your orgasms, and your soul, Cara. And before this night is over, you will beg me to accept them all."

With a swift motion, he had her off her feet and was striding purposefully toward the bedroom. He stopped and looked down—his face unwavering, his metallic eyes determined. "Tonight you will submit, mate." He walked inside and kicked the door shut before placing her on her feet.

Chapter 35

Cara let instinct take over as she took several steps back from the determined warrior standing between her and the bedroom door. His face intent, his body tensed for action, he mirrored her steps until her thighs met the bed. She searched around for an escape but could find none. The gentleness of his hands on the base of her T-shirt surprised her, as did the swiftness with which it was tossed over her head. Desire rushed through her; God she wanted this man. He stepped into her and reached for the button on her jeans. Heat enveloped her as the zipper was tugged down before her jeans and thong were pushed to pool at her feet; he even assisted her in lifting first one and then the other knee to free her legs. With a gentle push to her chest, she fell back on the bed.

She sat in a daze as Talen quickly rid himself of his dark shirt and jeans before leaning down and tugging her thick socks off her feet, his eyes hot and intent on hers the entire time. She shivered in the early light as he knelt and softly kissed the arch of one chilled foot.

"You are my mate, Cara," he kissed up her leg, hips, and belly, his breath heated with desire. "The prophets ordered us three hundred years ago to find a mate"—he continued moving up, placing soft kisses on each breast before gliding across her neck to her face—"and I waited for you." His mouth descended gently, kindly, on hers, and his strength surrounded her.

Cara knew he spoke the truth even before she opened herself up to the intense emotion rushing through him—even before he deepened the kiss until all she could do was feel. She whimpered deep in her throat as she kissed him back, her tongue dueling with his as her hands ran through his ebony hair, down his strong neck to his muscled shoulders—he was all smooth skin over hardness, and she arched against him in desire, in blatant invitation.

He chuckled as he released her mouth and nibbled down one delicate ear to lave the twin puncture wounds already healing in her neck before turning to her breasts. "You are so pretty," he rumbled against her skin, causing her to clutch her hands into his narrow waist before moving over his rock hard butt.

"You have a great ass," she replied in a throaty murmur as she traced her own path up his corded neck to bite his earlobe. He reacted by pressing into her and puckering his lips around one distended nipple. She gasped and pushed him to the side, fully aware that he rolled to his back only because he wanted to—she immediately took advantage to perch on his groin before leaning down and peppering his incredible chest with fierce kisses and nips. His hands went to her rear and then up her back as she moved farther south.

He stilled as she swiftly took him in her mouth—the tangy spice of him causing her to moan in enthusiasm. She had wondered about this. One hand reached gently down to cup his balls as she ran kisses up and down his length before again taking as much of him into her mouth as she could—she concentrated on the tip as one small hand tried to encircle his girth. A hand in her hair tried to tug her away and she gave a low chuckle, causing him to buck beneath her.

Then she was under him. He moved too fast for her to follow—one second she was playing and the next she was sprawled on her back with him buried in her to the hilt. She didn't have time to breathe before he moved—hard and fast and out of control. He was too big, the pleasure too intense, almost painful, the orgasm slamming into her from deep within—all she could do was clutch his shoulders and cry out at the exquisite waves blasting through her.

She came down with a whimper only to have him whip her back up again, driving into her, one hand tangled in her hair, the other hand holding her hip as he pummeled.

God she loved him.

She gasped as the spiraling feeling deep within her womb, within her heart, started again and her hands clutched at his hard buttocks, pulling him even closer into her. Talen slowed a bit and nipped Cara's lower lip none too gently. He raised his head and pierced her questioning eyes with his. "Mine."

"Talen?" Cara asked softly, her hands frantically moving up to his broad shoulders as she tried to pull him deeper within her. "Don't stop," she moaned, clenching around the full length of him.

"Say it, Cara." Talen emphasized his guttural command with a firm tug on her hair.

Cara's hesitation incited something primitive inside him that roared through him with savage force. Her empathic shields nonexistent with him, she understood what she'd done.

"But," was all she got out before he pulled out and flipped her over onto her belly. With rough hands, he pulled her to her knees while she tried to find balance with her hands. He entered her in one surge. He had told her she would submit to him this night. He started to move. To pound.

Cara felt overwhelmed. Her legs spread wide by his large hips, his grasp on her hips keeping her in place. Huge and indomitable, an untamable force behind her. She couldn't move and had no control over the situation. Maybe he didn't either. His relentless pounding forced her toward an even bigger orgasm, if that were possible. Her whole being focused on that orgasm. She wanted it more than breath itself.

Then suddenly, buried to the balls in her, he stopped.

She whimpered and tried to move back against him to keep him moving. Firm hands on her hips held her still until one strong hand lifted to catch in her hair and angle her head so he could see her face.

His voice deepened to something unrecognizable when he rasped, "Who do you belong to?"

She struggled, barely able to concentrate on mere words when that orgasm was within her reach.

"Cara," he tightened his hand in her hair, the slight pain catching her attention.

"What?" she breathed, trying to move forward and back again.

"Say it," he growled, his voice rough and demanding in her delicate ear.

"But," she began.

"Now," he emphasized his demand by withdrawing and slamming into her again.

Even in her aroused state she knew what he wanted. What he demanded. She paused, her heart thundering as she looked around his masculine bedroom with new eyes. Everything looked different. Finally, with a soft sigh of release, she focused over her shoulder into his eyes and said, "You. I belong to you."

He swelled even larger inside her as he released her hair. She closed her eyes and leaned down on her folded arms. It was true acceptance and they both knew it. With her surrender, his control vanished. She felt it escape him. With a bruising grip on her hips, he pounded in and out of her as the roaring in his head, in his balls, took over.

His teeth latched onto her shoulder, her orgasm hit with a howl from her, and she saw blackness for a moment.

Her body fiercely milked him until he came with a hoarse shout, filling her beyond completely. He held her in place, buried to the hilt, as the aftershocks of her orgasm enhanced his. Finally, with a final kiss to the puncture marks in her shoulder, he pulled out.

Cara was asleep instantly and didn't hear Talen go to the bathroom and return with a damp towel to gently clean her off. She turned into his arms as he snuggled her close and didn't hear the satisfied "mine' he murmured before following her into sleep.

Chapter 36

Cara awoke alone in the bed and sighed as she stretched overworked muscles. Again. She might as well get used to it. God, she loved that stubborn, chauvinistic, bossy vampire. Her gaze landed on the pretty flowers dotting her dresser and her memory shifted through the time he'd brought her the tree, his feet shuffling as he tried to make her happy. To bring her peace.

All right—he could be sweet, too.

She wrapped a dark blue blanket around herself and went in search of her husband. Her mate. She had something to tell him. A couple of things, actually.

He sat in a comfortable wooden chair on the deck looking thoughtfully out at a lake illuminated by morning sun. His eyes warmed as he watched her walk barefooted over the smooth wood, and he reached out two hands to tug her onto his lap. "Morning, mate," he murmured, placing a gentle kiss on her head.

"Morning," she breathed. She snuggled closer into Talen's warmth and couldn't help the soft kiss she placed against the steady pulse in his corded neck.

With their connection, she felt his heart roll over in his chest when her smooth lips met his skin. His arms tightened, and he stared at the deep green of the awakening lake ahead of them.

Talen remained quiet for a moment, apparently gathering his thoughts. "I love you, Cara." One strong hand reached out to intertwine with hers as his tone deepened. "I know I should grant you freedom—tell you that your life is your own to lead and promise to let you go." Resolve overpowered regret in his voice.

"I take it you're not going to say that?" Cara asked wryly, her warm breath against his neck, liquid warmth heating her from within as his love vibrated around them both. Much like their future, the lake sparkled clean and pure ahead of them. Pine and sweet, early tulips scented the air.

His hand enclosed around hers. "No." He slid a two-karat square diamond ring onto her left hand.

"Talen," she breathed. "It's beautiful." The platinum setting was simple, classy, and elegant. In other words, perfect.

"The ring reminded me of you," he said softly, turning her hand over to place a gentle kiss against her palm. "You're my mate, and I'm keeping you." He shifted. "But I can give you time to accept me. To accept us."

"Really?" She stretched like a well-fed cat in his arms. "How much time, Talen?"

He placed a gentle kiss on her head. "As much as you need."

"So we would kind of like, date each other?" The idea of him showing up for a first date, yanking at a tie, wondering if he should kiss her good night all but made her snort.

His heart warmed against her—through her. He apparently liked the sound of that. "Yeah. Like courting."

"Oh. Well, where would I live while we courted?" Her satisfied grin filled her voice.

"With me." His voice turned firm.

"Oh. What bedroom would I use?" She tried not to giggle at him. He really was trying to be sweet.

"Ours." It was more of a growl.

"But how will we sleep in the same room and not have sex?" She flipped his hand over, tracing the intricate mark on his palm with one finger. He hardened beneath her.

"Making love is part of courtship, wife." Every muscle in the lean body holding her tensed to full readiness.

"No, it isn't," she countered and dissolved into the laughter she had been repressing. A bird twittered high above in response.

Talen shifted her so he could see her amused face. "Are you laughing at me, mate?"

"I don't need time, Talen." She leaned forward and brushed a gentle kiss across his frowning mouth. "I love you. I want to be married to you."

Emotion, hot and sweet, plowed through him at her words and filled *her* with light. With love. He took her mouth in what started as a gentle kiss but quickly slid into something deeper, hotter. They both breathed heavy when he lifted his head and her giggles had long disappeared.

"Besides"—she dropped a quick kiss on his now smiling mouth—"it'll take both of us to keep your son from turning into an arrogant, bossy vamp like his father." She didn't need Emma's words to know the babe she carried was a boy. She was finally accepting the enhanced abilities she'd denied for so long; without them, she wouldn't have met Talen.

"Son?" He stilled to stone around her. "A baby?"

She lifted her head to his—she hadn't considered he might not welcome fatherhood. The wide smile lighting his dangerous face dispatched her fears.

"A babe?" he asked again, the green in his eyes swirling right through to dominate the gold.

She nodded. "You're happy?" A tiny thread of concern remained.

Talen placed a soft kiss on her upturned nose. "Ecstatic." He leaned back to stare at the lake while joy whipped through him and straight into her heart. "We need to go get Janie—I want my family all in one place."

His words spread the joy to her. "All right. She should be awake by the time we get there. I love you, mate."

He hugged her close. "Forever, Cara."

Chapter 37

"Janie, are you there?" Zane wound through the dream world with a sigh of frustration; this was her universe and he was only a guest. Where the heck was she?

"Hi, Zane." She popped out from behind a swaying tree with pink leaves scattering around her.

"Nice tree," he said with an appreciative smile. The oddest scent of powdered brownies clung to the branches.

"Thanks." Her responding smile was slower than usual. And tinged with sadness.

"It's all right, Janie Belle." He stepped forward to place a brotherly arm around her tiny shoulders. "The king is one of the fiercest warriors ever born; he'll find your Aunt Emma." Zane hugged his best friend closer. "And besides, we're gearing up to assist if necessary. The Kurjans don't stand a chance."

"I know." Janie hugged him back. "But I can't see it. I can't get a sense of Auntie Emma." Pixielike features turned to him in concern.

Zane shrugged. "Maybe you're not supposed to see everything, Belle."

"Well." For a four-year-old, the feminine pique was pronounced and brought a smile to Zane's full lips. He changed the subject. "How's your mother?"

Janie's smile came more easily this time. "She's good.

Ready to be with Aunt Emma again." Janie could already see her baby brother in her head—his magnificent power would only be balanced by his incredible heart. She wished he'd hurry up and be born.

"That's good, Belle. Make sure she rests up, our fight has just started."

Janie nodded. She didn't correct him, but in truth, the fight hadn't even begun. Once it did, the world they all knew would change. And even with her powers, she couldn't see the ending—she couldn't see the world that would emerge from the rubble. Determination mixed with faith in her soul as she looked at the young warrior before her. Together they would make it right.

She hoped.

Please read on for an excerpt from Rebecca Zanetti's brand new Dark Protectors novel!

VAMPIRE'S FAITH

The Dark Protectors are Back!

Vampire King Ronan Kayrs wasn't supposed to survive the savage sacrifice he willingly endured to rid the world of the ultimate evil. He wasn't supposed to emerge in this time and place, and he sure as hell wasn't supposed to finally touch the woman who's haunted his dreams for centuries. Yet here he is, in an era where vampires are hidden, the enemy has grown stronger, and his mate has no idea of the power she holds.

Dr. Faith Cooper is flummoxed by irrefutable proof that not only do vampires exist . . . they're hot blooded, able to walk in sunlight, and shockingly sexy. Faith has always depended on science, but the restlessness she feels around this predatory male defies reason. Especially when it grows into a hunger only he can satisfy—that is if they can survive the evil hunting them both.

CHAPTER 1

Dr. Faith Cooper scanned through the medical chart on her tablet while keeping a brisk pace in her dark boots through the hospital hallway, trying to ignore the chill in the air. "The brain scan was normal. What about the respiratory pattern?" she asked, reading the next page.

"Normal. We can't find any neurological damage," Dr. Barclay said, matching his long-legged stride easily to hers. His brown hair was swept back from an angled face with intelligent blue eyes. "The patient is in a coma with no brain activity, but his body is... well..."

"Perfectly healthy," Faith said, scanning the nurse's notes, wondering if Barclay was single. "The lumbar puncture was normal, and there's no evidence of a stroke."

"No. The patient presents as healthy except for the coma. It's an anomaly," Barclay replied, his voice rising.

Interesting. "Any history of drugs?" Sometimes drugs could cause a coma.

"No," Barclay said. "No evidence that we've found."

Lights flickered along the corridor as she passed through the doorway to the intensive- care unit.

"What's wrong with the lights?" Faith asked, her attention jerking from the medical notes.

"It's been happening on and off for the last two days. The maintenance department is working on it, as well as on the temperature fluctuations." Barclay swept his hand out. No ring. Might not be married. "This morning we moved all the other patients to the new ICU in the western addition that was completed last week."

That explained the vacant hall and nearly deserted nurses' station. Only one woman monitored the screens spread across the desk. She nodded as Faith and Dr. Barclay passed by, her gaze lingering on the cute man.

The cold was getting worse. It was early April, raining and a little chilly. Not freezing.Faith shivered. "Why wasn't this patient moved with the others?"

"Your instructions were to leave him exactly in place until you arrived," Barclay said, his face so cleanly shaven he looked like a cologne model. "We'll relocate him after your examination."

Goose bumps rose on her arms. She breathed out, and her breath misted in the air. This was weird. It'd never happen in the hospital across town where she worked. Her hospital was on the other side of Denver, but her expertise with coma patients was often requested across the world. She glanced back down at the tablet. "Where's his Glasgow Coma Scale score?"

"He's at a three," Barclay said grimly.

A three? That was the worst score for a coma patient. Basically, no brain function.

Barclay stopped her. "Dr. Cooper. I just want to say thank you for coming right away." He smiled and twin dimples appeared. The nurses probably loved this guy. "I heard about the little girl in Seattle. You haven't slept in—what? Thirty hours?"

It felt like it. She'd put on a clean shirt, but it was already wrinkled beneath her white lab coat. Faith patted his arm, finding very nice muscle tone. When was the last time she'd been on a date? "I'm fine. The important part is that the girl woke up." It had taken Faith seven hours of doing what she shouldn't be able to do: Communicate somehow with coma patients. This one she'd been able to save, and now a six-year-old girl was eating ice cream with her family in the hospital. Soon she'd go home. "Thank you for calling me."

He nodded, and she noticed his chin had a small divot—Cary Grant style. "Of course. You're legendary. Some say you're magic."

Faith forced a laugh. "Magic. That's funny." Straightening her shoulders, she walked into the ICU and stopped moving, forgetting all about the chart and the doctor's dimples. "What in the world?" she murmured.

Only one standard bed remained in the sprawling room. A massive man overwhelmed it, his shoulders too wide to fit on the mattress. He was at least six-foot-six, his bare feet hanging off the end of the bed. The blankets had been pushed to his waist to make room for the myriad of electrodes set across his broad and muscular chest. Very muscular. "Why is his gown open?"

"It shouldn't be," Barclay said, looking around. "I'll ask the nurse after you do a quick examination. I don't mind admitting that I'm stymied here."

A man who could ask for help. Yep. Barclay was checking all the boxes. "Is this the correct patient?" Faith studied his healthy coloring and phenomenal physique. "There's no way this man has been in a coma for longer than a couple of days."

"It shouldn't be," Barclay said, looking around. "I'll ask the nurse after you do a quick examination. I don't mind admitting that I'm stymied here."

A man who could ask for help. Yep. Barclay was checking all the boxes. "Is this the correct patient?" Faith studied his healthy coloring and phenomenal physique. "There's no way this man has been in a coma for longer than a couple of days."

Barclay came to a halt, his gaze narrowing. He slid a shaking hand through his thick hair. "I understand, but according to the fire marshal, this patient was buried under piles of rocks and cement from the tunnel cave-in below the Third Street bridge that happened nearly seven years ago."

Faith moved closer to the patient, noting the thick dark hair that swept back from a chiseled face. A warrior's face. She blinked. Where the hell had that thought come from? "That's impossible." She straightened. "Anybody caught in that collapse would've died instantly, or shortly thereafter. He's not even bruised."

"What if he was frozen?" Barclay asked, balancing on sneakers.

Faith checked over the still-healthy tone of the patient's skin. "Not a chance." She reached for his wrist to check his pulse.

Electricity zipped up her arm and she coughed. What the heck was that? His skin was warm and supple, the strength beneath it obvious. She turned her wrist so her watch face was visible and then started counting. Curiosity swept her as she counted the beats. "When was he brought in?" She'd been called just three hours ago to consult on the case and hadn't had a chance to review the complete file.

"A week ago," Barclay said, relaxing by the door. Amusement hit Faith full force. Thank goodness. For a moment, with the flickering lights, freezing air, and static electricity, she'd almost traveled to an imaginary and fanciful place. She smiled and released the man's wrist. "All right. Somebody is messing with me." She'd just been named the head of neurology at Northwest Boulder Hospital. Her colleagues must have gone to a lot of trouble—tons, really—to pull this prank. "Did Simons put you up to this?"

Barclay blinked, truly looking bewildered. He was cute. Very much so. Just the type who'd appeal to Faith's best friend, Louise. And he had an excellent reputation. Was this Louise's new beau? "Honestly, Dr. Cooper. This is no joke." He motioned toward the monitor screen that displayed the patient's heart rate, breathing, blood pressure, and intracranial pressure.

It had to be. Faith looked closer at the bandage covering the guy's head and the ICP monitor that was probably just taped beneath the bandage. "I always pay back jokes, Dr. Barclay." It was fair to give warning.

Barclay shook his head. "No joke. After a week of tests, we should see something here that explains his condition, but we have nothing. If he was injured somehow in the caved-in area, there'd be evidence of such. But... nothing." Barclay sighed. "That's why we requested your help."

None of this made any sense. The only logical conclusion was that this was a joke. She leaned over the patient to check the head bandage and look under it.

The screen blipped.

She paused.

Barclay gasped and moved a little closer to her. "What was that?"

Man, this was quite the ruse. She was so going to repay Simons for this. Dr. Louise Simons was always finding the perfect jokes, and it was time for some payback. Playing along, Faith leaned over the patient again.

BLEEP

This close, her fingers tingled with the need to touch the hard angles of this guy's face. Was he some sort of model? Bodybuilder? His muscles were sleek and smooth—natural like a wild animal's. So probably not a bodybuilder. There was something just so male about him that he made Barclay fade into the meh zone. Her friends had chosen well. This guy was sexy on a sexy stick of pure melted sexiness. "I'm going to kill Simons," she murmured, not sure if she meant it. As jokes went, this was impressive. This guy wasn't a patient and he wasn't in a coma. So she indulged herself and smoothed his hair back from his wide forehead

BLEEP

BLEEP

BLEEP

His skin was warm, although the room was freezing. "This is amazing," she whispered, truly touched. The planning that had to have gone into it. "How long did this take to set up?"

Barclay coughed, no longer appearing quite so perfect or masculine compared to the patient. "Stroke him again."

Well, all righty then. Who wouldn't want to caress a guy like this? Going with the prank, Faith flattened her hand in the middle of the guy's thorax, feeling a very strong heartbeat. "You can stop acting now," she murmured, leaning toward his face. "You've done a terrific job." Would it be totally inappropriate to ask him out for a drink after he stopped pretending to be unconscious? He wasn't really a patient, and man, he was something. Sinewed strength and incredibly long lines. "How about we get you out of here?" Her mouth was just over his.

His eyelids flipped open.

Barclay yelped and windmilled back, hitting an orange guest chair and landing on his butt on the floor.

The patient grabbed Faith's arm in an iron-strong grip. "Faith."

She blinked and then warmth slid through her. "Yeah. That's me." Man, he was hot. All right. The coming out of a coma and saying her name was kind of cool. But it was time to get to the truth. "Who are you?"

He shook his head. "Gde, chert voz'mi, ya?"

She blinked. Wow. A Russian model? His eyes were a metallic aqua. Was he wearing contacts? "Okay, buddy. Enough with the joke." She gently tried to pull loose, but he held her in place, his hand large enough to encircle her entire bicep.

He blinked, his eyes somehow hardening. They started to glow an electric blue, sans the green. "Where am I?" His voice was low and gritty. Hoarse to a point that it rasped through the room, winding around them.

The colored contacts were seriously high-tech.

"You speak Russian and English. Extraordinary." She twisted her wrist toward her chest, breaking free. The guy was probably paid by the hour. "The jig is up, handsome." Whatever his rate, he'd earned every dime. "Tell Simons to come out from wherever she's hiding." Faith might have to clap for her best friend. This deserved applause.

The guy ripped the fake bandage off his head and then yanked the EKG wires away from his chest. He shoved himself to a seated position. The bed groaned in protest.

"Where am I?" He partially turned his head to stare at the now-silent monitor. "What the hell is that?" His voice still sounded rough and sexy.

Just how far was he going to take this? "The joke is over." Faith glanced at Barclay on the floor, who was staring at the patient with wide eyes. "You're quite the actor, Dr. Barclay." She smiled

Just how far was he going to take this? "The joke

is over." Faith glanced at Barclay on the floor, who was staring at the patient with wide eyes. "You're quite the actor, Dr. Barclay." She smiled.

Barclay grabbed a chair and hauled himself to his feet, the muscles in his forearms tightening. "Wh—what's happening?"

Faith snorted and moved past him, looking down the now-darkened hallway. Dim yellow emergency lights ignited along the ceiling. "They've cut the lights." Delight filled her. She lifted her voice. "Simons? Payback is a bitch, but this is amazing. Much better than April fool's."

After Faith had filled Louise's car with balloons filled with sparkly confetti—guaranteed to blow if a door opened and changed the pressure in the vehicle—Simons had sworn vengeance.

"Louise?" Faith called again. Nothing. Just silence. Faith sighed. "You win. I bow to your pranking abilities."

Ice started to form on the wall across the doorway. "How are you doing that?" Faith murmured, truly impressed.

A growl came from behind her, and she jumped, turning back to the man on the bed.

He'd just growled?

She swallowed and studied him. What the heck? The saline bag appeared genuine. Moving quickly, she reached his arm. "They are actually pumping saline into your blood?" Okay. The joke had officially gone too far.

Something that looked like pain flashed in his eyes. "Who died? I felt their deaths, but who?"

She shook her head. "Come on. Enough." He was an excellent actor. She could almost feel his agony.

The man looked at her, his chin lowering. Sitting up on the bed, he was as tall as she was, even though she was standing in her favorite two-inch heeled boots. Heat poured off him, along with a tension she couldn't ignore.

The man looked at her, his chin lowering. Sitting

up on the bed, he was as tall as she was, even though she was standing in her favorite two-inch heeled boots. Heat poured off him, along with a tension she couldn't ignore.

She shivered again, and this time it wasn't from the cold.

Keeping her gaze, he tore out the IV.

Blood dribbled from his vein. She swallowed and fought the need to step back. "All right. Too far, Simons," she snapped. "Waaaay too far."

Barclay edged toward the door. "I don't understand what's happening."

Faith shook her head. "Occam's razor, Dr. Barclay." Either the laws of physics had just changed or this was a joke.

The simplest explanation was that Simons had just won the jokester title for all time. "Enough of this, though. Who are you?" she asked the actor.

He slowly turned his head to study Dr. Barclay before focusing back on her. "When did the shield fall?"

The shield? He seemed so serious. Eerily so. Would Simons hire a crazy guy? No. Faith tapped her foot and heat rose to her face, her temper stirring. "Listen. This has been fantastic, but it's getting old. I'm done."

The guy grabbed her arm, his grip unbreakable this time. "Did both shields fail?"

Okay. Her heart started to beat faster. Awareness pricked along her skin. "Let go of me."

"No." The guy pushed from the bed and shrugged out of his gown, keeping hold of her. "What the fuck?" He looked at the Foley catheter inserted into his penis and then down to the long white anti-embolism stockings that were supposed to prevent blood clots.

Faith's breath caught. Holy shit. The catheter and TED hose were genuine. And his penis was huge. She looked up at his face. The TED hose might add a realistic detail to a joke, but no way would any responsible medical personnel insert a catheter for a gag. Simons wouldn't have done that. "What's happening?" Faith tried to yank her arm free, but he held her tight.

Dr. Barclay looked from her to the mostly naked male. "Who are you?" he whispered.

"My name is Ronan," the guy said, reaching for the catheter, which was attached to a urine-collection bag at the end of the bed. "What fresh torture is this?"

"Um," Faith started.

His nostrils flared. "Why would you collect my piss?"

Huh? "We're not," she protested. "You were in a coma. That's just a catheter."

He gripped the end of the tube, his gaze fierce.

"No—" Faith protested just as he pulled it out, grunting and then snarling in what had to be intense pain.

God. Was he on PCP or something? She frantically looked toward Barclay and mouthed the words security and Get the nurse out of here.

Barclay nodded and turned, running into the hallway.

"Where are we?" Ronan asked, drawing her toward him.

She put out a hand to protest, smashing her palm into his ripped abdomen. "Please. Let me go." She really didn't want to kick him in his already reddening penis. "You could've just damaged your urethra badly."

He started dragging her toward the door, his strength beyond superior. A sprawling tattoo covered his entire back. It looked like…a dark image of his ribs with lighter spaces between? Man, he was huge. "We must go."

Oh, there was no we. Whatever was happening right now wasn't good, and she had to get some space to figure this out. "I don't want to hurt you," she said, fighting his hold.

He snorted.

She drew in air and kicked him in the back of the leg, twisting her arm to gain freedom.

Faster than she could imagine, he pivoted, moving right into her. Heat and muscle and strength. He more than towered over her, fierce even though he was naked. She yelped and backpedaled, striking up for his nose.

He blocked her punch with his free hand and growled again, fangs sliding down from his incisors.

She stopped moving and her brain fuzzed. Fangs? Okay. This wasn't a joke. Somebody was seriously messing with her, and maybe they wanted her hurt. She couldn't explain the eyes and the fangs, so this had to be bad. This guy was obviously capable of inflicting some real damage. His eyes morphed again to the electric blue, and somehow he broadened even more, looking more animalistic than human.

"I don't understand," she said, her voice shaking as her mind tried to make sense of what her eyes were seeing.

"Who are you? Why were you unconscious in a coma? How did you know my name?"

He breathed out, his broad chest moving with the effort. The fangs slowly slid back up, and his eyes returned to the sizzling aqua.

"My name is Ronan Kayrs, and I was unconscious because the shield fell." He eyed her, tugging her even closer.

"I know your name because I spent four hundred years seeing your face and feeling your soft touch in my dreams."

"My—my face?" she stuttered.

His jaw hardened even more. "And that was before I'd accepted my death."

Made in the USA
Coppell, TX
31 December 2023

27092801R00187